Mace Fox

Masonry Ink
Book Two

SH Richardson

MACE FOX
MASONRY INK

USA TODAY BEST-SELLING AUTHOR
SH RICHARDSON

Copyright

Copyright 2023 by SH Richardson

All rights reserved
Published by SH Richardson

Mace Fox: Masonry Ink is a work of fiction. Names, characters, places, and incidents are all products of the authors ridiculous imagination and are used fictitiously. Any resemblance to actual events, locales, or persons, living or dead, is entirely coincidental. Except as permitted under the US Copyright Act of 1976, no part of this publication may be reproduced, distributed, or transmitted in any form by any means, or stored in a database or retrieval system, without the prior written permission of the author.

First Edition:
Formatting: Liberty Parker
Cover design: Raven Designs
Cover Photograph: Raven Designs

Information address: Shrwrites@gmail.com

Prologue

For three weeks I hunkered down in this courtroom. My mother sat next to me and held my hand as we listened to the harsh testimony day in and day out. *Chad Jenson,* the accused, was charged with first degree murder along with a laundry list of lesser charges. That smug motherfucker with his high-priced lawyers and paid psychiatrists had confessed yet at the same time swore he was innocent. They rambled on and on about temporary insanity due to steroid use induced by female provocation. He was made out to be the injured party while they pissed on my sister's character and cut her down for sport. They were relentless in their smear campaign, appealing to the misogynistic ideals of the handpicked jury made up of ten men and two old women raised to glorify the patriarchal belief system. His entire defense was a bunch of bullshit that never failed to give me the shits the longer the trial lasted. I stayed strong through it all, the rock my mother leaned on while they crucified my baby sister in front of a captive audience. Maya Fox was the sweetest girl in the world, and she never stood a chance.

I understood how someone like my starry-eyed little sister could've fallen for such a tight-laced golden boy. He was massively tall, broad shouldered, with sandy blond hair that was a bit too long and sat wildly atop his head. She would've found him cute, charming, and incapable of becoming the monster he turned out to be. She would've fallen head over heels in love and gifted him her whole heart, as any teenage girl would've if the high school's star football player paid them the slightest bit of attention. She would've ignored the red flags and denied her misgivings about their relationship. Her delicate nature would've influenced her intelligent mind into believing that jocks were naturally more aggressive. She would've taken his fists as long as he said he was sorry because she believed in forgiveness even when motherfuckers like that cockroach didn't deserve it.

Evidence documents revealed the many times she asked for help only to be denied by antiquated laws that favored rape culture over the cries of women. She kept her abuse a secret from our mother, never confided in me, and I was her big brother. If only I'd known the extent of her suffering, I would've put an end to it by snapping that fucker's neck where he stood, sealing him inside a steel drum, and burying his ass under a concrete slab. Nobody lifted a finger to stop the madness until it was too late. Until her beautiful face was marred with scars and smears of dried blood. Until her bright light was extinguished for good, left in plain sight under the shade of a maple tree in the middle of a neighborhood park. Until her death was declared a homicide, one of the statistical many attributed to girls under the age of eighteen by men who professed their innocence because they acted out of love. That concept made absolutely zero sense to me. How the fuck do you hurt the person you're supposed to cherish and protect? Well, I found out how, straight from the horse's mouth.

During his cross examination, the defense attorney asked the accused to explain what happened the night of the murder. His well-rehearsed diatribe left a bitter taste in my mouth and caused my fists to clench at my sides. My teeth chattered from repressed anger subdued by a precarious safety valve primed to blow. All I needed was five minutes alone with that fucker, and I'd make him pay the ultimate price. Rather than risking a jail sentence that would've left my mother alone to face this shit show, I watched and listened with focused attention.

"She asked me to meet her at the park, so I said yes, of course. I planned to break up with her anyway; she was starting to get clingy, kept demanding more and more of my time even though she knew I had football practice and stuff."

"I see. Then what happened?"

"She showed up to the park like we agreed wearing one of those skimpy dresses; you know the kind, the one's that show off a girl's breasts." He motioned using his hands as cups.

A deep growl ripped from my chest in outrage.

"And then what?"

"I told her it was over, and she went crazy on me! Started begging for another chance, said she was a virgin when we met and I was her first, which was a lie. Three other guys from the team said they slept with her during the school year. Who would *you* believe? When I called her out on it and tried to walk away, she said she would tell everyone that I was abusing her. I could've lost my football scholarship. I don't remember what happened after that. Things got hazy; I was sweating. Next thing I know, she's lying on the ground dead, so, I panicked."

"As any young man in the same situation would have, Mr. Jenson. I have a teenage son of my own, and I'm not sure if he would've acted any differently," his attorney said.

"Objection! Is there a question on the table, or is the defense council simply pontificating?" the prosecutor shouted.

"Sustained," the judge ordered. "Save your grandstanding for closing arguments, counsellor. I won't have that in my courtroom."

On and on he testified, lying his fucking ass off. It took everything I had in me not to leap across the council's table and beat his brains in, anything to make him shut the fuck up. He accused her of taunting him into losing control, said she knew he had a hot temper but kept pushing until his mind went blank and he snapped. My gut twisted with acid as I listened to the gasps of the jury when he begged them to see things from his perspective. Their sympathetic gazes embittered me as they took in the slumped shoulders and crocodile tears of the *poor boy* who was so deeply in love he just couldn't think straight. My seventeen-year-old sister was made out to be some fucked-up temptress who brought this all on herself by not heeding the warnings or using common sense. Fucking lies, all of it; only I knew the real truth.

A broken promise, the last-minute decision to have a few beers with my squad before taking a later flight, and my failure as her big brother to keep her safe.

I was the one who left her to that fate.

I killed her, the same as if it were my hands around her neck.

I observed his every movement, this pillar of the community as described by his lawyers and character witnesses. He was raised by his devout Christian parents who claimed to have taught their son right from wrong and to follow the word of God. Clearly, they fucked up the lesson plan, or he skipped right over the chapters on killing. The sad irony about that was, he, too, had a younger sister who attended the trial along with their folks. She was a tiny thing of grade-school age, and I wondered if she knew that her brother was a coward and a murderer? A few years from now, they might find themselves in the same boat if she decided to date one of the popular kids. How were they going to protect their daughter from some rich kid with roid rage without paying lip service to their son?

I prayed he felt my eyes on him.

You're going to die soon, I swore.

The hatred bubbling inside me would one day be let loose for that bastard to witness. He would see it all. The pain in my heart that slowly morphed my innards into a detached being, separate from the compassionate man who valued life, twisted into a savage animal conceived for destruction. That person or entity would someday be waiting for him outside those locked gates of the state prison when or *if* he was ever convicted. That *being*, once uncaged, would ignore his pleas for forgiveness the same way he ignored my sister's pleas for mercy.

I sat stock still during the entire ordeal, barely breathing, for fear that my foundation would crumble to ash on a hard wooden bench reserved for members of the public. I'd lived the life of a trained soldier, killing the enemies of my country in the name of patriotism, duty bound above all else. War made me immune to scenes of death and carnage, or so I'd believed. The day the prosecution presented the colored crime scene photos taken hours after my sister's body was discovered broke me in half. It was the only time I blinked back tears remembering her beautiful face as it once was and the last conversation she and I had together before my expected return.

"What day will you be home, Macey?"

"The day after tomorrow, as soon as I get my discharge papers. Why? You miss me or something, squirt?" I teased.

"I...of course I do, silly. I can't wait to see you again."

She sounded strange, not her usual upbeat self when I called most Sundays. I chalked it up to typical teenage angst, being a high school senior, hanging out with friends while juggling homework and maintaining a social life. Then I recalled my mom writing to me about a new boyfriend she started hanging out with and how she didn't think he was good enough for her. She never went into specifics, but I took the opportunity to ask about it.

"Everything okay, kiddo? How are things going with the young man you've been seeing? He's on the football team, right?"

"Yes, he's a defensive linesman." She went quiet all of a sudden, which concerned me.

"Anything I should know about? You guys serious?" I asked, knowing that it was not a good idea to push her into telling me something she wasn't ready for. Girls were strange that way.

"We, um..." She took a deep breath. "I can't wait for you to come home, Macey. It's been so long since the last time I've seen you." She sniffled.

"What is it, baby? Talk to me," I nudged.

"I..." She hesitated. "You're sure it's the day after tomorrow that you are coming home, right? I can count on you to be here, you promise?"

"Of course. Don't I always keep my promises?" I assured her.

Her sigh of relief was immediate.

"I'll tell you all about it when you get her. I'd rather do it in person."

"Roger that," I confirmed. "Day after tomorrow. See you then, squirt."

I arrived home to police cars, homicide detectives, an endless string of questions, and a distraught mother begging God to take her instead of her sweet baby girl. She waited for me as long as she could before deciding to meet up with her boyfriend, alone, to end their relationship. He hadn't taken it well and refused to let her go in peace. *She waited for me.*

The four chambers of my heart thickened behind my chest wall as the judge spoke into the microphone attached to the bench and pulled me from my thoughts. He dismissed the jury to deliberate while my mother and I were left stunned and detached at having heard the details of my sister's last hours on this earth. Two days we waited, barely speaking, not sleeping, picking over our dinner plates, until we finally received the call letting us know that the decision was in. We arrived to a packed house, confident that despite all his bullshit, Chad

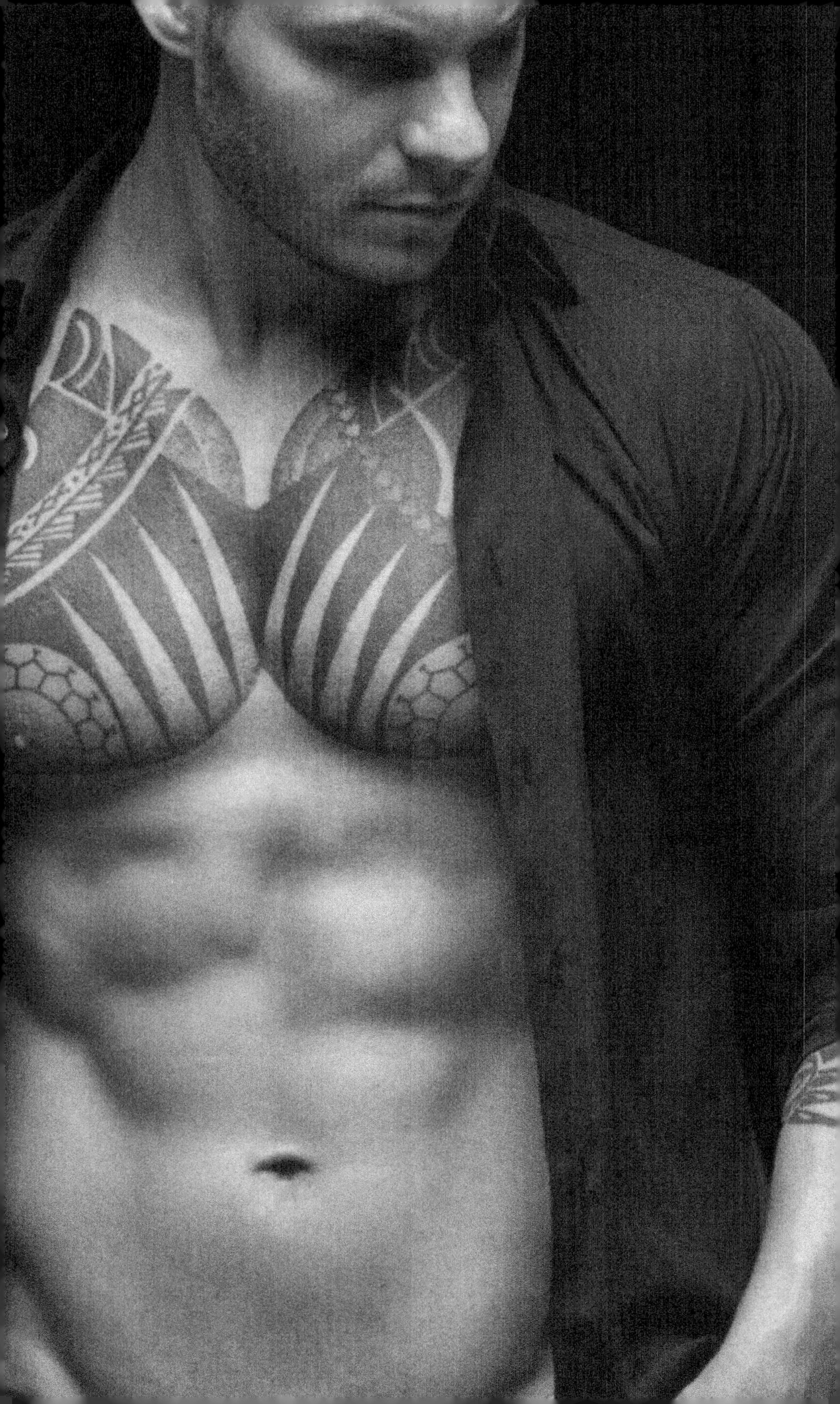

Jenson would get his just due and my sister would have her justice.

"Madam Foreperson, has the jury reached a verdict?" the judge asked.

A plumpish-looking middle-aged woman stood with a folded piece of paper in her hand of which to read from and delivered the decision.

"On the charge of murder in the first degree, we, the jury, find the defendant, Chad Jenson, not guilty. On the second charge of voluntary manslaughter, we, the jury, find the defendant, Chad Jenson, guilty. On the third charge of..."

Not fucking guilty?

I tuned the rest of it out, all except the quiet sobs of my mother as she held me around my waist, her tears soaking clear through my dress shirt. The defense attorneys shared congratulatory hugs with their client and thanked the twelve men and women for their time and impartial decision making. The prosecution spoke to us about the unfairness of the judicial system as a whole and how they wished things had turned out differently. They needn't have bothered. In my silence, I vowed that it would be. I'd fucking see to it, and not only for her, but for all of them. The ignored, the marginalized, the forgotten.

The sheriff's deputies cuffed that piece of shit and led him away to a prisoner transport vehicle waiting out back to carry his ass from the courthouse to his new jail cell. As he passed, his mother reached out her hand, and he assured her that everything was going to be fine, that he loved her and she shouldn't worry. Before I could turn away, he caught my eye and smirked triumphantly, proof positive that deep down, the cunt knew he'd gotten away with murder.

A month later, they sentenced him to fifteen years in the state penitentiary with the possibility of parole after eight and a half. A goddamn slap on the wrist for taking a life, but enough of a reprieve to refine my skills while I waited for his release. Until then, others would pay the heavy cost for his atrocities against my family. The threads holding my sanity together would be stretched. Some would feel the pain of a thousand tears; the rest would burn in fire and blood.

War and pain. I would become wrath until the day of reckoning arrived.

I'll never be on the wrong side of the clock again.

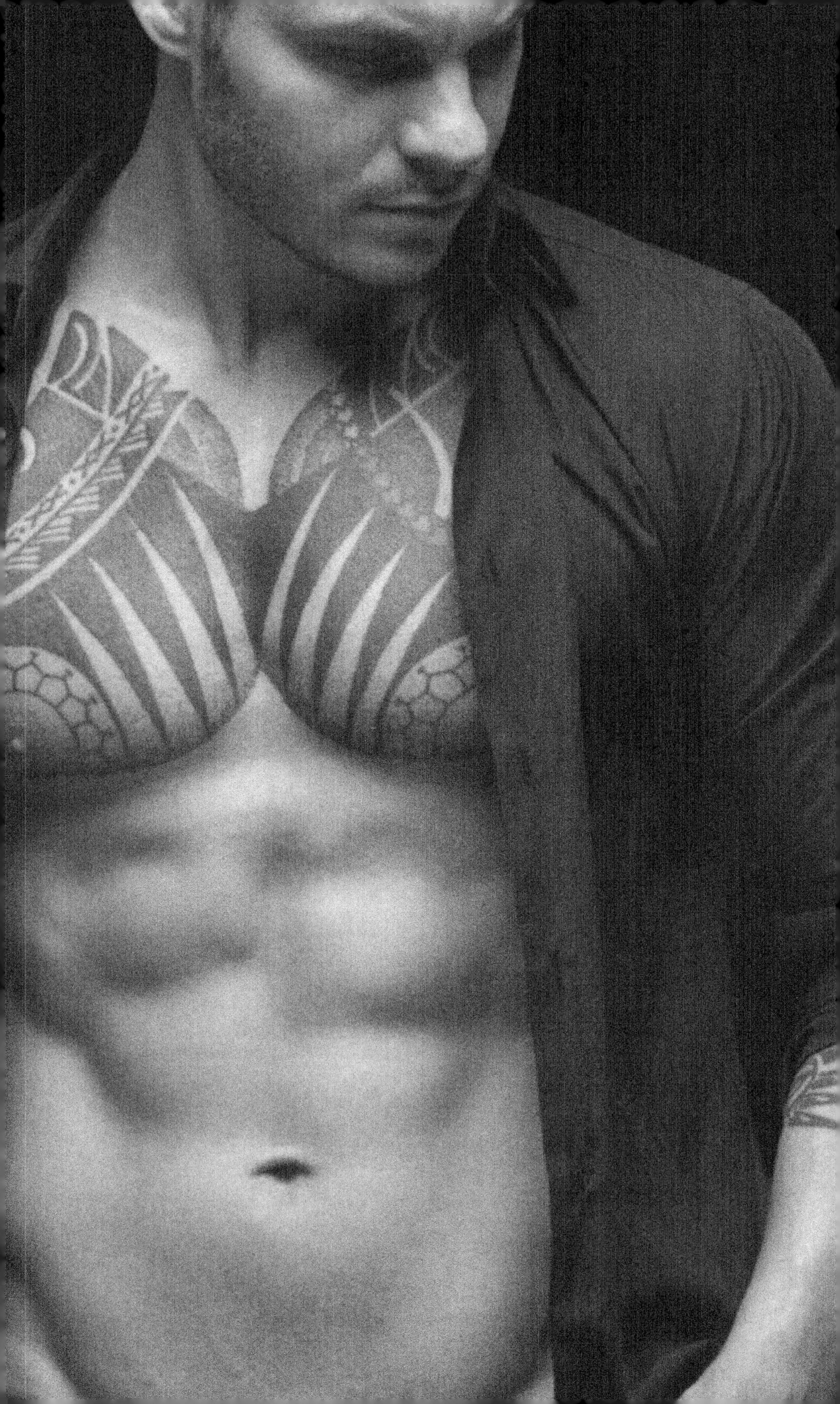

Chapter One

True

Oh God, please don't let this be happening.

"Please, please, please. This. Can. Not. Be. Happening."

Of course, this was happening, because why on earth would the cosmic powers that be want to make things just a little bit easier for me? My mother would say that ending up in a small southern town in the dead of night was my just deserts for running away from my golden goose. A woman whose only talent in life was spreading her legs for the highest bidder was entitled to her opinion, I suppose. She would be wrong, of course, but then again, she was wrong about a lot of things. I stopped counting on her support when I was a child, which was a blessing and a humbling reminder that I was indeed alone in this world. She hated me about as much as I hated her and was the last person I'd ever reach out to if I were in trouble, which was *exactly* where I found myself tonight—in big fucking trouble.

The Greyhound bus I was traveling on had experienced engine trouble on its way to Saratoga Springs, New York. It was the furthest I could journey with very little cash and no credit cards. I'd underestimated a few things in my haste to get away, namely the price of *two* plane tickets due to the infant carrier, which only got us as far as Mississippi. Who knew that flying south to end up north was cheaper than a non-stop route to the east? I certainly didn't, so unfortunately, that was the end of our air travel. From there, I had just enough money left over to purchase two bus tickets, totally clueless about the physical toll sitting for long hours would have on my worn-down body. Meandering with a newborn was hard enough under normal circumstances; doing it after giving birth a mere twenty-four hours prior? Yeah, damn near impossible. I was exhausted, scared, and anxious, so when the bus made yet another pitstop, I decided to get off and take a bathroom break.

Ten minutes, the driver said.

I should've paid closer attention.

I struggled to carry the baby and myself inside a handicap stall, which was the only one big enough to fit both of us. I sat her on my lap while I one-handedly pulled my pants and underwear down while squatting over the paper-covered seat. The cool porcelain felt so good against my bottom, I breathed a sigh of relief and allowed myself to relax to the sound of the trickling stream of urine. I only remembered closing my eyes for a minute, two at the most, but when I went back outside, the bus was gone, along with my duffle bag and ticket receipt. Left in the middle of nowhere. Fucked sideways.

I choked back a sob that lodged itself in the back of my throat and forced myself to stay calm. I'd come too far, done too many terrible things to turn back now. Then I heard that voice, the one that haunts me, *"Families stick together no matter what. Never forget we are family."*

I must've walked for hours; at least it felt that way. I hadn't seen a single car on the road since I started this little trek; the wildlife kept us company for most of it. By the time I crossed the city limits into the small town of Remington, Virginia, I could barely feel my legs anymore. My shoulders ached from switching the carrier back and forth between each arm. My feet shuffled along the pavement, every step sending a wave of wetness down my core, soaking the maternity pad to the hilt. I soldiered on, forward, always forward. That evil voice in my head egging me on, taunting me. *Give up,* it said, but I ignored it. Even if I had to crawl, I'd never stop moving towards freedom.

I came across a small strip mall in the heart of town. Everything was closed except for a tattoo parlor whose sign read *Masonry Ink*. It was filled with people going in and out, the sketchy kind you read about in books but hardly ever saw in real life. Regardless, it was my only hope. I took a chance that someone inside could recommend a cheap motel, halfway house, or woman's shelter nearby. It was a stupid thing to do, I'd be the first to admit, but I left the baby outside by the door since I'd only planned on staying for a minute. Someone pointed me in the direction of the person in charge, and for the first time all night, my legs refused to cooperate. The sheer beauty of the dark, muscled, tattooed man took my breath away. The guy was a fucking tank. My eyes homed in on his arms—they were built for holding a woman securely on her feet and beckoned me to burrow my weary self between them. My heart plummeted to my stomach with a yearning so deep it struck me odd. Such a weird response to a stranger, I thought to myself.

I shook it off, carefully walked over, and tapped him on the shoulder, but before I could ask about local accommodations, my world was flipped on its axis. Some blond-haired ass clown ran inside bouncing around like a jack rabbit as he held my baby in his arms asking if he could keep her. I went totally apeshit on his ass right there in front of everyone just before all hell broke loose. The few people milling around were ushered out by the owner, or more to the point, *thrown* out. A closed sign was slapped on the door, and the fire-breathing hulk of a man commenced to tearing me a new asshole with no lube.

"You left an infant outside, alone, to ask for a place to stay?" he growled.

"I didn't..."

"You left an infant outside, alone, in this neighborhood?" he repeated, deadly calm.

I tried to take my baby and leave, but it was too late. He saw right through my *I am woman, hear me roar* bullshit and called me out on it. He fired off question after question, none of which I had an answer for, until he calmed his shit long enough to address me rationally and without foaming at the mouth. By then, I was bone-tired, despondent, and barely keeping it all together. I was so flummoxed by his growling and rumbling that I even inquired about the *Help Wanted* sign posted on the window mid-tirade. That really set him off.

"Woman, if you want to be able to sit down tomorrow, you better start talking, and it better be good. You got one minute."

"I beg your pardon? Did you just threaten to spank me?" I gasped.

"Minute's up," he snapped.

Defeatedly, I asked. "Is there a cheap motel nearby, one that's within walking distance?"

It took him a long time to answer, too damn long. I wasn't sure what he was thinking, but whatever it was made him run his fingers through his hair and shake his head as if to clear it. I took a step towards the door and must've swayed on my feet, anxious to get on my way, when my baby decided now was a good time to cry out in hunger.

"How old is that baby?" he whispered, almost as if he was afraid of the answer.

"Two days old and in need of a diaper change, some milk, and some peace and quiet, so if you don't mind, I'll just be moving along now. No harm no foul."

His chest deflated some, thank goodness, but his gaze was

hot enough to burn a hole in my head. He struggled to keep the base out his voice as he looked me up and down.

"I'm trying really hard to understand why someone like you would be out and about, traipsing through the tulips with a micro-mini hatchling fresh from the womb. Where"—he stepped closer and leaned forward—"the fuck is your man?"

"Look....," I started tiredly, "I'm going to be straight with you, whoever you are."

"Mace Fox," he announced haughtily.

What could I say? I had no one and nothing to my name, a newborn baby who was starting to fuss in her carrier, and I was so fucking tired of looking behind my back waiting for the other shoe to drop that I just wanted to close my eyes for a few hours and recharge. Funny, how after everything I'd been through, the one thing I hadn't felt since I stepped inside Masonry Ink was a sense of fear. *Why aren't I afraid of him like so many others?*

I shook it off as a byproduct of fatigue, stress, and engorged breasts playing tricks on me. Mace Fox was unlike any man I'd ever met in my life, I'd give him that, but I simply couldn't fall for his dominant bull in my weakened state. That was saying something considering the company my mother used to keep in our rundown apartment back in Montana before I left to get married. Those bums didn't hold a candle to this growly alpha pain in the neck, but it wasn't just his good looks that set him apart. I genuinely believed he was concerned for my welfare. Yet another sign that I was on the brink of an emotional breakdown and needed to get as far away from him as I possibly could.

"Well...Mace Fox, I have exactly forty-eight dollars and fifty-two cents to my name. My man is no longer in the picture, nor is it any of your concern. I'm dog-tired and hungry, and as you can probably hear, so is she. The last thing I need is a lecture on personal safety from someone who looks like he was just released from a chain gang, so please, don't talk... point."

"Name," he mumbled.

"What?"

"What. Is. Your. Name?" he repeated as if I were learning impaired.

"Nancy Jennings, Capricorn, pleased to meet you. Now... can I go?"

The lie fell from my lips so easily I almost believed it myself. The identification I'd stolen from the real Nancy Jennings was near perfect to the naked eye; it's why I chose her to begin with. It worked perfectly when I purchased the plane tickets, and with any little luck, it would continue to do so. Her life wasn't in jeopardy. As far as the world was concerned, I was the five-foot-five blonde-haired, blue-eyed, twenty-seven-year-old organ donor from Montana. She was everything I wanted to be but never got the chance.

I watched her from a short distance away at a neighborhood coffee shop, the sun highlighting her hair with streaks of gold. She laughed at something she'd just read in the book she carried, and I wondered what it was like to be so carefree, not worrying what her husband, if she had one, was going to ask of her once she returned home. Two hours had passed in a blur before she stood to excuse herself to the lady's room. She left her book tucked neatly under her purse without a second thought that someone like me would steal it, which was exactly what I did. I exchanged her life for mine and that of my unborn child in hopes that one day, she'd be rewarded for her generous donation. She was my hero, and Lord knew I needed one.

Everything was going to hell while I stood there thinking about my amateur thievery. I blew out a long-suffering breath and sat down on one of the artist's stools with the baby carrier in my lap. *Just a minute to bounce back*, I said to myself, just a minute to gather my wits. As soon as my ass hit the cushion, there was an audible *squishy* sound from my saturated maternity pad. I glared at the large man in front of me, my face as red as the stain I undoubtably made, ready to continue our little showdown. Hopefully, the material was washable.

Instead of going for round two, he glowered at me once more before reaching into his back pocket for his cell phone. His lips firmed as he punched in the numbers so hard, I thought the devise would break into pieces.

"That's great! Call the cops or child protective services. See if I give a shit, you asshole."

"Shut it, woman," he snarled. "Nobody's calling the suits, so calm the fuck down."

My baby girl wouldn't be put off any longer, so while he made his call, I moved into mommy mode right there in the open. I lifted her from the carrier, released my heavy breast, and placed the nipple to her mouth, relieved when she took to suckling without any coaxing. And what do you know? Mace Fox was a gentleman. He turned his back to give me some privacy without being asked. That was certainly unexpected. He looked the type to brazenly stare at a pair of tits, being a manly man and all that. *Guess momma was wrong again.* I listened in as he barked at someone on the other end.

"It's Fox," he hissed. "Need a favor." *Silence.* "No, not that. Get your head out of the gutter. Got a woman here with a kid from out of town. Need a spot to dump their asses in for a bit. Quiet, no visitors."

Dump?

That isn't very nice.

"Appreciate it, babe. Be there in twenty."

He disconnected his call and took a few cleansing breaths. By then, I'd caught my second wind and was ready to grab my baby and move along. With his back still turned, Mace Fox pocketed his phone and addressed me with measured speech.

"Don't know you," he started. "And you don't know me, but what I do know is this. You just had a baby, and you're all alone, barely holding on to consciousness. You're cramping and bleeding heavily. I know that because you're favoring the right side of your stomach and you keep discretely checking your postpartum underwear ever so often for leaks. You're broke, and you have nowhere else to go. What are you going to do?"

"I'm fine…" I looked down at my baby girl in my arms. "We're going to be fine."

"Sure, you are," he grunted. "A real tough chick."

"I'm far from tough. What I am is a mother, and no one is going to take my child away."

He whipped around, eyes ablaze, and lit into me.

"Then be a mother now when it counts and let me help you, Nancy. Not asking for gratitude in trade. Believe it or not, there are still men in this world whose only desire is to do somebody a good turn without having expectations. I assure you, that's all this is; an opportunity to rally."

Maybe he had a crystal ball underneath all of those tattoos of his; either way, Mace Fox was spot on with his assessment. Every second that passed, my body betrayed me, serving as a reminder that even though I had the will, I most definitely didn't have the way. He made a compelling argument, but could I believe him?

"Am I safe with you?" I asked.

"No," he answered without hesitation. "But…you'll be safe regardless."

Tennessee Williams once wrote, "There's a time for departure even when there's no certain place to go." Deep down I knew that today was not one of those times. The man was like granite when all I'd ever known in my life was pumice, but I'd been fooled before by men who say one thing and do another. I was a failure who'd given up a lot of things I wanted out of life, but I wouldn't sacrifice my baby's wellbeing for anything. I had to put myself aside and focus on what was best in the long run, and right now, I couldn't physically protect my child from a homicidal ant. With a stiff upper lip and steel in my spine, I did what any mother would do, given the situation.

"I'll accept the help, for now, but only because you asked so nicely," I replied tiredly.

"Good. Now grab the kid. Let's roll."

"I, ah…would you happen to have a towel?" I asked, earning myself another grunt. *Lovely.*

Now would be a good time for the earth to swallow me.

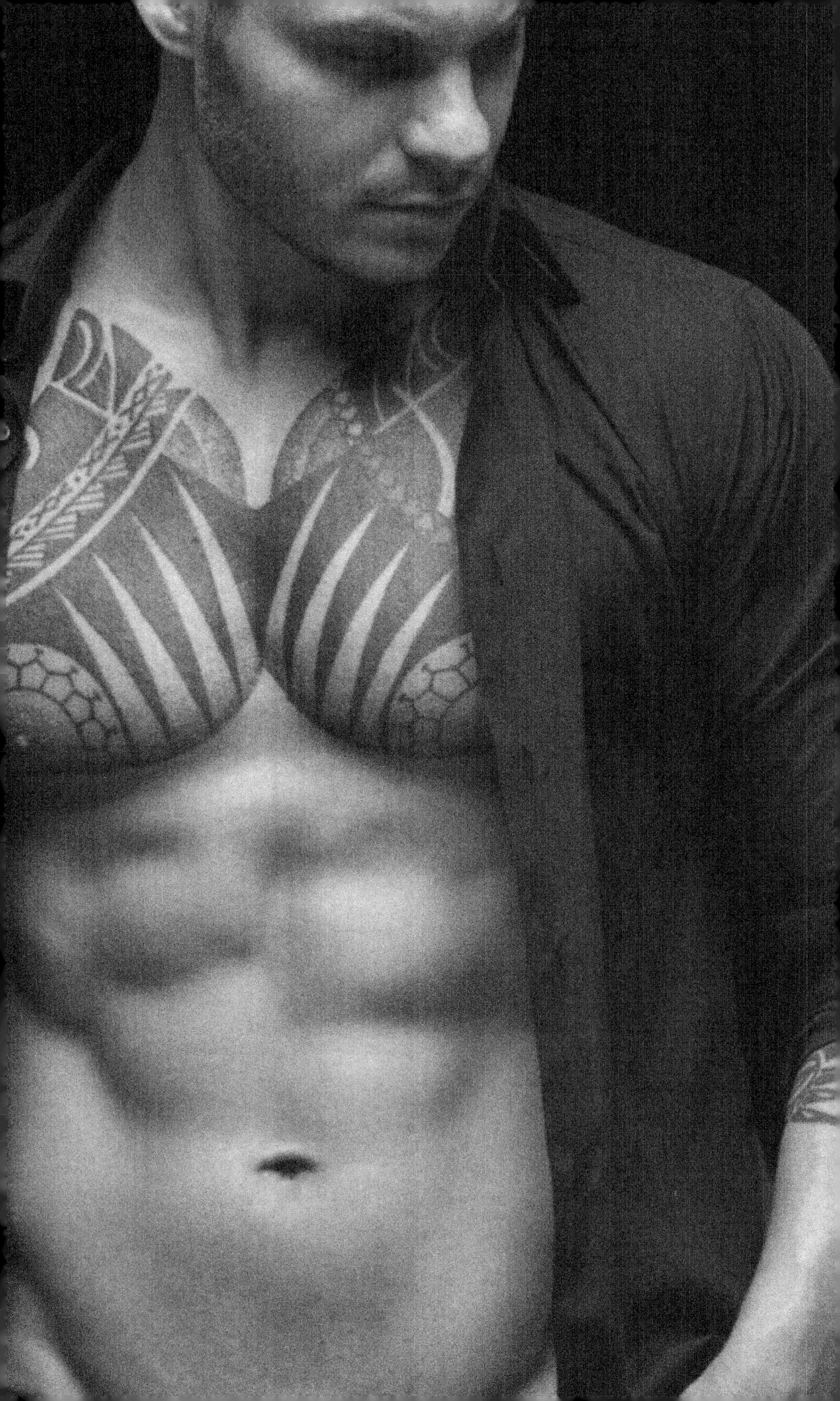

CHAPTER TWO

MACE

I HAD no fucking business taking on another headache. That was all I could think about on the ride back to Masonry Ink after I'd left the penniless woman and her kid with an old friend better equipped to handle female shit. It was her fiery mouth, all pink and pouty, drawn up into a cut little sneer that prompted me to react without considering everything that was on my plate. Between seeing to the shop's daily operations, countless hours spent tattooing pieces for my elite clientele, and schooling a new member to our team, I just didn't have the time for any more bullshit. One look into her shit scared blue eyes, and I'd folded like a plastic lawn chair.

It wasn't that Dread needed me to hold his dick while he took a piss; it was getting him on board with what happened *after* closing, deep in the streets, when no one was watching. He got a taste of it when his cunt of a step-mother showed up acting batshit crazy, damn near killing his woman in the process. We rallied behind him and took care of that shit quick fast, which kept him from going back in handcuffs, but he still wasn't privy to the full brunt of our covert activities until recently. I was right to bring him on board as more than just an artist. My fear was that it was too much too soon for a man fresh off a three-year parole sentence.

Still, most days, I felt like watered-down paint, stretched thin to cover the walls, applied as a filler to mask and conceal dirty stains under the sheetrock. The world was going to hell quicker than we could keep up. What were once *one-off scenarios* was becoming all too common place, especially now that social media ruled the lives of *woke* folks, and the shit was getting old. Toxic masculinity, misogyny, cyberbullying, gang life, all fucked-up terms thrown around like confetti to make society seem civilized, when in reality, it was an overflowing cesspool of misery. Case in point, a lone woman traveling at night, unprotected, with a newborn. The fuck? You can't make this shit up. She was damn lucky not to have made the top story on the six-o'clock news. Another innocent casualty of street violence in the books for small town Remington. *Jesus, fuck.*

People were in danger—women, children, and elders especially. The pigs didn't seem to care a fuck, victim blamed before they bothered to hear the full story, or were plain old lazy bastards who avoided the paperwork in lieu of a box of donuts. More often now they were coming to me for help, at their wit's end with nowhere else to turn, hoping for a small sliver of relief from the elements that plagued their worst nightmares. Their pain became my pain till I was damn near obsessed with it. I knew firsthand what would happen if you found yourself on the wrong side of the clock. Once I took something on, that shit was as good as handled, the same as with the little mother and her pink bundle of joy.

One glance at that tiny little baby and the panicky air surrounding her, and I knew Nancy Jennings was up to her pretty, blonde eyebrows in tragedy. I should've given her a few bucks and sent her on her way; probably would've saved my ass a lot of trouble in the long run. If I had to blame my call to action on anything, I'd say it was that spark in her eyes when she squared up against Kaden, arched her back like an angry little kitten, and threatened to leave Masonry Ink even though she was hurting. The strangest feeling of foreboding came over me, a sign that if I allowed her to walk out the door, I'd never see her alive again. In hindsight, the thought pissed me off once I realized that my reasoning was stoked in the primitive need to protect the beautiful woman who clearly had no one else to watch her back.

Nancy Jennings.

That was a load.

The name she used slipped from her tentative lips as she tried it out for size, thinking I would fall for the bullshit. Little did she know, facial recognition inside the doorway of the shop pegged her the second she stepped inside. Kaden designed the software to give us sophisticated information in real time with the discretion to dig deeper if the need presented itself. That shit saved our asses more than once. The guy was a computer genius, a hacker whose skills rivaled the best in the business when he wasn't getting on my damn nerves. The identification may have been fake, but her fear? That was very much real, and she reeked of it down to her cute little toes.

According to the preliminary transcripts, her real name was True Boardman, twenty-eight years old, married to some redneck cop from a shit-ass town in Montana. An only child to a single parent living hand to mouth but somehow managing to keep the lights on without ever working a full-time job. No further explanation was needed for that one—some poor bastard was fitting the bill, or several someone's. I'd bet my left nut she made her money on her back and was probably damn good at it to have kept it up for so long. I continued reading along, feeling defensive hackles rise on the back of my neck.

There were other things about her that struck me odd, her

medical records being one. There were no signs of unexplained injuries chalked up to clumsiness, usually part and parcel of domestic violence. No broken bones, stress fractures, or overnight stays in the ER. There were also no reports of prenatal care or certificate of live birth for the state of Montana in the days prior to her arrival. On the flipside, there were no reports of a child abduction, so I surmised the kid indeed belonged to her. There was a driver's license issued in her fake name along with a few credit cards that were reported stolen by their owner, closed and reissued. I glanced at the black-and--white DMV photo on top of a mound of papers. It was a good likeness for a farsighted idiot distracted by tits and ass, but not to a man like me. I made it my business to notice the particulars about a person, especially strangers. She couldn't have picked a worse place to stumble into if she'd tried.

I shook my head to clear out the wariness and ran the printouts through the shredder in my office. It was late, exhaustion a constant reminder that I'd been awake since early morning and wasn't likely to get much sleep with what I had planned for our next engagement. No matter how hard I tried, I couldn't stop my mind from racing with self-doubt over the decision to send that woman and her kid away. I was a man. What the hell did I know about the kind of doctoring she needed? The last time I was within ten feet of a baby was when my sister, Maya, was born. I was seven, nearly eight at the time and hated the idea of being a big brother to a crying, messy, shitty-ass little Muppet. That all changed the day my parents bought her home from the hospital and I took one look at her chubby pink cheeks as she held my finger in her tiny hand. My heart swelled to the size of the moon, and from that day forward, she owned me.

My parents had been trying for years to have another child only to be disappointed again and again by negative pregnancy tests. My father, who was a tough old Army dog, decided he was tired of being treated like a piece of meat when Mom was ovulating, would often complain good-naturedly at her expense.

"Lay off me, woman. Drained me twice already, both times before breakfast. Let a man regroup, for Christ sakes. I'll give you more of my magic stick once my belly is full." I recalled him saying to her one day, although at the time, I didn't know what he meant by it. She'd laugh it off like it was no big deal, but soon enough, failure turned to disillusionment and their joy began to die right along with dreams of ever having another kid. Like most couples, they simply gave up trying, then, lo and behold, Mom turned up pregnant, and nine months later, Maya came screaming into the world. Misfortune struck again a few years later when my strong-as-an-ox father was taken away from us after suffering a massive heart attack. Overnight, Maya became my responsibility as more than just her older brother. I was her provider, protector, and her hero until the day I failed at all of it.

Fucking hell.

The ache in my sternum that never went away obnoxiously pounded out a reminder to not continue down that train of thought if I had any hopes of falling asleep. It dawned on me then that I hadn't been laid in a while, something else I needed to see about, and damn soon. I carried my weary body up the stairs, stripped down naked for a quick shower, wrapped a towel around my waist, and lay on top of my bed for the next few hours, wide the fuck awake.

So much for not going there.

The ceiling fan rhythmically twirled, cooling my skin from the scorching steam of the shower. The synchronized blades failed to calm my wayward thoughts the more I watched them rotate. What the fuck had I gotten myself into with this chick? Never had I ever called on a friend to get me out of a bind with a complete stranger. What was it about her situation that made it so different from any other woman on the run? Things were slowly returning back to normal at Masonry Ink after the shit with Dread and his psycho bitch mother, and here I was, adding more trouble to the pile. Who was I kidding? Even with all that out of the way, I still had enough going on to keep my eyelids from closing, starting with Angelica and her non-relationship/relationship with Jagger.

The two of them would probably never sort out their shit long enough to act on their feelings, so of course, the rest of us were made to suffer through their Romeo and Juliet melodrama like spectators at a football game. I promised to stay out of it as long as it didn't affect the business or work environment, but their daily skirmishes were starting to do my fucking head in. I blew out an uneven breath and tried counting backwards from one hundred, willing my mind to go blank so I could get some damn sleep. I'd almost made it to fifty before another complication breeched my subconscious mind.

The same night fake Nancy showed up, Dead Man took off to parts unknown without so much as a backwards glance. One look at the distressed female, and I knew it was just a matter of time before he made his exit. He'd been the same mysterious, brooding, hothead since our apprentice days, only back then, he struggled to find his *reason*. I gave him one the night I ran across a little girl being forced to perform unspeakable acts to please her father. Nonetheless, it left me a man short, not only in the shop but in other ways, critical ways that could leave us open to risk. It was a problem that had me second-guessing our next takedown, but I wouldn't allow it to deter me. When sleep finally arrived, it came with dreams of flowing blonde hair and electric blue eyes that flared to life behind a brilliant smile.

Kaden showed up to my apartment bright and early the following morning, which was his usual MO. How any human could survive, let alone function at a high level, on less sleep than the average horse was beyond me, yet he somehow made it work. He peeked around the corner suspiciously, checking for signs of who knows what, before settling himself on the couch like he owned the place. Blond hair askew, brightly-colored tats on display, he'd put you in mind of a California surfer dude if it weren't for the intensity behind his lopsided grin.

"What happened last night, Mace? You send the little momma packing, or what?" he asked.

"Something like that," I mumbled on my way to the kitchen for coffee.

The man had entirely too much energy for this time of the morning.

"What's that mean, something like that?" he questioned. "Did you fuck her?"

I opened my mouth to answer, then closed it. Here's the thing about Kaden—when he's on a roll, it's best not to engage unless you want an eye tick for the rest of the day.

"Hey, man, no judgment. My dick got hard when she snatched that baby-carrying thing away from me, and I'm not ashamed to admit it. I think I might have an Oedipus complex or something 'cause the bitch I fucked last night? Yep, you guessed it. Made her call me daddy till I nutted all over her face. That's not weird, right?"

Don't answer. Don't answer. Don't answer.

I repeated that over and over in my head.

My brain usually felt as if it was underwater until that first cup of coffee did its thing. Three hefty gulps, and I was ready to be a contestant on *Fuck My Life*, the sequel.

"Took her over to Sal's. Figured another woman could help get her shit sorted, you feel me? New baby, tired as fuck, just needed a place to lay her head down before moving on. Felt bad, so I made a call. No big deal," I lied.

"Damn, that's fucked up, bro. Food poisoning sucks." He smiled, tapping his fingers against his knee. "Think she'd let me borrow a cup of her breast milk for my breakfast? I'm picturing

Fruit Loops or Captain Crunch. Bet that shit's bussin' like sweet cream with a sugary twang."

"Motherfucker, what? It's too goddamn early…you know what? Forget it." The guy was fucking brilliant with an IQ through the roof, but staying on task without dumb shit flying out of his mouth was a long shot. I blew out a frustrated breath because what the actual fuck?

"We all set for tonight?" I asked, causing him to sit up ramrod straight and quit with the silly-ass grinning. He answered with a head nod in the affirmative.

"What time are we leaving?" he asked.

"Ain't gonna be no *we* this time, Kaden. Going in alone."

"The fuck you say? Let me get the peanut butter out of my ears 'cause it sounded like you told me to go fuck my sister. You didn't say that right, Mace? Because we both know our success depends on how well we work as a unit. No *Lone Ranger* shit, remember? You almost had me going, man, you funny motherfucker."

"Does it look like I'm joking? Need you here to watch over the mother and her kid. Keep them safe in case shit gets hot and I don't make it back. Help them on their way with whatever they need—cash, transportation, safe contacts. Whatever they need, Kaden, hear?"

He pulled at his hair.

"Then take Jagger or Dread to watch your back, Mace. You can live out your big boss fantasy some other fucking time. This is bullshit," he snapped.

"Don't need 'em. Besides, Jagger is on Angelica, and Dread has Michelle. Like I said, going in alone, so save your sweet talk for the ladies. I don't want to hear any more about it. End of."

"Mace, I'm begging you. Let me call in Dead Man. Wherever he went, he'll come back if he knows you're in trouble. Please."

"I'm not *in* trouble, Kaden. They are. Crossed the line

slinging that poison at the middle school. Little kids don't know the difference between meth and the damn Avengers, walking around strung the fuck out, dropping like flies. Gave the cops plenty of chances to clean that shit up. Now another little boy, too young to have tasted his first piece of pussy, is being buried in a goddamn superhero casket. Why the fuck are we still talking about this?"

I threw my coffee cup against the wall. The pieces shattered into dust.

"All I'm saying is that we have a better chance if we stick together," he protested.

I took a few cleansing breaths. "The cops failed, but I won't, Kaden. Dead Man needs this time alone. Don't fuck that up because of me. I know what the hell I'm doing."

"But…"

He swallowed his next retort fully aware that it might come with consequences and repercussions, namely my fist in his gut. I acknowledged his silence with a hard stare that meant our discussion was over even though Kaden looked about ready to pop. My inflexibility on the matter was hard for him to understand without spending time inside my head, where the miseries were kept. The crew at Masonry Ink were my life; their safety was all that mattered to me, even more than my own. Always would be, no matter what.

Kaden stomped his way out the private entrance and back downstairs to the shop. Arguing with one of my closest friends left a hollow feeling in my bones. It wasn't a victory, more like a cease fire for the time being. I walked outside barefoot in a pair of sweats, head hung low, shoulders bunched, full of remorse. The fresh air took away some of the sting at having to shut down Kaden's genuine concerns. I was still thinking about it when I heard my name called and knew right away who was about to walk up on me, unwelcomed. Ashley Benjamin.

"Hey, gum drop," she greeted with a small wave. "Fancy seeing you here."

I ignored her.

Her cheerfully husky voice matched her beautiful face when she flashed me a smile. The way her hips swayed as she walked closer to where I stood would've brought the average heterosexual man to his knees. That wasn't us. Sexual attraction never entered my mind when I thought about Ashley Benjamin; it was never about the fuck between the two of us. Our relationship meant more to me. She had a piece of my heart, which was also the reason why her betrayal cut much more deeply.

I promised Memory a few weeks back that I would consider letting the women from the junkyard off the hook after they endangered my men when we were tasked as escorts. Everything worked out, thank Christ, but I wasn't ready to end the deep freeze just yet. I gave her credit for not giving up, but Ashley was way too selfish to understand the magnitude of her actions, how the very idea of something happening to her on my watch would've broken me in half. Perhaps I expected more from her, or maybe I was just being an asshole. Either way, I tipped my chin and turned my back on her, just like all the other times she tried to reconcile our rift. Eventually, we'd have our time to wade through the bullshit, but today wasn't the day, and she was no longer my concern.

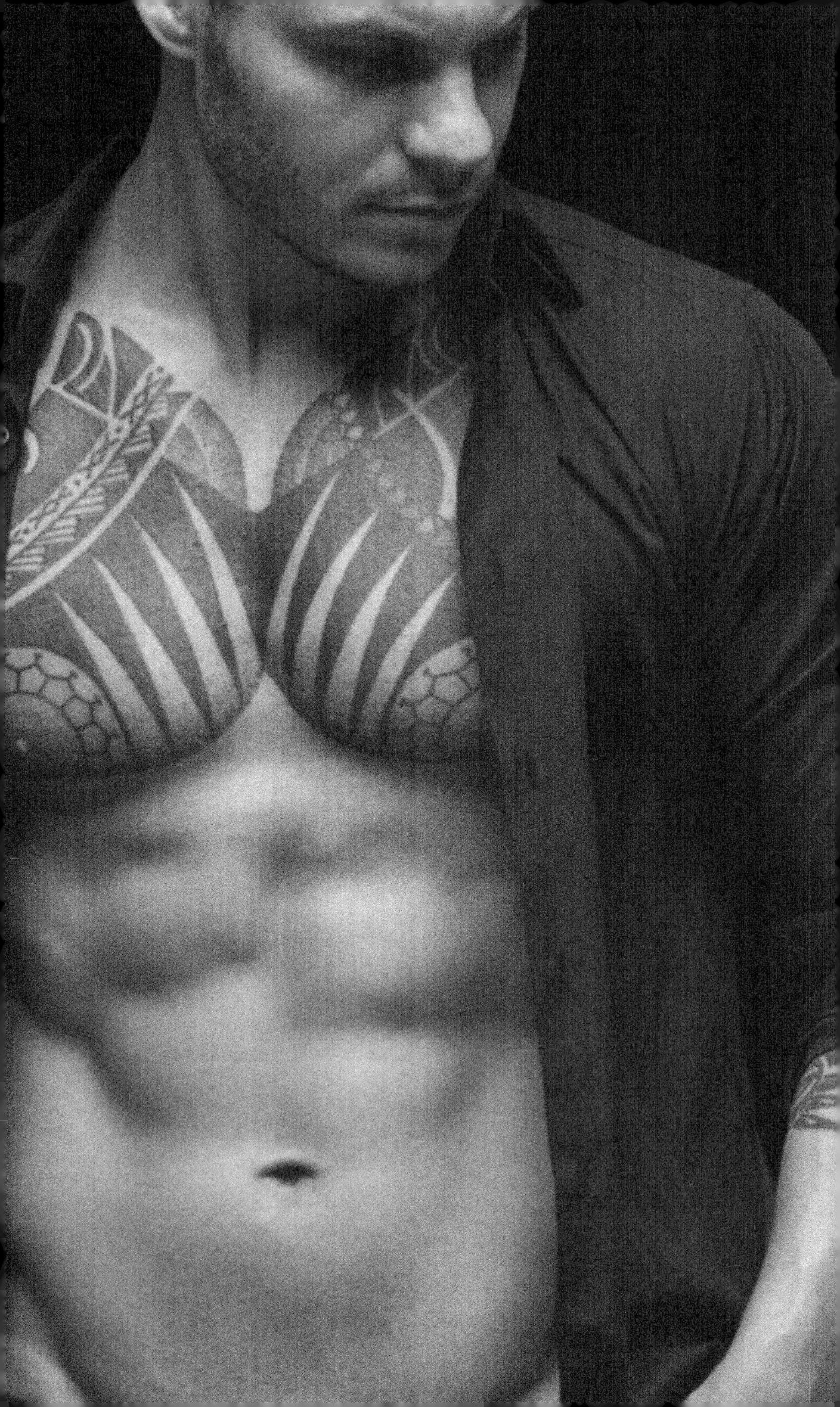

Chapter Three

True

It'd been two weeks exactly since I swallowed what was left of my pride and accepted help from Mace Fox, tattoo shop owner extraordinaire. We barely said two words to each other the entire trip over to his "friend's" house, but once we reached our destination, he changed into this whole other person right in front of my eyes. They hugged and kissed like prepubescent teenagers, laughing and giggling until they remembered someone else was standing outside, namely me. I swerved to avoid the sudden feeling of jealousy and insecurity I felt at witnessing their connection and openly eyed the ebony enchantress. She was a stunningly beautiful woman around my age, tall and slim, her hair stylishly cut short on the sides and back yet naturally curled on top in spiraled ringlets. Any trepidation I felt about showing up at this woman's house uninvited died a quick death the minute she smiled at me from the doorway and ushered us all inside towards her living room.

Mace Fox made quick work of the introductions, then proceeded to ignore the fuck outa me while he and the goddess made small talk. Being the odd man out and all, I stood off to the side, silently counting to one hundred. I was just that embarrassed. Since neither one of them was paying me any mind, my eyes took a slow perusal around the lovely space while the two of them rounded first base. The inside matched the outside in its simplistic beauty. Modern leather furniture, large black-and-white photos of inanimate objects adorned the walls, and a woodsy smell with a floral note tweaked my nose, most likely incense of some sort. The whole vibe created a warm aura about the place, peaceful and classy, like the owner. I reluctantly tuned them back in after a few minutes.

"You sure you're okay with this shit, Sal?" Mace Fox announced. "Nancy and her kid here need some looking after. Not sure how long. Could be a week, could be longer."

"Of course, big daddy, anything for you," she practically purred in response.

I threw up a little in my mouth at the moniker until they both started to laugh as if it was the funniest thing in the world. Call me slow, but I didn't get the joke.

"Good." Mace sobered. "I'll be in touch."

And then he was gone, leaving us behind with an unknown person in an unknown place.

"Well, you look dead on your feet, girlfriend. Let's get you all squared away."

Her comforting words triggered something inside me. My legs began to shake with nervous tension, but I couldn't allow her see the full extent of my desperation in case my next statement hit home and she believed my bullshit.

"You really don't have to do this, Sal. That was your name, right? Sal? I'm sure we'll be fine in a hotel or something for the night. I appreciate the help and all…"

The rest of the words failed to form. All I could do was stare at a spot on the wall, lost in a pit of defeat. It was all empty talk. I had no plan, nowhere else to go, fucked, for lack of a better word. She seemed to understand my reluctance. Her eyes softened as she stuck out her hand.

"Come, beloved," she urged. "The hard part is over now. You can do this. You're safe."

"I..."

She moved towards me, arms wide and welcoming. I all but fell into them. She wrapped them around my shoulders and led me towards a hallway where the bedrooms were located. Inside a smaller-sized room I assumed was a spare, my eyes took in the immaculate space complete with fresh linens, a chest of drawers, and a faux sleeping basket outfitted for baby Kayla. I was stunned stupid by her outpouring of kindness. Hot tears ran down my cheeks in a rush as my chest heaved from pent-up anxiety. There were no words to describe what I was feeling, so I didn't bother with trying to convey them. A humble thank-you would never be enough.

Sal's Florence Nightingale routine didn't stop there. She fed me a big plate of homemade lasagna dripping with melty cheese, tangy sauce, and garlic bread. Once my belly was full, she ran a warm bath sprinkled with Epsom salt, an indulgence I desperately needed after hours of sitting on a rickety bus. The entire time I soaked, she sat outside the door rocking baby Kayla in her arms so I could see for myself that my child was safe and sound.

When I couldn't stop the tears from falling, Sal was there to dab them dry with the sash of her cotton housecoat without passing judgment on my weakness. When I fought against fatigue, too afraid to close my eyes, Sal was there to reassure me that no one could get in without tripping her state-of-the-art alarm that was expertly installed by the best technician around. And when I had a nightmare that first night after finally drifting off to sleep, Sal was there to whisper in my ear that I was good and would stay that way as long as she had breath in her body.

I couldn't help but wonder why she would go out of her way for a stranger without even batting an eyelash at the say-so of a man like Mace Fox. I assumed they were lovers once or perhaps still, and at some point, I'd be forced to listen to their flesh slapping against each other every night like clockwork. I was surprisingly wrong all around. I hadn't seen or heard from him since he left us here to fend for ourselves. Not even a phone call to see if we were alive or dead.

Still, Sal was a godsend. If it weren't for her, we surely would've perished on the dark streets of Remington, alone. I barely made it out of bed those first few days. Luckily for me, Kayla slept most of the time, as newborns normally do, rousing only for feedings or diaper changes. Sal worked during the day, which meant we had the house to ourselves until early evening when she got off. The solitude gave me plenty of opportunity to drown myself in self-loathing with the help from a heaping dose of post-partum blues to keep things interesting. The tears were abundant along with the feelings, so many fucking feelings, I didn't know where to put them all. Everything from vulnerability, paranoia, to downright nothingness, the void was so deep, it swallowed me whole and regurgitated me back up. The worst of which was all the guilt behind my actions, the lying and stealing. I wasn't that person. I didn't know who I was anymore.

Sal's persistence kept me from falling over the edge when all I wanted to do was stop existing. She'd sit outside my door for hours reciting the ups and downs of her day, sharing stories from her childhood and those of her favorite aunt, who lived close by. She worked as a medical transcriptionist at a OBGYN office in town, which sort of made her even more perfect to look after us while we recovered. Wholesome meals with fruits and vegetables along with baby supplies were posted in the hall several times a day. All I had to do was walk out to grab them.Mace Fox appeared to be a pretty calculating guy, which had to have been the reason why he called on her in the first place. I reminded myself to thank him later for his forethought if I ever saw him again. Bit by bit I started to feel marginally better until one day, I cracked open the door and participated in the day's story time.

I learned that Sal was short for Sally, as she was named after the *Peanuts* character who just so happened to be Charlie Brown's younger sister. She argued that the name wasn't savage enough for someone like her and that she wouldn't be caught dead mooning over an asshole like Linus for any length of time. Too emotional for her tastes, and the whole blanket and thumb sucking thing was a complete turn-off—her words, not mine. That crack became an opening for fellowship, and I considered her the closest thing I ever had to a real friend. Her reward for guiding me towards the light? Lies on top of more lies. Every word that came out of my mouth was a falsehood, so much so, I started to believe the bullshit myself.

To Sal, I was a country girl from Montana whose marriage collapsed for reasons unknown, and after years of trying to make it work, I fled on a bus in hopes of getting as far away as possible. She accepted those details as if it were nothing, never pressuring me to say more. I was convinced that my place in hell was marked with a gold placard labeled *Deceitful Cunt*. Put me in coach—I was officially the most valuable player in the lying game, and I couldn't let this go on a minute longer.

I smelled the aroma of coffee coming from the kitchen and knew she was getting ready to leave for work. I bundled Kayla up in her carrier and went in search of Sal, needing to speak with her about a few things that had been on my mind.

"Good morning, little momma," Sal greeted while taking Kayla from my arms and smacking a quick kiss on the bottom of her little foot.

"Morning, Sal." I smiled. "Are you about ready to leave?"

She wore scrubs with little pink baby bottles on them today.

"Yeah, but I have a few extra minutes if you need to talk, Nancy. What's on your mind, girl?"

Hearing that name coming from her lips twisted my insides

and burned through my digestive tract like acid reflux. Every fucking time I answered to it, I betrayed her well-meaning soul with willful cowardice that wasn't getting any easier the more our friendship evolved. Sal was the last person on earth who deserved my shitty treatment of her. For as much as I wanted to spill my guts, unburdening myself of my darkest secrets, I knew, once the truth was out there, she'd not only toss my ass to the curb, she'd realize what a complete and utter trash human being I was.

There was too much to risk.

She took a seat at the breakfast nook holding Kayla while I grabbed a glass of orange juice along with a pre-pumped bag of milk, another gift from my Good Samaritan. The day after we arrived, I started to receive unidentified items in the mail addressed to Nancy Jennings. An electric breast pump with enough feeding supplies to outfit an entire tribe of pregnant women. That along with diapers, wipes, onesies, and various other girly outfits for Kayla, plus a wardrobe of comfortable sweatsuits for me to wear. One of the packages even included postnatal underwear with matching nursing bras that felt like heaven against my battered nipples. I could only imagine the cost, none of which sat well with me, which prompted this little get-together.

"I can't continue to accept these generous gifts from you, Sal. It's too much."

She gave me a look that screamed, *Bitch, please.*

"I know, I know, I haven't got a pot to piss in, but that doesn't mean I'm a mooch. I guess what I'm trying to say is that I don't understand your motive. Why would you make your home available to someone like me, a stranger, and with a kid, no less? I can't wrap my head around it."

"Because Mace asked me to, that's why, girlfriend," she replied with a shoulder shrug.

"It can't be that simple, Sal. It's been my experience that

people don't go out of their way to help others unless there's something in it for themselves in return. Once you're indebted to someone, the premiums grow into payday lending. Oleander plants are beautiful to look at, but they're still poisonous, so why the helping hand? What's in it for the two of you?"

Her eyebrows pinched together as she walked into my space. I'd offended her.

"I'm just grooming you long enough for that pussy of yours to bounce back into place so I can put you out on the street corner, make me some real money." She snapped her fingers. "Or maybe I'll sell you wholesale to some of the boys who like a little cream in their coffee. Yeah, I could get top dollar for a fresh little hick like you, straight off the farm with hay still sticking from behind her ears. I bet your momma would be really proud to see her daughter turned out and swallowed up by the streets with a few bodies under her belt."

I gasped at her hurtful comments. "I'm sorry…"

"Gotta say, beloved, that shit sounds wacked after everything we've shared. Thought you knew me better than that. Guess I was wrong about you."

"Put yourself in my shoes, Sal. What you think about all of this?"

"Your shoes?" she snapped. "You mean those cushy ballerina flats you're wearing? 'Cause from where I'm standing, you got it made, sister." She clicked her tongue and looked me up and down.

Her words were like daggers, piercing my heart with subcutaneous strikes meant to wound, not kill. Could she see the truth I'd been so desperately trying to hide behind? Sal didn't know me, not the real me, yet somehow…her passionate speech, the distant tone, the sheen in her eyes as she fought to beat back the sorrow. I recognized the spitefulness as her way of telling me I was being unappreciative, that things could've been a whole lot worse had it not been for her friend Mace Fox. She wasn't affronted on her own behalf; no, she was offended in support of the man who came to our aid when no one else would. *Man, I really fucked that up.*

"I didn't mean to upset you, Sal." I reached for her hand and held it. "My life was shit growing up, and it progressively got worse until I no longer recognize friend from foe. Not that I *had* many friends, but you get the idea. I just can't help the feeling that I'm being played."

"Wow...Is that what you think I'm about, Nancy? That all of this is some master plan we cooked up one day with a little help from Dr. Evil?" She stuck her pinky in her mouth like Mike Myers in *Austin Powers*.

"Of course not. I'm just not used to being cared for in this way." I shrugged.

"Well, that's a relief, 'cause there's a crib and travel playpen scheduled for delivery this afternoon. Sign for it, and I'll help you put it together when I get home from work."

"Sal...I can't."

"Look," she interrupted with a stiff hand. "We've all been there, Nancy. Down on your luck and going through a hard time. That shit's not new, beloved. Get in the back of the line."

"No disrespect, Sal, but you have no idea what you're talking about. Look at yourself and then look at me. You have a great house, a good paying job, and friends whom you clearly care about and who care about you. There's no comparison between my life and yours."

She pinned me with a shake of her head at my little meltdown.

"Poor little Nancy pants," she tutted. "Life has you by the proverbial ball sack, and it's the end of the fucking world. Gurl, cry me a river with pistachio nuts. You aren't that bad off, and even if you were, it's just a speed bump in the road to betterment. Shit rolls downhill and all that. Look on the bright side; make some fucking lemonade."

"Not compared to you, that's all I'm saying," I challenged.

Her face turned grim as she lowered her voice to barely a whisper.

"What you see isn't the finished product, beloved. God isn't done with me yet. Back in the day, I was a mess, until my Aunt Corrine sought help from an atypical man who had a reputation for getting things done. He offered me the one thing I needed—a safe place to go when I was ready to get off the streets, no strings attached, no ulterior motives. When I begged him to take the only thing I had of value in return for his kindness, he turned me down flat. Instead, he told me I was worthy, that there was more to life than selling pussy to the lowest bidder so I could buy more drugs. He saved me...and he'll save you, too. That's why, when he asked me for a favor, I didn't hesitate in saying yes. I owe him everything."

Holy shit.

She was talking about Mace Fox.

"Sal, I..."

"Besides," she announced, preparing to leave out the door, "I haven't paid for shit. Nope, not one red penny. Does it look like I'm made of money? I work for a living."

I stood there with my mouth hanging open in shock.

"Get some rest, Nancy, and try not to worry so much you'll give yourself gray hair."

Not likely now that my mind was blown. *Holy shit.*

How the fuck did I get here?

Montana
Five years prior:

The funeral service for my mother-in-law was a veritable who's who of Sorensen, Montana. Everyone was there, from the owner of the local bakery to the mayor and his entourage, who never failed to press the flesh, especially during an election year.

My husband's mother was a kind woman by nature, quiet and reserved, conceding to her husband for pretty much everything. We were all in shock from her sudden death, having spoken to her the day before, when she seemed perfectly fine and in great spirits. I wasn't aware of any illnesses that plagued her, and according to the obituary, she passed peacefully in her sleep of natural causes. My heart broke for my husband when he was delivered the news. Their bond was very special to him; I envied their closeness. Mourning one's mother was not something I ever had to worry about. I looked forward to the day mine departed this earth. She deserved to rot in a pit of fire as far as I was concerned. *Good riddance.*

The crowd of well-wishers had all but disbursed with the exception of Ryan's father, the town sheriff, who also happened to be his boss. We decided to hold the repass at our house far removed from the gloomy place where the body was found just days before. I was putting away the many trays of sweets, casseroles, and sliced fruit when Ryan walked into the kitchen with a crestfallen look on his face. His dark suit was a mess of wrinkles, and his tie hung haphazardly around his neck, hair a bird's nest of strands. How I wished I could take his pain away.

"My father is taking my mother's death pretty hard, True," he said, leaning against the doorjamb, watching me as I worked.

"That's certainly understandable. They were married, what… twenty-five years?"

"Twenty-seven," he corrected.

"Hmm…long time."

I continued my task not knowing what more to say in this situation. My own mother was very much alive and well, living across town in the seedier part of Sorensen. She'd declined my invitation to the funeral for obvious reasons—she'd slept with half the male population in attendance, including the mayor, so it wouldn't have been a good look. For once, I was grateful for her forethought, albeit selfish in nature. Having her around on the worst day of my husband's life would've cemented my neighbors' beliefs that I was a tramp, the same as her. Guilty by association and all that. *Thanks, Mom.*

I dwelled on that narrow escape a little too long. Soon enough, the air in the room turned cold, bitterly cold, as if the air conditioning was turned to blizzard. The hairs on the back of my neck stood on end, and I felt my hands begin to shake. A bad omen? I looked over my shoulder at my handsome husband and frowned. Something wasn't right. I could tell by his body language, the coiling of his muscles beneath his shirt, and his terrible habit of biting his thumb nail to the quick when he was nervous.

"My family is important to me, True, more important than anything in this world. You're a part of that, you know, a very special part," he finally said.

"I feel special, Ryan. You, of all people, know what it was like for me growing up with my mother as a role model. Your family has treated me like one of their own since the beginning, and I appreciate that more than you'll ever know. Anything I can do to help ease the burden of your mother's loss, just ask. I'll always be there for you."

"Oh, True." He smiled. "I was hoping you'd say that."

I smiled back at my husband, having done my best to sound like the supportive wife I always aimed to be. Of course, I didn't mind helping out his dad if the situation called for it. What wife would? I didn't suspect he'd know much about grocery shopping, housekeeping, or dirty laundry; that was Mrs. Boardman's job, rest her soul.

Ryan moved with deliberate steps, head down, angling towards where I was rinsing out the dirty glasses to go in the dishwasher. He reached for my elbow and gently, yet urgently, led me in the direction of our living room near the entrance of the house. There, in the loveseat, sat my father-in-law, drink in hand, suit jacket and tie removed, dispassionately waiting for our arrival. He was a large man, well over six feet, fit and muscular from all his years in law enforcement. Ryan favored his father in the looks department with his dark hair and brown eyes. Watching the two of them together was like seeing a spitting image of the older man in his younger years. He'd always been affable towards me once Ryan and I were officially dating, the same with his wife. My soul wept for him while at the same time, my senses were leery.

"Are you leaving now Mr. Boardman?" I questioned. Confused.

"Ask your husband, True," he slurred.

I looked to Ryan for direction, but his eyes were void of any emotion. I felt the strange need to pull myself away and run from their presence, to seek safety elsewhere for the time being, but where would I go? Ryan was my only family aside from my mother, and I'd die before I asked her for help. The room began to sway as I concentrated on my breathing, in and out, in and out, in... *Stop being ridiculous,* I told myself. Everything would be just fine as long as my loving husband was by my side. We were a team, and he was my paragon of strength.

Ryan squeezed my hand, and I flinched. He turned me around by the shoulders to face him.

"It's been a rough day for all of us, True, but there's something you can do to make it better. I'm asking you this because I know you can...for me...for our family."

"I don't understand, Ryan."

"You know I love you, right, True?" he responded. "No matter what, I'll always love you."

"Of course, I do, but..."

"He needs you tonight. One night, that's all I'm asking. You'll do that, won't you? It doesn't mean anything, and I swear once it's over, we'll forget it ever happened." My brows pinched together before the meaning of his request finally sunk in. My knees buckled, but I refused to go down, not in front of them.

"Ryan, what are you saying?" I shouted.

"It's one night, True." His finger ran along my cheek. "One favor to secure your place and make us all proud. You're the only woman in the house now. Do it for your husband."

"Are you seriously asking me to…" I couldn't bring myself to acknowledge this foolery.

"You'll do fine, True. I have faith in you."

"Ryan, please, you can't be serious. I'm your wife. Think about what you're asking. This will ruin us! I love you, please," I begged.

He grabbed the back of my neck and held me in place.

"Then show me how much and do what I ask."

"Please don't do this. It's wrong."

Hot tears slipped down my face in waves. Just when I thought this was some kind of a sick joke, Ryan looked to his father, nodded his head once, released me from his hold, and walked out the door without me.

"My son certainly understood the assignment, True. I applaud him for that. All that talk of love, though? Must say I'm a little disappointed, but that's boys for you. Did you know that I always wanted a girl child? A little princess to call my own, someone to spoil rotten with love and affection. My newly departed wife wasn't so keen on the idea once Ryan was born, said she couldn't stand the idea of having another child, especially not with me," my father-in-law stated matter-of-factly.

"Mr. Boardman, I think perhaps…"

"Oh, now, none of that, True. Please call me Rich, or father, even daddy if you'd like."

I was going to be sick.

I tried to appeal to his rational side.

"Grief is a terrible thing, Rich. I'm sure in time, you'll realize that it's just the heartbreak and sadness you're feeling and sleeping with your daughter-in-law is not the solution. Today was heavy for everyone. Let's take a moment to reflect, maybe say a prayer for your wife. I'm sure she'd appreciate that."

"That's..." He barked out an uproarious laugh. "Thanks, True, I appreciate the sympathy."

He downed another shot of whisky and stood from the chair. I took a step back contemplating my next move. My eyes searched for a way out. It was the sneer on my father-in-law's face that dared me to try. I moved one pace to the left only for him to toss his glass at my head, barely missing. His action caught me off guard. I gasped then froze, my heart nearly beating out of my chest.

"Don't you fuckin' move, bitch, or I'll make sure you regret it!" he shouted.

My back stiffened from his harsh timbre.

I silently prayed for my husband to return home and take me away from this nightmare.

"What have you done to Ryan?" I accused. My voice trembled. "I refuse to believe that he came up with this foolish idea all on his own. You must've threatened him in some way, but why? How could you do that to your own son?"

"Ryan does what I tell him to, missy. Get that through your head. He comes from my loins. Without me, he would've been nothing but a stain on the mattress."

I stood there in complete shock.

It'd been less than five hours since we buried his wife, a woman he'd been married to for the better part of his adult life, but did he give a fuck? Judging by his salacious smirk and the noticeable hard-on bulging his pants, I'd say the answer was unmistakable. The man had lost his mind along with any sense of right and wrong.

I jutted my chin in challenge. "I won't be a part of this... insanity. Get out of my house."

"Don't you mean *my* fucking house?" he snapped. "Look at you..."

He approached. Confidence oozed from his strut, the swagger of a man in complete control.

I'd never felt so scared and alone.

"Up your own ass, thinkin' you got any say in what goes on around here. I was the one who convinced Ryan to marry you straight out of high school. Did you know that? He wanted to wait, sow his wild oats for a while before settling down, mind filled with cunt. He didn't want you!"

I blanched at his outburst.

Liar.

"He took the job as my deputy because *I* told him to. He married you because *I* told him to. He agreed to let me have you for one night"—he grabbed me by the throat and leaned down an inch from my nose—"because *I* told him to. Now, you can either accept that, or shit's gonna get really uncomfortable for you. What's it going to be?"

One night.

Ryan gave me away.

I am weak.

My nightmare began after the death of another.

That night, I would've given anything to trade places with her.

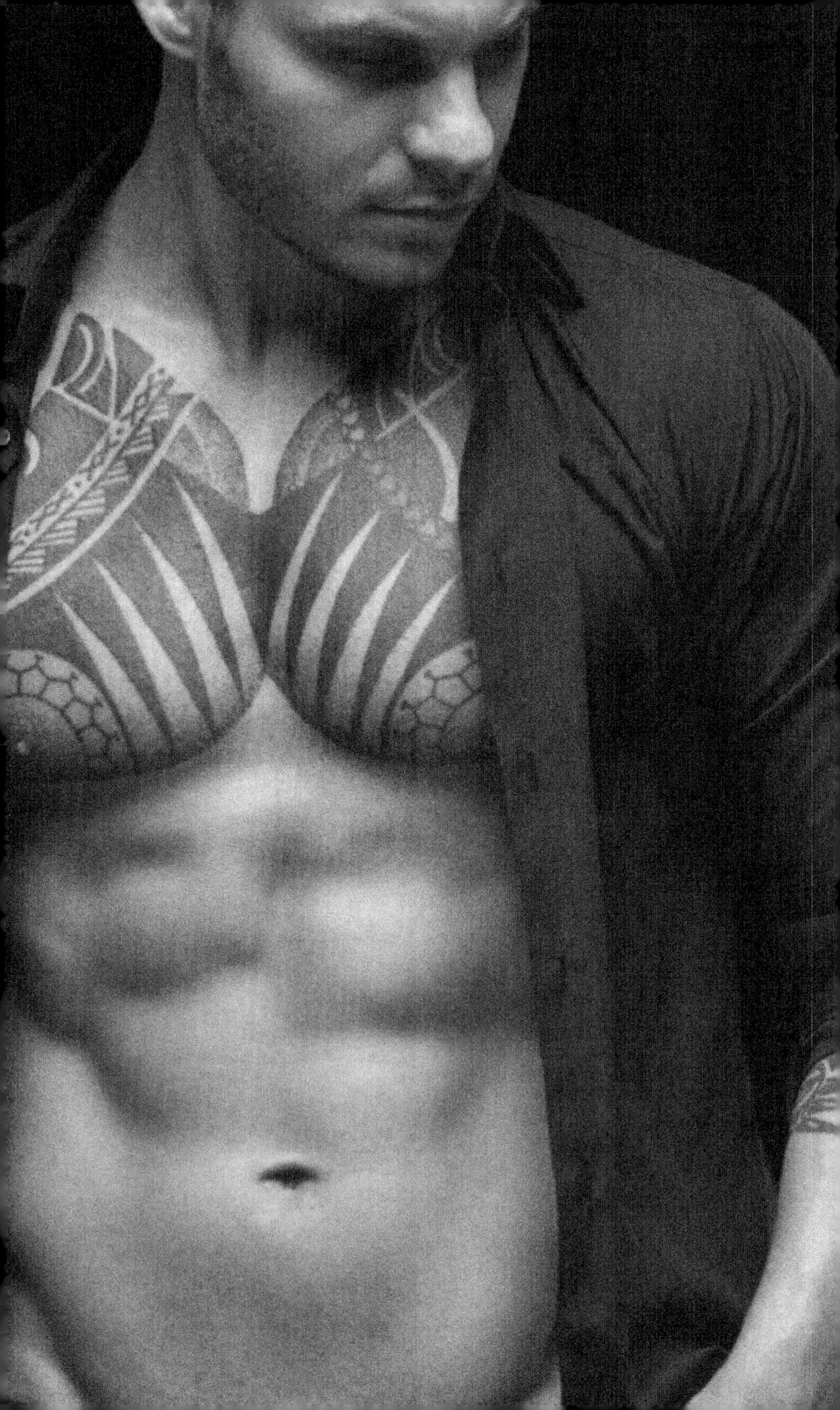

CHAPTER FOUR

MACE

"WE NEED to slow it down, Mace. Shit's getting out of hand," Jagger bellyached.

"Yeah, that last job we did was completely fucked up. Homey's gonna need a colonoscopy bag for the rest of his life after you Barry Bonds' his ass. Didn't think you were ever going to stop impersonating a cleanup batter till that fucker was dead," Dread responded, sketching a picture of something in his notepad.

There must've been an alien invasion that abducted my crew and body-snatched their asses into a bunch of women. At this rate, I'd have to ask Angelica to add a box of tampons to the weekly supply order if they kept on much longer.

"Not to mention that shit with the meth lab. They're still looking for body parts in the burnt-out wreckage," Jagger added, shaking his head.

Waah. Waah. Waah.

We were all sitting around my office after a particularly brutal encounter that took place the night before. I was two seconds away from tossing all of their asses outdoors if they didn't stop riding my ass about shit that was over and done with. The only one who wasn't crying like a bitch was Kaden. He was too focused on pacing around the room, adjusting his nut sack, and giving me the evil eye like he had been since the night I took down the meth lab solo. He had a right to hold on to his grudge, but as far as the other two, they had T-minus zero to back up off my dick before I cleared this motherfucker out with some lead. I wasn't sorry for what I did. Given half the chance, I'd do that shit again in a New York minute.

The cunt we tracked down was a third-generation restaurant chain owner's son who thought it was acceptable to sexually harass his employees, both male and female, whenever he got the notion. He deliberately targeted the underprivileged who couldn't afford to lose their jobs as a consequence of reporting his behavior to the police. Shit went on for months. When someone did finally tell, he accused that young woman of stealing from the cashbox and had her arrested, even though she had zero access to the till. He offered to drop the charges if she dropped to her knees in return. That's when a friend of hers decided he had enough and tried to do something about it. He's now serving six months in county lockup for misdemeanor assault. The good news was that his cell mate was a prospect for the B9's and took a liking to the guy, reached out to Python, the club president, who then reached out to me.

The smarmy motherfucker managed to piss me off and gross me out all at the same time. I'd be the first to admit, I lost my cool, but it was totally worth it to see the look on his face when I took a bat to his cock sack after he bragged about molesting the thirteen-year-old daughter of his father's secretary. He offered her up in exchange for his freedom, did it as a means for getting out of his predicament. His fucking gall enraged me, thinkin' we were anything like his repugnant ass, hard up for little girls. I felt the blood echoing between my ears as I grabbed him by the throat and happened to look down. Asshole was fully erect and smiling.

I saw red.

I saw motherfucking red.

I beat that disgusting prick to within an inch of his life and only stopped because Jagger snatched me around the shoulders and held me back. That trust fund pedo had it coming, plus a lot more if I had my way. Now his rich daddy can buy him the best wheelchair on the market and usher him around while he drooled all over himself, sippin' on canned peaches for dinner. I gave less than half a fuck that that piece of shit got roughed up, which was exactly what I told my crew. I sat back in my chair and glared at their concerned faces.

"My operation. My call. Don't like it? Walk the fuck away. Feel me? I don't need pussies on my team, and I sure as shit don't need y'all second-guessing my motives."

"Mace," Jagger spoke, "it's not that we want out. It's that…" He looked to the others.

"What, motherfucker? Spit it out," I snapped.

"You seem to be enjoying it, bro, and I get it, I really do. Some of these cocksuckers deserve to rot in hell, but we're risking our freedom with every new person we take on. You going rogue a couple weeks ago didn't help matters much either. Blowing up a meth lab and two people in the process is not operating under the radar, bro. That's being lit up like a fucking Christmas tree. Why can't you see that?" Jagger griped.

"You scared now that you got a new bitch, Jagger?" I accused. "Take your punk ass somewhere else with that shit. Your frilly panties are showing, hoss."

"That shit was low, Mace. It's got nothing to do with that, but you're too far gone to listen to reason. We care about you *and* Masonry Ink. Losing either is not an option for us."

"Too far gone? Big dog, I started this fucking shit, and you got the nerve to speak to me like this? Chest all swollen, ready to throw hands. Pussy got you thinkin' you're a bad motherfucker all of a sudden, see me outside the next time you feel like testing me."

Jagger recently started dating some chick named Kira, who moved in upstairs at his apartment complex. She took in his massive muscles and asked if he could help her lift some boxes, a smooth bitch move perfectly executed, and his dumb ass fell for it. I had to listen to Angelica and Dread's woman, Michelle, grumble about it for hours last week when he paraded her ass into Masonry Ink for everyone to see. Angelica hadn't taken the news well, and I was starting to get worried about her fragile mental state. She insisted that she was fine with it, but I knew her better. She was devastated, withdrawn and despondent, similarly to when I found her on the street as a scared little girl. I refuse to let her backslide over whom Jagger decided to stick his dick into. She'd come too far to let a broken heart derail all of her progress.

But that was for another time.

Today was about me.

"I don't need a fucking intervention, and the next time you all decide to give me one, you better think long and hard about what it's going to feel like with my foot broken off in your asses. I'm not off the grid, far fucking from it. End of. Now…is there anything else you want to say before I completely lose my shit?"

"We trust you, Mace," Jagger declared. "We'll follow your lead, all the way to hell if we have to, brother. We just…"

"Yeah, I won't hold my breath. Now, get the fuck out."

The big man, along with Dread, piled out my office without another word. Kaden stayed behind, shoulders tight, knees locked in place, and battle ready. I learned long ago that the man was a critical thinker; scary smart, he used only the facts to form a judgment. Once he was in, he was all the way in. His manic behavior, poor impulse control, and frequent womanizing were the only things that seemed to calm his beast long enough for him to function properly without killing someone. He was my friend, and his insight was invaluable, but my stance was not up for debate, no matter what he had to say.

"What I said to them goes double for you, Kaden, so say whatever the fuck is on your mind and get the fuck out. I got work to do."

He finally stopped his pacing.

"You think I don't know what's going on, Mace? Think you can clown me into thinkin' your shit isn't two seconds away from affecting all of us? I know everything, motherfucker, why you've been distracted, why you've been taking on more than we can handle, and why you almost killed a man without considering the consequences for everyone involved."

"So, what? Want a fucking medal?"

"You could've ended this a long time ago, Mace. You had the connections, coulda put the cash up for bids the second that prick hit the joint, but instead, you chose to wait, do the deed yourself. Now he's up for parole, and you're spiraling. Tell me I'm wrong," he raged.

"Not wrong, Kaden. Not completely right either," I challenged. "He's not getting out. No way they grant that bastard parole. I refuse to believe that could happen after what he did."

"You need to prepare for the unimaginable, Mace. Stranger things have happened, but this, you…" He pointed towards my face. "Lost, man, you're completely fucking lost."

"Appreciate the psychotherapy, especially coming from you. Now, if you don't mind…"

It was my way of dismissing him and his bullshit concerns for a second time in a matter of weeks. If I wanted my head shrunk, I'd track down Hank and make an appointment. They tried to keep it on the down low, but I knew he was treating Dread afterhours at his office. The yuppie male model slash psychiatrist was good at getting his patients to open up about their past trauma, but I didn't need a shoulder to cry on. What I

53

needed was peace and quiet to figure out who my next mark was going to be. Unfortunately, there were a lot to choose from and very little time to plan. My operational framework was clear as cut glass, and my crew could either get on board with that or get the fuck outa the way. I wouldn't be held down by anyone. Kaden sucked his teeth in a snit and turned on his heels, marching towards the exit.

"One last thing," Kaden announced before reaching for the door. "He's tracking her. Put out an all points advisory along with a description."

"Who's tracking whom?" I asked.

"True Boardman's husband, the cop."

Fuck.

I expected that at some point, but shit if the timing wasn't ideal.

"Can you lead him away for a while until she and kid are stronger, able to travel?"

Kaden was a beast behind the keyboard. If anyone could buy us some time by using trap doors and Trojan Horse software, it was him.

"Already on it," he announced but made no effort to move along.

"You got something else to say?"

"Yeah," he hedged. "There was no mention of the child in any of the bulletins, Mace. Any idea why that would be? What kind of father doesn't look for his baby girl who's presumably missing along with her mother?"

Fucking shit. Damn good question.

I had no answer.

"We wait, keep watch, and hope he follows the trail to nowhere. By then, they should be out of our hair and someone else's problem to look after. Keep me posted. Let me know if you hear anything else of concern," I instructed.

"Roger that."

Once my office was cleared of all the riffraff, I was able to exhale a breath I didn't realize I'd been holding. A part of me wanted to run over to Sal's and gather up little momma and her baby girl in my arms and steal them away from here. The feeling was as foreign to me as it was shocking. I swallowed it dry, no chaser, while mentally chastising myself for contemplating such foolishness. Sure, she was beautiful, and like Kaden, my dick moved to half-mast when she entered Masonry Ink, but they weren't mine to shield and never would be. It was best for all involved that I maintained my distance. It was safer that way… and still…

What else are you hiding, True Boardman?

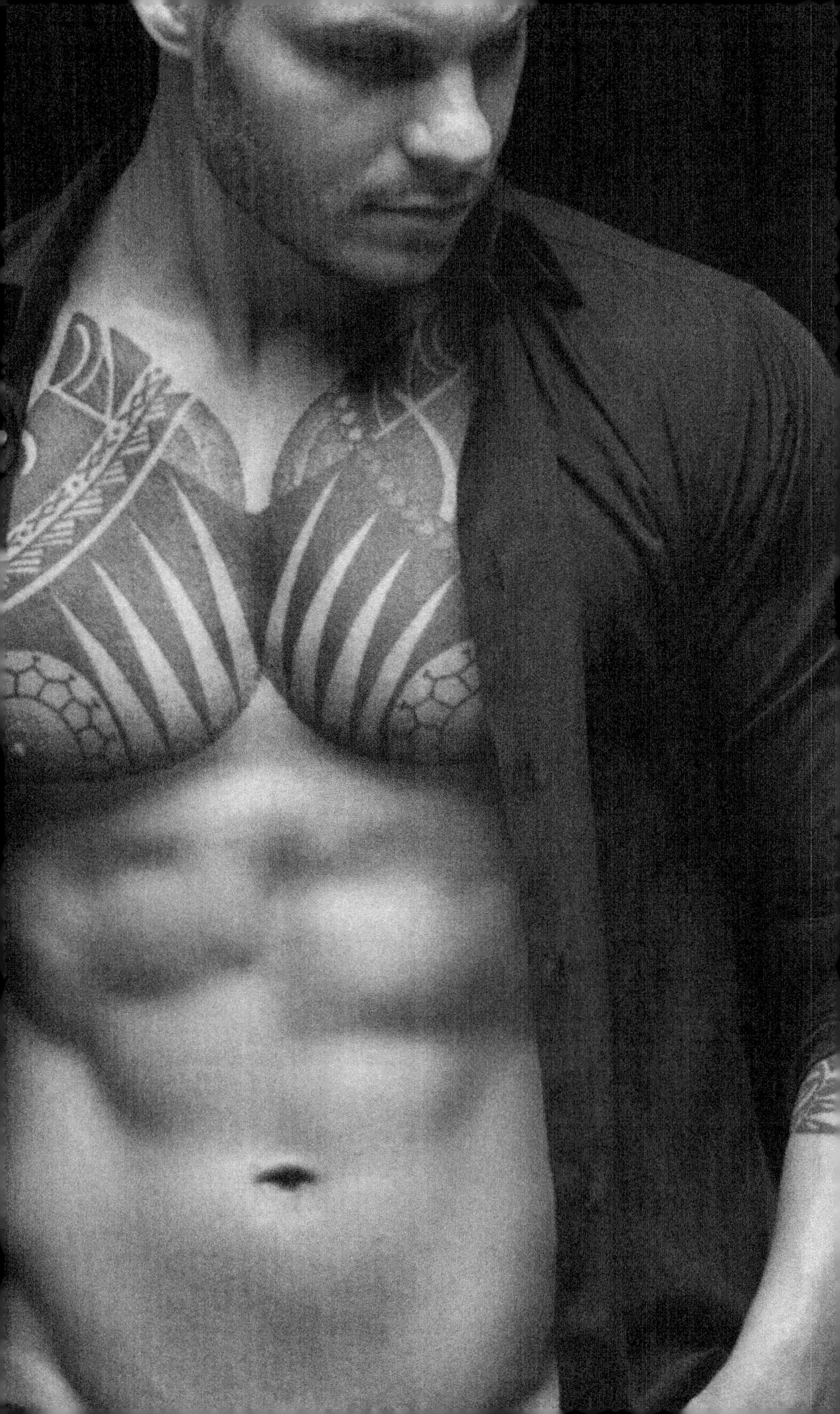

CHAPTER FIVE

TRUE

"IT'S VERY nice to meet you, Mrs. Lafontaine. Sal's told me so much about you," I stuttered while extending a hand to the kindly old woman in front of me. She was impeccably dressed to the nines and reminded me of Olympia Dukakis in *Steel Magnolias*. A tiny woman with the grace of a Southern belle who spent her younger days sipping on mint juleps, surrounded by gentlemen callers. Her radiant laugh lines told the story of a life well enjoyed, the remnants of a monumental romance full of passionate adventure, and oodles of love. It was easy to see why Sal spoke so highly of her and with profound reverence.

There was just one minor problem.

"Looks like she left a few things out as well," she snickered good-naturedly.

"Now that you mention it," I agreed, surprised.

"I see we've managed to shock another niece of mine. How many does that make now? Three, four? The look on their faces is always priceless, if I do say so myself."

"Works every time," Sal joined.

"Now, enough of the shenanigans. Please, call me Corrine. Come in and take a seat. We have much to discuss, and you must have a lot of questions."

I tried to keep my staring to a minimum while piecing together the familial connection between Sal and her well-beloved Aunt. Sal being African American while Corrine was Caucasian was obviously a running joke that the two of them loved to play on unsuspecting idiots like myself. I swallowed my embarrassment and followed them into the seating area that looked like a professionally staged furniture store. Photos lined the mantle of the fireplace, both black and white and in color; there were even a few of a young Sal wearing pigtails, smiling at the camera, cute as a button. Aunt Corrine had vases with fresh cut flowers on the coffee tables; I'd bet money she had a standing order each week with the florist. I sat along the edge of the loveseat, too afraid to wrinkle or crease the delicate fabric that probably cost more than I could make or steal in a year. I looked around for a comfortable spot to place Kayla's carrier and settled on a carpeted space on the floor closest to my foot.

"Is that the little bundle of goodness, Nancy?" Aunt Corrine asked.

"Sure is." I smiled. "This is baby Kayla."

"Land sakes, isn't she the most precious thing this side of the Mississippi?"

She covered her mouth with both hands in excitement as she took in my daughter's pink cheeks and chubby thighs. Her gummy smile was infectious, and I couldn't help but to return her joy with some of my own. Kayla was no longer the frail little creature that came screaming into the world at a whopping five pounds one ounce. She'd thrived over the last several weeks, drinking her fill of breast milk combined with supplemental formula when I wasn't producing enough to sustain her hearty appetite. She was an absolute beauty destined to be a heart-breaker when the time came for her to start dating. The perfect mix of mother and father, a sprinkle here and a dash there, Aphrodite herself got in on the handiwork. Sure, I was biased, but who wouldn't be? She was my redemption and I her martyr. Her life would never be anywhere near as traumatizing as mine. Of that, I was certain. I had momma bear instincts and wasn't afraid to use them against anyone who dared to threaten my child's safety. That instinctive behavior was new to me, but it wasn't the only thing that had changed recently.

Kayla wasn't alone in her healing, bless her sweet soul. Gradually, I allowed myself the freedom to explore outside the confines of my cozy little bedroom. Granted, it was mostly in the backyard at first, but I started to feel a sense of safety in the bubble that Sal had created for us. Baby steps and all that. Soon, I began to feel bolder and more confident as the days passed.

I practiced my social skills on the mailman, Rob, when he delivered packages and asked for my signature. Hellos and goodbyes evolved into short chats about the weather, the local news, and our favorite television shows before getting personal. Rob was a divorced father of two sons who couldn't wait to retire from walking endless miles so he could spend more time with them. I was an old friend of Sal's visiting from out of town for a while before deciding my next course of action. He bought the lie just like everyone else, beamed excitedly while he ate up the bullshit, unaware that I was completely full of shit.

The real test was behaving around people I didn't see on a regular basis while pretending to be Nancy Jennings. Sal insisted, after much debate and paranoia, on dragging me to her office for a proper post-natal checkup, where I'd been given a clean bill of health. Once again, the invoice was mysteriously paid in full and no questions were asked regarding my past or personal life. Nancy Jennings was listed as the name on top of the chart, but other than that, I was a ghost. Coincidentally, the best pediatrician in the state just so happened to have a private practice in the suite next door and agreed to see Kayla at the same time. I was ready to call bullshit on the whole entire thing until I realized that Sal was right—my baby needed to be examined by a professional, and as her mother, it was my job to see it done. According to her growth chart, she was in the top percentile and was progressing on schedule. Physically, we were both fine and dandy. The daily bouts of sadness began to subside as my postpartum depression removed its chokehold from my soul, hence the reason why we were here visiting with Sal's Aunt Corrine.

I was done taking benevolent handouts, or as Sal liked to call them, requisite gifts from a humble tributary, whatever the fuck that meant. Ryan wasn't looking for me, or better still, he'd never be able to find me while I played the role of Nancy Jennings. As long as I remained in the shadows, kept my head down and my mouth shut, I could pull off what I had planned and get what I needed to move on, namely money. That all required a little help.

"Are you sure you don't mind keeping an eye on her during the day, Corrine?" I asked.

"Of course not, dear. What else do I have to do besides worry about Jerome and Michelle? And this one isn't much better." She pointed to Sal. "Do you see all of these gray hairs? It's because of my beautiful niece, I assure you, Nancy."

"And there she goes, blaming me for her stock in Henna Hair Dye," Sal joked.

"Jerome and Michelle?" I wondered aloud.

Sal told me that her aunt was a widow and had been for a while now since her husband of thirty-five years, Peter, passed away. As far I as knew, they never had children of their own, and I didn't recall Sal ever mentioning the two.

"Oh yes. They are a lovely young couple trying to make it on their own in this big bad world. They rent out my guest house in the back." She pointed towards the window. "Jerome is an amazing artist, and Michelle is a beautiful and caring young woman who attends classes over at the community college while working part-time at the retirement home. The two of them are very special to me, and I consider them family, just like you and baby Kayla here. One big happy family, and we take care of each other," she preened.

Corrine smiled fondly at the now sleeping baby. Her little snores were audible throughout the room. For as much as I wanted to believe her words, I couldn't take them in as gospel; they were way too familiar since I'd heard them once before. Her declaration left me feeling hollow, as if a hand reached inside my chest and its contents were removed by force. The only thing I ever wanted in my life was a place to call home. A kind husband who loved me with a fierceness so intense, our glow would light up the earth for a thousand years. Nevertheless, there would be no laugh lines or cultured ambience surrounding my morally bankrupt character once I reached old age. Hell was my journey's end, one way, no stops.

"Are you alright, dear? You look a bit pale. Would you like a glass of water?" Corrine asked.

"No, I'm fine. Thank you for offering."

"Oh, she's just wondering how long it's going to take for her to be able to sit down again after Mace tans that ass a new shade of pink. Just sayin', gurl, I don't think bogarting that man's space without an invitation is the right way to go. Maybe you should think on it a bit more."

"I thought you understood, Sal. It's the only way," I replied.

"Oh, I understand, Nancy. I just hope you're ready for the fallout." She smirked.

"Hush now, child. She knows what she's doing," Aunt Corrine interjected. "Besides, there are worse things to worry over than having a handsome man catch fire over a beautiful woman. Angry or not, he'll do the right thing, mark my words."

My cheeks bloomed crimson at the thought of Mace Fox taking my ass in hand and delivering a solid blow across my cheeks. I tried in vain to hide behind a curtain of my hair, but any fool could see how the threat affected my libido. That man did all sorts of crazy shit to my body with just a look and a growl. Considering my history, it was strange, yet not completely unpleasant. I set those thoughts aside for the time being and concentrated on the original topic brought to the table. All it took to refocus was a quick glance at the sleeping infant, and I was back on track. Every decision I made from here on out would be in Kayla's best interests. I swore to do for my daughter what my mother never once did for me.

"Should we go over the feeding schedule, Corrine? Kayla isn't normally fussy when it comes to food, but I don't want there to be any surprises," I announced.

"Of course, dear. Let me grab a pen and paper, and we'll get right to it," Corrine agreed.

"Oh Lord. Guess her mind's made up," Sal blurted on an exhale.

Damn right, it is, I thought to myself.

For Kayla, it had to be.

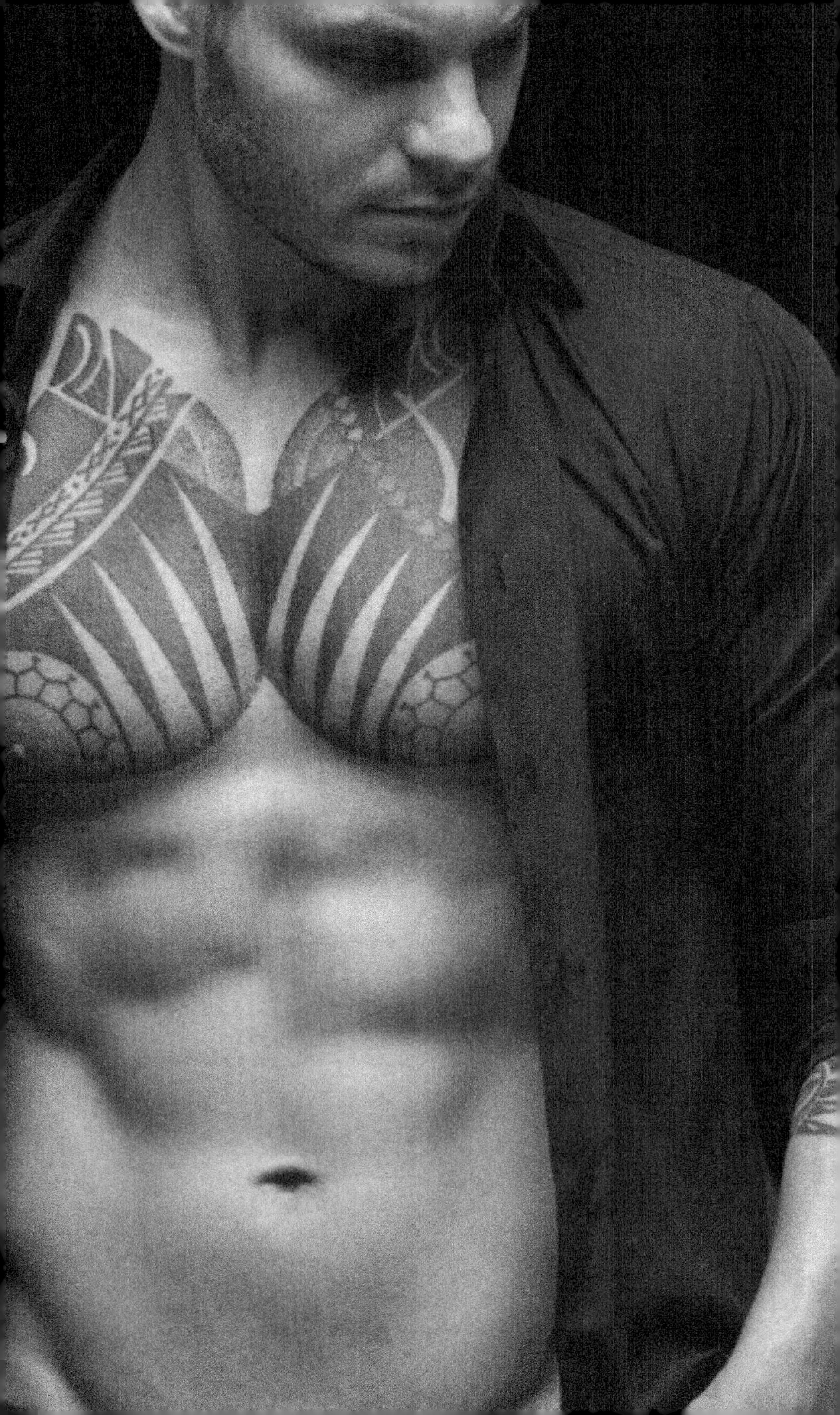

Chapter Six

Mace

I needed away from all the bullshit.

My crew had lost faith in me, questioning my every move, moaning and bitching like a bunch of wet pussies. That shit didn't sit right with me what-so-fucking-ever. We were supposed to be a goddamn team, not break apart like the damn Beatles. They knew the mission and why it mattered better than anyone, but they could never fully understand its toll. I was the one who had to listen to the sob stories of beaten-down women stuck between a rock and a hard place. I alone was the one who had to look into the eyes of all the confused and traumatized kids after someone they trusted betrayed them. I was the one who had to first send them away, encourage them to go to the authorities wasting more time, knowing help would never come, or if it did, it would be too late. Until one of them had to deal directly with the burden of hope, they could all get in line and take turns sucking my dick.

I heard the cries in my head.

I carried the scars on my soul.

I saw the faces in my nightmares.

Sanctimonious assholes had no fucking clue.

After my talk with Kaden, I decided to jump in my truck, destination unknown, and just fucking drive till my head was clear. Once I hit the I-20 heading south, I knew where I'd end up and why my subconscious decided to lead me there. Two hours later, I pulled into the driveway next to an old Toyota Tercel, knowing full well that a brand-new Mercedes Benz was parked inside the garage hardly driven. I'd given her the car as a gift for her birthday, to which she'd adamantly refused to "mess up" by putting miles on the speedometer. I shook my head and laughed to myself as the front door swung open before I could even put my truck in *Park*.

"Oh, Macey! What on earth are you doing here?" she screeched from the porch.

"What? Sons aren't allowed to visit their mothers anymore? I must've missed the memo." I smirked, exiting the driver's side.

"Of course, you are, darling. I'm just surprised to see you, is all."

She wrapped her arms around my middle, squeezing me for dear life. The familiar embrace was so comforting, I swallowed past the lump in my throat and took in her unmistakable scent. I became aware of just how much I'd missed her in that moment and never wanted to let go. Belinda Fox was a five-foot-nothing ball of high energy who took no shit off anyone, including her hardheaded son and overbearing husband. Blessed with dark features, which I inherited, her ageless beauty only intensified as she grew older. She made mom jeans and a T-shirt look damn good against the afternoon sun.

"Let's get you inside and put some food in your belly, son. You look thin," she commented as she stepped away, taking in my worn expression and bunched shoulders.

"In a minute, Ma." My eyes cut to the gated backyard. "Something I gotta do first."

She wavered but didn't object. "Sure, take your time, honey. I'll see you shortly."

I watched her retreat on a long inhale and made my way to the locked gate that separated the side of the house from the back. Nothing much had changed since I lived here as a kid. The lawn was impeccably manicured courtesy of a neighborhood teenager I paid handsomely to make it so. The flowers, on the other hand, were all Moms. Rows and rows of brightly colored blossoms stretched skyward towards the rays. In the corner was a square cutout for vegetables and seedlings that my mother picked and canned every year as a donation to the local church. It was her small way of giving back while also staying busy. When I was a boy, it was my absolute favorite place to spend my time. I'd lost count of the number of frogs that were captured around the garden before Ma ordered me to set them free. Once Maya was born, it became *ours,* and I still saw it that way in my mind's eye.

The metal structure I needed to see was still intact, the same as when my father built it years before. It was weathered and aged now, but I wasn't afraid of it not being sturdy enough to hold my weight, so I claimed a seat on the belt between the chains. I allowed the peace to engulf me. My shoulders sagged with relief, and I felt thirty pounds lighter. Little girl giggles filled my ears, and my heart galloped wildly in my chest as I recalled a memory from the past that was as fresh today as it was when it happened.

"Push me higher, Macey!" she squealed.

"Remember what happened the last time, Maya. Mom and Dad will have my ass if you fall off again and need more stitches," I reminded her.

"Nuh-uh, they won't have your ass. They already have one of their own."

"Don't say *ass*, Maya. Jesus you're a little brat." I turned my head to hide my smile as I listened to her evil little snicker.

"What if I promised to hold on tighter? Like this," she tried to negotiate by grabbing the chains in her little fists and squeezing with all her might.

"Sorry, kiddo, no can do. You're not old enough to understand this yet, but Mom can be really scary when she's angry. One time, she even grew claws and fangs when this kid from school accidentally hit me with a baseball during recess. I never want to see that side of her again, crazy protection mode. And don't even get me started on Dad."

"That's silly." She giggled. "Momma doesn't have fangs."

"Don't believe me? Ask her yourself, but don't say I didn't warn you."

"You'll protect me, too, won't you, Macey?" she asked. "You're the biggest, baddest, bestest big brother to ever live! No one would dare touch me as long as you're around."

"I'll always protect you, Maya, I promise." I leaned in and kissed her forehead.

She smiled brightly. "Good! Can I have a push now?"

We spent that afternoon with the sun shining on our faces, laughing the day away in our own little world. I'd been thinking about her a lot lately, the way our family was robbed of its heart and its future. My mother was forced to bury not only a husband but her miracle child in a span of less than five years. It was unfair and brutal, a disgusting tragedy no one should have to live through. That familiar burning of hatred I'd been missing since my crew decided to put me in timeout returned with a vengeance. I wasn't wrong in my methods. If anything, I was too fucking soft on some of those cunts, but not anymore.

I swallowed down the golf ball in my throat, wiped at my eyes, and focused on restoring my breathing to its normal pace. I found my mother waiting for me in the kitchen sipping a glass of sweet tea, her favorite. She didn't ask what I was doing in the backyard; she didn't have to. It wasn't the first time she'd caught me out there communing with the dead. Before I could get comfortable taking a seat at the breakfast nook, there was a big-ass hoagie sandwich placed in front of me made just the way I liked it—extra pickles with light mayonnaise. Next to it was a glass of ice water and an orange cut into wedges, another one of my favorites. I felt like a twelve-year-old after a summer afternoon of playing in the streets with my friends.

"You look tired, son. Long hours at the shop?" she asked, pulling up a chair next to me.

"Same as always, I suppose. You know how it is."

I took a huge bite of my sandwich that tasted like heaven.

"Heard there was a mystery woman who showed up out the blue with a baby in tow," she casually commented, playing with the edge of one of the place mats.

"Angelica talks too damn much."

She playfully swatted my arm. "Oh, leave her be. She's only looking out for your best interests, and we both know she's your number one fan."

"Figures you'd take her side, like always. Did she snitch to you about Jagger as well, or was it strictly mind Mace's business day on the other end of that phone? She needs to clean her own pile of mess instead of worrying about mine."

"Hmm…I wonder who she learned that from? Sure wasn't me."

We shared a knowing smile filled with fondness as we mulled over the woman who came to signify so much to the both of us. Short on resources at the time, I'd convinced my mother to take on the burden of a distraught twelve-year-old girl not related by blood, and to my surprise, she agreed without hesitation. Angelica became a second daughter to her and the little sister I'd give my life for, when she wasn't running her mouth or getting herself into trouble. Par for the course of working at a tattoo shop with a bunch of alpha men, I guess.

"Sooo…Who was she, this mystery woman? Is she as pretty as Angelica said, or was my girl just blowing smoke up my butt?" She wiggled her eyebrows.

"Geez, Ma, please don't say *butt* in front of me while I'm trying to eat."

"Your father said far worse, and you never complained. Besides, don't change the subject."

I'd rather go blind than lie to my mother about anything, but the subject of Nancy, AKA True, was a delicate one. Angelica had placed me in an awkward situation by running off her mouth about shit that didn't concern her in any way, something I'd have to remedy once I returned to Masonry Ink. As for my mother, the less she knew, the better.

"Sorry to disappoint, but she was just someone who was passing through and needed a helping hand. Chances are, they already left town and started on their new life."

She worried her bottom lip between her teeth, gave me a sullen look, then stood from her seat and rounded the table. My answer wiped the smile right off her face. Gone were the moments of bliss we shared before we starting talking about Nancy slash True. I thought perhaps she was angry that I'd kept it from her until I heard the sniffles coming from her stance by the sink. She was crying, and the sound struck so hard in my chest I nearly collapsed as I marched towards her.

"Hey, now." I engulfed her in a hard embrace. "What's all this about?"

"It's nothing. I'm being silly, is all." She tried to blow it off, but I wasn't having it. My mother almost never cried. Something I said struck a nerve, and I needed to know what.

I turned her around to face me so I could look into her eyes.

"Want to tell me what bought on the waterworks? Gotta be more than just some random chick coming into the shop."

She swiped at a lone tear rolling down her cheek and shook her head as if to clear it.

"I guess I got a little excited at the prospect of finally becoming a grandmother. You never talk about a special woman in your life, so when Angelica mentioned this one, I put one and two together and came up with baked goods, overnight visits, and presents piled high under the Christmas tree. Lord knows Angelica is way too young and immature to start pushing out babies, and since you're at that age where men start to settle down, I figured, hey, maybe this was a sign or something," she explained on a shrug.

"Gave this a lot of thought, have you? There's so much to unpack there I don't even know where to start, Ma." I scrubbed a frustrated hand down my face.

"I have to listen to Marsha Buckland bragging about her six grandchildren every Sunday during church. It's non-stop as soon as the sermon if over. It's like she's taunting me with snap shots, videos, Polaroids. I didn't even know they still made those."

I loved this woman more than life, but she was so far off base she wasn't even in the ballpark. Nancy slash True was beautiful, I'd give her that. Her supple tits and sassy mouth made my dick hard, I'd admit to that, too, but the rest of that maternal delusion boarding on insanity? Not gonna happen.

"Tell you what I'll do." I kissed her temple and rubbed her shoulders. "I'll knock up the next chick that walks into my shop with a baby as long as you promise to never, and I mean never, ever cry over something as silly as when I'm getting married. Deal?"

"Deal," she chirped. "Now sit down, finish your lunch, and tell me all about what's been happening at Masonry Ink."

"That I *can* do."

I spent the rest of the afternoon making my mother laugh with tales of oversized men crying through their first tattoo session. The whole time, staring out the kitchen window, I watched that empty swing set and stewed in the darkest recesses of my mind. There was more work to be done, and this short trek down memory lane was just what I needed to fortify my commitment.

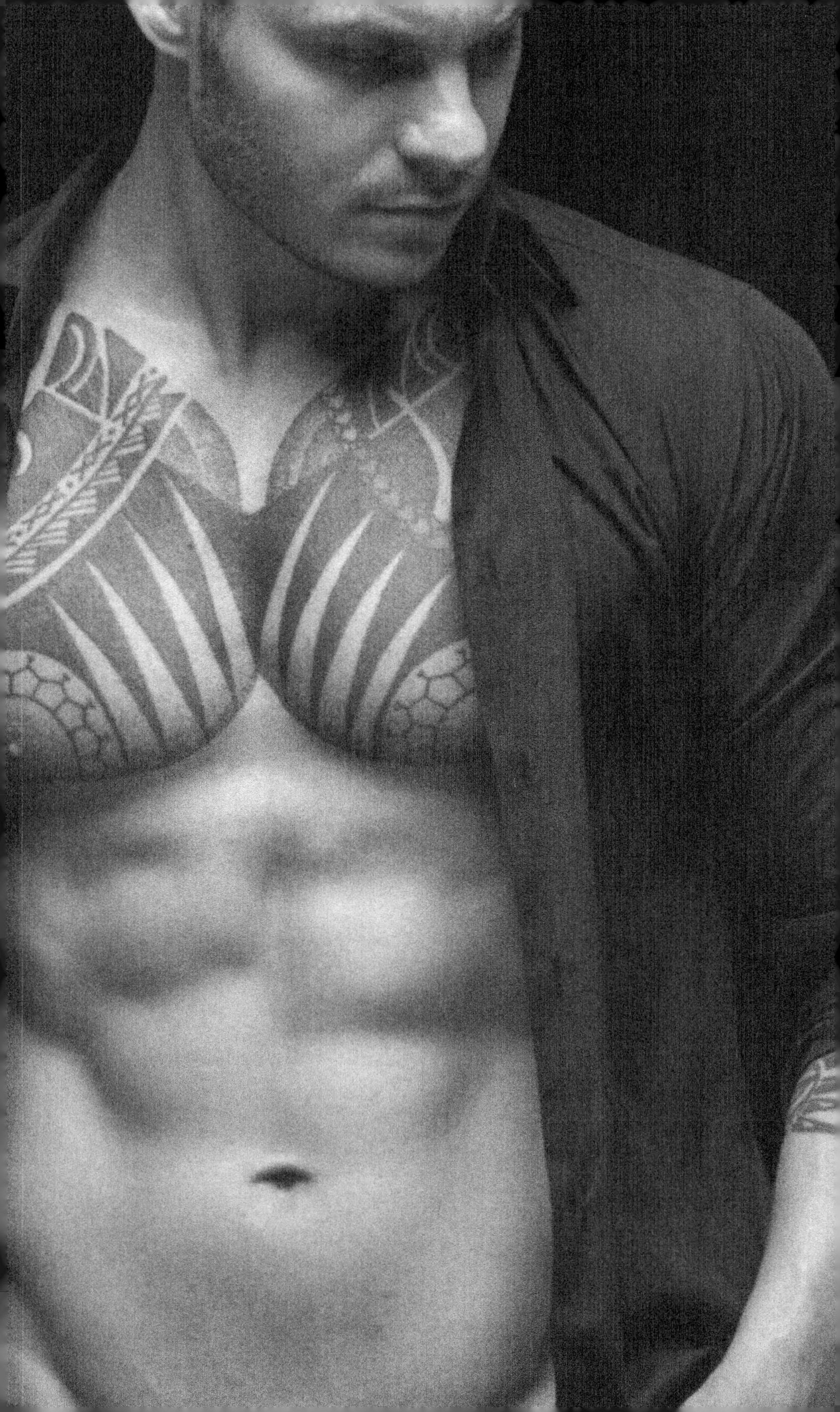

Chapter Seven

True

I NEVER THOUGHT it would be this hard leaving Kayla in the capable hands of Aunt Corrine, but the experience was pure torture. Gut twisting, heart pounding, shoot-me-in-the-ass torture, plain and simple. I went over the instructions with her again even though they were written down in a notepad on the coffee table. I reminded her that Kayla needed her favorite toy to cuddle with before she took her afternoon nap. She was an older lady without children, so I felt it prudent to educate her in the proper way to hold a baby after feeding to extract the best burps so she wouldn't get gassy. And of course, I had to mention Kayla's new favorite television show, *The Bubble Guppies*, so she knew to cut it on for her promptly at twelve.

That whole thing took well over an hour, then I moved on to my baby girl. I peppered her chubby cheeks with all the kisses, played with her little toes, and sniffed her belly button long enough to memorize her scent. I lingered as long as possible before Sal ushed me out the door, and since she was my ride, I had no choice but to comply, albeit under duress. I was close to tears by the time we sped away from the curb.

"You sure about this, Nancy? It's not too late to back out," she asked for the third time.

"As sure as I'll ever be. Now stop worrying and put the petal to the metal. I want to get there early, before the crowd arrives and I chicken out."

"Suit yourself. Remember, I warned you."

We pulled up in front of the strip mall a few minutes later. Sal barely slowed down enough for me to jump out of the car. My reluctance to leave Kayla bit into her time, and she was running late to her office. I wasn't exactly dressed for success. Today's jogging suit was jet black; it seemed like the appropriate choice for a tattoo shop, so I went with it. The lot was completely dead this time of the morning, and I felt a strange sense of déjà vu as I approached the door to Masonry Ink. I took a deep breath, stepped inside, and froze. I felt my ass cheeks start to warm on their own accord. Sal's warning echoed around in my head, filling mine with doubt. I counted backwards from ten and pushed forward remembering the end objective—my daughter's welfare. I'd only ever been inside this place once, and that was the night I arrived, but to see it in all its glory without a crowd of people was something to behold. The interior was stunning. Modern with a rugged appeal, it looked more like a massage parlor with its separate cubicles and dim lighting. Music blasted from the rear of the shop, so I followed the sound in stealth mode since I wasn't exactly sure who was back there.

I passed a few open workstations and was just about to enter the last one when a hand clamped over my mouth from behind before I could let out a scream.

It was a man.

Hard body, chest thundering, well-endowed man.

"The fuck you doing sneaking around, woman?" he hissed into my ear.

The most I could offer was a whimper and a head shake until he released his hold.

"I came to work. I didn't steel anything, I swear. Please, I'm sorry."

The second he spun me around, I recognized the blond Adonis who'd found baby Kayla outside and refused to hand her over. He seemed almost jovial during that first meeting. Today, not so much. His eyes bore into mine nearly trance like until he seemingly snapped out of his stupor long enough to whip out his phone, press a few buttons, and holler into the receiver.

"We got a serious fucking problem in the shop. Better get your ass down here quick fast," he told the person on the other end.

"This really is a big misunderstanding, you'll see..." I tried to explain.

"Shhhhh...I'm thinking about baseball terms," he replied.

I stood there like an idiot not knowing what to do next. He, on the other hand, relaxed his stance, folded his colorful arms over his chest, and shamelessly stared at my tits. *Who does that?* I felt so uncomfortable under his gaze I started to fidget, shuffled my feet, and turned my body sideways to escape his scrutiny. I had so many questions, like who did he just call? Why was he staring at me like the cat that ate the cream? Why was he here so early even though the place was empty? And what the fuck was so goddamn funny?

I heard a door slam followed by heavy stomping down a stairwell but couldn't tell where the hell it was coming from. This building was all one story, not a high rise, or at least I thought so. There was a distinct sound of growling followed by a string of curses that would make a sailor applaud. That's when the world around me seemed to shrink and my heart decided it was a good time to vacation in the Ozarks.

"It's all over now, little momma," the blond remarked. "Stay thirsty, my friend."

"What?" I snapped. "I'm not thirsty…but, yeah, thanks."

"Speaking of thirsty." He grinned. "I got a bowl of Captain Crunch in the back. Think you could spare a cup…Oh shit, never mind. He's coming."

The blond disappeared somewhere in the shop, and I was left with a very pissed-off, half-naked Captain Bravado Mace Fox storming my way. I couldn't afford to mess this up. The life of my daughter depended on it, but sweet Jesus, the man was stacked. He must've been sleeping when he got the call, so I'll start with the fact that he was wearing black silk underwear with noticeable morning wood, and nope, wasn't even trying to hide it.

If that weren't enough to short-circuit my girly parts and cause my hips to wiggle, he was rocking some serious bedhead to match his angry scowl and five-o'clock shadow. If this was his way of intimidating me, he definitely went about it the wrong way. Golden, colorful man flesh from his waist up and thighs down, hitching a ride on his muscle train, left me beyond speechless. I was entranced. Someone say, *abra-fucking-cadabra, snap out of it, bitch*. I was a goner until I heard the click of the safety being released from the gun he was holding.

Have mercy.

"Where's the kid?" he grumbled, two inches from my face.

"Kayla," I corrected. "Her name's Kayla, and Sal's aunt, Mrs. Lafontaine, agreed to babysit for me while I…" He interrupted before I had the chance to finish my sentence.

"Warning," he rumbled, "I woke up from a good dream for this shit, left my nice warm bed, and I haven't had any coffee. I give less than half a fuck what you're doing here, Nancy. I want you to turn around and march your ass back to Sal's and stay there. It's not a request."

I saw his lips moving, but for the life of me, I couldn't make out a word he said. It came across as *grunt, grunt, hiss, hiss, vroom, vroom, growl*. What the hell did I do now?

Shit, this was awkward.

Stall, True, stall.

I stood straighter. "Can you show me to my desk? I know you were looking for a bookkeeper, and I've decided to accept the job, starting today."

"The fuck you say?"

"My desk." I shrugged. "Can you point it out to me? And, not for nothing, I don't think you're wearing the appropriate attire for a conducive work environment. I suggest you go back to wherever you came from and put on something...more."

I waved my hand around to indicate his lack of clothing hoping he'd take the hint and remove his hard dick from my eyeball. No such luck.

"Told you I was having a good dream," he rasped.

Mace made no moves to cover up, put the gun away, or even acknowledge my question about where I was working for the day. Instead, he stood there looking like a big ol' slice of strawberry cheesecake after a crash diet. I thought my statement was self-explanatory; perhaps Mace wasn't smarter than a fifth grader and needed me to spell it out in simpler terms.

"Of course, of course, my mistake." I flashed a placating smile. "Sooo...where's my desk?"

"No," was his one-word reply.

No? "What do you mean, no?" I shrieked.

"I mean hell to the fuck no! Now, since I didn't studder and you seem to be feeling better than when you ran up in my shop a few weeks ago, I'm going to assume you'll want to be moving on now. Glad you stopped by. Now get lost."

He turned to leave, giving me the perfect view of his amazing ass. Talk about a dump truck. This guy had globes for days. I had to take the offensive. Things were getting desperate, and I was losing ground. He couldn't turn me away. I needed this. Kayla needed this. He left me no choice but to resort to drastic measures. I screamed bloody murder at the top of my lungs until he stopped moving, turned back around, lost the hard-on, and gave me his utmost attention.

"Don't you dare dismiss me, Mace Fox! I'm not done talking to you yet, so until I am, you're going to stand there and listen to what I have to say!" I screeched.

He thought about it for a second.

"Fine. Speak. My feet are getting cold."

Rude much?

"I know you've been giving Sal money to help pay for our expenses. She all but admitted it to me, but I wasn't in the proper position to do anything about it before today."

His brows pinched together. "So?"

"So?"

"It's what I said. So, fucking what?" he confirmed with an exasperated sigh.

He wasn't making this easy.

"So, it's not cool, paying all that money, supporting us financially even though we are strangers to you. You know as well as I do that there are no free rides in this world. Everyone expects something, or else why do it?" I flung my hand out.

"Got all I need, thank you, and you don't owe me shit. Now...we done?"

I wasn't making any headway with this guy. For some reason, he was intent on getting rid of me like yesterday's trash. If I had any chance of living without fear, I had to make him understand why I needed to do this. I had to give him something, something that would force him to stop and hear my despair, hear *me*.

"When I begged him to take the only thing I had of value in return for his kindness, he turned me down flat." Sal's words felt like poison in my veins, but I had to try harder.

"Please...you don't understand..."

"We're done here, Nancy. Have a good life," he dismissed.

True, I wanted to shout. *True fucking Boardman is my name, and you will acknowledge me, Mace Fox.* Instead, I took a shot. How else was I going to make him listen without laying down the law as if he owned the place? Okay, perhaps I didn't think that one through, but still…

"I *am not* a fucking charity case. I earn my own way, Mace Fox, in any way that's required. I have a daughter who's counting on me to protect her, and for that, I need money. The clothes she wears, the formula she drinks, even the Pampers that diaper her little tush, you bought. I am her mother, the only person she has in this world, and I won't fail her by relying on a man, any man, for a damn thing. So, you *will* give me this job. I'm not taking no for an answer. Deal with it," I whispered, defeat heavy on my shoulders.

I was out of breath by the time I finished my little spiel. The only thing left to do was wait for an answer. Mace mumbled something I couldn't make out yet suspiciously sounded like, "I don't have time for this bullshit."

I waited through the hair pulls, the chest hair scrubbing, and the neck rubs. I even waited through an ass crack scratch and wedgie pull. That was fun.

Until…

"Trial run," he stated.

Fucking finally.

I jumped up and down, punched the air a few times, and even gave myself a high-five by using both of my own hands. I was ecstatic, until I saw the look on his face. My new boss was not impressed with my little celebration dance.

"Two weeks. You get your travel money up, then you and the kid get gone. Stay out of my face, make it so I don't need to wear earplugs every day, and try not to give me a bunch of shit. Office is that way."

He pointed to a closed door at the end of the hall and walked away.

"Is there something I should start doing while I wait for you to get dressed?" I asked.

"Nope. Sit in there till I get back, and don't touch anything!" he shouted over his shoulder.

And that was the last I saw of Mace Fox…

For two whole days.

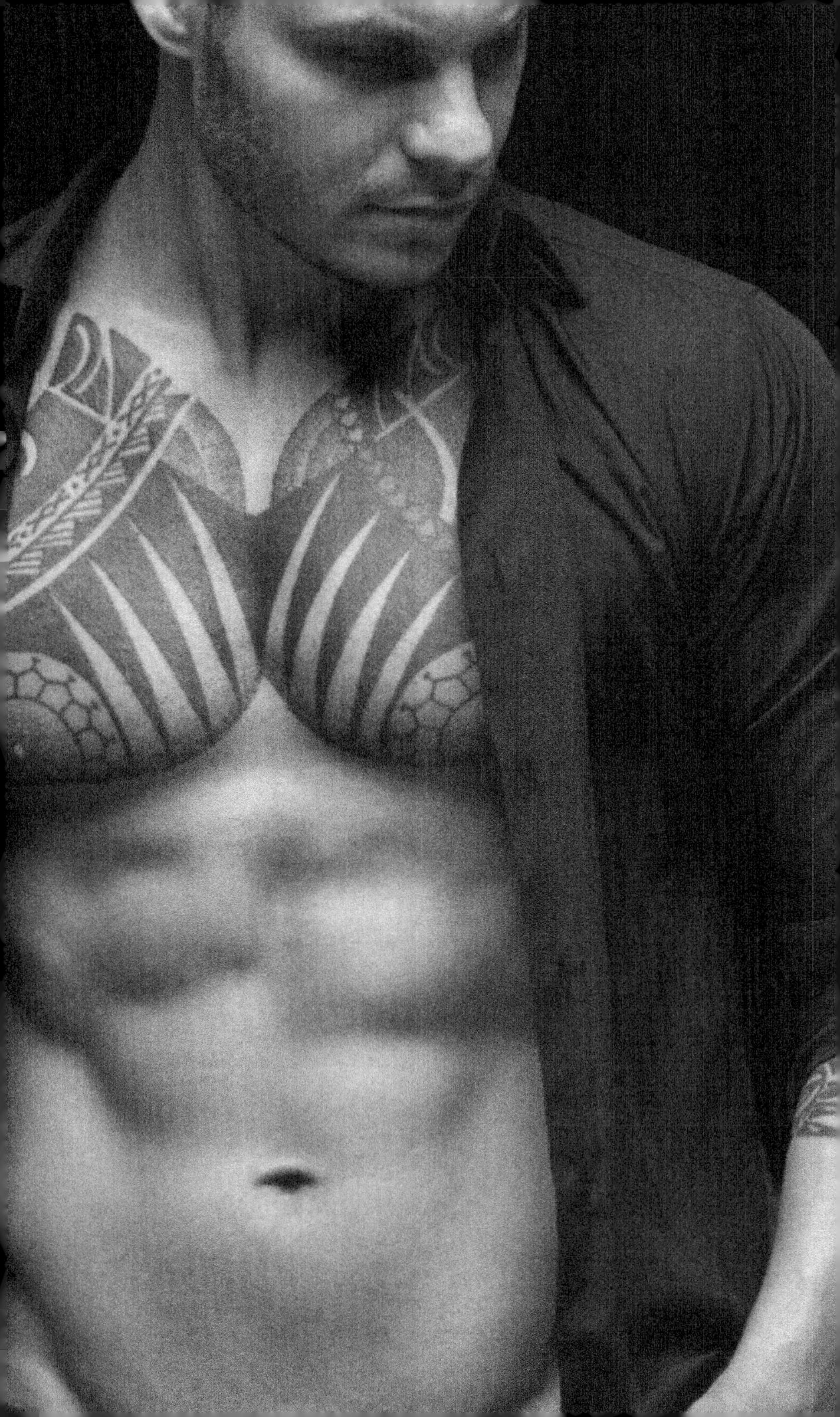

Chapter Eight

Mace

I PURPOSEFULLY KEPT my distance from Nancy slash True, electing instead to communicate strictly with Sal regarding anything she and the kid might've needed. No expense was spared for their care, checkbook wide open, and the motherfucking thanks I get? She showed up here, in my shop, covered head to toe in black fleece, making demands as if I owed her something. I don't put up with emotional blackmail from anyone, certainly not from some chick I happened to do a good deed for out of the kindness of my heart. I would've told her to kick bricks the second she started mouthing off had it not been for my lack of sleep. I'd just closed my eyes when I got the call from Kaden urging me to hustle my ass downstairs. One look at the *new* and improved woman before me, she could've asked for the moon, and I would've tried to lasso that shit with a rope to get it for her.

Her poorly timed ambush had rocked me to the core and made my morning wood stiffen to the point of pain. In what could only be described as a cruel joke played by Satan himself,

True Boardman was absolutely fucking stunning. Over the last several weeks, her appearance had changed so drastically, it was hard to believe that she was the same woman who'd just given birth before stumbling into Remington alone. Gone was the haggard, sickly-looking, stringy blonde little weakling. Her cheeks had rounded out and sported a healthy glow about them. Her muscle mass was more in line with her height and weight thanks to a healthy diet. Her hair was long and shiny, pulled high on top of her head in a ponytail, and her cerulean-blue eyes sparked with fire when she pleaded her case for employment. Sal had told me weeks ago that she didn't trust either of us and thought we were running a game. Despite all of that, she took me head on, for her daughter's sake, and wouldn't take no for an answer. I stared her down holding on to my shotgun, listening to her pleading voice while it tap-danced along my heartstrings, then BAM! I was certifiably fucked.

I stormed my way back upstairs, stowed my weapon, and angrily reached for my cellphone. Reception connected me to the appropriate desk, where I proceeded to lose my ever-loving mind on the person I believed was partially responsible for this shit show.

"This is Sal, how may I help you?" she greeted cheerfully.

"What in the half a fuck do you think you're doing?" I thundered.

"Oh, hey, big daddy. So nice of you to call."

"None of that cute shit, Sal. I want to know what the fuck she's doing here. I told you when I dropped them off not to let her roam around the streets alone. I explicitly ordered you not to have her contact me directly for any fucking thing. Now, with all that being said and you being an intelligent person, I want to know why you disobeyed our agreement, Sal?"

"Look, Mace, I tried to stop her, but she wouldn't budge. Got all up in my shit when I told her it was a bad idea. I don't know what she's running from, we never talk about that, but whatever it is, she's scared to death of relying on someone else to take care of her kid. I'm really sorry I didn't warn you, but I assumed you'd just send her back with her tail between her legs."

"Cunt move, Sal. Thought we were better than that. Thanks for the raw ass fuck."

I heard a gasp on the other end.

"Go straight to hell, Mace, you arrogant bastard. You asked *me* for a favor, remember?"

"Yeah, and thanks to you and your girl, I've regretted it ever since, bitch."

She hung up on me, then, pissed as all get-out.

As mad as I was about the situation, I couldn't fault Sal for basically doing the exact same thing I did. Folded in half like a card table behind a sob story and pair of blue eyes. Fucking hell. I decided not to return to the office. Instead, I chose to make her little ass wait until I was in the right headspace to deal with this shit. I closed my eyes on a heavy breath thinking how much I wanted to hit something. That was exactly how I felt when I got dressed and took off out the back exit towards my truck. She needed to learn early that I wasn't the one to manipulate, dictate orders to, or box into a corner to get your way. I drove a few towns over and rented a hotel room, disengaged the tracker every member of my crew had installed, shut off my phone, and decompressed. Forty-eight hours inside the sweet pussy of a waitress I picked up at the bar, and I was back to feeling like myself again.

Two days was the longest I could stay away without rousing suspicion from the rest of my team. You would've thought I was gone for a year by the way they lit into me the second I hit the door. I should've stayed away longer, but fuck it, I was here now. I braced for the backlash surrounding Nancy slash True, and as I expected, they didn't disappoint.

"Well, well, well, if it isn't Mr. Disappearing Acts himself," Angelica snarked, stacking magazines at the front desk. "Next time, take the stray cat with you, Mace. We're not running a damn shelter around here."

I gave her the side eye and kept walking.

"Big boss man! I see I'm not the only one with new booty in his life. Who's the pussy now, motherfucker?" Jagger smirked from between a woman's legs as he tattooed her inner thighs.

I flipped him the finger.

His laughter echoed off the walls as I passed Dread, who gave me a chin lift from behind his sketch pad but didn't comment. This was the one time I appreciated his brooding, strong, silent façade, but there was still one more prick left to be dealt with before I reached my office, and he was the worst of the bunch. I tried to prepare my mental state, but it was always a toss-up with Kaden. Either he'd be somewhat reasonable, or I'd have to waste the next hour trying to get him to focus on work and not what was going on with our newest addition. The fool probably had another one of his crazy stories to tell involving a baby rattle and a monk behind a dumpster in Little Italy. I sometimes wondered if he believed his own bullshit, or perhaps maybe his coping mechanism was permanently switched to the lunatic setting.

Before I reached the end of the hall, I heard chatter coming from behind the closed office door.

"That's it. Push it more in the back. Use your legs, Kaden," she ordered.

"I can't! It hurts my ass cheeks every time I try and squeeze it in. You have to help me," he answered with a loud grunt.

"Aw, come on. Show me what those muscles can do. I thought you had skills," she taunted.

Oh, hell no!

What the fuck?

I broke into a trot, determined to kick the two love birds out on their asses for having the brass to bump uglies in my space. I cleared the entryway like a raging bull and froze, eyes wide, fists clenched, confused as a motherfucker.

Nancy slash True was sitting behind my desk wearing another jogging suit, pink this time, shouting orders at a sweaty and discombobulated Kaden, who was bent over a box in the corner as he struggled to lift it.

"The fuck's going on in here," I growled.

"Ask little momma," Kaden whined. "I'm out of here. I'm a lover, not a human crane."

"Thanks anyway, She-Hulk." She smirked. Her eyes hardened as she took me in.

He rushed out of the room without his usual pageantry while the tough chick and I engaged in a heated staring contest. She turned up her nose as if she'd suddenly smelled shit and twisted her cotton-covered ass towards the wall, giving me her back. I might have been all wrong about the whole screwing thing, but I sure as shit wasn't wrong about her attitude. The woman was hell fire pissed that I'd left her for two days, and it was killing her not to blow up and read me the business. She was smart to hold that shit in after what I just witnessed.

"What were you doing in here with Kaden, Nancy?" I snapped.

"What does it look like, genius? Moving those stupid boxes of candy out of the way." She flipped her wrist to indicate the obvious, her indignation slipping through.

"Just checking to see whether or not I need to break out the Lysol disinfectant spray."

Her eyes narrowed into slits as she crossed her arms over her full chest.

She was set to explode in three, two, one...

"Why did you leave me alone for two days without a word, Mace?" she sneered. "Anything could have happened while you were missing in action. A tropical storm could've swept me away, a serial killer could've chosen me as his next victim, or a herd of farm animals could've escaped through a fence and I was eaten alive by a pack of wild goats! Did you even stop to think about that while you were off doing…whatever you were doing?"

I smiled despite myself.

"Nothing was going to happen to you, Nancy. Calm your ass down."

"Something could've happened," she muttered softly, her voice cracking at the end.

She tried to hide her face, but I could see the tears streaming down her cheeks. What was it about beautiful women crying that made me want to hurl myself off a bridge? I realized then how badly I'd fucked up with my little stunt. She wasn't annoyed or acting bitchy for no reason. She was scared shitless that I wasn't around to protect her from the ghosts that ate away at her spirit. Regret and shame burned through my veins. How could I have been so goddamn careless with her fear knowing that this woman had no ties in Remington other than relative strangers? I needed to rectify my mistake damn fast, reassure her that she was covered even in my absence.

"I had your back."

"Yeah, right," she scoffed, wiping her cheek with her shoulder.

"I said… I had your back." I bristled, scrubbing a hand over my unshaved stubble.

"That's awesome, Mace. Give yourself a round of applause," she responded sharply.

She stormed from my desk and moved to a smaller one in the opposite corner of the room that wasn't there two days ago. It was then I noticed she had taken the initiative to rearrange things in the office space and every surface had been cleaned to a shine. Knickknacks were added from the storage closet here and there, which gave it that homey feel. Papers were stacked in neat piles, a flowery cloth covered the wood, and there was a coffee cup on the edge of my desk that held pens and pencils in neat order. That was a nice touch and totally unexpected.

"I see you kept yourself occupied while I was away despite having to slay a dragon, fight off a gang of angry munchkins, or any of that other shit you just mentioned," I noted.

Nothing.

Not a sound.

I flopped down in my chair completely worn out by this bullshit already. This was exactly why I didn't want her here in the first place. Sure, I was making fun of her in a tongue-and-cheek kind of way, mainly for my own benefit. I believed in giving it to you straight, and if I wanted even a hint of peace today and for the next two weeks, I was going to have to give her some harsh truths.

"Listen, Nancy, working at Masonry Ink is not just a job..."

"Let me guess," she interrupted, "it's an adventure?"

A deep grumble bubbled up from my chest as I tried to ignore her smart-ass remark.

"No." I exhaled through my frustration. "But we are a family, and we respect each other and treat this place as if it's our home. When you inserted yourself into the bookkeeper position, you didn't really give me a choice of whether or not to hire you. I made the decision based on blind faith since I don't know you from a can of paint, Nancy. I don't like feeling pressured, so I took off for a few days, and now, I'm back."

"You agreed to let me work here, Mace, or was that just so I would shut up and take the hint when you didn't come back? You could've just said no and saved yourself the gas money. I'm a big girl. I can take it. Since you clearly don't want me here, I'll just grab my shit and go. See how that works? Simple."

She jumped up in a huff.

"And have that shit on my conscience, wondering what happened to you and the kid? No fucking thanks, tough chick. I'll stick it out until payday."

"So... now you want me to stay?" Her brows shot up to her hairlines.

Fuck, this woman was getting on my nerves.

"Like what you did to the place. Let's see what else you're good at doing."

That sounded more sexually charged than I'd intended, but fuck it, whatever worked. The suffocating silence that followed was necessary to ease some of the tension in the room. The three-minute conversation left me feeling completely unbalanced with a heavy sense of guilt from the damage I caused. I made a woman live in fear for two whole days over nothing, who cried with relief when she realized she was safe all along. Wave after wave of disgust turned my stomach sour because of my actions.

"What's with all the boxes of gum drops? You got a sweet tooth or something?" she asked, breaking the silence.

"It's a long story and nothing you need to concern yourself with, Nancy."

"It is my concern when I have to stack those heavy things. I mean, look at all of those." She waved her hand around towards the corner of the office. "What's the deal?"

"Let's talk about the job instead," I ordered, changing the subject. "It's for a bookkeeper, so I assume you have some experience in that field."

I steepled my fingers and waited for her to answer.

"Nope, not a bit," she replied. "But I'm a fast learner once I set my mind to something. How hard can it be? I already stacked the invoices, separated them by color, and put them on your desk. I can probably finish them in about an hour once I get going."

"Is that so?"

"Yep! I'm way ahead of you, boss," she boasted.

Nancy slash True perked up from her seat and grinned brightly. Her beautiful face transformed when she smiled. Shame I was about to wipe it away; it was a good look. I pressed a hidden button beneath my desk that triggered a panel nearest to the door to spring open. Inside were stacks upon stacks of paperwork that needed to be digitized using updated software that Kaden created. He was always concerned about cyber thieves getting ahold of our information and cleaning us out, so he worked tirelessly to combat an attack. I tried to keep up with the changeover, but the shit got away from me. Hence the reason I was looking for a bookkeeper. It was also a testament to the success of Masonry Ink considering the stacks of paperwork were only three months old.

"Are those…"

"Last quarter's invoices. Every single one has to be categorized appropriately, reviewed for accuracy, and logged electronically for good old Uncle Sam. You up for that?" I asked.

Her shoulders slumped in defeat before she shocked the shit out of me by cracking her knuckles and shaking out her fingers.

"Show me how to do this, Mace. I'm all yours."

For the next few hours, I instructed her on the basics of the software and how the coded number sequences corelated to the services or stock order. From there, she was on her own, and I was able to step back and away from her alluring scent. The light touches on my arm when she did something right, the way her voice hitched when I leaned into her, the way she said my name as if it were a prayer, all of it was fucking with my head, the big and the little one. Two weeks couldn't come fast enough.

Two weeks of pure torture.

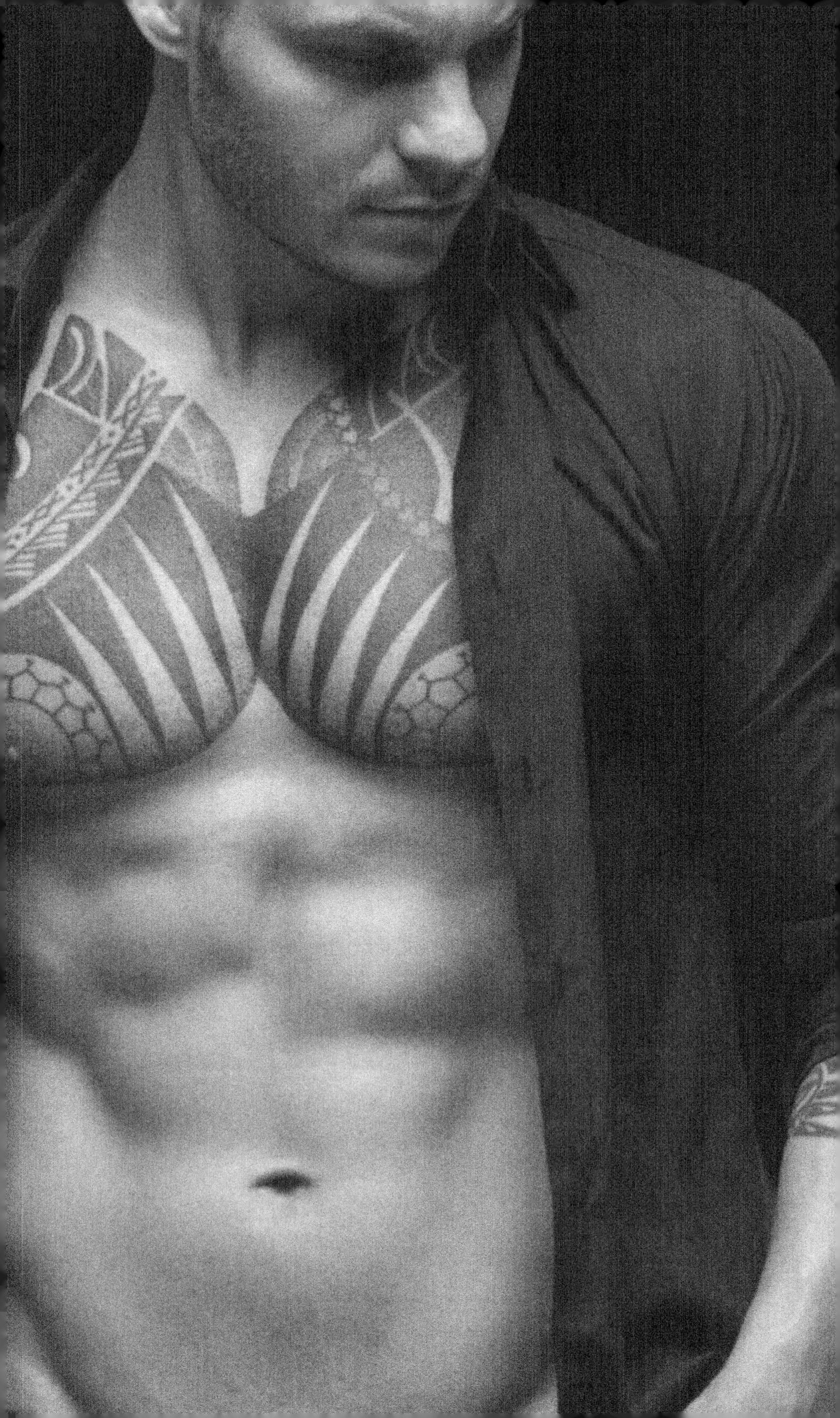

Chapter Nine

True

"You're not allowed back there," the dark-haired beauty protested from behind the front desk when I cleared the entryway. "Mace's orders, I'm afraid."

"Do you know how long they'll be in there? I have a lot of work to do."

"Nope, didn't ask," she responded dryly.

"Damn, that really sucks," I whined.

I'd just arrived at Masonry Ink, eager to start hacking away at the mountain of paperwork waiting for me inside. I wasn't expecting anyone else to be around this early except for Kaden; he seemed to be more of a morning person, or perhaps he slept here somewhere like Mace. Either way, by the time I showed up at eight, he typically had the lights turned on, workstation cleaned, and the closed sign flipped to open. Come to think of it, he was the only one of the staff who ever made it in before noon. The meeting must've been really important for everyone to rearrange their schedules, but it was still biting into my plan to get ahead.

It occurred to me then that I hadn't been formally introduced as the new accountant for the next two weeks. Kaden happened into the office on the day Mace came back, and I took that opportunity to ask for his help moving the boxes of candy out of my way. I'd caught glimpses of the rest of the crew on my way to the bathroom or when it was time to leave. Other than that, I spent most of my day hiding out, too afraid to interact with these lively strangers. The young woman at the desk didn't seem interested in having a friendly conversation. I assumed it was because she didn't know me. Since Mace hadn't taken the time, I decided to remedy that myself.

"I'm Nancy, by the way, the new accountant." I stuck out my hand.

"Charmed, I'm sure." She never looked up from her task, nor did she return the salutation.

"Do you have a name?" I prodded.

She exaggerated a sigh, tone sharp as a paring knife. "Angelica."

The fuck's up her ass?

"Nice to make your acquaintance, Angelica."

She rolled her eyes so hard I thought they were going to pop out and bounce across the floor. I took that as my cue to retreat and sat in one of the waiting room chairs. I had hoped to be saved from her shitty attitude by an announcement that the meeting was over. Since that wasn't to be the case, and I was trying to come out of my shell, I pumped myself up to believe that perhaps I could bond with the princess of Masonry Ink. If I were going to learn how to make new friends, I needed to tuck in and take a shot, be bold and all of that. Call me cuckoo for Cocoa Puffs, but I wanted her approval since she meant so much to Mace. I went with the female ally approach and ran with it, foot firmly inserted into mouth at full speed.

"You must be relieved to have another set of X chromosomes

around this place. I'd imagine being the only girl surrounded by crude burley men all day must be exhausting," I kidded.

That seemed to get her attention. Unfortunately, she didn't share in the joke. In fact, she appeared downright indignant judging by her narrowed eyes and puckered lips. Clearly, I'd said something wrong, but I had no idea what.

She sneered then pointed a finger.

"Those burley men you were flapping your gums about are my brothers, and I don't take kindly to no drifter bitch spewing shit about them. Do you know how many women like you have been through here looking to land themselves a quick fuck or a quick buck? That puts you squarely in the *been there and done that* line, Nancy. Mace might have a soft spot for you, but to me, you're nothing more than a rolling stone, passing through on her way to con some other fool into thinking she's worth a damn. Stay in your lane, little momma. This one is taken."

"I'm not looking for any of that, Angelica. You don't know shit about me," I fired back.

"Right, like I've never heard that before," she snapped. "Warning, and you only get one. Hurt Mace, and we're going to have a serious problem. You feel me, cupcake?"

I was shocked, no, I was appalled. Hurt Mace? Why would she think that?

How dare she blow up at me for trying to have a polite conversation with a fellow co-worker? I wasn't asking to become besties or anything, so why all the hostility?

My retort was cut short by the men piling out of the back room, none of them smiling, or even talking for that matter. Mace approached the front desk eyeing me suspiciously before turning his gaze to Angelica, who was nonchalantly buzzing around, all sunshine and rainbows.

"Everything okay here?" he asked.

Angelica was quick to answer, "Peachy keen, boss."

Bullshit.

"Everything's cool," I muttered, playing along. "Just waiting for you guys to finish up."

"You can head on back now, Nancy. We're done," Mace said.

I walked away with my wounded pride barely intact after that merciless tongue-lashing. For the next few hours, however, I stewed over everything she said about me. In truth, I was a drifter with no real home, a heartbeat away from being cast out amongst the other rubbish. I had no license to make assumptions about anything or anyone inside these walls.

I was naïve to think that I could change the past and be looked at as someone worthy of friendship. I never had that creature comfort growing up until Ryan took an interest in me. Being acquainted with the daughter of the town whore, as most people called her, wasn't something the citizens encouraged or supported. Soon enough, I gave up trying and resolved myself to being alone. It wasn't until my sophomore year of high school that things finally changed.

Ryan Boardman was hardly a stranger, more like a mystical being, similar to a unicorn. We'd been schoolmates all our lives, yet he never once took notice of me, until one day, during lunch, he asked to sit at my table. I was eating alone as always, so I gave him a shoulder shrug, uncertain of his motives. He was the son of the town sheriff, third generation, star quarterback, and every girl's secret crush, including mine. He had a bad reputation with a long line of broken hearts just waiting for their number to be called, but on that day, he chose me. I often questioned what made a guy like him want to go out with a girl like me. My mother told me to milk it for as long as it lasted, which wouldn't be long if I didn't put out. She liked to say that a woman with a wet pussy could have any man she wanted if she knew how to work her assets. We were married the day after we graduated high school, and I never asked for her advice again.

I was head over heels in love with the man of my dreams. I had the family I always wanted. I felt cared for and relevant for the first time in my life. For five years, he was my everything, the other half of my soul. One request took that all away and dammed me to hell.

I felt my bottom lip start to quiver as I recalled the memory. I swore to myself that I would never think about that unfortunate time, yet there I was, blubbering over a stack of papers like an idiot. I knew in my heart that it wasn't the years of happiness that caused the flood gates to open, but the years that followed which gave me grief. I was wrong about everything, including the definition of a family. I envied Angelica for her willingness to protect her own. She looked me straight in the eyes and made her intentions clear. Fuck with them, and she'd make me eat my own teeth. How could I argue with that? It was everything I wanted for Kayla, a tribe to have her back, a place to belong, respectability and pride. I might not have had any of those things, but as her mother, I would make certain she would.

I stayed in my own head longer than what was reasonably acceptable during working hours. I thought a glass of water might clear my musings and set me straight for the rest of the day. It was still early enough that the shop was pretty quiet. Mostly young girls too afraid to come at night, anxious for the experience of getting their first tattoos. I walked past a giggling bunch on my way to the kitchenette and startled.

"Need thicker skin to work around here, little momma," warned a rumbly voice.

A younger man, perhaps in his early twenties, blond, gorgeous, and full of tattoos was using the sink to rinse off what looked to be tiny paint brushes. He wore well-worn jeans and a tight black T-shirt that showcased his beautiful ink. His cheekbones were sharp enough to cut through a window pane, like some sort of a cosmic superhero. I was too embarrassed to meet his eyes, which I'm sure were just as beautiful as the rest of him.

"Didn't realize anyone was in here." I skirted past him to grab a paper cup.

"I'll put up a sign next time," he replied with a grunt.

Charming.

Fuck's sake. I watched him from the corner, sipping from my drink as he meticulously handled each brush before wrapping them securely inside a silk pouch. They must mean a lot for him to be so careful with them, perhaps an heirloom?

"Little momma, if you keep staring at me like that, I might get ideas. My woman, Michelle, would beat my ass if I got those ideas, so do us all a favor and look at the ceiling or something. It's creepy. My dick has a mind of its own and only recently been tamed."

He was adorably cheeky with crazy blond hair that reminded me of a younger version of Brad Pitt. And just as I previously gauged, eyes uncased in long lashes, as blue as the ocean and much too pretty to belong on any man. I gave him a small smile that he returned before finishing up with his brush cleaning. He was nicer to talk to than Angelica. Perhaps it was all of my new maternal instincts kicking in, but I had the strangest urge to bake him a warm batch of chocolate chip cookies. *Weird.*

"I'm Nancy, by the way, but I've heard that before, you know, little momma," I hedged. "Why is everyone calling me that? Is it a tattoo shop thing, using nicknames?"

"Don't know about that, but there's a whole lot of reasons a person is given a name, not all of them good," he replied. "It's nice compared to mine."

"Oh yeah? And what's that? Baby Face Nelson?" I poked fun.

"Name's Jerome, but they call me Dread."

I couldn't help it; I laughed harder than I had in a month of Sundays. Who in their right mind would name this absolute sweetheart such a ridiculous label? What were they afraid of, being recruited into his boyband? I sobered quickly once I realized he wasn't laughing with me.

"I meant no offense. Wait a second." I snapped my fingers.

"Are you the same Jerome and Michelle who live with Mrs. Lafontaine in her guest house out back?"

A look of fondness clouded his eyes along with a lip twitch before he answered. "That old bat is going to be the death of me, and so is that kid of yours." He smirked.

I perked up at his mention of Kayla.

"Stopped in the main house to check in with the old lady on our way out. Michelle caught sight of that baby girl. Had to drag her ass outside kicking and screaming. I promised to knock her up someday just so she'd get that mushy look off her face." His eyes turned dreamy as he smiled to himself. "She'll have that. On my life, she'll have that."

Ahh...young love.

Delusional fools.

"Is this a private party, or can anyone join?"

I looked up, up, and up some more.

Sweet Lord above.

If an NBA basketball player, a power lifter, and a male model decided to have sex and make a baby, nine months later, this guy would've popped out. I knew I was gawking at him like a fool, but it couldn't be helped, nor would I apologize for it. He was hands down the biggest dude I had ever seen up close and personal. I felt the heat of a blush on the tips of my ears and knew my face was probably red as a beet. *Totally worth it!*

"Been a couple of days now. Glad you finally left your cave and graced us with your presence," his deep voice grumbled as he smiled down at me.

"Jagger, Nancy. Nancy, Jagger," Jerome said by way of introductions.

"Nice to meet you, Jagger," I stuttered.

"Nice to finally meet you, too, Nancy. Welcome to Thunderdome."

Hearing that fake name took some of the wind out of my sails, but I somehow managed to play it off. The two men shared a grunt and went on about their business. Jagger grabbed a juice bottle from the fridge while Jerome sanitized the sink, ridding it of the strong solvent smell. I returned to the office with a pep in my step and a smirk on my face, that disastrous conversation with Angelica all but forgotten. I couldn't wait to get home and tell Sal all about my day. *Home.*

What a magnificent word.

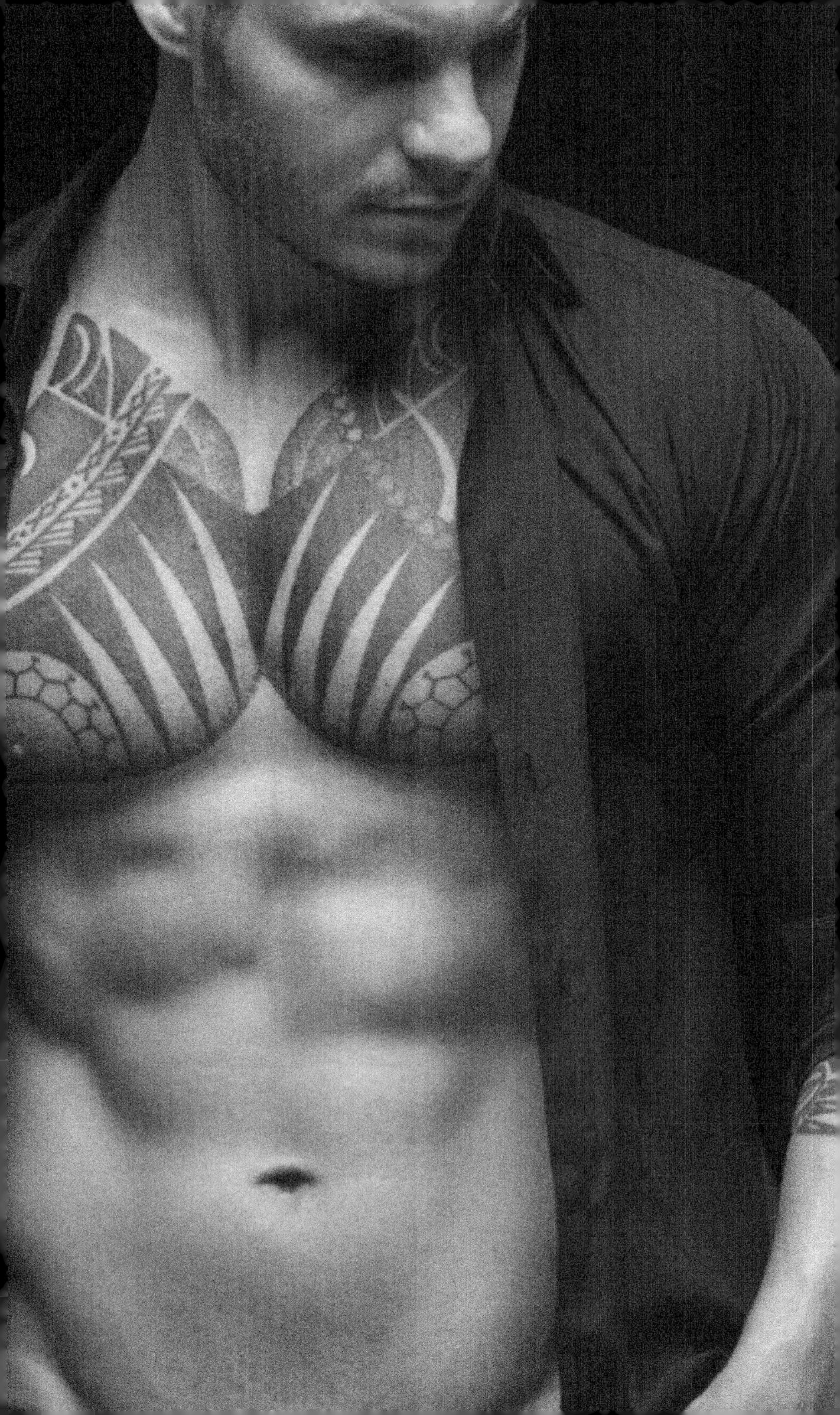

Chapter Ten

Mace

EARLY MORNING MEETINGS sucked dirty dick, but unfortunately, this one couldn't be helped. We were on the move tonight, preparing to attack with the utmost disrespect. Our latest intel suggested that the mark was escalating and time was running out for us to intervene. I was sitting in my office after the huddle going over the details, and every angle was coming up fucked. On the one hand, he was just a kid of barely voting age, but I knew from experience that age was nothing but a number when dealing with an obsession. I felt the burn of bile rolling around in my gut before the inevitable clutch of my heart nearly doubled me over in pain. My mind conjured up mental imagery using presumptions from the past with specifics from the present, what I knew versus what I construed. She wasn't Maya, I told myself while thinking about the young girl. She wasn't my little sister, and I hadn't made a promise to protect her. Everything felt topsy fucking turvy, and I wasn't getting anywhere.

I recalled the young girl who plopped down and cried her eyes out to me not thirty days ago. She'd been given my name by her dentist after he'd fixed the chipped tooth. She confessed that she'd gotten it from a backhanded punch delivered by her ex-boyfriend, the prick. We had previously handled a delicate job for the doc involving his cheating wife and her crackhead lover. He had a hunch that they were plotting to kill his ass and split the life insurance money, but since he had not proof, no one believed him. Once we got involved, the dope fiend serendipitously overdosed from a tainted bag of heroin, and the wife was arrested for trying to hire an undercover hitman. We set her ass up, recorded her making the deal with Dead Man, turned the tape over to the authorities, and the bitch went down for an attempted murder plot. In turn, the grateful doc paid it forward and referred the girl to Masonry Ink, so I agreed to meet with her.

Her commentary made my asshole clench more than a few times as she struggled to tell it. The shit that punk's been putting her through was level ten, hardcore, savagery. He ignored the protective order issued by the court, broke into her bedroom, and shit on the fucking floor, after having jacked off on her bedspread. Bold as fuck, he then left a message on the wall written in blood that he'd be back to finish what he started. By the time the cops got there, he was nowhere to be found. When the police eventually tracked him down, he had an airtight alibi for his whereabouts and she was told there was nothing else they could do.

Their hands were tied, but ours weren't. The ache only intensified once I tried to take an impersonal approach to the planning strategy. This shit was very personal, and it was getting to me worse than it ever had before.

"Would you like me to grab you a cola, Mace?" I heard a short distance away.

Fucking hell.

I forgot she was in the room.

"Not thirsty," I snapped.

I tried to keep my tone even, but I knew it came across as a bit hostile. It wasn't intentional; she just caught me at a bad time. Nancy slash True took my rejection on the chin and made her way back over towards her stack of papers. I watched her luscious ass wiggle and bounce in another one of those jogging suits I bought her, this one red. There was nothing sexy about the outfit, but she made that shit look good. Her slumped shoulders, on the other hand, deflated my impending hard-on and gave me a quick reality slap. She was only trying to be nice, and I pissed all over that for no good goddamn reason other than I felt like being an asshole.

Get your shit straight, Mace, and fix this.

"You been getting along alright at Sal's?" I called from my seat.

She gave me a guarded smile.

"Sal's been amazing. I wouldn't have made it without her kind generosity," she replied.

"Glad it all worked out."

She nodded her head before returning to her work, but I could tell she had more on her mind. Her mouth opened and closed several times like a goldfish before she mustered up her courage.

Her brows knitted in concentration.

"I met the other tattoo artists today, Jerome and Jagger. They both seemed very nice…"

"But…" I urged her to continue.

"They never asked me any questions about, you know, the obvious. Who I am or what I'm doing here. What's my background? It was strangely accepting for a place like this."

"Uh-huh." My hackles went up. "By *a place like this* you mean a dump full of inked-up morons who don't know how to mind their own business, is that it? Where men walk it like they talk it? Got some fucking nerve, woman, disrespecting my shop like that."

"I…" She hesitated then shook her head a few times.

Fucking great job, dickhead.

Her eyes sparkled with sheen before she spoke low and slow.

"You mistake me, Mace. My fault for not being clear. I was five years old the first time I realized that having a family was the only thing I wanted out of life. The first day of kindergarten, as a matter of fact. All the little girls were dressed in new clothes and shiny shoes, but that wasn't what cinched it for me. It was the mothers and fathers who waited outside the steel doors, waving goodbye to their children, tears in their eyes, trying to act brave knowing they would miss them terribly for the hours they spent away."

She paused her story with a self-deprecating laugh. I wanted to interrupt her, stop her from torturing herself by reliving the past, but there was meaning in her message that she wanted me to hear.

"Want to know what I did on that first day since my mother was too busy shacked up with her latest married man to walk me to school, Mace?" she asked.

I shook my head.

"I picked out a blond couple in the crowd and pretended that they were my parents, that they were proud to have me as their daughter, and I waved goodbye to them until my tiny arms gave out and it was time to go inside. It was the best worst day of my life, but I got through it, that day and all the days that followed."

I was still a little lost as to what that had to do with meeting some of my crew in the shop until she took a deep breath and gave me the rest.

"I've never known that type of unconditional acceptance, Mace, not for a long time. There was a boy once who used to come along with his father when he *visited* my mother. I was young, maybe three or four years old, but at the time, he meant everything to me. He taught me to play Go Fish, fed me gummy bears, made me laugh. Then one day, he just stopped coming, and I was left alone to fend for myself. Sal is the second person

I've ever considered to be a friend to me. At my age, that's not only pathetic, it's scary as hell. How am I supposed to teach my daughter that not everyone is the enemy and there are good people in the world when I hardly know any myself? I can't screw this up, Mace. Her life depends on it."

The question wasn't rhetorical, so I gave it to her straight.

"You don't," I hissed. "You teach her to go with her gut and to use the instincts that God gave her. If she thinks a motherfucker is bad news, chances are they're bad news. Teach her to never second-guess her decisions, to never go back for more once a person shows their true colors."

I stood from my chair and walked to her side of the room. I needed to be sure that what I told her next would stick. I wasn't a father, but I was raised by the best one who ever lived, and he taught me well. What little he missed, years serving in the Marines took care of, proficiently. She couldn't know all the trials and tribulations suffered by my crew or even myself, but she felt our bond, our connection to one another, and that made me feel proud as fuck. Nancy slash True wouldn't be around long enough to witness the full brunt of our allegiance to one another, but hopefully, I could impart a little wisdom for her to take on her journey.

I stepped right up into her grill; barely an inch separated our lips. The flecks of blue in her eyes were more pronounced at this distance; they called to my inner beast like a siren. *"What secrets are you hiding, True?"* I wanted so badly to ask but didn't. I had her attention, judging by her sharp intake of breath and the pinkening of her cheeks. She was just as affected by our proximity as I was. My chest vibrated with pent-up emotion. She smelled of peaches and uncertainty, both of which made my dick hard, but I had a point to convey.

"Teach her to fight no matter what and to never give up until the whistle blows."

"I'm not a baseball fan, Mace. I wouldn't know where to

start with that explanation. I'm jaded and cynical about life. The last thing I want to do is pass that on to my baby girl."

I held back a smirk for obvious reasons.

"You won't, Nancy, not possible. A mother's love is the strongest love in the world."

"What if I can't?" she argued. "I'm a weakling whose only claim to fame was pulling a runner from her husband." Her panic-stricken eyes flashed with alarm. She'd revealed too much.

I moved impossibly closer. Leaning over the desk, I could almost taste her sweet lips.

"Took moxie to do what you did. That first night you arrived, weak and spent, you never backed down when I pressed for answers, not once. You made a desperate choice, not knowing if I was full of shit or some hustler looking to get one over on you when I offered to help. You're stronger than you think, Nancy Jennings, a fuck of a lot stronger."

She turned her face away at my use of her fake name. Whatever connection or spell we were under was broken in an instant. Perhaps that's why I referenced it; she needed to stay as far away from me as humanly possible. Piling more shit on top of an already full plate wouldn't do either of us any good. She was on her way out, and I was on the fast track to hell. My insides twisted damn near painfully once I forced myself to take a step back and away from her vicinity. My eyes dropped to her pink pouty mouth and imagined her meeting me somewhere in the middle, reclaiming her hold and taking it further than either one of us expected.

Her image glimmered into a wisp of air. In a heartbeat she was in front of me. Steady hands reached for the loops on my belt and tugged, surging my hips forward. Our height difference landed my bulging cock against her belly. She exuded strength with an element of sureness when moments ago, she touted weakness as her shortcoming. My chest expanded with pompousness knowing that she chose me as the vessel to step out of her comfort zone. I grumbled a warning, spread my legs wider to give her better access as she dove right in.

"The fuck you playing at, woman?"

"Just enjoy, Mace," she purred, licking her lips.

"This a joke?" I hissed.

"No jokes. I want the taste of your cock in my mouth so I'll always remember it. When you come, I'm going to swallow it all down, every drop, and savor it as it coats my tongue."

Her right hand skimmed the seam of my inner thigh with enough pressure to stimulate my hardened cock to the point of pain. I smirked knowing she wouldn't take things any further, but she surprised me. True dropped to her knees and stared up at me through hooded eyes. Fingers nimbly unbuckled my jeans and slowly lowered my zipper.

I closed my eyes in anticipation of that first long draw from root to tip as she deep-throated me with abandon. The wetness of her cusped pink tongue as she used it to pass through the slit of my cockhead. It felt so real I hadn't realized someone was yelling my name until the very last minute. Lord knew how long I stood there daydreaming about a fucking blowjob, but it was embarrassing as all hell.

"Mace, what the fuck? Didn't you hear me calling you?" Angelica shouted in the doorway.

I chanced a glance at Nancy slash True, but she seemed to be immersed in her work.

"Sup?" I snapped to attention.

"Big Tony is outside asking for you, something about a job."

"Be out in a minute. Get him a drink and make sure he's comfortable."

"Yeah, whatevs," she sassed.

I caught the sideways look she gave True before slamming her way out the door. Funny how I just realized that when she mentioned meeting the crew, she conveniently left Angelica out as being among them. Women and their moods.

Not my fucking problem.

Big Tony was here with the specs on the house we'd be infiltrating tonight, and I needed to see to him real fucking fast. That was something I could wrap my head around and distract me from the sudden need to fuck the shit out of my new accountant. Causing a psycho prick some pain would set everything to rights and deliver retribution for a woman long denied by the system. I got my head back in the game with a little kick in the ass.

Cowards are they that torture the harmless.

I was once again the bringer of righteousness lurking in the darkness.

I was malicious truth in suffering.

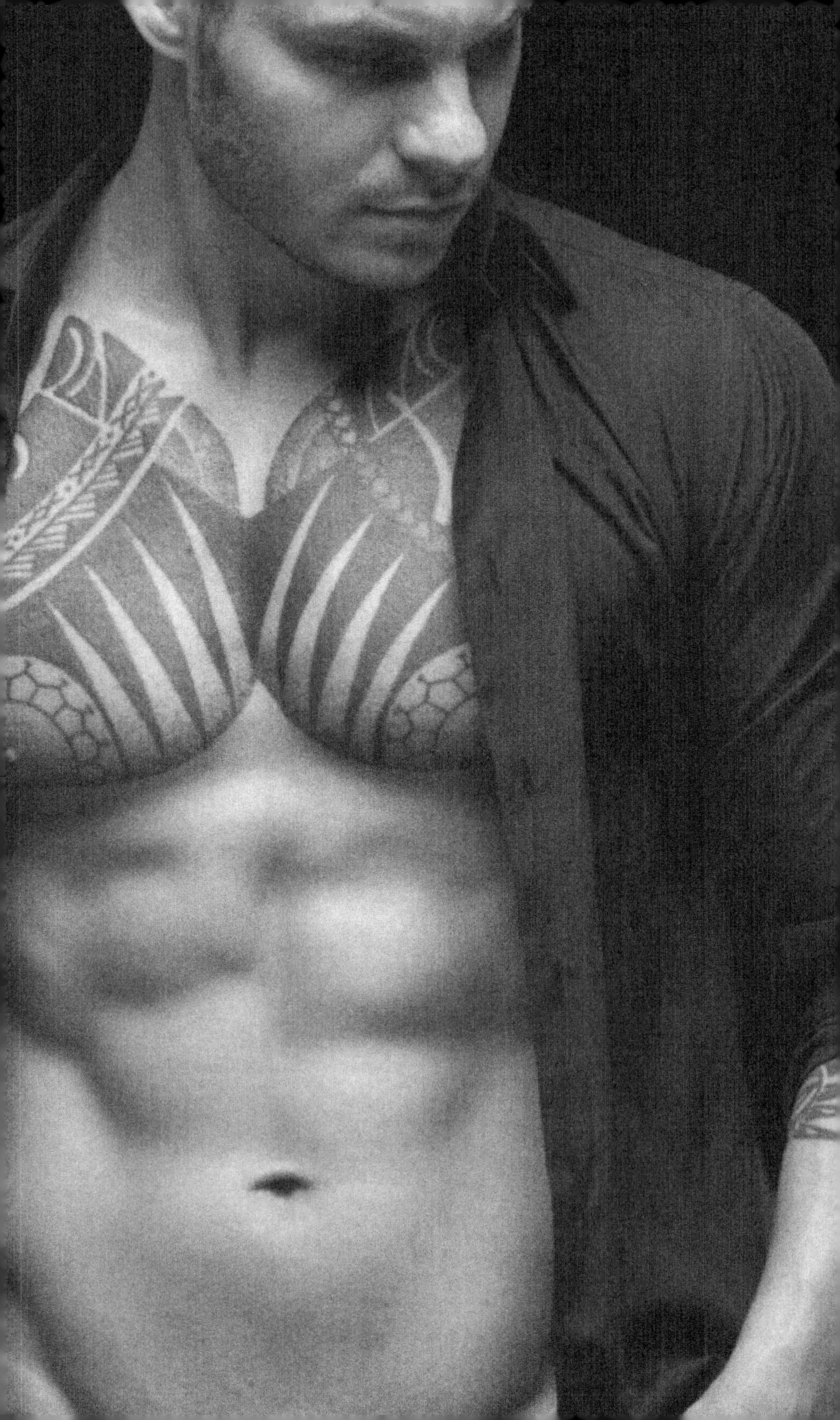

Chapter Eleven

True

Kayla was an absolute beast to put down tonight thanks to Mrs. Lafontaine and her reluctance to stick to the napping schedule. She was under the impression that every waking moment of the day should be filled with some sort of fun activity regardless of the havoc it caused in the evenings. My baby girl and her sensory overload would not go out without a fight while that affable old woman was probably tucked in her bed, nice and warm, sawing wood. I was definitely going to revisit this topic with her again since I was the one who had to deal with the fussy infant at the end of the night.

Sal announced she was going out with friends shortly after we arrived, so I had the whole house to myself. Once Kayla was finally asleep, I drew myself a hot bath and soaked until the water cooled and my skin pruned. I stepped out from the bathtub and wrapped myself in a terrycloth bathrobe that Sal let me borrow. I hadn't realized how exhausted I was until I sat down on the couch with a steaming cup of tea and reached for the remote control. I fell asleep sometime during the opening credits of *The Crown* and was awakened by fists pounding on the front door.

I shot up from the cushion and stopped dead. *Please don't let it be him.*

Had he finally found me?

My knees started to shake so badly I could hardly stand, my first instinct being to protect Kayla. The second was to get ready to bolt. The house was fortified, I knew that from the tour Sal had given me on the first day we arrived, yet my fear was crippling to the point of hysteria. *Please, God, make him go away...*

I could smell his disgusting aftershave in the air all around me. It burned like hot garbage, singeing the insides of my nostrils. It stole my breath away and gagged me, the intensity was that brutal. *True, suck me like you mean it, doll,* his voice demanded inside my head. My throat worked feverishly to stop the bile from expelling from my lips as I remembered the taste of him on my tongue. It was a bitter, salty reminder that I was a coward who accepted defeat and abandoned hope whenever *he* came calling. Well, he could have me, but I'd never let him near my daughter. I'd die first.

I crept to the door and placed my ear against the wood. I heard heavy breathing and grunting from the other side, but I didn't dare open it. *Please, just go away and leave us alone,* I prayed silently, my forehead pressed against the door. Another hard knock, and I damn near collapsed. I covered my mouth with my hand knowing that if I screamed, he'd attack in an instant. Hot tears streamed down my cheeks unchecked while I prepared for the imminent pain that always followed when he visited me. *Forgive me, Kayla, I'm so sorry.*

"I can hear you breathing, Sal, open the fucking door." I choked back a sob of relief at the familiar voice booming behind the barrier that separated us.

"Mace, is that you?" I whispered back.

"Yeah, it's me. Open the fucking door, Nancy," he snapped.

I gathered the ties on my robe, securing them tightly before disengaging the alarm. Mace was dressed in all black from head to toe, his large body leaned against the frame in an effort to stay upright, or so it appeared. His skin was pasty white with droplets of sweat between his creased brows. His dark eyes met mine, and instead of explaining his sudden appearance, he thundered with a strange demand.

"Care to explain why the fuck you were crying a second ago, Nancy?"

"What?" I stuttered, taken aback by his sudden hostility.

"The tears, woman. I heard you. Now fucking explain," he demanded through bared teeth.

The second I opened my mouth, he leaned forward, let out an inhuman groan, and almost toppled over. He was favoring his right side, applying pressure with this hand while using the other to brace himself. Between his splayed fingers, I watched in horror as droplets of crimson coated his skin as he fought valiantly to hold it back.

"Mace, ohmygod, what happened to you?" I shrieked in horror.

"Work-related injury," he responded.

"Someone stab you with a tattoo gun because they didn't like color? What sort of work-related injury ends with you being cut?"

"The none-of-your-fucking-business kind. I need to see Sal. Where the fuck is she?"

Ouch, that hurt.

"Out with friends for the evening. Not sure when she'll be back."

"Fuucckkkk..." he groaned before doubling over.

I immediately went to his side, hoisted his huge arm over my shoulders, and carried slash dragged his ass indoors. That was no easy feat, but I chalked it up to one of those strange stories you read about, where mothers were able to lift cars to free their children before sudden death.

A bit dramatic, but you get the idea.

I deposited him on the couch with a shove before my mind went into overdrive. What the hell was I supposed to do now? I've never worked in the medical field, and I certainly wasn't a doctor. Hell, I couldn't even remove a splinter from my finger. Maybe I should call one of the guys from the shop or nine-one-one for an ambulance. I stood there, looking around as if the answer would fall from the sky and hit me in the head or something. Deciding that was never going to happen, I inched a little closer for a better look.

"That looks pretty bad, Mace. Should I call someone for help?" I offered.

"No," he barked angrily, moving his hand from the wound.

I could see it clearly now. It looked like a knife attack, a razor-thin line speckled with blood seeped through clear down to the white meat. The sight of it turned my stomach and forced me to look away.

"I'm not sure what I should be doing here other than trying not to vomit. You're going to need stitches, a round of antibiotics, and maybe a tetanus shot."

"Sal has a first-aid kit around here somewhere. Grab it along with a needle and thread. Hurry."

I searched through the cabinets in the kitchen first before making my way to the bathroom. I found the box marked with a red plus sign, rummaged around inside to make sure it was full of supplies, checked on Kayla, who thankfully was still asleep, and made my way back to the living room. Mace had somehow found an old sewing kit that Sal must've kept in the hallway closet and was pulling a damn Rambo on himself using a running suture. He never flinched or made the slightest noise of discomfort. I might've been impressed if it weren't for the ick factor. I waited until he was done before moving to help with the bandage.

"Thanks." He sighed. "Could've done it myself."

"Of course, you could've. That's why I'm helping you, silly."

"Real tough chick," he grumbled.

We slipped into an uncomfortable silence as I applied the last of the dressing. Mercifully, the color was returning to his cheeks, which gave me hope that he wouldn't bleed to death all over the furniture. He definitely could've used a change of clothes, but those were in short supply around here. Sal never brought any dates home, and the only thing I had to offer were onesies and burping cloths. Sal did keep a bottle of tequila in the freezer, said it was for medicinal purposes. I'd say this was as medicinal as one could get.

I hurried over to the fridge, grabbed the booze along with a glass, and presented it to Mace, who swiped for it none too gently. He declined the glass, ripped off the top, and chugged straight from the bottle. Three more huge gulps, and he relaxed into the cushion with a long-winded exhale. Our close proximity moved from weirdly awkward to straight-up uncomfortable, at least on my part. I felt it was best to extend the same courtesy he'd shown me by not asking too many more questions. I doubted he'd answer them anyway.

He interrupted my thoughts. "Haven't had to do that since I left the Marines. Didn't like it then, definitely hate that shit now."

I gasped. "You were a marine?"

He smirked. "Ooh Rah…"

"That explains why you were so good at the whole self-care thing," I replied.

"I'm good at a lot of things, woman. You should see what I can do with a piece of rope and a birthday candle." He grinned.

My imagination took me straight to the gutter, and my pussy

was *not* okay. My nipples started to tingle from the dirty image of hot wax dripping over their hardened peaks, increasing their sensitivity, and I had to stifle a moan. If I spoke now, it would be to beg him to show me exactly what he could do with a candle. To save myself from any further embarrassment, I sat down in the seat directly across from him, face glowing crimson clear down to my kneecaps.

"Just need a minute to catch my breath, then I'll get out your hair," he remarked.

"Sure. Take all the time you need, Mace."

I appreciated him trying to make me feel more comfortable with the situation, but the man was full of shit. If the blood loss didn't knock him on his ass, the shots of tequila would surely inhibit his ability to travel on his own. Luck was not on his side if he thought for a minute that I would wrap up my sleeping baby and haul his drunk ass home, no matter how much I owed him. I tried to sit still, but I was one of those people who couldn't stop their knees from bouncing whenever they were nervous. I was pretty much doing a river dance without wearing the clunky shoes.

"Wanna tell me why you were crying when you answered the door?" he mumbled.

"Not really."

"Wrong answer, babe. Try again."

Slurred speech, sleepy eyes, *and* blood stains.

I could deal with *one,* but the alpha male trifecta on a sexy beast like Mace Fox, and I might as well start waving a white flag in surrender. The rugged veneer made him appear savagely masculine and virile without so much as trying. He captured my attention with his penetrating gaze, and I gave up trying to avoid the question.

"I was afraid when I heard something moving around in the dark." *Someone.*

"You cry when you're scared, like the other day in my office," he slurred.

"Sometimes...but I'm used to it."

He grimaced before a look of understanding crossed his brows as if he knew more about my past than he was letting on. His guarded expression screamed dominance, honor, and trust. A bone and blood hero who kept the secrets of the realm.

"It's good to feel scared. Lets you know you're still alive, breathing." He groaned.

"Do you ever feel afraid, Mace?" I'm not sure why I asked him such a stupid question. He was sturdily built and could rip my arms off if he ever felt the need.

"Every damn day," he whispered.

I let his answer hanging in the air around us.

What could possibly cause this man such worriment to affect his daily life? He always seemed so in control, so deceptively calm, I questioned whether or not he was being truthful with me or only saying what he thought might make me feel better. I rejected the pang of curiosity. Everyone was entitled to their secrets, and I had plenty. Mace was starting to fade, but right before, he pinned me with a hard gaze.

"Do not tell my crew that I came here tonight, wounded. Swear on your motherfuckin' life, Nancy. Swear on the life of your baby girl," he demanded.

"I swear, Mace."

"Real tough chick," was the last thing he mumbled before the empty bottle tumbled from his grasp and fell to the floor by his foot.

His breaths were even, and he looked semi-comfortable, so I decided to leave him be. I grabbed a spare blanket from the closet and draped it loosely around his arms and legs, careful not to irritate his bandaged side. I watched him sleep for hours. The urge to climb into his lap, nestle beneath his chin, and soak up all of his suffering was persistent. If only he were mine, this imposing figure who at the moment looked so peaceful in his slumber. I would whisper into his ear that he was safe with me, that I was *his* protector for the night, and nothing and no one would harm him. I pondered whether or not he would welcome my comfort, or would he turn out to be just like every other man in my life, a taker? Knowing I wouldn't find the answers in the dark, I finally went off to bed, reminding myself of the obvious. He came looking for Sal, not for me. She was part of his family, one of the select few people he cared about. I closed my eyes and dreamed that one day, I could be one of them, too.

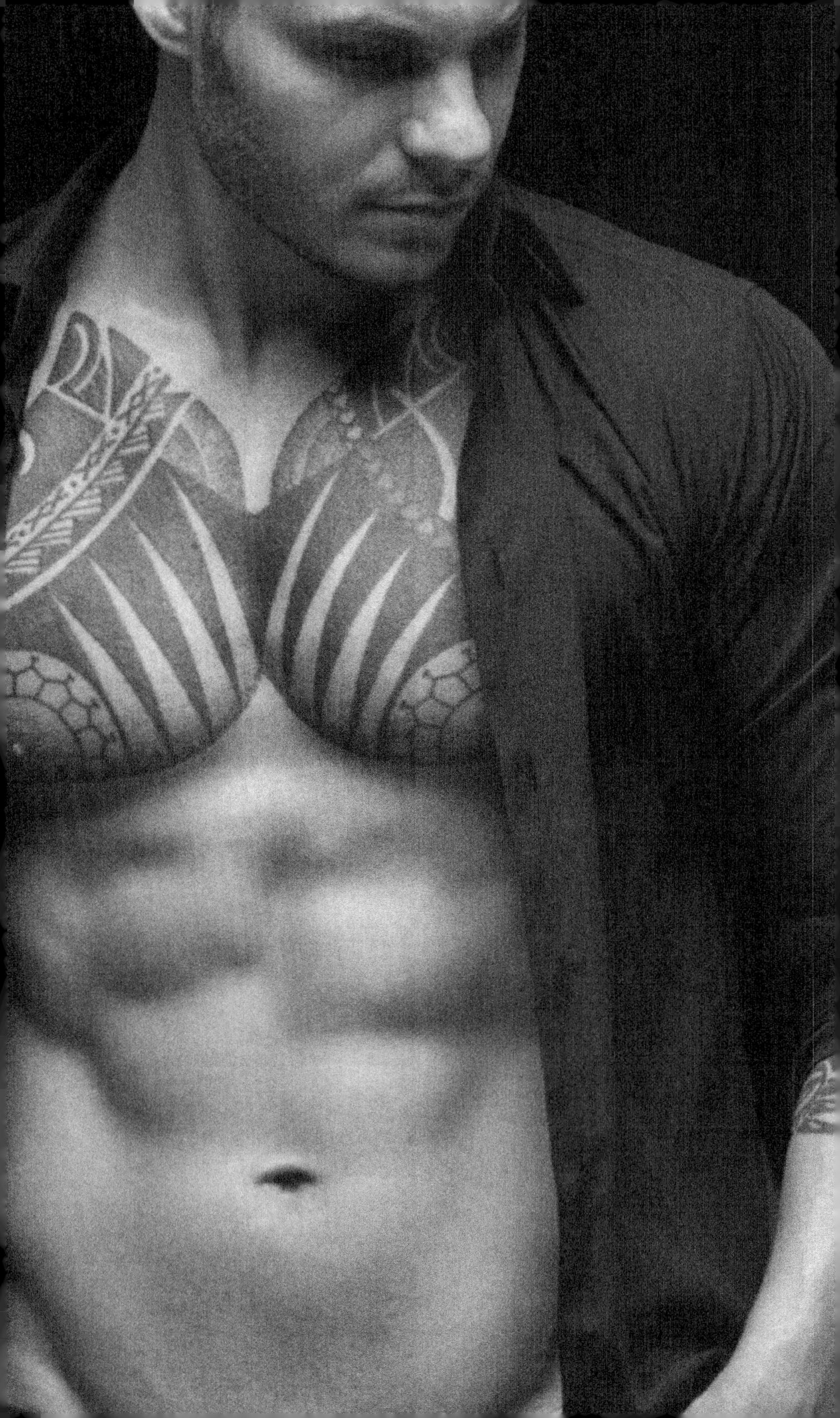

Chapter Twelve

Mace

I FUCKED up big time last night, and that shit can never happen again. I went over to Sal's because I knew she would patch me up and keep it on the down low if I asked her to. Admittedly, it was a dick move even for me. I'd saddled her with a strange woman and her kid to look after. I'd called her a bitch over the phone because she stayed loyal to a friend, which, incidentally, was the same shit I was going to ask her to do. Her not being home created an obstacle I wasn't physically able to circumvent, and I'd carelessly involved Nancy slash True as an accomplice to my misdeeds. *Stupid, stupid, stupid.*

I could hear her crying from behind the door, low at first, then louder, more panicked. It dulled the searing pain along my ribs and sent me spiraling into beast mode. I wanted to rip it off its hinges, storm inside, and beat the dog shit out of whoever had made her upset. When she finally let me in wearing an old house robe looking like a scared little rabbit, the first thing I demanded to know was what caused the sob fest. I should've let her be, stumbled my ass back to the truck, and used a piece of tackle wire to sew my shit up. That would've been the right thing to do.

She was clueless about what we did in the dark and the cold-blooded means we used to rectify the wrongs done to vulnerable citizens. I took a huge gamble asking her to cover for my ass after my amateur fuck-up. It wasn't blowback from the cops I was worried about; it was the ire from my crew if they ever found out. They would never trust me again if they cottoned on to the fact that I'd acted alone without backup for a second time. As far as they were concerned, the operation went off without a hitch, and that was all they were ever going to know. We had a code of honor, and I busted that shit wide open without so much as a twitch.

We caught that little fuck who was terrorizing his girlfriend gearing up to break into her house again and convinced him what a bad idea that would be. At first, he denied it like the punk bitch he was, said she was making up lies. Female exaggerations, he called it. Wasn't until Jagger slapped the shit outa his ass a few times that he finally cut the bullshit and copped to stalking her, leaving fucked-up messages at her place, hoping to win her back. An hour more of whooping on his pussy ass, and the boys were satisfied that he learned his lesson. I wasn't so convinced.

Call it... gut instinct.

Something about his unorthodox demeanor rubbed my ass raw; I just couldn't shake it. The tight set of his jaw when we mentioned her name, the hard-on in his jeans when we questioned his unwillingness to take no for an answer. The spiteful tick of his eye when I told him that she had moved on and he should do the same. I added all that up in my brain, and that prick came out phony as a three-dollar bill. Oh, he cried and begged for another chance to do right, pleaded with us to show mercy, but I wasn't fooled by his Oscar-winning performance. Fucker even pissed himself for good measure.

I kept hearing my sister's voice as she begged someone to

believe that her life was in danger. I felt her hopes dash to ash when she was told not to worry, that most of the time, guys get the hint after a few missed calls and that she should try to avoid him, even though they attended the same school together. I smelled the stench of fear in the air, like on the battlefield before a big campaign against the enemy. It shook me to my core, painfully so, almost as if someone had reached inside my chest, grabbed ahold of my heart, and jerked it back and forth. I turned off my humanity and allowed nature to be my guide. I denied my conscience, my compassion, my ego and relied solely on my predatory instincts.

I watched and waited. Cautiously optimistic that I was wrong.

I wasn't.

Didn't take that lecherous prick twenty minutes from the time we left him on the side of the road before he was in his car and on the move again. I broke rule number one of our code of conduct, to never engage a target alone. Soon as he stepped out from the driver's seat, I clocked his ass with an uppercut to the chin before he knew what hit him. Problem was, I never saw the blade hidden inside his boot until it was too late and I was already slashed. I jumped back in surprise, steaming pissed. *In the hush of night, we bled for our acts of wickedness.*

"The same thing is going to happen to that little bitch when I get my hands on her. Wait and see, cowboy. Your little ambush didn't do shit but slow me down," he taunted.

"I'll give you one chance, motherfucker. Leave now and save yourself a world of pain," I warned, holding on to my side.

"You might get me muscle brain, but not before I make her cunt bleed with my cock and my blade." He pointed his knife in my direction. "I warned that whore what would happen if she ever tried to leave me. She's mine. If I can't have her, no one will. I'll show her not to fuck with me. I'll show all of you what happens when you mess with my property!"

Blood rushed between my ears and created a tunneled echo inside my brain. The last thing I recollected was grabbing him by the shirt collar and kneeing him in the gut until he choked out a cough. When my senses finally came back online, I found him lying on the asphalt propped up against his car, dead as a dog. His neck was snapped, and the only downside to the whole thing was that I couldn't remember doing it. I made a call to my buddy Python, President of the B9's motorcycle club, and within minutes, all traces of his deranged ass were swept away from existence. Gone. *Poof.*

I had to show my face at Masonry Ink today if I wanted to keep up appearances. I made sure to rebandage the gash across my ribs with heavier tape so the blood wouldn't seep through my homemade stitches. The hard part was trying to fake normalcy around a bunch of guys who were trained to spot discrepancies in any individual who walked into the shop. The most I could hope for was a well-rehearsed misrepresentation of the truth, enough so that I wouldn't feel like the biggest piece of shit who ever lived.

I walked down the steps from my apartment around noon, and as luck would have it, ran headfirst into the one person I needed to stay the fuck away from. *Kaden.* With Dead Man being gone, Dread playing the role of follow the leader due to his inexperience, and Jagger with his nose wide open behind some bitch, Kaden's antennas were always pointed skyward. Bastard took one look at me and knew something was off.

He advanced.

Nostrils flared.

"Before you even try to play stupid, know this." He pointed at my chest. "I already had my dick jerked this morning, so save your breath. Tighten your shit up, Mace. You're headed for a padded room if you don't pull your head out of your ass."

"The fuck you mean, Kaden?" I played dumb.

"So, that's how it's going to be, huh?" He shook his head.

"You trusted another motherfucker to get your ass out of something big last night instead of your brothers, Mace." He looked me up and down, twisted his mouth up in disgust. "I *eat* pussy, asshole... I don't play one on TV."

He pissed me off with his bullshit assumption. Granted, it was true, but still.

"Who the fuck you think you're talking to like that, brother? You forget yourself, hoss."

He clapped right back.

"Know *who* you are, Mace, also know *what* you are. Give my best to Python and the B9's since you're rocking with them now." He pinned me with a sneer. "And go fuck a goat while you're at it...dickhead."

He muscled past me with a hard shoulder check, letting me know he wasn't done with this conversation. It made sense that he would have knowledge of the phone call I made last night— he scanned the LUDs each week and submitted a report during briefings. In the midst of his bouts with insomnia, that once every seven days usually changed to every twenty-four hours. The monotonous task occupied his thoughts, or so he said. I shook off his accusation, 'cause really, what did he know? That I made a phone call to an old friend? It lasted seconds, could've been a fucking hang-up or a butt dial. The next time he decided to square up with me, he'd better be prepared to throw down. He needed his ass whooped anyway on general principle.

My guilt-ridden mood turned downright indignant by the time I stepped inside my office. Nancy slash True was busy working, papers strewn all over the place, a pen in her mouth and two more sticking from her hair. Taking more bullshit was not on the menu, so whatever she had to say about last night was fixing to be background noise, not open for discussion.

Today's jogging suit selection was yellow, and for the life of me, I couldn't remember why I picked out that color. Not only was it blindingly loud, it made her look like a twelve-year-old boy or a wilted daisy plucked from the ground. There was nothing sexy about it, not like the night before when she wore a simple house robe while she dressed my wound. She was naked underneath, I imagined, freshly bathed and smelling like cocoa butter. Her closeness made my mouth water. But this shit right here? Hell no.

The brightness frustrated me.

Her silence frustrated me.

The goddamn fucking world frustrated me.

I kicked the inside of my desk, unintentionally startling my shimmering employee. Her expression changed in an instant to one of concern. Her brow quirk practically reached her hairline, but before she could speak, I snapped.

"That outfit"—I waved my hand around—"is doing my fucking head in. I can't be looking at that shit all day, Nancy, not unless you want me to put a bullet in my brain. You're a goddamn beautiful woman and should be seen as one, not some asexual tomboy."

Her cheeks turned bright red.

"I'm sorry, Mace. I could go work in another room if you'd like. The laptop is portable, so I can carry it anywhere. Perhaps in that empty workstation out front?"

I blew out a heavy breath. "No. We don't allow anyone in there when Dead Man is gone."

"Oh, I see," she mumbled. "I could call Sal and..."

I jumped to my feet and stalked towards the door.

I was sick of being couped up inside these walls waiting for the next unfortunate person to call on me for help. Sick of the tingly quills along my skin when I thought about that cocksucker who had to be neutralized last night. Lastly, I was sick of looking at Nancy slash True in another one of those fucking jogging suits. Rather than losing my mind or picking another fight with Kaden, I made an executive decision.

"Let's go," I ordered, anxious to get away.

"Go where?" she squawked.

"Anywhere but here," I barked. "You work for me, remember? So, when I say jump, you say how high and get that ass moving."

"I have to be back before five to catch my ride home," she fretted.

"I got you covered, but we need to leave now."

She hesitated for a second before reaching for the phone on her desk. She pulled out a slip of paper that was stowed inside her pocket and dialed a number. She waited a beat until someone picked up and hesitantly asked for Sal.

"Um, hey, Sal...I won't need you to pick me up today. Mace is going to..."

The conversation paused.

"No, it's not like that, Sal. He just..." She cut her eyes to me then turned away.

"I promise, okay? See you at home later."

She slowly slid the handset from her ear and gently placed it on the receiver. I headed towards the back exit knowing she would follow. I felt as if I were being stalked by the sun—it burned my skin; the warmth on my back quickened my stride. We stood by the passenger side of my pickup while I fished out the keys, engaged the locks, and ripped open the door. As soon as she stepped up to the running boards, I had the perfect view of her well-covered ass sticking right in my face. I licked my lips fighting the urge to bite into it like a ripened apple.

"Where exactly are we going, Mace?" she asked.

"Get in and find out," I hedged, not really sure myself.

I held open the door while she climbed inside and buckled her seat belt. I walked around the front thinking to myself, where were the gray skies when you needed them?

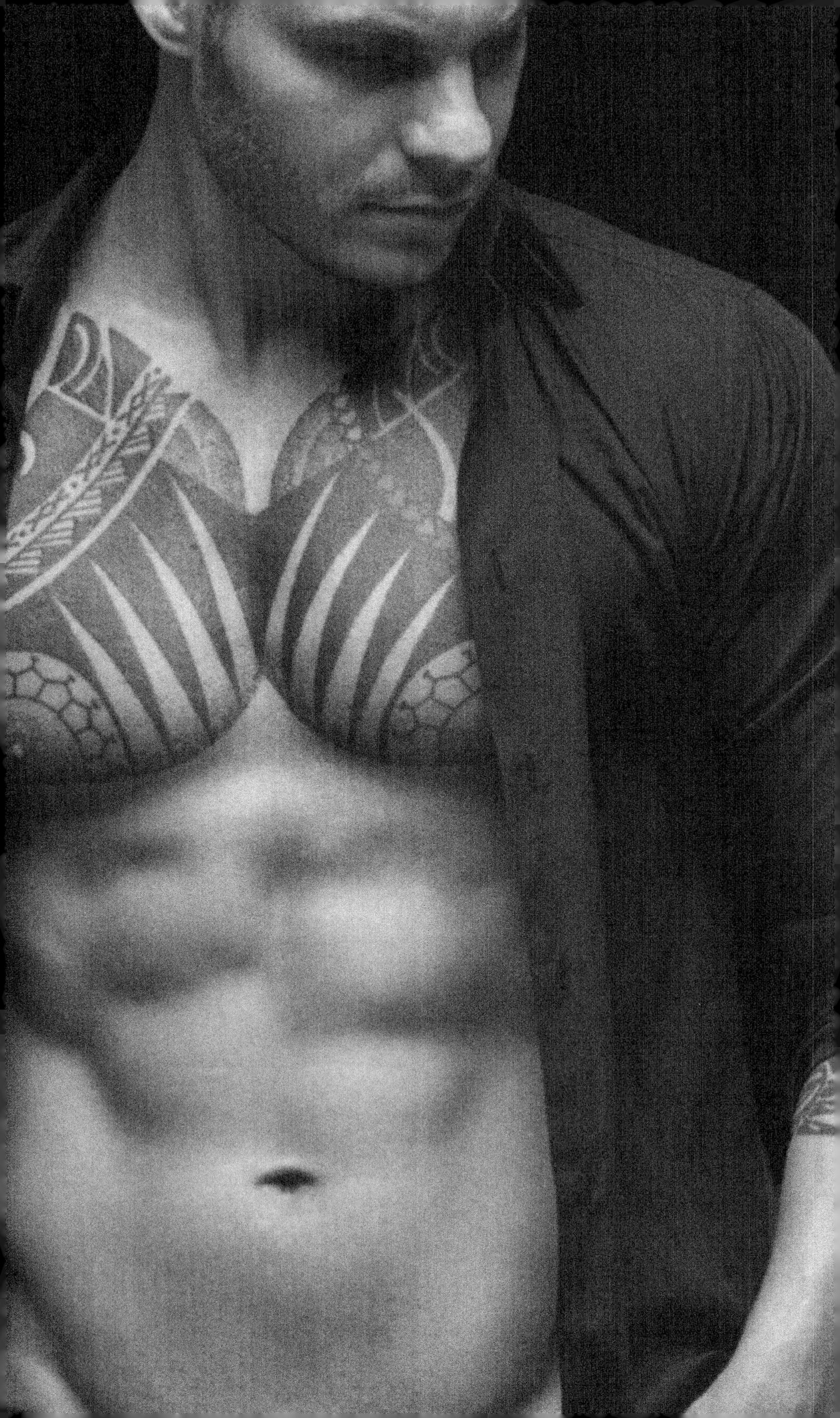

Chapter Thirteen

True

MACE'S IDEA of a getaway turned out to be an impromptu shopping spree at a local Target superstore. Apparently, my wearing jogging suits to Masonry Ink every day had somehow become a deal breaker for him. I held the reminder on the tip of my tongue that he was the one who bought them in the first place, so he really only had himself to blame. The entire ride was a cacophony of grumbles and hisses about daisies and sunshine, which was oddly strange considering it was coming from a man with a knife wound. I finally just gave up caring a shit. He could figure out his own issues with botany. I sat quietly in my seat and enjoyed the scenic view of downtown Remington and all the wonders of this quaint little hamlet.

I watched in awe the many faces of smiling people enjoying their everyday life. I pictured Kayla and me putting down roots and making this place our home instead of the stopover I had originally planned. She deserved to grow up shrouded by kind, loving folks who wouldn't look down on her because her mother was a whore. I considered asking Mace what he thought about the idea of me sticking around a while longer. One peek at the disgruntled man, and I figured now wouldn't be a great time to engage him in hypotheticals.

He pulled into a parking spot and was out of the truck before I had the chance to blink. It took every effort to keep up with his long strides as he stalked through the women's section, pointing out various items, snatching shit off the racks, and tossing them in my general direction. He rushed past several blue-haired old ladies, towering over them, snarling as they clutched their pearls. As we passed, I felt the need to apologize for his brashness on his behalf, but they weren't having any of it. They turned their noses up and scurried towards the produce section, far and away from Hurricane Fox to avoid the damage path.

I accepted two new pairs of jeans, two novelty T-shirts, and a pair of comfortable sneakers before I no longer had the will to continue. I wrung my hands together to control the panic building deep within my bones. It didn't help. Droplets of sweat flowed down my temples. All sorts of bizarre illustrations popped into my head as I glanced at the other shoppers. They were watching me, reporting my every move in real time. My breaths started to come shorter and quicker the longer I stayed trapped inside the store. Even the damn mannequins were spying on me. Laughing to one another, at the same time pitying my efforts to stay hidden. *He* was out there somewhere, waiting, plotting, scheming. Had I covered my tracks enough to finally be free? I tried my best to recall the steps only to have the echoes of his cruel taunts nearly double me over in agony.

"I'm going to fuck you for the rest of your life."

"Your pussy belongs to me."

I couldn't take it anymore. While Mace paid the bill, I grabbed up the bags and hightailed my ass back to the truck, completely overwhelmed. *Check your shit, True,* I told myself. I was so close, too close to have it all snatched away. My ears pricked up against the light breeze to the excited lilt of Sal's voice when I phoned her about my road trip with Mace. She'd romanticized the outing as some sort of hook-up plan between the hot tattoo shop owner and his lonely accountant. I could picture her bouncing on the balls of her feet as she sang, *Nancy and Mace sitting in a tree...K.I.S.S.I.N.G.* She thought of me as this little lost soul, sweet, innocent, broken down but ready to be built back up. She was so wrong. I wasn't innocent, I was less than nothing, and her steadfast support made me shudder with revulsion.

"Not a fan of being left at the fucking cash register alone, Nancy," I heard barked. "Know it's not Neiman Marcus, but show a little courtesy, woman."

I was so deep in my own head I hadn't realized I wasn't alone anymore. His deep rumble made the hairs on the back of my neck stand on end.

"I'm sorry, Mace. Didn't mean to embarrass you back there. Just needed to get some air, gather my thoughts." I turned my head slightly to the right so he wouldn't notice the unshed tears as they pooled in my eyes.

"Save your thinkin' for when you're sitting on the toilet, not wasting my time."

"Duly noted, boss. Just need another minute."

I sat on the curb, not at all anxious to get back inside his overcompensating monster truck and head back to work. I gathered that he wanted to speed past whatever happened last night. I respected that decision. What I couldn't wrap my head around was this sudden outing, and with *me* of all people. I assumed he had friends, the guys who worked at the shop. Hell, Angelica would've made an even better choice. The excuse about the clothes? Wasn't buying it. Something else was going on, and I refused to move another inch until he spilled his guts.

Mace glanced around the parking lot before returning his hard expression to me. He quirked an inquisitive brow, glowered down at me, then folded his big arms over his chest.

"Still got places to go, Nancy. Get that ass moving," he ordered.

"Don't you have a wife or a girlfriend you'd rather spend your time with instead of your temporary bookkeeper? I'm sure she wouldn't appreciate you out and about with another female. I know I wouldn't."

He scowled. "That your way of asking who it is I'm fucking, Nancy? Awfully forward of you. What is it with you women always wanting to know where I stick my dick?"

You women? How many are we talking about?

I sucked my teeth. "That's not an answer, Mace."

"First off, this isn't spending time; this is doing something to keep my mind off hurting a motherfucker back at Masonry Ink. I meant what I said before we left. To clarify, beautiful women should be seen wearing something other than baggy-ass jogging suits on a daily. My shop's got a rep to protect. *That* is the reason why *you* are here, the only fucking reason," he emphasized with annoyance.

"As far as your other question, no wife, no girlfriends, but when my dick needs a kiss, I've got a cornucopia of lips ready to pucker up, don't you worry. We done with story time?"

I couldn't help but laugh at the absurdity of this situation. He said what he said, and I got it, I truly did. He wasn't one for attachments. *Duly noted.*

Mace had a lot of responsibilities— he owned a business, took care of his employees, served the community. Ever since I started working to prioritize the expenditures, I noticed little things at first. Cash donations to the local food bank in the name of Masonry Ink. School supplies twice a year like clockwork to Remington Elementary, Remington Middle, all the way up to Remington High. Charitable contributions for small businesses weren't that unusual, but then there were others I had no idea how to categorize. A mobile wheelchair for an unknown recipient, bought and paid for by Masonry Ink. An eight-seater minivan, again bought and paid for by Masonry Ink, recipient anonymous. Remington Community College yearly tuition paid, not only for one student, but for several. Why keep such good deeds a secret, and where was all the money coming from?

Judging by the invoices, it all seemed on the up and up, but I had my misgivings. Still, there was nothing complicated about how I found myself alone with my boss. It was the absence of connection he needed, someone he didn't give a fuck about, or ever would for that matter.

A stand-in for his dearest kinfolk... and I felt every bit the lonely intruder.

Mace held on to his side as he struggled to sit next to me on the curb. I cringed thinking of how painful that gash must feel today as opposed to last night. Aside from an audible grunt, he pretended like everything was fine and dandy. *Such a man thing to do.*

We sat unbothered by the crowd of shoppers wandering in and out of the parking lot. It was the perfect setting to allow my imagination to take hold and curiosity to force my unbridled tongue to wag.

"Did you always want to be a tattoo artist, Mace?" I whispered into the open air.

It took several moments for him to answer, so low I barely heard it.

"No. I had other plans after I left the military, but...things changed."

He said no more, but I did.

"Growing up, I watched my mother destroy the lives of so many people with her selfish actions disguised as a means of survival. Love was a game to her, an emotion she never felt but claimed to know everything about. All the men in our town saw her as an easy lay, and she saw them as her meal ticket. 'They have to pay to play,' she would always tell me. I promised myself that one day, I would find the man of my dreams, and he would always choose me. I thought it was a simple thing to ask, you know? Turns out, not so much."

"That how you found yourself alone with a newborn babe roaming the streets of Remington? Your man cheat on you...with your mother?" he asked.

I almost laughed.

What does it say about a person when cheating in a marriage would've been the preferred experience over the eventual outcome? It was a conversation best left for another time, or not at all. The last thing I wanted was to watch the look of disgust as it floated over Mace's face at my full disclosure. So, I did what anyone would do in my position and changed the subject.

"So...who was it?" I asked, chancing a glance.

"Who was what?" he grumbled.

"The person who pissed you off back at Masonry Ink."

His stare took on a faraway look, and his scowl deepened as he concentrated on the back tires of the monster truck. I anxiously waited for a name Jagger, Angelica, Jerome, but to my surprise, it was none of them.

"Me," he says. "Pissed myself off."

"Huh, I can see that being a problem for a certified alpha male," I offered.

"Fucking right it is. Hard to kick your own ass without falling headfirst into the dirt."

He stood from his spot on the curb with a huff. Clearly, our conversation was over. I followed his lead and made my way over to the passenger side of the truck while he clicked the fob to open. The silence made me feel uneasy, that I'd somehow overstepped by asking questions. He seemed more tense than when we first left Masonry Ink, if that were even possible. His shoulders were bunched up to his neck, and his hands fidgeted along the steering wheel. The silence inside the cabin was deafening until finally, I had no choice but to break it.

"I usually have lunch around this time, Mace. I also need to, um…you know…pump. Please tell me there's a sandwich somewhere in the back seat, maybe a can of Coke? I can feel my stomach beating the shit outa my liver, and it's not a pleasant feeling. Surely, you didn't get all those muscles by starving yourself to death."

His lips twitched just a tad in the corner.

He groaned in mock outrage. "Eating in my truck is a surefire way to getting kicked out of it, Nancy. It's not just a means of transportation. This here's my baby." He patted the console pridefully. "And it's definitely not a place to whip out your tits unless you're ready to see a grown man drool."

"So…no sandwich, then?" I teased.

Mace blessed me with a genuine smile that touched my soul. Both rows of straight white teeth, plump lips, and a sparkle in his eye that felt like silk along my heated skin. It was infectious and hearty at the same time, relieving me of the need to consume actual food. I could've stared at his handsome profile for hours, but then I noticed his brows pinched together, his nose scrunched up, and I just knew. *Fuck my life.*

I could've died right there in my seat.

"Looks like you sprung a leak, little momma." Mace ogled. "Try not to stain my upholstery, yeah? I got a bucket in the back, if you need it."

"Don't be an asshole. What are you, twelve?" I scoffed.

"Are you talking about my dick again? Thought we went over this already, but just to clarify, I'd say it's closer to an eleven, but I'd doubt you'll miss that extra inch." He smirked.

"Jesus Christ, you're an idiot."

I folded my arms over my chest in order to hide my engorged breasts. The air conditioning wasn't helping. I usually had this under better control, but like I said, the hour was later than usual. Mace must've sensed my discomfort, or maybe he just felt sorry for me. Either way, he somehow maneuvered the truck into the turning lane and executed a three-point turn into the middle of oncoming traffic.

"Where are we going now, Mace?" I shrieked.

"Got a buddy that owns a diner, makes the best corned beef Reuben sandwich I ever had. We'll stop and grab one on the way to Mrs. LaFontaine's so you can feed the kid."

"Or you could just pull over and give me a little privacy," I offered.

He lifted a hand and pointed a finger at himself. "Driver…" Then pointed at me. "Passenger. End of."

How could I argue with that? I loved Reuben sandwiches.

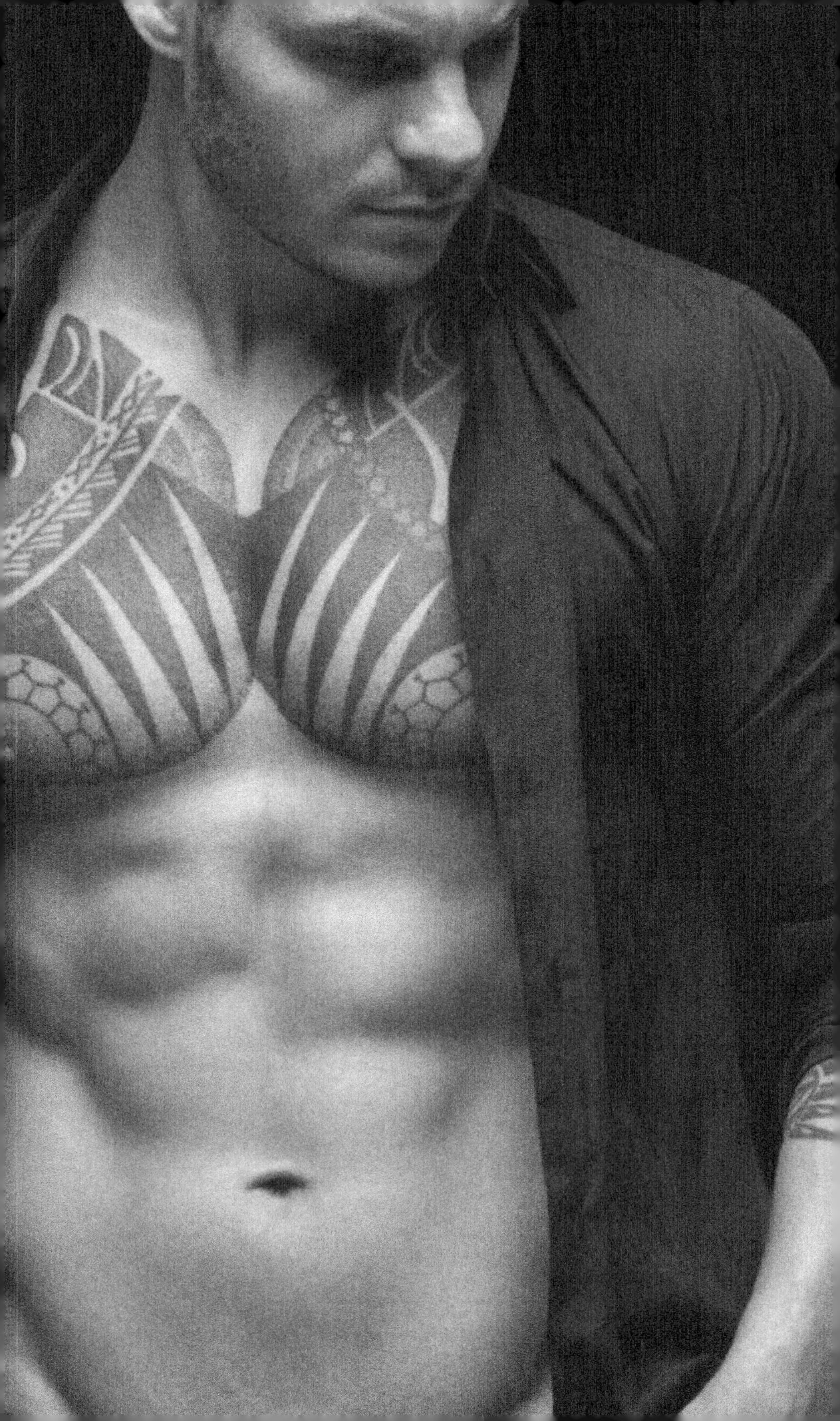

Chapter Fourteen

Mace

I was this close to telling her the truth.

That I knew her history and why she ran out of the store like her ass was on fire. Once you've witnessed real fear from another human being firsthand, you recognized it as easily as you recognized your own name. I should've been more careful with her. My need to get away overshadowed my common sense, but it was too late to dwell on that now.

I drove in silence through old town Remington headed towards the residential section of the city. Nancy slash True stared stoically out the window, convinced that I was somehow thoroughly repulsed by the wetness of her stained jogging suit. What she couldn't know, and what I refused to confess, was that there was nothing in the world more lovely than witnessing a woman's body transform as it prepared to provide nourishment for a child. Took all I had in me from turning into a prehistoric caveman the longer I stared at her tits encased in yellow sunshine. I could remember the look in my father's eyes as he watched my mother expose her breast, position my sister across her lap, and encourage her to latch on with a satisfied smile.

"You're too young to understand, Mace, and I don't expect you to," he spoke, "but there ain't a man livin' that don't get a hard-on seeing his woman like that."

"Eww, Dad. Mom's boobs are gross," I replied with all the disgust of a typical seven-year-old boy. He simply smiled with a knowing look on his face.

"Best fucking feeling in the world, son. You'll find out for yourself one day, mark my words."

True Boardman wasn't my woman, but that didn't stop the ache in my chest or the longing my soul tried to penetrate into my very foundation. I wasn't deserving of becoming a father, or a husband for that matter. A woman would have to be a damned fool to hitch herself to a hard-ass like me. I could fuck the shit out of any woman I chose to be with, but the intimacy part was where I was lacking. Getting close meant the possibility that one day, they could be taken from me at the hands of another motherfucker out to test the weight of his cock. The very idea of having to go through another loss, that emptiness, the feeling of helplessness, crippled any desire I had of loving or being loved. My pool of willing bodies was small by choice; not just anyone could go ten rounds with a heavy weight, and yes, I was talking about my cock. Nancy slash True might have been a tough chick, but she belonged to someone else, and like a kid with a shiny new toy, I was never big on sharing.

I pulled the truck to a stop in front of the Lafontaine house and cut the engine. She jumped out in a rush, but I lingered a bit. She needed the space to deal with her self-consciousness and to escape inside. I grabbed the paper bag with the sandwiches and made it to the door as Corrine Lafontaine blasted me with a blinding smile and open arms.

"Mace Fox! Get your handsome self over here and hug my neck," she squealed.

"How you doing, Corrine?" I asked, crouching down to her stumped level.

"I'm right as rain, Mace. Please, come in, take a load off."

She relieved me of the bag and pointed me towards the direction of her sitting room. I got the same feeling in the pit of my stomach as I always did when I visited this house. She reminded me a lot of my mother in some ways, imposingly strong despite her size, considerate to a fault, and deeply compassionate. Our first encounter was far from ordinary as the pint-sized woman barged into my office at Masonry Ink like a tidal wave, helped herself to a seat, puffed up like a peacock, and lit all the way into me. I remembered it like it was yesterday.

"I was told you're a man who knows how to get things done," she stated plainly.

"Oh yeah? And who told you that...Ms...?"

"Mrs," she corrected with her chin held high. "Corrine Lafontaine. Now you know me, and I know you, Mace Fox. How I came about that information is totally irrelevant, unless, of course, I was misinformed? Besides, you wouldn't want me to snitch now, would you? My source is reliable, I assure you."

I could only blink at her bolder-than-fuck attitude. She knew the answer to her question without me having to co-sign; she wouldn't have been here if she weren't a hundred percent sure of my credentials. Corrine Lafontaine didn't strike me as the type of woman who went off halfcocked, and for that, she had my attention.

"Go on," I nodded.

This old broad was a savage. Dressed to the nines in designer wear, gold and diamonds blinging on her fingers, and to top it off, a goddamn string of fresh water pearls wrapped around her delicate neck. She had that old lady smell, the kind that you run into at the supermarket right after service lets out. Flowery mixed with decrepitude, but not all the way broken down. This woman took pride in her appearance and wasn't the least bit intimidated walking into a tattoo shop after hours. I respected the hell out of her just for that.

"I need you to track down my niece, who's in a bad way, and bring her home. I won't try and sugarcoat things to make it seem more palatable, Mr. Fox. Things are pretty bad. In fact, I'd say it was a matter of life and death. I can pay whatever you want as soon as the job is done, no questions asked. Do we have a deal?"

"What are we talking about here? Drugs? Sex work?"

She sighed. "Both, I'm afraid. One does usually follow the other in most cases. I should warn you now, my niece is black, as in African American. Now, if that's a problem for you, I'd certainly understand. I know from television that some of you good old boys don't care too much for our darker brethren. It's disgusting, but…to each their own. Now, can you help me or not?"

I hesitated, not wanting to turn her down flat. Junkies were a tricky bunch, cunning and manipulative, anything to get their next fix. I didn't know how long her niece had been out there, but she wasn't a victim turned away by the police. She was a willing participant, more likely to slit my throat if I tried to pull her out before she was ready.

"Look…I appreciate you…"

"She wants to come home. Look." She slid a folded piece of paper across the desk. I picked it up and started to read it.

Dear Aunt Corrine,

I'm so sorry for what happened. Don't give up on me. I'll find a way to make it home, I promise. You are always in my heart.

Love, Sal.

"I tried to do it myself, but that snake of a flesh-peddler she calls her *sponsor* dislocated my shoulder. I was in a sling for weeks. I came to find you as soon as I was able to drive. It may already be too late. Please, I'll give you anything you want," she pleaded.

She left my office a short time after more details were given, more begging from an individual who swallowed her pride to save someone she loved. I made no promises, brought it up to the crew the next day, and came to a decision. Dead Man was completely against it. Jagger and Kaden were neutral. We all knew you could never trust a junkie. In the end, it all boiled down to mind over matter. If that wannabe Iceberg Slim didn't *mind* twisting the arm of an old lady till' it cracked, then his pointless parasitic life didn't much *matter*. Once we tracked him down to a sleezy motel on the outskirts of town, I ended his reign of terror. Not for the crackhead passed out on the bed, but for the old woman who couldn't fight back.

Corrine's laugh from somewhere close by shook me from my recent memory, and I watched her start to pick up various toys scattered throughout the floor. Surely, one tiny baby didn't play with all that shit, did she?

"Nancy will be out in a minute, Mace. Little Kayla was happy to see her momma earlier than usual, so she's taking advantage."

"In no hurry, Corrine. I'll drive them over to Sal's when she's done. No use heading back to the shop this late in the day."

"Wonderful." She smiled. "That's very nice of you."

"Corrine, can you help me with something?" Nancy slash True called from the bedroom.

"Be right back."

I was content just sitting around on the couch while the ladies did whatever the hell they were doing. The slash along my ribs had been giving me a fit the entire afternoon made worse by hunkering down on a cement curb. Corrine would never let me back in her house if I bled all over her fine English furniture.

"Oh Mace, I'm so sorry. Look at the time. Do you mind holding her while I put the roast in the oven? Jerome and Michelle can't make it for Sunday dinner this week, so we're having it tonight. Didn't he tell you? Silly boy. Well, no matter."

"Hold her, who?"

I nearly choked on my own tongue when she handed me a tiny person dressed in one of those ruffled snap footie things with a matching headband. This couldn't be she same baby that was barely big enough to fit in my hand the last time I saw her. This one had rolls for days, chubby round cheeks, and a mop of blonde hair that curled around her ears. My breath caught on a gasp I was so taken aback. She was absolutely beautiful and looked so much like her momma it was uncanny.

"What am I supposed to do with her?" I ask.

"She's well fed and should be drifting off to sleep any moment," Corrine said with a head shake. "Just sit as you were, and if you're feeling adventurous, rock her a little, but not too hard. Wouldn't want her to throw up her meal now, would we?"

Corrine took off into the kitchen, leaving me with my arms full of powdery fresh-smelling infant. I was entranced. What happened next took me all the way out. She grabbed my finger and squeezed. At the same time, she smiled looking right into my eyes. I stiffened and took a few shuddering breaths, unprepared for the warmth as it pulled at my heart strings.

"I can take her, if you want, Mace," her mother whispered nearby. Freshly changed into a new shirt, hair brushed, skin glowing. I much preferred the wet titty look.

I had no idea how long she'd been standing there, nor did I care.

I wasn't ready to give her back. *Not yet.*

"I got her," was all I could muster.

She stayed in my arms while her mother went into the kitchen to eat her sandwich. I'd lost my appetite, full off of baby drool and contented belly farts, too powerful to have come from such a delicate little thing. The longer I held her, the more she smiled, until she dozed off making sucky noises with her pouty lips. When it was time to leave and her mother took her from me, I felt empty inside, like a part of me was missing and I desperately wanted it back. As we drove away from Corrine's, I watched her closely in the rearview mirror, afraid she'd disappear and I'd never get to see her again. Exactly the type of shit I tried to avoid in my life. I caught a strange look from the passenger side on my last sneaky peek. The kid's mother was staring at the speedometer with her eyebrows raised.

"Let me guess." She smirked. "Trying to save on gas, that why you're driving so slow, Miss. Daisy? I can get out and run faster than this thing is rolling."

"Shush it," I grumbled. "Precious cargo."

"Just saying, it'll take us an hour to get to Sal's at this rate." She snorted.

I laughed despite my sour mood.

"Guess you'll have to put up with me a little longer, then," I said to her.

"Pfft. You're not so bad...except when you're scaring old ladies shopping at Target."

"You should see me at Walmart. That's where I really make 'em scatter," I joked.

She settled into her seat with a coy smile that made me wonder. What regular man in his right mind would give up his beautiful wife and precious little daughter? I scrubbed my hand over my face. Anger rolled off my shoulders in waves. If they were mine, I'd never let them out of my sight, not for a minute, not for an hour. The thought of it made my skin break out in a cold sweat. Her husband must've been a damn fool. If they were mine, I'd...

But... they aren't yours.

Cue the bucket of ice water. With that bitter truth, the ache went away.

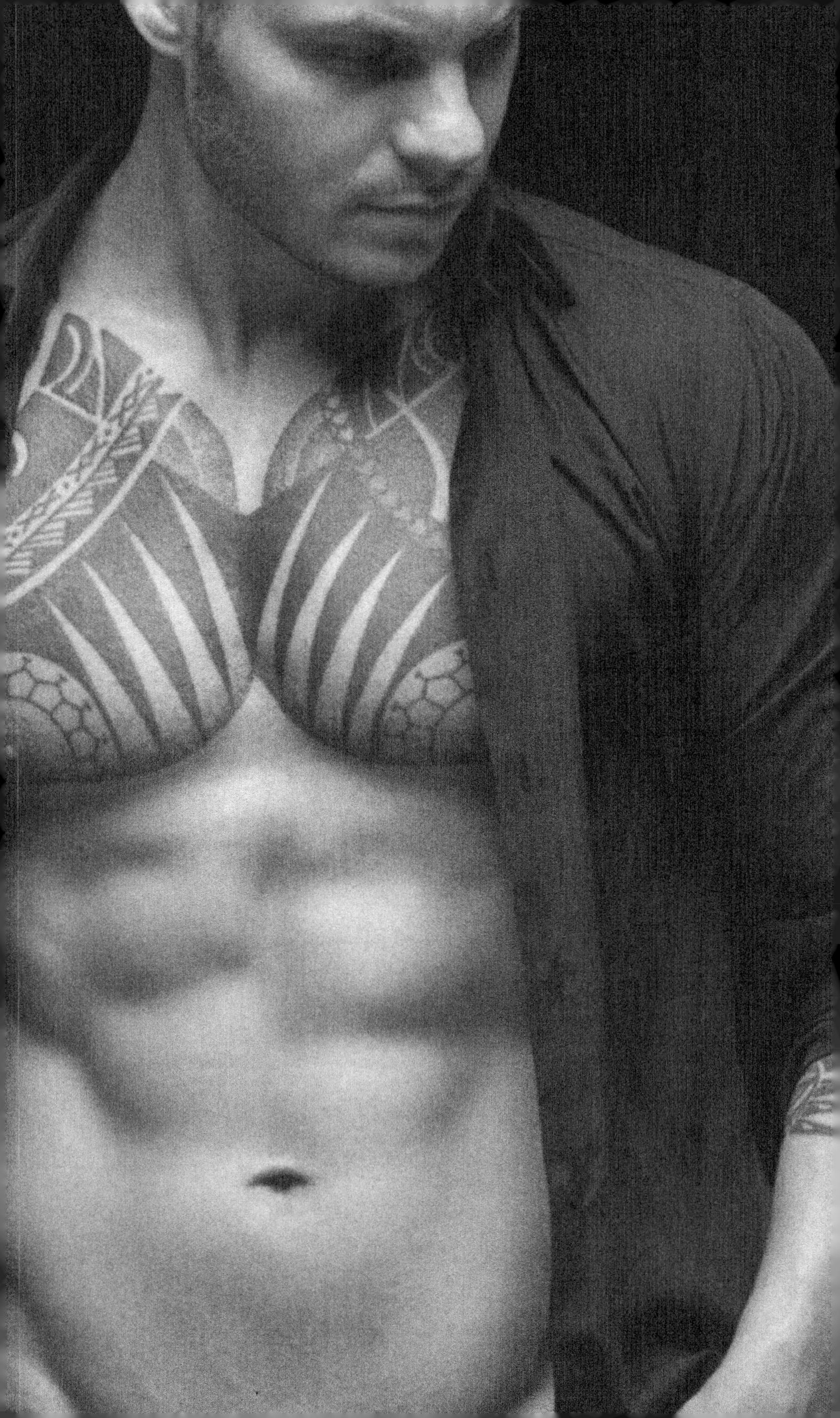

Chapter Fifteen

True

Bizarre occurrences.

That's the only way I could think of to describe being kicked out of the office for the third time today while Mace met with someone who wasn't looking to get a new tattoo. How did I know they weren't potential customers? Well, the first gentleman who came forward was screaming about disgusting skin vandalism and how they should all be outlawed. I failed to see what someone like him would need to discuss with a man who creates tattoos for a living, but I digress. His meeting lasted all of ten minutes, and he wasn't any happier when he exited as he was when he entered. If anything, he seemed even more pissed.

I was anxious to get back to work when visitor number two arrived, an older black woman carrying a bible, requesting a sit-down with Malik Bird owner slash operator. I thought Mace would send her away, obviously having entered the wrong place, 'cause who the fuck was Malik Bird? Instead, he welcomed her in while asking me to make myself scarce for a while. That was how I ended up cleaning out the refrigerator in the break area.

Their meeting lasted over an hour, and by the time the woman left, it was well into the afternoon and I hadn't accomplished a damn thing. Oh, but that wasn't all.

The third visitor was a child, a boy, no more than thirteen years old, carrying an old backpack and in dire need of a Big Mac hamburger and a hug from grandma. I made the mistake of looking into his empty eyes as we passed each other at the office door. I recognized myself as a scared young girl in that young man, begging to be seen yet quietly hiding in plain sight. I wondered who he was and where his parents were. More importantly, what put that faraway hopeless look on his face as if the world and everyone in it had forgotten about him?

Bizarre occurrences or perhaps something more?

I stood near the reception desk hoping to get back to work for at least a few minutes before Sal came to get me. Hushed conversation from my left took my attention away from the closed door long enough to be a distraction.

"I can't believe he bought that bitch here again, Michelle, said he had a back piece that's going to take him a few hours to complete and he wanted her to keep him company. It's like...he's throwing that shit in my face or something, trying to make me jealous."

Angelica was crouched in the corner talking on her cell phone to whom I assumed was Jerome's girlfriend, Michelle. I'd noticed the two younger women spending time together outside of Masonry Ink, grabbing lunch or coffee during the afternoon when they both had a break. Michelle was absolutely stunning with her long red hair, freckled nose, and lovesick irises that sparkled every time she glanced at her other half adoringly.

I tried to look busy so she wouldn't think I was eavesdropping, which I obviously was, unintentionally, of course.

"What claim, Michelle? He doesn't owe me anything," she hissed. "I'm not his woman. She is, and you and I both know why that's for the best."

Who are they...?

"Jagger can eat a dick and die, for all I care. If that fake triple-D dingbat is who he wants, then I say more power to him. Go nuts. But what he's not going to do is try and make me feel like shit about you know what."

You know what? Holy shit! What, what...

This place was better than an episode of *Days of our Lives*. Angelica was in love with Jagger, who was dating a woman with fake breasts and a learning disability. Who knew? I tried, I really did, but I couldn't help the sudden snigger that developed when I pictured this woman in all her big-tittied glory. Since I wasn't in the loop, I had to draw my own conclusions, and with my limited experience, the result wasn't pretty. I pictured Jessica Rabbit with a Dr. Seuss book turned upside down while she tried to read it out loud.

"If you're going to listen in on someone's private conversation, you could at least have the common decency to turn around before laughing, bitch!"

Shit. Busted.

"Oh, I wasn't..."

I stopped mid-sentence. No use in trying to deny it now. She'd caught me red-handed. I squared my shoulders, looked her straight in the eyes, and prepared myself to march down tongue lashing lane, courtesy of the dark-haired beauty with mist in her eyes.

"I apologize, Angelica. That wasn't my intention. You have every right to be upset with me. I promise it will never happen again."

I pleaded in earnest hoping she could hear the sincerity in my voice. I never meant to make an enemy out of anyone here at Masonry Ink, and I certainly wasn't gaining any brownie points by acting like a creeper. Her hard expression softened ever so slightly then vanished all together when we were joined at the desk.

"Sorry for the, um... cliterference, ladies, but my man sent me on a mission," I heard announced before turning around to see who the voice belonged to.

Angelica barely held herself together as she faced off with the buxom bombshell wearing a halter top and skinny jeans. Her makeup was flawless, *two hours in front of a mirror sipping water from a straw* flawless. I might have been a little slow on the uptake, but one look at those protruding nipples, and I knew this was the woman Angelica had been talking with Michelle about on the phone. This wasn't their first meeting, I surmised; the air around us practically crackled with tension.

"What the fuck do you need, Kira? Can't you see we're busy?" Angelica snapped.

The two of them exchanged dirty looks while I stood there with my mouth hanging open. First impression, this Kira chick was up to something, that much was clear. The way she smirked, batted her eyelashes, and used her perfectly manicured fingers to drum along the wooden surface of the reception desk was all show. It was about to go down.

"That man could tie me up, ask me to get on my knees, and suck his dick from the back, and I'd do it in a heartbeat," she purred. "Oh, wait a second." She tapped her chin as if she were really thinking about something. "I did that last night. Oops."

Ugh.

Smooth, lady, real smooth.

Angelica looked in my direction from under her dark lashes, and I could see the fire dying within her soul as her shoulders deflated. It was the most heartbreaking thing I'd ever witnessed in my life. Tearing another woman down for pleasure should be outlawed. She was crushed by the remarks but fought hard not to show the damage the words left behind as a consequence.

"We do not care, Kira. Now, what do you want?" she replied stoically.

Kira kept at her, undeterred.

"*Whew*...that man is a pure beast in the sheets. He has me walking bowlegged every night. Have I ever told you about the first time we fucked? That man blew my back out with one stroke."

I'd heard enough of her bullshit.

"Hi, I'm Nancy. Can I help you with something?"

I plastered on the fakest smile I could muster, stepped closer to her person, and tried to block Angelica from this bitch's taunts. We might have gotten off on the wrong foot, but I'd be damned if I stood idly by and watched her be ridiculed. She took her evil eyes off Angelica just long enough to acknowledge me. Disdain dripped from her fangs. She reminded me of a rabid squirrel scurrying about looking for nuts, no pun intended.

"Hi, I'm Kira...Jagger's woman," she boasted. "He needs a few extra packages of Round Shader needles for the client he's working on. Said to grab it from the front."

I pointed to a spot over her shoulder. "They're on the shelf just over there."

She didn't even bother to look, knowing full well where they were before she approached.

"I'll tell you that story next time, Angel." She smirked, turned, and walked away.

The poor girl's skin turned white as a sheet at being called Angel. The dig held a hidden meaning, something private, I was sure of it.

Angelica appeared so lost and dewy-eyed. It was easy to forget how young she really was by the way she carried herself. Most of the time, she was a hellcat, but today, she was just a girl in love who needed a friend. I wanted to convey a few words of encouragement, but everything sounded so disgustingly contrived in my mind. I gave it a shot anyway.

"Costume jewelry looks just like the real thing until you get it wet," I told her.

"What's that mean?" She simpered.

"It means Jagger will come around, and when he does, she'll be kicked to the curb so fast it'll make her silly little head spin. She can crow now, but she'll be the one crying later."

"Yeah," she said as she stepped from behind the counter, eyeing me wearily. "But she does get to *have* him, which is something I never will." She paused with one final look.

"It's as it should be, Nancy. Stay the fuck out of my business next time." *Ouch.*

Bizarre occurrences.

I wondered what tomorrow might bring.

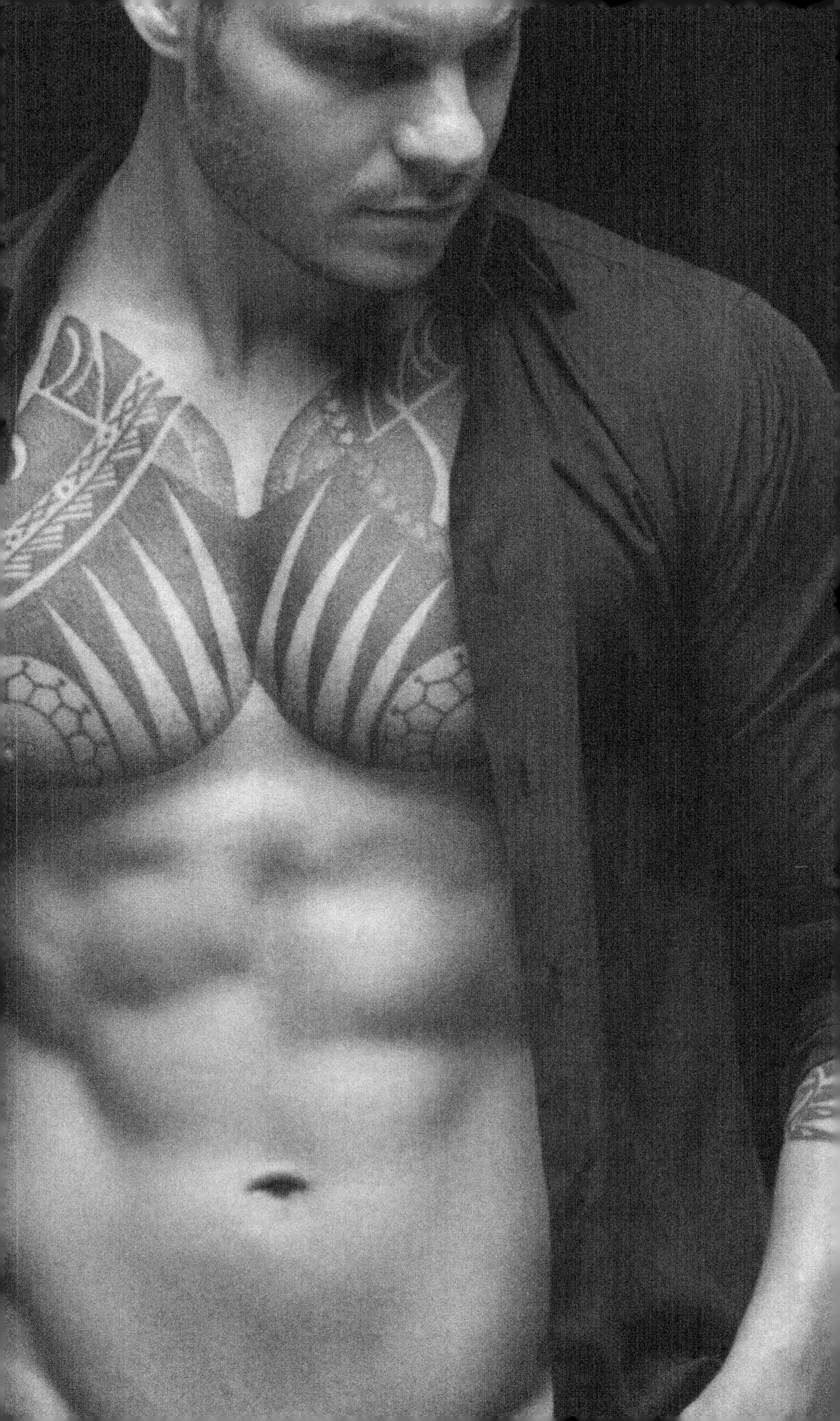

Chapter Sixteen

Mace

"What the hell is this?"

"What the fuck is what?" I snapped, dumbfounded.

"This!" she shouted. "Are you seriously trying to play macho-man stupid right now, Mace Fox? You know exactly what I'm talking about, and I want an explanation, damnit."

Two weeks had come and gone, and my soon-to-be ex-employee was standing in front of my desk, frothing at the mouth, over heaven knew what. Not counting this little hissy fit, she'd actually been the perfect accountant—arrived on time, stuck to her hour break, kept her head down. Her attention to detail and old-school work ethic was commendable, and she'd definitely be missed. Right now, though? She was getting on my fucking nerves. She huffed out a frustrated breath, planted her arms on her shapely hips, and gave me the stink eye for several long minutes. She tapped her foot expectantly as if to say, *I'm waiting*, and when I wouldn't budge, she threw an overstuffed envelope down so hard, it *smacked* when it landed.

"The fuck, woman, it's payday." I shrugged.

"Yeah, if I worked for the President of the United States or something, not slinging paperwork at a tattoo parlor. This has to be a mistake, an oversight perhaps. I think you should go back and re-check the records."

"I'm not seeing the problem, Nancy." I steepled my hands and stared right back. "No oversight. That's"—I waved in her general direction—"two weeks' pay."

"Not seeing the problem?" she blustered. "Not seeing the problem? Mace...look at all this money. It's...it's...ohmygod, I think I'm going to be sick."

I tried my best to ignore her little tantrum, but she looked damn cute in her new jeans, T-shirt, and running shoes. She thought I was kidding about those fucking jogging suits until I took the liberty of ordering more shit in her size and had them delivered to Sal's with strict instructions to never wear them again or she was fired. It seemed to have worked. Today was the day she'd been waiting for, so why she was carrying on like a banshee in my office was a mystery to me.

"Don't even think about blowing chunks in my space, Nancy."

"But, but..."

Enough of this fuckery.

"How many hours did you work? What was the hourly wage?"I pushed.

She pulled up short and thought about it, the answer out of reach.

"Take a seat," I instructed.

The second her ass hit the chair, I commenced to educating her on how we rolled at Masonry Ink. Once again taking time out of my day to do what I vowed I wouldn't, which was dealing with unnecessary bullshit.

"You never asked how much the gig paid, Nancy. You never even bothered to ask shit about the job before you took it, *took* being the operative word," I reminded her.

"That still doesn't explain the stack of cash, Mace."

"Then allow me." I fixed her in place with a hard look.

"Everyone here works as a unit, from the artists, designers, receptionist, and yes, even the bookkeeper. We all get our fair share of the earnings regardless of who brings in the most or the least. My name is on the deed, but this is our home, our business, and our pride. It's been that way since I opened Masonry Ink, and that's never going to change. Get over it."

"I don't know what to say," she answered in a low voice.

"Then don't say anything. Now that you have enough cash, you and the kid should be set up nicely, wherever you decide to go tomorrow."

She recoiled at my mention of her leaving.

I'd long suspected that she wasn't as keen on the idea of taking off as she was before. Truth be told, I wasn't so geeked on the idea myself, not after spending time with her chubby little baby. Foolishly, I'd been taking liberties where I shouldn't have over the last few days, stopping by Corrine's house after Sal drove them away to work in the mornings. Sleepless nights turned into early days with nothing to deflect my dark thoughts. I'd been fighting against the pull of darkness ever since I cancelled that prick stalker, but the kid had a way about her. She calmed my inner workings and quieted the storm that always seemed to be brewing.

I was falling apart.

This year, unlike every other since it happened, was different.

I realized that what Kaden said about me was the truth and was likely to push me further into the bowels of the dark abyss before long. It was the anniversary of his sentencing, that sham of a bid he managed to con out of the jury. I saw his face everywhere I went, smiling, laughing, reminding me that I could've stopped him if I'd only kept my word. It wasn't just my imagination on this unholy day; it was the size of his brass balls whenever I received a letter in the mail addressed by him. I kept them bound in a stack hidden beneath my closet, too afraid to open them, too angry to read his words.

What would be the point?

I'd give him the chance to say his piece to my fucking face when I put a bullet inside his skull and watched him bleed out by my feet. Only then would I entertain his bullshit apology, if that's what they were. Fuck those letters.

My visits to the kid started with a yearning to once again smile at nothing in particular. I missed the spontaneity of laughter in my life, the ease of which it made everything infinitely clearer, and the way it caused my cheeks to stretch. She gave that to me when I thought it was lost for good.

The excuse I gave Corrine that first time was that I was there to check in on Dread, make sure he was following all her rules while living in the guest house. Since I was the one who asked her to rent out her space, the lie was easily believable. When she left me alone with the kid to go check on a bottle in the warmer, I focused on her deliberate smile meant only for me. It was as if she'd recognized me from before and started to make cooing noises. One squeeze of her tiny fingers, and all the pressure that was suffocating me seemed to evaporate into thin air.

I took a deep breath.

Then another.

The weightlessness I felt only lasted long enough for Kaden to fuck it when he announced to the crew that the family of the dead stalker had gone to the cops about their missing boy. I fed him some bullshit about it being a coincidence, assured him that wherever he ghosted to had nothing to do with us, that he probably felt the squeeze of our negotiation and thought it was in his best interest to take a long vacation. He knew I was full of shit; the others, not so much, but they suspected. When he slyly asked my thoughts on the situation, I looked him dead in his eyes and told him I had none. End of.

I lied so easily that it shook me.

Who the fuck was I turning into?

The second time I showed up at Corrine's, I told her I was there to check out her alarm system, that there had been a string of break-ins in the area and I thought it prudent to be on the safe side. She once again left me with the kid, but instead of feeling the levity I sought through her smile, it was the spring of hot tears that followed her light. Everything spilled out of me and onto her chubby cheeks as I leaned in to get a whiff of her baby smell. Parole hearing, murder, death, kill. Wasn't long before we were both blubbering together, reacting to each other's emotions. I made my excuses to Corrine and got the hell out of there, but fucking hell, how I wanted to go back. She held the power in her little fists to stop me from destroying myself, a burden no child should be responsible for. My behavior was beyond trifling, and I never went back for thirds.

"Mace? Did you hear what I said?" My thoughts returned to the present.

"Sorry. Can you repeat that?"

"I was thinking, or, well, hoping that perhaps, if you don't mind, that I could stay on a little while longer in Remington. This little town has kinda' grown on me."

I sighed, pissed that I wasn't paying attention when she originally bought it up.

"I'll have to run it by the other guys, see if they're okay with you sticking around. You and I both know this isn't the normal employer slash employee situation we're talking about. When I first bought you on, I told the crew it was temporary, till you got back on your feet. Not sure they'll agree to much else."

"I see," she answered in a low tone.

"I'm responsible for everyone's safety, Nancy. We're a team, and no one person is bigger than the group. You need to figure out your next move, be diligent, and prepare to answer questions if the crew asks. Can't expect them to stick their necks out unless you're willing to give something in return. It's how we operate. We look out for one another through thick and thin. I'm not saying you should worry, Nancy. You'd be surprised how accommodating they can be once they accept you into the fold."

"I don't know if I can do that, Mace." Her cheeks turned rosy.

"Your choice how much you want to share. We don't keep secrets from each other; you should know that by now. Think it over. Sal okay with you staying in her space?"

"Yeah, we've talked about it. She doesn't mind."

It wasn't enough that she wanted to stay in Remington and continue working at Masonry Ink. It'd been weeks, and she still didn't trust us enough to reveal her real identity. She ran from her cop husband with his kid, which made her a liability I couldn't afford to underestimate. She wasn't aware that I was privy to that information and every other fact concerning her life in Montana. Logically, I should've denied her on the spot, sent her on her way now that she had a pocket full of cash and was in relatively better health since giving birth. Since I was clearly a dumbass, I proceeded in the opposite way.

"Where were you headed the night you arrived at Masonry Ink, Nancy?"

Her face turned ashen, stricken.

It took her a minute before she finally answered.

She turned away slightly to avoid my gaze. "Somewhere… anywhere…a starting point, I suppose, a place that would offer us the freedom to exist without all the pain. I saw a brochure once that mentioned a little town in upstate New York, and I thought I'd give it a try."

"Starting point, huh? Away from your mother's reputation?"

"Among other things," she replied.

I mentally tried to talk myself out of asking the next question, not wanting to push if she wasn't ready, but I ignored that sharp stab of warning in my chest.

"And the child's father, a husband, I assume, where does he fit into the equation?"

"He doesn't!" she screeched. "Kayla will never meet her father, not while there's breath in my body, Mace. I'll never go back, and no one can make me."

"Calm, woman. We're just talking here," I said gently.

I'd clearly struck a nerve, but why? The way she bristled when replying to my question was telling. Was her husband a pussy-ass wife beater? A cheater? I hadn't realized that my hands were balled into fists until my knuckles cracked under the strain. I took a deep breath, prayed for calm, but pressed on.

"Still, has to hurt knowing you slipped away with his baby. Would hurt the fuck out of me not knowing I had a kid in the world, unprotected."

"How'd you know I was married, Mace? Maybe I'm a single mother whose baby daddy didn't want anything to do with her or her kid. Maybe I'm just like my mother, you think of that?"

"You look like the marrying type of woman to me, Nancy. Now it's confirmed."

"Well...I know what you're thinking, and you're wrong. My husband never abused me, cheated on me, left his socks in the corner, or forgot our anniversary. He's a non-factor, and I prefer to leave it that way, if you don't mind."

That was clear enough.

"I'll talk to the crew, get their buy-in to keep you around," I assured her. "Till then, don't worry about it. Come back on Monday business as usual. Any plans for your new-found fortune? Don't spend it all in one place."

"Something of my own," she whispered. "I earned this standing up and not on my back."

Not like your cunt mother.

"You did good, Nancy, damn good," I announced.

That made her smile.

A damn beautiful smile at that.

"Yes, yes, I did, didn't I?" She beamed.

Charm was a quality passed down from mother to daughter, I concluded. They each shared a tiny dimple on the corner of their mouths, a depression only visible when they were amused. I shook my head, putting a stop to those thoughts before they got started. She walked away with her envelope safely tucked in her jeans pocket, anxious to get back to work, before she unexpectantly turned.

"I think we're going to like it here, Mace."

I watched her sweet ass as she trotted away. *Real tough chick.*

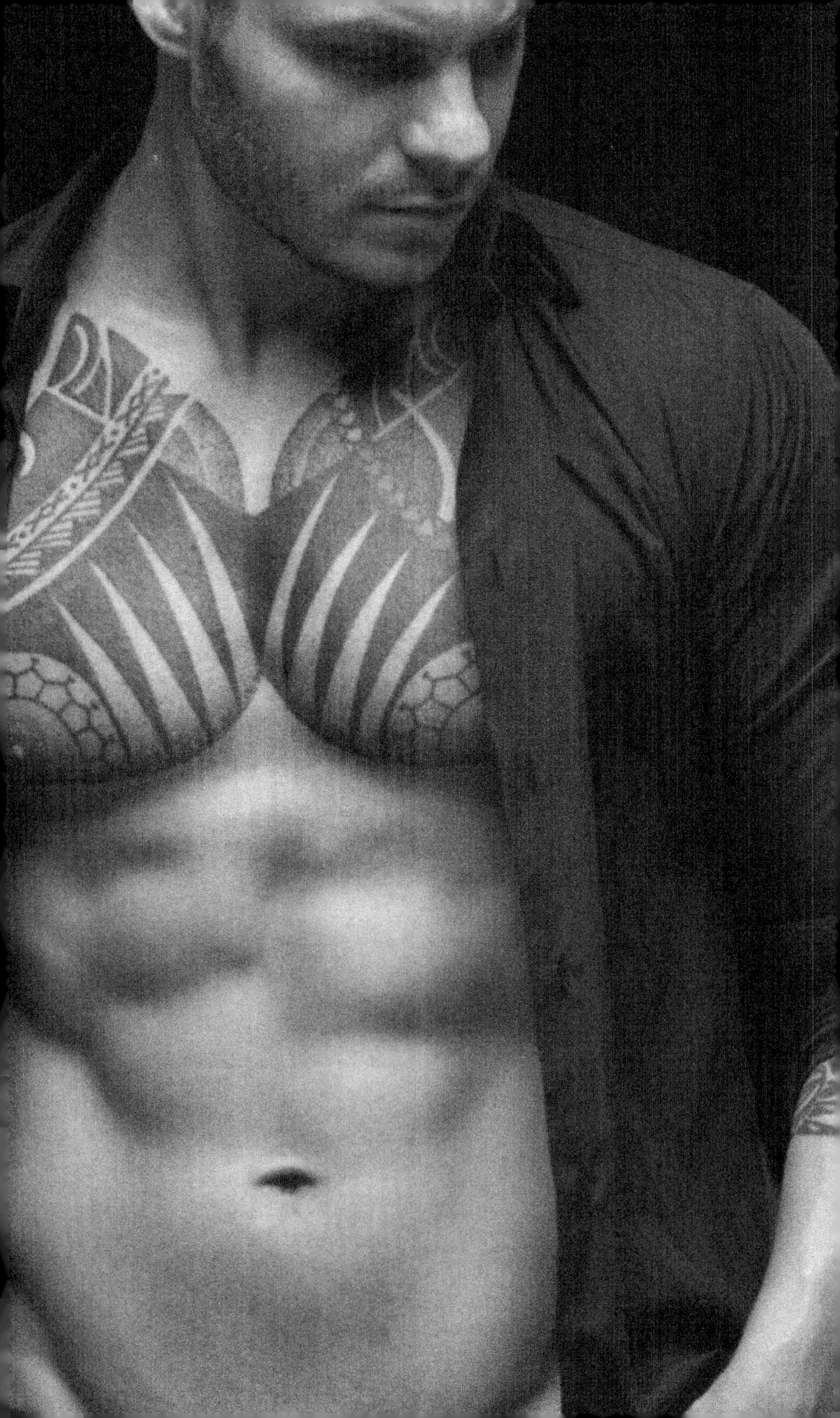

Chapter Seventeen

True

Lies, even those by omission, had a way of biting you in the ass when you least expected. As soon as I told Sal about my ginormous paycheck, she insisted that we go out on the town and celebrate my good fortune. I'd run out of excuses to give as to why I never wanted to leave the house at the end of the workday. Crying broke to justify my hermit impersonation worked thus far, but since that was no longer the case, I sullenly agreed to her invitation. Needless to say, my stomach had been tied up in knots ever since.

Thanks to Mrs. Lafontaine, we were able to make a day of it without the added worry of dragging around a fussy infant. We hit the spa for facials and massages, the salon for hair and nails, and we even managed a bit of shopping. Sal dragged me inside a cell phone store and added my name to her plan, or rather, Nancy Jennings' name. She thought it was a good idea in case of an emergency, so I settled on an open-boxed model at a reduced price. Who would I call anyway? Ghostbusters? My mother surely heard of my disappearance by now and would give me nothing but grief if I dared to contact her. I refused to even think about that tonight. This was a happy occasion, and since I hadn't had many of those, I planned to bask in it.

We were seated in a booth at one of the restaurants newly opened in developing downtown Remington. The place was called Kellogg's and specialized in authentic Southern-style cuisine—everything from fresh seafood to downhome smoked meats were available, and I was anxious to try them all. We made a fine pair judging by the looks of the other diners. Sal in her knee-length little black dress with sky-high heels, while I chose a more conservative outfit, a solid tank maxi dress that fell to my ankles with a pair of comfortable wedge sandals. I felt like a new woman for the first time in ages.

"I'm glad your tits are no longer a food source so we can have wine with our meals," Sal joked while making sucky noises with her lips.

"Don't let me stop you. Have at it. I'm a lightweight anyway when it comes to drinking, and let's not forget I still have to get up early and make the bottle."

"Now, what kind of friend would I be if I indulged, and you couldn't?"

"The happy kind?" I teased.

We shared a laugh while perusing the menu. Everything looked amazing.

"This place is the shit. I'm so glad we decided to come here," Sal remarked.

"Me too. I don't remember the last time I've been out to a restaurant. We really only had one diner back home, and I wouldn't exactly call it upper scale, more like eat at your own risk."

An older gentleman sitting at the table to our left gave Sal an appreciative glance with a flirtatious arch to his brow. She noticed and blew him a kiss before mouthing in his direction, *fuck off asshole,* and returned to her menu.

"Good thing you're sticking around, then." Sal reached across the table and took my hand. "Can't have you bored and hungry all at the same time in that shitty little town. I'm happy you decided to stay." *Boredom is the least of my worries back home.*

I smiled and made my selection when the waitress reappeared. I settled on the barbeque brisket sandwich with a side of fries and homemade coleslaw. Sal chose the half rack of dry rubbed ribs, a side salad, extra basket of cornbread, and the restaurant's signature honey butter. We were going to need a crane to move us out of our seats and into the car after all of this stuff.

We chatted about everything and nothing, Sal doing most of the talking. She had the better life anyway. My only contribution was the number of times Kayla managed to poop in any given day since I weened her off breast milk. My girl was a glutton, and my tits just weren't doing the job. Night after night, she'd suck me dry and still cried for more, all the while keeping everyone awake to the wee hours of the morning. After checking in with her pediatrician, we decided with much debate that I would switch to formula. I wouldn't be winning any mother of the year awards, but at least my tits would return to normal size and stop leaking all over my shirts like a bucket with a hole in it.

"So, beloved, what are your plans? Stay at Masonry Ink? Find a sugar daddy? Join the circus?" Sal asked around a bite of her buttered roll.

"I don't know." I sighed. "I actually enjoy working at the tattoo shop, even though Angelica hates my guts for some odd reason and doesn't mind showing me just how much."

I'd been confiding in Sal about my run-ins with the staff at Masonry Ink. I'd been venturing out from the office more ever since the guys encouraged me to do so—a wave here, a hello there. I discovered that Kaden was a hoot with his inappropriately crazy comments from left field, stories of sexual conquests, and overall weirdness. The guy was simply outrageous, but he brought a smile to my face whenever we crossed paths.

Jerome was pensive and brooding in his youth, so much in love with his girlfriend, I couldn't decide whether or not I wanted to hug him or strangle him. He was just so gosh dang cute. Then, of course, there were Angelica and Jagger. He seemed to be pretty down to earth, growly and larger than life, reminded me of a big old teddy bear. Angelica, on the other hand, was…how should I put this? A raging bitch on wheels. I accidentally walked in on the two of them during a heated conversation, and even though I apologized profusely, she told me she hoped I choked to death on a chicken bone. I hadn't eaten poultry since. Hence the whole *she hated my guts* thing.

"Don't worry about her. She's harmless," Sal remarked.

"You're acquainted with her?"

"Not really." She shrugged. "I know that she's been with Mace since before she was a teenager, lived with his mother for a few years, then, when she turned eighteen, started working at the shop. I guess what I'm saying is that her bark is bigger than her bite."

That was all news to me. Then again, what the hell did I really know about Mace Fox? *That he is sexy as shit and I wouldn't mind his face between my legs?* Fuck my life.

Sal checked her cell phone, the third or fourth time since we arrived, her brows furrowed.

"Is something wrong? You seem distracted," I inquired.

"No." She waved around a hand, finished typing a text, then clicked off the phone. "Just work stuff. No biggie." I knew she was lying, but I let it go.

The waitress returned asking if we wanted dessert, to which we both groaned and declined. We instead requested to-go boxes for all the leftovers scattered about the table. Three guesses as to what we'd be eating for the next few days. I'd just paid the bill when a shadow loomed over the table and engulfed everything in sight.

"Ladies." *Holy shit.*

I'd recognize that deep, gravely drop-your-drawers voice anywhere.

It hugged me like a well-worn sweater.

"Hey, big daddy," Sal chirped, bouncing in her seat. "Pop a squat."

His huge manly cock was eye level with the table, and I fought like the devil to keep from staring at it like a creeper. So close, I could reach out and touch it... just the tip.

"Can't." He held up a paper bag with the Kellogg's logo on the front. "Picking up take-out for the boys. Need to head back before they burn my fucking place down. The second I step foot out the door, all hell breaks loose."

All I could do was sit there like an idiot, mouth hanging open, knees shaking, totally at a loss for words. I just saw him yesterday when I waved goodbye at the end of my shift. I was thinking that must've been workweek Mace Fox, 'cause this guy? Sweet fuck was he an eyeful. It wasn't the clothes that were different. His typical black-on-black attire, the strain of his muscles as they fought to contain themselves inside the fabric, or the hug of the jeans around his manhood. No, it was something else I couldn't quite place, a calmness perhaps.

"Typical Saturday night at Masonry Ink, then?" Sal mused.

"Damn straight," Mace preened. "Stop by when y'all are done here. Should be a good time."

Sal gave me an inquisitive look, silently asking if I wanted to go.

"Maybe, we'll see. The night's still young," Sal answered for the both of us.

Mace rapped his knuckles against the table three times in quick succession before he turned to leave.

"Bye, Mace," I said to his back.

Geez, I was such a looser.

"Gurllll...if you could see the look on your face." Sal poked fun the second he was out of earshot. "You've been bit by the bug, beloved, no use in denying it. You've been bit by the Mace Fox bug...you got the sickness!"

Her loud allegations drew the attention of the other diners. I could feel my face heating up from embarrassment. I was tempted to crawl under the table and hide.

"Shush...will you settle down, Sal? No need to tell the world," I whisper-yelled.

"Just calling it as I see it, sister." She smirked.

"Not this again." I shook my head in denial. "Do I look like I'm in a position to fall for a man like Mace Fox, Sal? Look at me, I mean, really look at me. I'm homeless..."

She tried to interject, but I kept going, repeating my statement.

"I'm *homeless*, broke, and grossly undeserving of any man remotely as good as him. I'm nothing, Sal, less than nothing, which is why your assertion that I'm falling for him is not only wrong, it's downright ludicrous."

"Everyone deserves love, Nancy. The past doesn't matter when it comes to the heart," she pressed.

"You're a fool if you think it doesn't, Sal. Trust me, I've done the math."

"Then we're all doomed to be alone, beloved. A thought too cruel to consider."

"Well, I've already *considered* it, and it is what it is."

I finished my little after-dinner speech with a self-deprecating laugh that missed its mark. I fought back the tears that threatened to spill over and ruin my newly made-up face. Sal was pretty much doing the same. We both sat there, lost in thought, reflective, regretful, the mirror image of one another in black and white.

Tell her the truth, you idiot. She's your friend, I chastised myself.

I couldn't burden her with more of my bullshit, and she didn't deserve my failures. So, I sat there worrying my bottom lip with my teeth, the laughter and banging of plates becoming louder and louder by each passing second. Satisfied that we were no longer the center of attention, I gathered our to-go boxes and slid from the booth. Sal followed, and we walked silently to her car.

She stopped suddenly before hitting the key fob, smiled, and wrapped her arms around me in a generous hug, our little tiff forgotten.

"Soooo…are we going, or what?" she asked.

Confused, brows drawn. "Go where?"

"Masonry Ink, of course. Did you forget we got the babysitter for the whole night?"

"Uh…I'm not sure…"

"Oh, come on, it'll be fun." Sal was practically bursting with eagerness.

"I work there, remember? There's nothing fun about watching a bunch of overgrown men getting tortured for vanity purposes."

"You work Monday through Friday, beloved. Saturday night at Mace's place is a whole different experience. Besides, he invited us, and I'd hate to be rude." She stuck out her bottom lip in a pout, then hit me with the hand-holding begging gesture.

Her enthusiasm was infectious, and I found myself agreeing with a small shake of my head. So, off we went to hang out on a Saturday night at a tattoo parlor which just so happened to be my place of business. *Yay me!*

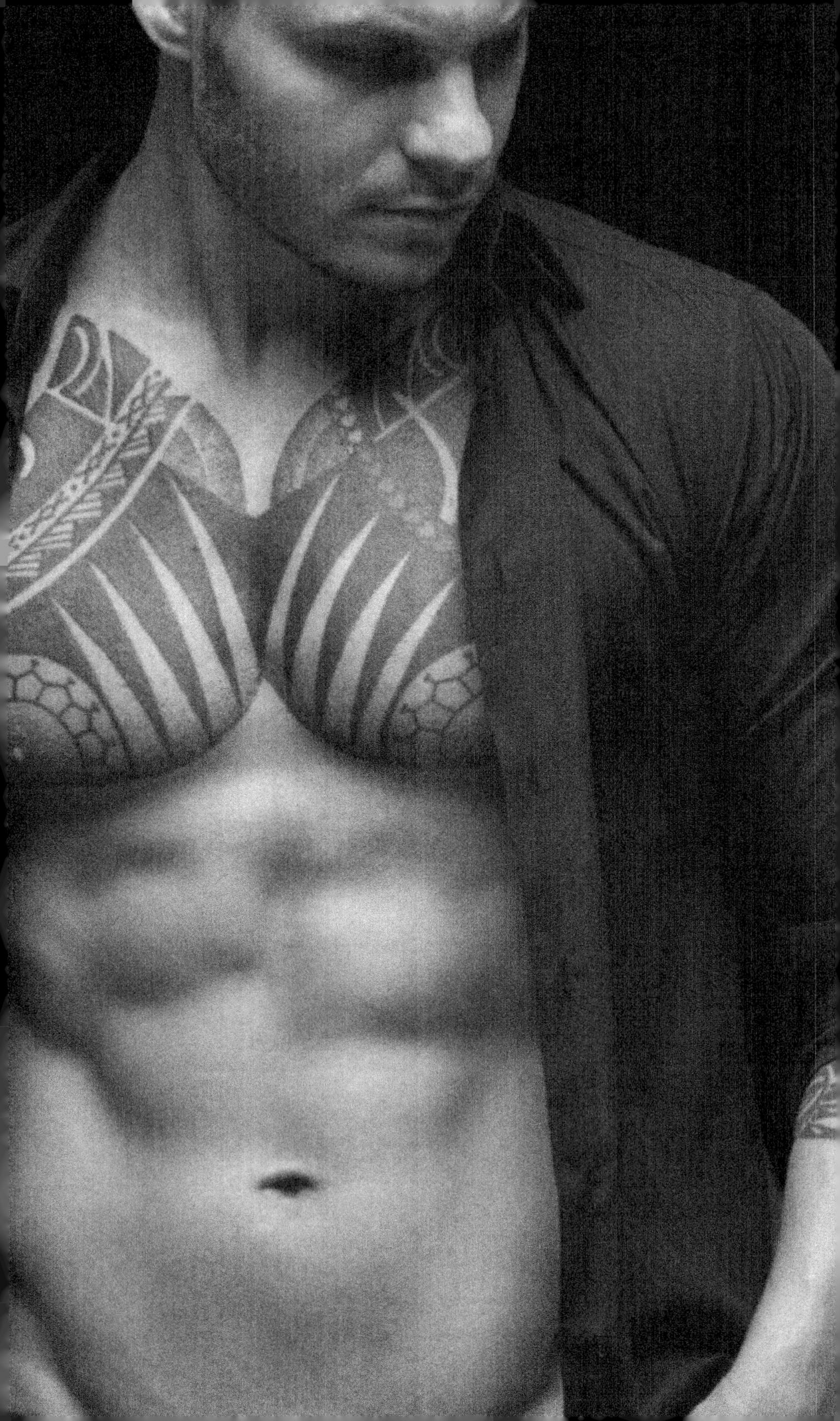

Chapter Eighteen

Mace

"Holy fuck! This must be my lucky night!" Kaden shouted in surprise. "Get over here, Sal, and let me check your tonsils with my tongue."

"Leave the woman alone, dumbass. She doesn't want your cooties," Jagger scolded him above the noise, making his way over to the entrance.

"Don't worry, boys, there's plenty of me to go around." Sal smiled, exchanging hugs.

She was comfortable in her element around society's lower class, but Nancy slash True was looking around like a deer caught in the headlights. She stood by, mouth agape, shocked as shit at the happenings going on inside the shop tonight.

DQ Newport, a local metalhead and aspiring musician, was set up in the corner shredding some cords on his electric guitar. A few women from the local strip club waiting their turn for services gyrated half naked to the deafening beats, eyes closed, titties bouncing, earning money off the clock from the group guys watching with hard dicks. There were easily over a hundred people milling around, some just kicking the shit, drinking and having a good time. Others looking to boost their stolen merchandise for a quick buck, club members wanting to get their old ladies branded with their mark, and regular nine-to-five professionals who cut loose on the weekends away from their wives and children. I knew every single one of these people, some more familiar than others but acquaintances all the same.

The rules applied to everyone in my house, and everyone abided by them.

No drugs, using or dealing. Weed was acceptable, but only if they smoked outside. That shit tickled my nose and made me sneeze. Allergies were a bitch.

Shit talking was commonplace, but if anyone got heated, they took it to the ally out back. No cheap shots and no weapons, mano a mono. The only head knocking allowed inside Masonry Ink was done by me, and I never lost a fight.

Women were to be treated respectfully until such time they agreed to be treated with the utmost disrespect. I tried to keep that shit away from my bathrooms and storage closets as best I could, but you know, it happened. Nothing like catching a five-hundred-pound biker going at it with a club whore, a circus clown, and one of his brothers...or two. I don't judge other's preferences, but when I was the one who had to clean that shit up? Yeah, that's not going to fly.

"Hey, little momma." Kaden finally noticed her skulking behind Sal. "Come over here and squeeze those milky tits against my chest. You look fucking gorgeous tonight."

She tried for a simple wave in greeting, but the fool all but attacked her. His arms circled her waist, lifting her off the ground. She wasn't happy with his handsy bullshit, and neither was I.

Crazy prick.

I watched the exchange from the security monitors inside my office. I'd kept this part of our outfit hidden from my little accountant during normal working hours. She didn't need to know how state of the art this place really was, far superior to any other tattoo parlor around. She normally stuck to her side of the office and would've never noticed the console blended into the wood paneling embedded into the wall. It's how we managed to stay on top of things while the outside world remained oblivious. Plus, it was cool as shit.

My reasons for inviting them here was twofold. One, I was sick of getting the play-by-play via text message from Sal without actually being there in person in case she needed backup. And two, we'd lost track of her cocksucker husband a few days ago. He was on the move and undoubtably headed straight for us. For all we knew, that motherfucker could've been parked three doors down, and we wouldn't have the advanced warning to stop him. She put me in a box by not opening up so we knew what we were dealing with, leaving me handcuffed with no recourse but to rely on Sal. I was so frustrated with the back and forth that I made up an excuse to interrupt their little celebration and pressed my own agenda. I wanted her where I could see her, near me, where I could touch her, close, where I could imagine sliding my cock inside her.

Where the fuck did that thought come from?

I noticed on the monitors some of the men sizing her up, looking for an opening, about to make their move. I couldn't blame them one bit. She looked amazing in what I assumed was a new dress and fuck-me sandals. Her long blonde hair had been styled in layered waves as it hung along her shoulders, down her back, to just above her ass. Speaking of asses, she really did have a nice one, firm and round, perfect for fucking while I palmed her luscious tits. My dick came to life behind my zipper thinking of all the ways I could bend her little body to suit my physical needs. I tamped that shit down quicker than fuck after smacking myself upside the head. She was a married woman with a baby, and even though she'd left the prick, I would never take on that kind of responsibility. My reasons for staying single all these years was a small thing, really. Why should I be allowed to have something my sister Maya never would? She would've made an excellent mother if it weren't for me. It wasn't right that I should be allowed to go on with life, finding that happy you read about in books. I was undeserving of such a gift, penance for my wrongdoings, which I'd accepted until now.

I closed down the surveillance equipment and stepped out front to the common area. Bodies stood around everywhere, some drinking, others mingling. Jagger was working on an arm piece for a state senator who traveled six hours to my shop because of our stellar reputation. His constituents would shit themselves if they knew he was using his campaign contributions towards the three hundred dollars per hour for his ink. The man was as crooked as a dog's hind legs, a typical politician out for himself, sticking it to the people left and right.

I crept past them, not wanting to engage in useless conversation with the prick. I spotted Sal dancing with a group of women from the strip club. Arms raised above her head, she gyrated her lovely hips to the beat of the music, not giving that first fuck about being mistaken for one of them. She was a rare beauty with a heart too big for this world full of filth. She smiled wide as she watched me approach, then something made her brows pinch together, and her mouth formed a heated frown before she took off towards the opposite side of the room.

My eyes tracked her movements. One flick, and the noise around me stopped. True was pinned in the corner. I saw a flash of light before my eyes, and my ears started to echo. I felt like my gums were bleeding, wetness trickled down the front of my shirt, and I couldn't catch my breath.

Then it all went black...

"I knew you hit him too hard, dickhead. What the fuck were you thinking using that wooden table?" *Jagger.*

"That I didn't want my brother on death row for murder one? It was either hit 'im or shoot 'im. Dude was in the twilight zone, man. Nothing was getting through to him." *Kaden.*

"Yeah, well, you could've killed him, you idiot. Better hope he wakes up, asshole." *Dread.*

I was lying on something soft with a pillow under my head. The last thing I remembered was that cunt biker, whose name was Dope of all things, pinning True to the wall while he pawed at her face with his disgusting fingers. She shook her head no, but that bastard just kept on rolling, pushing his hips against her as she tried to move away. Her lips quivered with fear, eyes begging that cockhead through a curtain of tears to back the fuck off. How I managed to get to him before Sal was a mystery, but once I did, the only thing I wanted to do was spill blood.

"Move," Kaden hollered. "Let me stick my dick under his nose and use it as smelling salts. Guaranteed, that'll wake his big ass up."

Try it, and I'll rip it from the socket!

"Dude, you out of pocket for that shit. Smelling leftover pussy juice mixed with your spunk would kill him for sure this time. Put that thing away, you fucking idiot," Dread hissed.

At least one of them has some sense. Note to self: Dread gets a bonus next payday.

"Mace...open your eyes, brother. Can you hear me?" Jagger called from somewhere close.

I groaned.

Pain shot up through my spine, circled my ass crack, around my shoulders, and skidded to a halt at the base of my skull. I tried to lift my arms, the weight of them unusually heavy, but that wasn't all. I was bound around the chest with something sticky wrapped around my back so tightly I felt like a goddamn human burrito.

"The fuck happened?" I managed through gritted teeth.

"We, uh...had to restrain you, Mace," Dread replied wearily.

Flashes of what happened appeared before my eyes like a scene from an action movie. Me grabbing Dope by the throat, delivering a right hook to his head, catching that fucker by surprise. When he didn't immediately go down, I continued my attack, strike after strike, humanity lost. In the midst of all that violence, I heard Maya call out to me...

"Where were you, Mace?"

"I needed you."

"You promised."

The rest was a haze of grunts, an insane amount of punching, and weirdly, a kiss. I was sure that last part was a figment of my imagination, yet the memory of it was so...exquisite.

"Restrain me?" I tried to sit up. "With fucking duct tape?"

"It was all we had nearby that would hold you," Kaden supplied.

"Get this fucking shit off me, Dread, that's an order!"

"Not sure that's a good idea, Mace," he replied.

Bonus fucking cancelled, asshole.

He looked between Kaden and Jagger for direction. The three of them had some kind of silent discussion at my expense. Fucking assholes. When I finally got my hands free, heads were going to roll, starting with whoever the fuck taped me up like a damn mummy.

"Do it," Kaden says.

Dread pulled a switchblade from somewhere, cut the edge of the bindings, and ripped those motherfuckers off, taking hair and skin with it. I rubbed at the tender flesh moving my limbs around to jumpstart my circulation. *How long was I like this?*

"Move away," I snarled.

"We..."

"Back the fuck up...NOW! Not the time to check the weight

of your cock, brother." Dread threw his hands up still holding the blade and backed away slowly.

I made the threat through a clenched jaw. I needed to get my bearings straight, figure out what the fuck happened and why I was, evidently, bashed in the head with a table. For the first time, I was able to see the entirety of the situation through clearing eyes. I was in my apartment above Masonry Ink, lying on my couch, a pillow propped under my head. Closest to me were Jagger, Dread, and Kaden. In the kitchen were the women, True and Sal. Sal was holding True in her arms, comforting her, but from what? Was she afraid of me now? I needed answers, and I needed them fucking yesterday.

"Start fucking talking," I ordered to no one in particular. "Don't stop till I've heard it all, got me?"

The three men took a collective breath and commenced telling me how badly I'd fucked up.

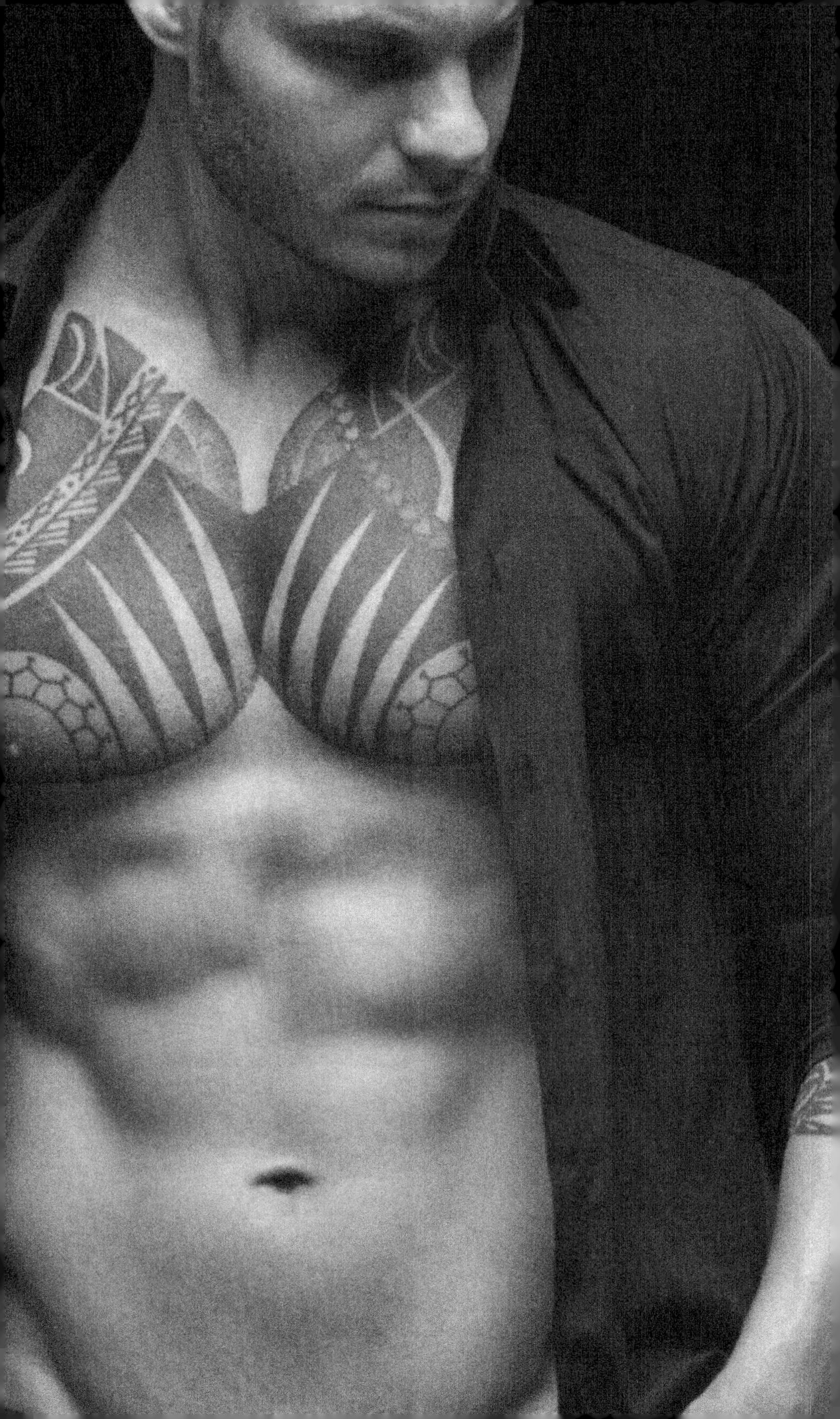

Chapter Nineteen

True

They are all very wrong.
Tragically so.

It took the strength of all five of us to move Mace from the polished shop floor to his upstairs apartment. I adamantly protested against the decision to restrain him, but my cries went unheard. Those binds, according to Kaden, were supposedly for my safety, yet the only thing they accomplished was bringing forth a flurry of emotions I'd kept bottled up for far too long.

Sal ushered me away from the scene and into the kitchen by my arm when all I wanted to do was wait for Mace to open his dark brooding eyes and look at me. She hugged me close, promising that everything was going to be alright, that Mace wasn't normally like the man who'd nearly killed another with his bare hands. I wanted to tell her to save her breath, that I didn't need her reassurance, just the opposite. I was awestruck by the powerful man who came to my rescue, fierce and unyielding. He never hesitated, not even for a minute, and I could only imagine what he would've done had I been his woman and not some random employee. If I hadn't known it already, Mace proved once again why Ryan was nothing more than a fucking coward and I'd made the right decision by running away.

The asshole who accosted me resembled a familiar stranger, returning time and again to remind me of my place in the food chain. Like him, he tried to take without asking, strongarm his desires onto my shattered heart against my will. When I told him I wasn't interested, he laughed in my face, spittle flew in all directions, and his bad breath made me gag. In a blink of an eye, he went from wearing a leather vest with colorful patches to donning a shit brown police uniform. The *clank* of the utility belt echoed in my head as he removed it from his waist.

"Who the fuck are you going to tell? The law?" he said "No one is going to believe you, True! I am the fucking law. Now get on your back and take this fucking you got coming to you."

Sweat and tears.

They were all the same.

I was trapped in the corner with nowhere to run; his nearness stole my voice and crippled my soul. I contemplated giving in to his demands, the same as I always did when presented with the alternative. Beaten dogs eventually learn to avoid the pain by tucking tail at the first sign of trouble. My hindquarters had been severed five years ago, along with my pride, my faith, and without measure, my vital spirit. My mind had checked out until a roar of brutelike ferocity bought me back to life when I heard his battle cry.

The darkened sky opened up to reveal a luminous aura as I witnessed him transform into a savage before my very eyes. I drank from his strength as if I'd been stuck on a desert island drying out from lack of moisture. I wanted more, as much as I could get, until I was ravenous from greed. Each blow felt like the breaking of a link against the chains wrapped securely around my neck. Strike after strike, I shed a tear for every time my voice was silenced by rough hands and loud grunts of pleasure. The splashes of blood that coated my new dress were God's elixir; I wanted to bathe in it, bottle it for when I needed a reminder that there were real men in this world. Real men like Mace Fox.

"He's awake. We should probably get back in there." Sal regarded me carefully.

I came back to myself. "Sure."

We marched into the living room in time to see Mace ripping at the industrial tape wrapped around his arms. He barely spared us a glance before he demanded that everyone step away from his person, far away. He'd calmed some since the incident, but I could see the animal lurking below the surface of his deep grimace, ready to strike if needed. He asked what happened, which I found strange considering he was there, smack dab in the middle of all the fists of fury. How could he not remember?

He should've been beating his chest like a silverback gorilla in the rain forest after declaring himself king of the jungle. It's how I saw him in those moments of sheer brutality right before Kaden struck him in the back with a table. Mace was completely out of control by that point, but God forgive me, I never wanted it to stop. He was fighting for *me*. For the first time in my life, I was the prize to be won, and I was worth the effort.

Jagger regaled him with the good, the bad, and the ugly. Nothing was glossed over.

"I was working on the senator, heard screaming, thought our asses were being held up or something. Wasn't till' I got out front that I noticed you whopping some fucker's ass," Jagger stated.

"I was closer, near the door," Jerome supplied. "Saw that fucker pushing up on little momma after you did. By the time I got there, he was already down. Seems you didn't notice that part, Mace. Split that prick's head open like a cantaloupe."

That explains the blood.

Mace sat stoically and listened to every word. The only telltale sign that he was affected either way was the slight tick to his jaw when it was mentioned that I was jostled in the fracas. He took that bit of information on the chin, steeled his features, and carried on. His eyes tracked my movements, as subtle as they were, assessing my level of comfort with all the talk of beatings and blood, I assumed. He needn't have worried. I was perfectly fine with all of it, right down to that asshole needing to be carried out by his fellow associates.

"The other members of the Rabid Free Riders weren't too happy that one of their brothers took a beatdown, but I handled it," Kaden said. "But, Mace, man...this is exactly the fucking shit we've been talking about. Busting heads, blacking out, running off halfcocked with your dick in your hand. Something's gotta give, bro."

"Blowback?" Mace finally spoke for the first time in a long while.

"They're a small operation, less than twenty strong out of West Texas, just passing through. I comped all of their ink, told them the next trip to bring the rest of their brothers and club whores for freebees," Jagger said.

A wave of guilt washed over me all of a sudden. Here I was, in a room full of people, most of whom I'd lied to for the better part of six weeks now, and they all, in one way or another, had covered my back. How could I continue to lie to their faces after everything that had happened? I wanted to drop to my knees and beg their forgiveness, but I never got the chance. The door burst forth with a crash so loud it shook the entire floor.

"You fucking bitch!" Angelica shouted as she ran straight for me. "I should rip your eyes out."

There was no time to duck before she struck me across the face with a harsh blow. She went for a second, but Jagger grabbed her from behind, pinning her to his chest.

"The fuck, Angel," he growled.

"I knew that bitch was nothing but trouble from the first day she arrived!" she shouted, struggling against his hold. "I'm going to slaughter her."

Sal advanced, stepping in front of me, using her arm to create distance. "Back the fuck off, Angelica. This is not your business," she ordered.

"Eat me, you dried-up crack whore!" Angelica screamed in her face.

"Whore? Bitch, I will mop the floor with your scrawny ass," Sal countered.

The two women were toe to toe, venom dripping from their lips as they traded insults. For a tiny thing, Angela sure packed one hell of a wallop. My cheek burned from her smack, and I knew for certain it would leave a mark. I couldn't blame her for being angry with me. This was all my fault. Saying yes to that thug would've been so much easier.

"ENOUGH!" Mace bellowed.

Angelica, who seconds ago was on my ass, folded into herself and covered both of her ears with shaking hands. The fight in her melted away faster than fresh snow after a heavy rain. I made a move towards her until Mace shot me a scowl, warding me off wordlessly. He wobbled to his feet still feeling the effects of hardwood hitting brain. I watched as he bent near her head and spoke quietly, the rest of us bystanders not privy to their conversation. Moments later, she shook her head in agreement to whatever Mace was saying and lowered her arms back to her sides. I swooned from the trusting bond they had with one another. I needed that feeling in my life so badly, especially now.

"Please don't fight because of me," I implored. "You're all friends, family, and I'm…" I struggled to come up with the right word. "I never meant for any of this to happen, I swear."

"It's all good, Nancy. We don't blame you. Fucker had it

coming," Jerome interjected. "Men like him never understand that no mean no. Next time, he'll remember that ass-whooping and step the fuck off. We'll always have your back, little momma."

"Thank you, Jerome, that means a lot."

I choked back the thick emotion that clogged my throat.

"Same here, beloved." Sal gave my hand a squeeze.

"Facts," Kaden added.

The twinge of guilt I felt earlier turned into a full-blown tsunami as I stared into each one of their faces. They weren't trying to bullshit me for their own gain; there was no reason for that. When they vowed to have my back, they meant it, all of it, but they'd been misguided in their outpouring of support. I didn't deserve it. If tonight's near-death experience taught me anything, it's that I couldn't allow the lies to continue, even if it meant facing their rejection.

Sal sent me a wry smile. "Nancy, we should probably get going…"

"True," I cried, turning to face her. "My name is True, not Nancy. T. R. U.E. True."

I looked to Mace for encouragement to continue.

A chin lift gave me the go-ahead to proceed on this total leap of faith.

I took a deep breath.

"My name is True Boardman, not Nancy Jennings," I whispered. "I was in a tough situation, to put it mildly, and I was forced to run away. My life wasn't the best…my husband… wasn't the best. I don't know if he's looking for me. I pray to God he isn't."

They were all listening, including Angelica.

"It feels so good to finally be able to say that without looking over my shoulder. I did some things I'm not very proud of. I escaped by stealing the identity of a woman who I thought looked just like me. Nancy Jennings was her name, so Nancy was who I became, for my freedom, and for the life of my daughter." I turned into a blubbering mess in front of everyone. It simply couldn't be helped.

"True is a beautiful name, beloved. It suits you," Sal said.

"I'm so sorry. I hope you can forgive me…I don't have any friends or family…Please, I didn't mean to cause so much trouble."

The dam burst unguarded before I could finish my plea. Hot tears spilled down my cheeks as I opened and closed my mouth several times, willing the words to convey what my heart already felt. I waited for the unavoidable reprimands from the victims of my heinous actions.

Kaden was the first to break the silence.

"Did the real Nancy have nice big fuckable titties like yours? 'Cause if that's the case, I'm tracking her ass down tonight, you feel me? Two holes are always better than one; that's just my opinion."

"Bruh…really?" Jerome chuckled. "Is everything about sex with you? How about you read a book sometime? Anything's better than standing around talking about pussy all damn day."

"Let me think about that." Kaden reached inside his jeans, scratched his manhood, pulled his hand out, and then snapped his fingers. "Nope! Books are stupid. Pussy is better! Dick lives matter, my guy. Raise your hand if you agree."

The blond buffoon was the only one who lifted his hand.

"Something is seriously wrong with you." Jagger shook his head.

"I'll try and remember that when I'm balls deep in some pussy *tonight*." He grinned.

Thanks to Kaden, the mood in the room seemed to lighten long enough for everyone to calm their tits. I felt marginally better after finally revealing a small portion of my truth. Then again, it was the least important aspect of a bigger lie. They were smart enough to know that there was more to the story and kind enough to let me tell it in my own time.

"Just as I thought, she's trash," Angelica snapped.

"One more word about my friend, bitch, and I'll stomp your little ass in the ground," Sal hissed as she squared her shoulders.

"Don't be that way, Angel. It's not like you to be so rigid," Jagger scolded.

"Eat a dick, Jagger. You can't tell me what to think. I'm entitled to my opinion, the same as the rest of you, and I say she's trash. I know from experience what it's like to trust a person unconditionally, only for them to stab you in the fucking back. Deal with it."

Jagger was visibly shaken but didn't rally.

"Everybody, shut the fuck up," Mace muttered, lips curled into a snarl.

I barely heard him above the shouting, but it was enough that we all snapped to attention. His demeanor turned weary, as if he could fall into bed and stay there for a week. A cloud of concern fell over the faces of the Masonry Ink staff; they were worried about him, and frankly, so was I. He was their leader, but who would be there for him if he needed a shoulder to lean on? How I wished it were me. I'd gladly draw him a bath, rub lotion on his sore shoulders, feed him a hot meal, and hold him against my bosom so he wouldn't be afraid. I would watch over him like a hawk and dare the gods to try and take him from me.

"Jagger, you get Angelica home safe. Kaden, take Sal and True to their house, check the doors and windows, lock 'em inside. I need to be alone now," he ordered.

Angelica snapped at his suggestion. "Dread can take me home. I'm sure Jagger needs to pick up his *woman* from her strip club job."

She rolled her eyes, flipped her hair, and with a huff, headed for the door with Jerome.

"All of you…get home safe." Mace used the last of his energy to give a final command.

He exited the room without another word.

Sleep well, my hero.

You deserve a peaceful slumber.

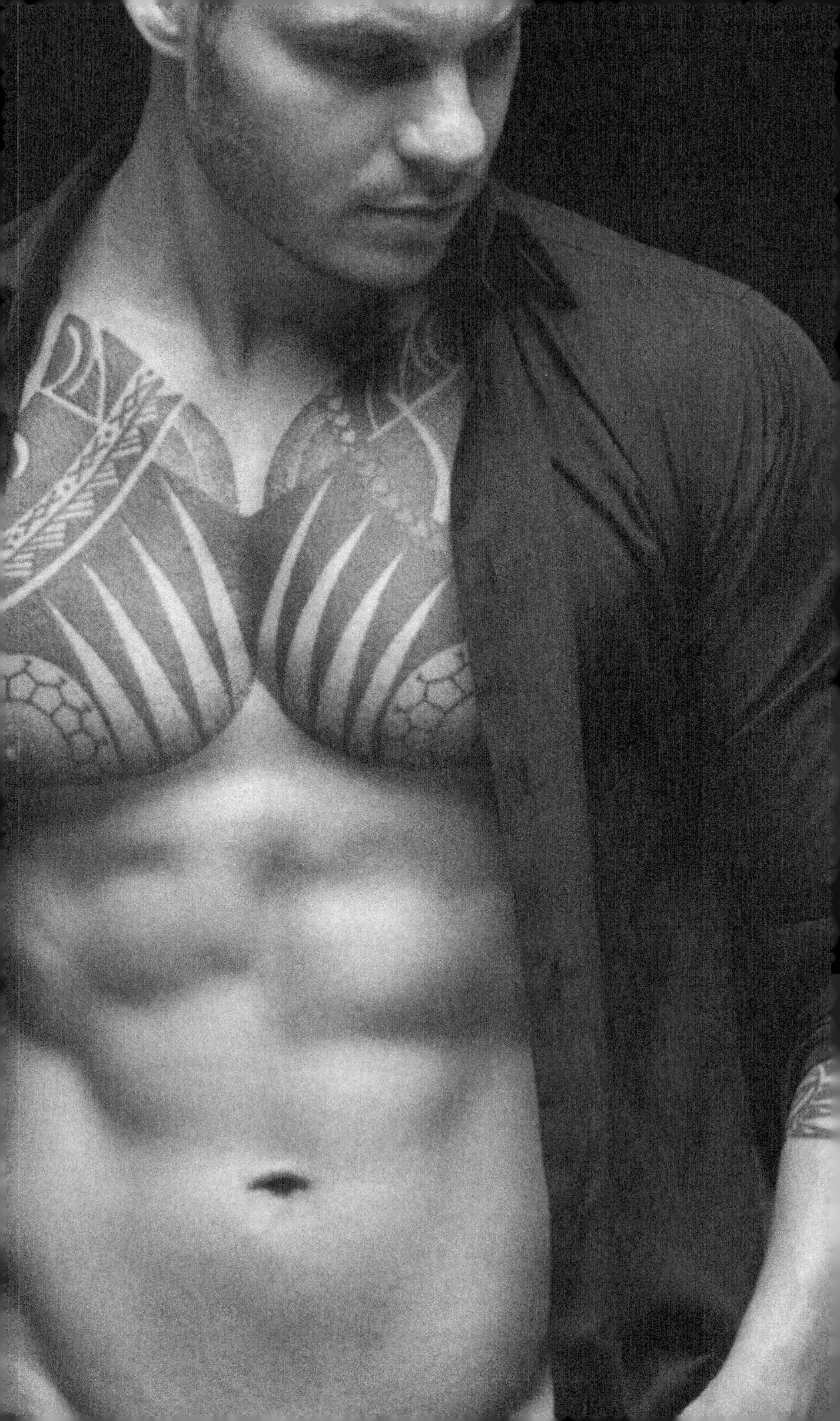

Chapter Twenty

Mace

My shop was a fucking mess. Not only that, my crew was doing the absolute most. As soon as I came down from my apartment this morning, I was subjected to hushed whispers and eye cuts whenever I turned a fucking corner. They were all just standing around like a bunch of vultures waiting for me to go apeshit so they could say, "See, I told you so!" I got it. I fucked up. I lost my cool on a motherfucker for trying to shoot his shot at a beautiful woman he wanted to take to his bed. Sure, he was highhanded, but we weren't exactly running a bible study group around here. I should've been able to better diffuse the situation without using my fists to cockblock. That said, they needed to ease up off my dick before I completely lost my shit.

I'd admit, almost killing the guy for trying to get laid was a new low, even for me. Judging by the blood stains on the floor and the broken furniture, I must've been a bear to try and wrestle to the ground. My crew had to hog-tie my ass to get me to stop inflicting pain, for fuck's sake. Worst yet, I couldn't even remember doing that shit. Maybe Kaden was right. Maybe I was two steps away from a padded room. The ever-present snake around my chest squeezed tighter, suffocating, relentless. Something had to give.

I reached out to the president of the Rabid Free Riders and offered an explanation as a sign of respect. I never copped to any wrongdoing, completely skipped the specifics, and merely reinforced the offer of freebees on their next visit. His bitch ass agreed like I knew he would, and all was right with their wannabe Wild Hog asses.

Rebuilding my credibility with the staff of Masonry Ink was going to take a lot more effort than a bullshit phone call. I always made life better for my crew; the five of them were my family with Dread being the most recent addition. Seeing the lack of confidence on their faces, the skepticism and mistrust, it shook my very foundation and sent me into a tailspin. I was supposed to be their leader, the person who everyone counted on to steer the fucking boat, and here I was, letting them down, one by one.

Angelica was retreating further into herself, instigated by having to witness Jagger's new pussy flouncing around the shop, showing out. He was either too caught up to notice her decline or wasn't giving a fuck. For him, I reckon getting blown was more important these days than seeing about his friend, whom he claimed to care about. That was my take on it. Kaden was acting more manic than ever; plus, that motherfucker hit me with a damn table, so there was that. Dread was still finding his way and navigating the pitfalls of free society, while Dead Man continued to be a damn ghost, running from his past. They were falling apart without my guidance, and I had no one to blame but myself. I'd dropped the ball on so many important things I wouldn't know where to start fixing them.

I was supposed to circle back and approach the team about the possibility of True remaining at Masonry Ink as the bookkeeper. She'd taken it upon herself to reveal her real name and that she'd escaped a tough situation, something I should've done weeks ago. Kaden was the only one who knew the circumstances of her being here. Thankfully, he kept the façade intact during her confession and never let on. Despite that, she left out so much that the whole thing sounded more like a bedtime story than an actual tragedy. We still had no idea what caused her to run in the first place, or the truth about the kid. I started to feel some type of way about keeping a man from his child, but I had to believe she had a damn good reason aside from being a cruel bitch.

I presumed things would be awkward between us when I arrived at work after Saturday's events, but instead of shying away, she seemed to be energized, plugging away at the stack of receipts, humming a catchy little tune with a coy look on her face.

Was she the one who kissed me?

Fucking hell.

Out of everything, that's the one moment I couldn't get out of my head. Why in the hell would she kiss me in the middle of that shitstorm? I intended to ask her straight out. I wasn't the fuck-around-and-find-out type of guy. I settled at my desk with a fresh cup of coffee, taken aback by the gleam in her eyes and the glow of her cream-colored skin.

"True?"

"Hmm?"

"We need to talk about what happened on Saturday night, what you saw, what you heard. Need to make sure you are okay with what went on. That crazy sonofabitch who couldn't keep his head? That's not me, and I really need you to understand that."

"Oh?" she chirped. "There's really no need. I thought it was very brave of you to swoop in and save me from what's-his-face. No telling what he might've done had you not been there, Mace. I appreciate you, more than you'll ever know."

Fuck me.

She swooned a little in her chair as her cheeks turned a light shade of pink. That strange little smirk returned to her lips as she stared at me from across the room, breathing shallow, eyelashes fluttering. I hesitated, trying to come up with the appropriate way to break it to her that I was no hero. What she saw was nothing short of savagery and should be thought of as such, not some fairytale white knight bullshit. If she'd romanticized my actions as me somehow staking my claim, I needed to put a stop to that shit ASAP. There was no future with me. On that point, it needed to be clear. Somehow, the idea of creating much-needed separation between the two of us nearly caved my chest in. I went through all the reasons in my head why there could never be anything between us, took a fortifying breath, and felt calmer about what I was about to do.

"Just so there are no misunderstandings, True. I would've done it for any woman I thought was in trouble. My actions were extreme, even for this place, but that doesn't make you special, only fortunate. My fault for asking you to come here knowing the type of crowd we get around here on a Saturday night. My miss. Won't happen again. You have my word on that."

"Yeah, sure, of course," she replied, deflated. "Nothing special."

I heard her mumble woefully. My words seemed to snatch the life from her soul, whereas minutes ago, she'd been floating on air. I immediately felt like the biggest dick in the world.

"True..."

"I get it, Mace. No worries."

My cell phone rang on top of my desk flashing my mother's name across the screen. I held up a finger asking her to wait a moment before continuing.

"Hello, beautiful mother of mine," I greeted cheerfully.

"Ohmygod, Macey!" she shrieked, hysterical.

"Mom, what is it?" I jumped to my feet.

Panic coursed through my veins like hot grease. My mother wasn't prone to histrionics, and I only ever remembered her crying on two occasions—once during my father's funeral, the other during the trial of my sister's killer. She was in the middle of having a complete meltdown, and it freaked me the fuck out. True caught my concerned shout and rose from her desk, brows pinched, mouth wide open as she wordlessly waited in suspense.

"They called me today. Victim services, they're letting him out! The bastard that killed my baby girl, they're letting him out on parole. Please, God, this can't be happening."

"The fuck you say?"

"They're releasing him, Mace! In a few weeks, he'll be a free man, while my baby is ...." She let loose with a pained wail. "DEAD! My baby is dead, and she's never coming back."

The serpent clamped down harder, constricting my air. I felt as if I were suffocating.

The hand holding the phone shook so badly that I barely held on to it. I went mute while my mother cried her eyes out on the other end of the line until I heard a whisper...

"Where were you, Mace?"

"I needed you."

"You promised."

My skin cooled while everything around me seemed to disappear. I closed my eyes, shutting down every unbidden thought and sentiment that came to mind.

"Mom...I want you to listen to me." My voice was strained yet unhurried. "I'm on my way. Shouldn't take more than a couple hours. Have Mrs. Hayes from next door sit with you until I get there, yeah?"

"Okay...okay...please, just hurry, son, I'm not..." She paused, sniffled. "I'll be waiting."

The line went dead, and so did I.

"Mace? Is something wrong?" True tentatively asked.

I saw her face etched with concern. *So fucking beautiful.*

"Mace?"

When we locked eyes again, I completely lost it.

I heaved a mighty gust of air, dying to break free from the serpent's hold, but it was no use. I raised my head skyward and unleashed a mammoth cry before grabbing hold of my desk and launching it over on its side, scattering its contents along with it.

"Kaden, Jagger, Jerome…HELP!" I heard screamed.

The shuffling of footsteps bounded across the floor. Strong arms reached for me, pulling, stifling, imprisoning my fury until it turned inward and arrested my movements. My knees gave out as my crew held on to me tightly before I hit the ground.

"We got you, brother," echoed around me.

"Don't you fuckin' break, Mace. Don't fuckin' do it, brother. Hold that shit in!"

I wasn't worthy of their trust. The flimsy tether that held my mental balance in check had ruptured so completely, I'd never be able to find all the fragments.

I failed them all.

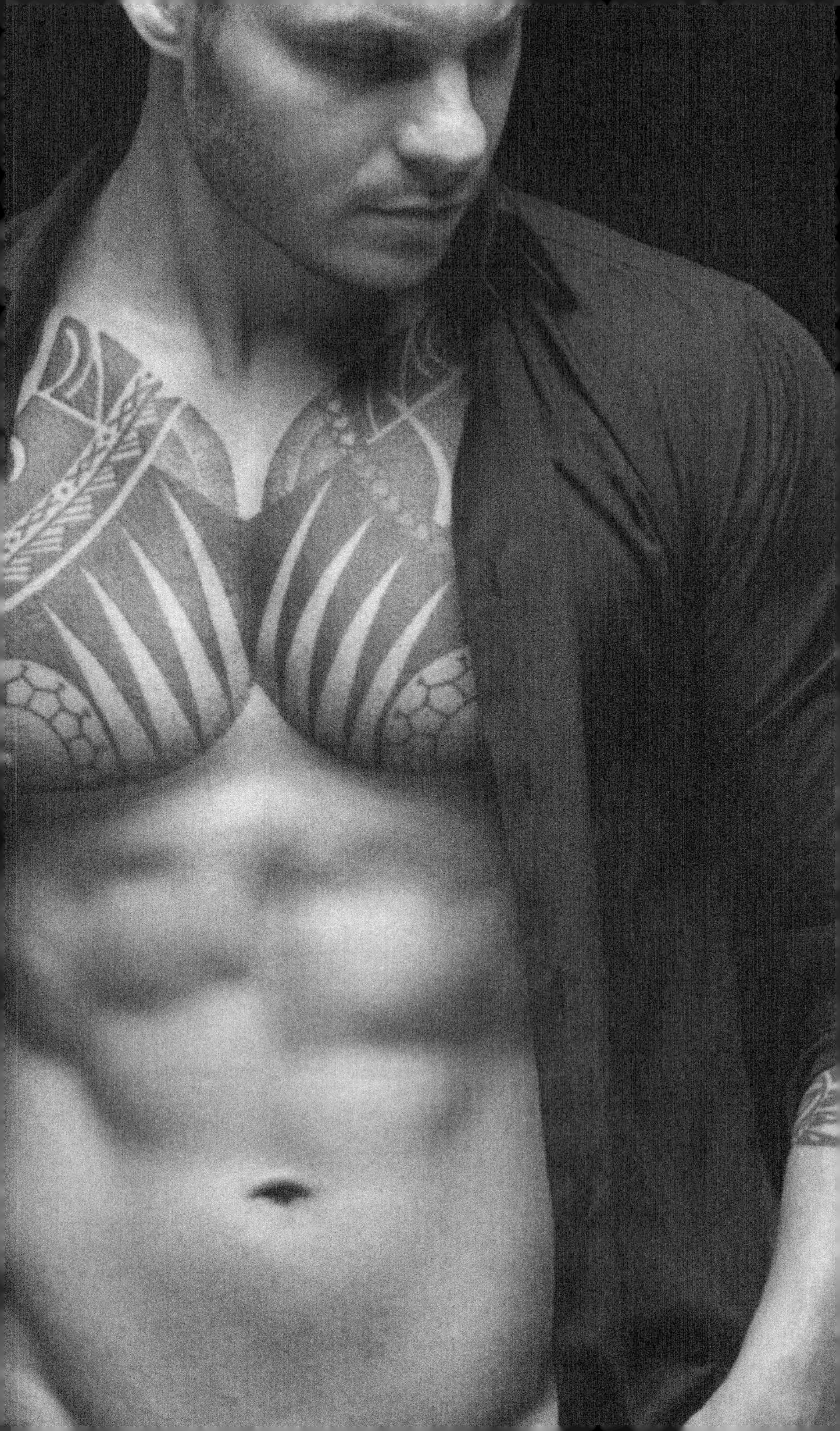

Chapter Twenty-One

True

Mace closed down the shop while he and Angelica hastily left Remington to visit with his mother after that disturbing phone call. I wished I knew what that was all about but understood why I wasn't kept in the loop. He'd said it himself, I was *nothing special*, so why would anyone want to confide in me? I was the insipid newcomer who couldn't exercise good judgment where men were concerned. I'd all but started that brawl which nearly caused a man to lose his life and a well-meaning champion a long-prison sentence. Maybe Angelica was right, and I didn't belong here at Masonry Ink. That revelation didn't stop the hollowness I felt in my chest at having witnessed the strongest man I ever met crumble to bits right in front of me.

Kaden escorted me out of the office and slammed the door in my face before I could see if Mace was going to be okay. I assumed it was because he didn't want me to see my boss in such a state, but with these guys, one could never be too sure. They had their own way of doing things, manly alpha males who preferred to use grunts instead of words as a means of communication. No matter. The temporary parting of ways was exactly what I needed to work through my salty feelings towards Mace and the straightforward remarks he used to rip my heart out. I only had myself to blame for letting my guard down, reading too much into folks just being kind and confusing it with acceptance. *Stupid, stupid, stupid.*

When are you going to learn your lesson, True?

Jagger offered to help me clean up the office by carrying the larger wooden pieces from the broken desk out to the dumpster in the alley. We didn't talk about my big *aha*-moment where I revealed my real name. As a matter of fact, not one of them even bothered to bring it up. The big man and I worked quietly, making headway with the scattered mess, till all that was left was a huge empty space where a tabletop once stood. Throughout the day, he seemed distracted, sullen, if his hunched shoulders and pained expression were anything to go by. I wondered if he was worried about his friends?

"Did you get a chance to speak with Angelica before she left, Jagger?" I asked.

"Naw." He straightened to his full height and put his hands on his hips. "She stopped taking my phone calls after I..." He shook his head. "She's not feeling me right now, so I just let her be. She doesn't want me around outside of work...or during work...or fucking ever."

Sadness surrounded his words like a dark cloak.

They made me want to comfort him.

"I'm sorry. Things will work out, you'll see," I said gently.

He gave me a weak smile. "I'm still holding out hope that she'll come around, sort out her shit. Until then, I got Kira to warm my bed. It's casual, but it works."

"As long as you're happy, I'm happy."

"Right...happy," he muttered, walking away.

Unconvincingly, I might add.

I grabbed the broom from the closet and commenced to

sweeping, my thoughts on the melancholy big man named Jagger. I'd met the woman he referred to as the one warming his bed, and she was not all that. Sure, she was beautiful, stunning even, with tanned skin, long legs, stylish blonde hair, and a body built for sin. On the outside, they looked like the perfect match, he with his oversized chest and tall features, her with a blinding smile, fit physique, and big doe eyes, but something was missing from the pair. A spark maybe, familiar chemistry, longing, or perhaps it was the absence of trust. I'd caught Angelica and Jagger arguing once. It was intense to the point of rapturous, a shining nexus between agony and passion. It stole my faculties in its force, so much so, I wanted to reach out and grab it. Only for a second.

Love was all around them, yet they refused to fight for it. They were probably all the better for it. I thought I knew about love, but I was tricked by its altered transitions and evil workings. Love was a confidence trick, like Three-card Monte, only I was the fool who believed I'd found the money card when in actuality, I'd gone bust.

Shuffle, shuffle, *flip,* and there was a marriage.

Flip again, and there was a home.

Bet it all, the last of my fortune, and *flip*...there was nothing. *Loser.*

In essence, I was absolutely no help with Jagger's conundrum, so I left it alone. Our cleanup efforts came to grinding halt when Kaden burst through the office door with an announcement.

"Truck's here!" he shouted. "Movers got the new desk ready to unload, if you guys are finished."

"We're good," Jagger confirmed.

"New desk? In less than twenty-four hours? How?" I asked.

"Standing order. This ain't the first time Mace fucked his furniture up," Kaden said, pointing to Jagger. "Remember that time Roscoe wanted to borrow some money for booze and got pissed when Mace wouldn't lend it to him? That was the first time the desk got broken. Only then, it was Roscoe's ass getting body slammed headfirst that caused all the damage."

"I bet he's still picking splinters from his cock." Jagger smirked.

"That's why the guy who makes 'em keeps a couple at his warehouse, you know, just in case."

"Well, that's .... Convenient," I replied.

"Yep. Clutch like a motherfucker." Kaden snickered.

It didn't take them long to get everything situated, the whole ordeal erased like it never happened. In the quiet of the office, void of the huge presence missing from his throne, I couldn't help the feelings of loneliness that chipped away at my heart. I shivered all the way to my bones, an iciness no amount of heat could warm. I wanted him here with me, close enough for when I needed to feel safe. Setting eyes on him from across the room felt like a shroud, completely protected. Sure, there were Kaden, Jerome, and Jagger right outside, but it was Mace who kept the daymares away. I could accept that I was nothing special to him, but what I could not accept was the possibility of never experiencing that feeling of safety ever again. There was a light tap on the door before Kaden stepped inside.

"You doing alright in here alone, True? Haven't seen you come out in a while. Thought I'd check on you, make sure you were cool," he asked, leaning against the frame with his hands in his pockets.

"I'm good," I replied with a sigh. "Just thinking about Mace. Have you heard anything?"

"Checked in, confirmed they made it safe."

"That's good. I was worried." I shrugged, playing it off as if the news meant nothing.

Kaden gave me a strange look before blinding me with his goofy-ass grin. A wisecrack was coming. The man couldn't help himself.

I waited…and waited…and waited, then POW!

"As I live and breathe." He hooted loudly before doubling over in laughter. Hands on knees, foot stomping, pointing an accusatory finger, two steps away from lying on the floor, in hysterics. Once he started humping the air, I lost the last of my patience.

"Kaden, what the hell?"

"Wait, wait." He sobered. "Does he know? Have you told him yet?"

"Know what?" I shrieked. "What are you on about?"

He straightened to his full height, smoothed down the front of his shirt, cleared his throat, and tilted his head to the side.

"You may not know this, True, and I'm not one to brag, but I've fucked a lot of women. Long hair, short hair, gapped tooth, hammer toe, don't matter to me none. I'm the emperor of the back entrance slide, and my cock has retired more pussy than social security, but again, I'm not one to brag." He fluttered out a hand.

"Clearly not." I cringed.

I also threw up a little in my mouth.

"That being said, I know all the signs, and I do mean all of them. The shortness of breath, the pinking of cheeks, the subtle glances when you think no one else is paying attention, and nothing beats a smile that says bend me over and smash my ovaries to smithereens."

What in the world of babbling bullshit is he talking about?

"I'm afraid you lost me somewhere around *emperor* and *gapped tooth*, Kaden."

"Then allow me to retort." He made a show of checking his nails, adjusting his junk, and running a hand through his hair before shuffling forward towards my desk.

He braced his hands on the wood and leaned into my space. "You've got a nine-by-twelve-inch yard sign staked inside your snatch that reads, *Welcome home, Mace,* and I'm here for it, babe."

"That's ridiculous," I sputtered, indignant. "Go away, Kaden."

I shooed him with my hand.

He laughed like a cackling hen as he made his way back towards the door. "Denial won't get that pussy slaughtered, True. Take it from me. Men like it when women are aggressive and know what they want. Shoot your shot, little momma, time's a wastin'."

"Goodbye, Kaden."

I could still hear his incessant squealing long after he was gone. Kaden had a strange way of expressing himself that took some getting used to, but I could tell it was his shield. We all had them in one way or another. He cared about Mace, though, and for that, he earned a place in my heart. I would suggest he see someone about his overactive imagination, though.

It was then, sitting alone, afraid and confused, that something got into me. I preferred to think of it as a moment of unconscious absurdity. Mace wasn't here to drive his point home about my not being anything special, and I needed that reinforcement. Old habits were impossible to shake once they took root within your psyche. When I lived in Montana, I had that reminder in the form of my only blood relative. On any given day, I could reach out to the one person who never failed to open those old wounds with a dull knife, twisting and pulling until she ripped my guts out. Stupidly, I reached for my newly acquired cell phone and made the call.

It didn't take long for her to answer.

"How many times do I have to tell you motherfuckers to stop calling here!" she shouted.

"Momma?" My voice trailed off. "It's me."

I heard the flip of her Zippo as she lit a cigarette. I pictured her lounging around on her fake leather couch with her fake cougar-length nails painted red, wearing the unseemly lingerie gifted to her by one of the many men who found themselves in her bed. The image was complete once I added a faux matching silk robe hanging open haphazardly in the front, exposing her modified breasts that were three sizes too big.

That was who she was. My mother.

"There's a reward out for any information leading to your whereabouts," she griped. "Plan to call that shit in as soon as I hang up. You know I need my cheddar, True."

"Sure, Momma, I understand."

"Had it made, girl. House, car, money, decent man. Took off without a word. Sneaky Pete. And here I thought I taught you better. Suck a man dry before you show his ass the exit and never leave the good stuff behind. You were always too stupid for your own good. Should'a aborted you when I had the chance, worthless little bitch."

And there it was.

The evidence I needed to corroborate Mace's point.

Thanks, Momma.

"I just called to let you know that I was doing okay, you know, in case you were worried." Sarcasm dripped from my words.

"Pfft. Far from worried." She heaved out a puff of smoke from her cigarette. "Thinkin' of taking a run at your man anyway, all alone in that big house, starving for pussy. Always liked Ryan. Chose poorly by picking you as a wife. Luckily, I'm here to restore our family's good reputation."

"You're nothing special."

"Could've been any woman in trouble."

"Fortunate."

I sat with the phone to my ear, silently weeping as her harsh words of validation seeped into my midsection and caused a spasm. That was the reason why I'd called. I got comfortable being around a group of people who treated me like my thoughts and feelings mattered. She was my only family, and I was destined to end up just like her, with a resentful daughter who hated my guts once she realized I was no better than a paid whore.

"I have to go now, Momma. Be well."

She wasn't finished with me yet.

"You got trouble coming, girl, big fucking trouble. I only wish I was around to see all your sweet turn to shit, you ungrateful little bitch. Had a man in your corner, and you fucked that all to hell. The deed on the house alone should've kept you satisfied long enough to claim half in a divorce settlement. What were you thinkin' by running?"

"He wasn't a real man, Momma, but I doubt you know the difference given your standards."

I hung up and promptly deleted her number.

She'd served her purpose.

I was back to being me again.

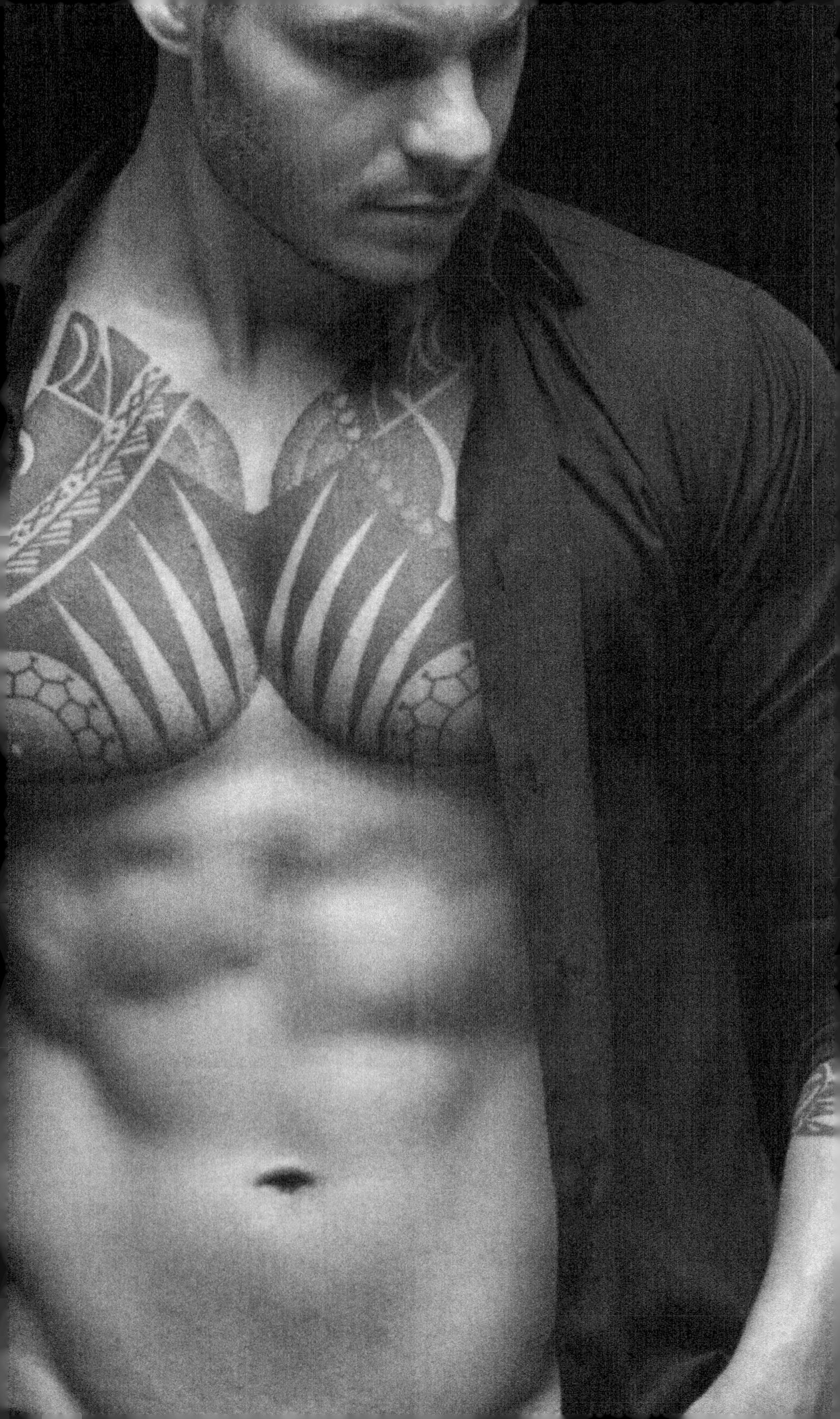

Chapter Twenty-Two

Mace

My beautiful mother.

A woman who bore two children, the youngest of which now resting below dirt, was beyond consolable by the time I arrived from Remington. The same woman who persevered through the greatest of tragedies, kept her family going after her loving husband departed this earth, was kind to neighbors, strangers, and old people couldn't form a complete damn sentence. One look,' and she shattered into a thousand pieces, right there on the floor, near my booted feet. What little strength she had left was lost to the anguish, which until now, she'd kept at bay with her grace and courage. I would've taken a bullet to the chest if it meant saving her from this nightmare.

I listened as she wailed about fairness and the absence of justice, how criminals shouldn't be allowed to take another's life without facing the same consequences. I watched helplessly as she begged the Good Lord to send her baby back so that she could hold her in her arms one last time. Her greatest state of affliction followed the denied access to her child while the investigation was ongoing, and the body was deemed evidence. I listened as she cursed God for his cruelty, for taking away the one person who deserved better than to be snuffed out by someone she loved. She spat obscenities towards the spiritual being who was once a constant comfort in her time of crisis but was now her nemesis. She'd lost her unwavering faith, and I was cast in a sea of regret for not taking bids to have that motherfucker shanked in the prison showers or during yard time when I had the chance.

When she grabbed me around my neck, demanding I do something, anything, to make the pain stop, my organs hardened behind steel plates, their value or relevance outlived. I was of no use to her after that. I lost my hearing, my sense of smell and taste. A touch felt like a thousand needles sticking in my flesh yet numb all at the same time.

"Where were you, Mace?"

"I needed you."

"You promised."

Maya's voice was fading inside my head along with all my happy memories of her. The little girl who always wanted me to push her higher was being sucked away bit by bit the longer I struggled with finding a balance between social consciousness and the growing need for retribution. She wouldn't have wanted this perpetual *emptiness* for me; it went against everything that made her such a unique individual. But she was gone now. *Dead and dust.*

Grudgingly, my mother took one of the sedatives prescribed by her doctor, and I made my excuses to step away for a while once she drifted off to sleep. Even in her state of slumber, she whimpered through painful sobs that shook her entire body wrapped snugly under a duvet. Angelica agreed to stay with her, not letting her out of her sight until I returned. I wouldn't need my GPS to navigate the route. I knew how to get there, the number of steps that led up to their driveway from the sidewalk, and the three people I'd find inside. Ten minutes later, I rang their doorbell and waited.

The door cracked open.

"Can I help..." His words trailed off.

Old and balding, he'd seen better days. One look, and he knew I wasn't there to talk.

"Honey, who's at the door?"

The wife, who swore her son could do no wrong, slipped in behind her husband.

The mother whose children are both alive and well.

Over her shoulder was the daughter, the sister. Too young at the time to realize what a piece of shit her brother was, she'd grown strong and beautiful since his sentencing. She made a move to speak but was silenced by the tension in the air. Did she know who I was? Did she give a fuck?

She stood stock still with her bright blue eyes and dimpled cheeks. She was perfect in every way, as all little sisters were to their big brothers, alive or dead. I caught a whiff of fresh baked cookies as it perfumed the mood around us. Fitting, I thought, since Maya loved her sweets, chocolate being her favorite. Soon enough, they'd all be back together again, one big happy fucking family while mine was on the verge of collapse.

I kept my ire bottled in its place.

We never spoke, not a single word, but we all knew how this tenuous connection would end. Losing a child was something no parent should have to endure, but at that moment, with the scent of cookies filling my nose, I promised them with a dip of my chin and the view of my back that they would soon know what that felt like. My word was my bond.

The following day, I kissed my barely functioning mother on the cheek goodbye and returned to Masonry Ink a shell of a man who'd lost his ability to give a fuck.

Angelica opted to stay.

She had her reasons.

Those being Jagger and his new bitch, but I didn't force her to rethink her stance. Spending time with the woman she thought of as her mother would be good for her mental state and even better for my guilt. Angelica required what I no longer had in me to give. That man succumbed to the savage master who seized his heart after staring into the eyes of his mother, who asked for the one thing that was beyond his reach. To bring her daughter back. If she knew that I was the reason for her torment, that I was the one who hadn't kept his promise, it would crush her already beaten soul into the ground.

I would make this right.

I hit the front entrance of Masonry Ink by mid-afternoon. The patrons as well as my crew were used to me sneaking in from the back by the hidden stairwell that led to my apartment. I stood there for a moment and took in my enterprise knowing it would have to sustain itself without me around to run it. Dread looked up from his sketch pad as he sat on the window bench near the door, his mouth twisted in concentration.

"Didn't expect you back so soon."

He peeked behind me, clearly looking for Angelica.

"She stayed," I grunted, ending his wonderment. "Meet me in the office."

"Sure, be right there."

I walked to the back of the shop and spotted Jagger talking with a customer. He, too, did a double-take and came up empty. I didn't bother giving him an explanation 'cause fuck him. After everything he'd done to fuck with Angelica's head over the last few weeks, he deserved to feel that stab of hurt in all four ventricles of his pumping heart. He could marinate on that shit the next time he flossed around with his bitch in front of her face. I gave him the signal to get his ass to my office pronto and left it at that.

Kaden was absent from view, but he'd undoubtably be around somewhere, shit-talking like always. I heard laughter coming from my office, so loud, I could make out the voices without even trying.

"Do it harder, Kaden! I want to feel the full effect."

"I'm telling you, True, it's going to hurt if I press down. Arch your back. You're a lot shorter than I am, so this isn't exactly the ideal position for it."

"Figure it out, bozo. This is your patented move, isn't it?"

What the actual fuck?

In my goddamn office? Not this bullshit again.

I busted through the door in time to catch them huffing and puffing, clothes askew, and guiltily fucking red-faced from exertion. True was down on her hands and knees laughing her ass off while Kaden was trying to pull her back up under her arms pits. I was ready to fuck this place up for a second time in less than a week. I was getting really tired of catching these two in my office doing shit that sounded an awful lot like fucking. Kaden loved women, and they couldn't seem to get enough of him. Guess True had a little of her mother's tastes inside her after all.

"The fuck's going on in here?" I bellowed.

"Mace...you're back!" True greeted me with a smile, straightening. "Kaden was just showing me his ..."

"Cock? Yeah, saw that," I accused.

"Take it easy, Mace. I was only showing her the Nuck-Chuck," Kaden added. "She asked me to. I swear to God, it wasn't my idea to go full out. It's her fault."

He pointed towards True.

"Like I give a fuck." I pinned them with an icy stare, hands on my hips, pissed as all get out but not knowing why.

"Kaden was telling me this story about growing up and some of the stuff he and his friends used to do to each other to keep from fighting." True shook her head, smiling brightly.

"And to be a dick, don't forget that part," Kaden interrupted.

"Right!" They shared a snicker. "Anyway...Kaden was telling me about this thing they used to do. He called it the Nuck-

Chuck 'cause well...you hold your opponent down, put your chin in the small of their back, push down as hard as you can or until they feel like they're gonna throw up, and just to say, that shit hurts like a mother!"

"It's worse when you try to get away, that's why you gotta lock that shit in hard, True." Kaden did this stupid little swirling thing with his hands, which caused another round of hysterical laughter. *Please, somebody shoot me.*

I knew Kaden like the back of my hand, and this was not him.

He was a whoring, spastic son of a bitch who *never* shared shit about his personal life with anyone, especially not with women. I leave for one day and come back to a friend I didn't recognize, hamming it up with some chick who'd just told us her *real* name? Jagger and Dread walked into the office with the same look of disbelief on their faces as I had.

"Um...what's so funny?" Jagger asked, watching the two of them grinning.

"Nothing." True answered. "Just... having a bit of fun."

I noticed my new desk had arrived, so I took a seat and made myself comfortable. Kaden and True were still carrying on as if they were the only two people in the room. It was the first time since she'd been here that I saw a genuine smile on her face for someone other than her daughter. My chest warmed with a strange sensation I chalked up to heartburn. It intensified the longer I stared at the two of them, then snapped like a rubber band when she touched Kaden's arm with affection.

"True!" I barked. "Need your full attention since this concerns you, too. Play touch the donut on your own time, yeah?"

"Of course, Mace, sorry." She had the nerve to snort in Kaden's direction.

"You'll be taking over for Angelica for now. Paperwork can wait. Not sure for how long."

"She didn't come back with you?" Jagger hissed. "What the fuck, Mace? Who's going to talk her down if she gets scared? You know how she gets if she's upset or can't sleep when that motherfucker invades her dreams. I can't fucking believe you thought that was a good idea."

His tone caused my eye to twitch, but I gave him that one play. His big ass needed to calm the hell down before I changed my mind about beating the shit out of him for ghosting her in the first place. Fucker had some nerve challenging my decisions where Angelica was concerned. Now would not be a good time for him to measure his cock against my mercy.

"She's fine, end of," I growled.

I held his angry gaze as a warning to not push his luck before returning it back to True.

"Talk to Corrine about adjusting your babysitting hours. She got a problem with that, we'll talk it through, see what alternatives we can come up with. Tell Sal so she's not blindsided. You okay with all of this?"

"Well...I don't have a car, so I'll need a ride to and from work if Sal can't do it. I'll also need to stop at Mrs. Lafontaine's on the..."

"I can give you a ride, True. A longggg ride," Kaden announced, smirking.

When he started to gyrate his hips, I slammed my palm down on the desk.

"You done, dipshit?"

"My bad, boss. I felt an itch down there. Please continue."

She smacked him lightly on the arm again, as her cheeks bloomed.

What is up with these two?

"I'll take care of it," I grunted. "Any other questions?"

Silence.

I pointed in her direction. "You start tomorrow. The rest of you are dismissed."

I watched my guys file out, playfully punching each other like kids at recess. I worried about their futures, ones that wouldn't include having me in it. How would they thrive after learning that their leader, their friend, chose to keep a promise knowing it would mean his death? Would they eventually forgive me for such a selfish act? I blew out a heavy breath, feeling overwhelmed yet set on my decision. Time was of the essence, and I couldn't waste any of it.

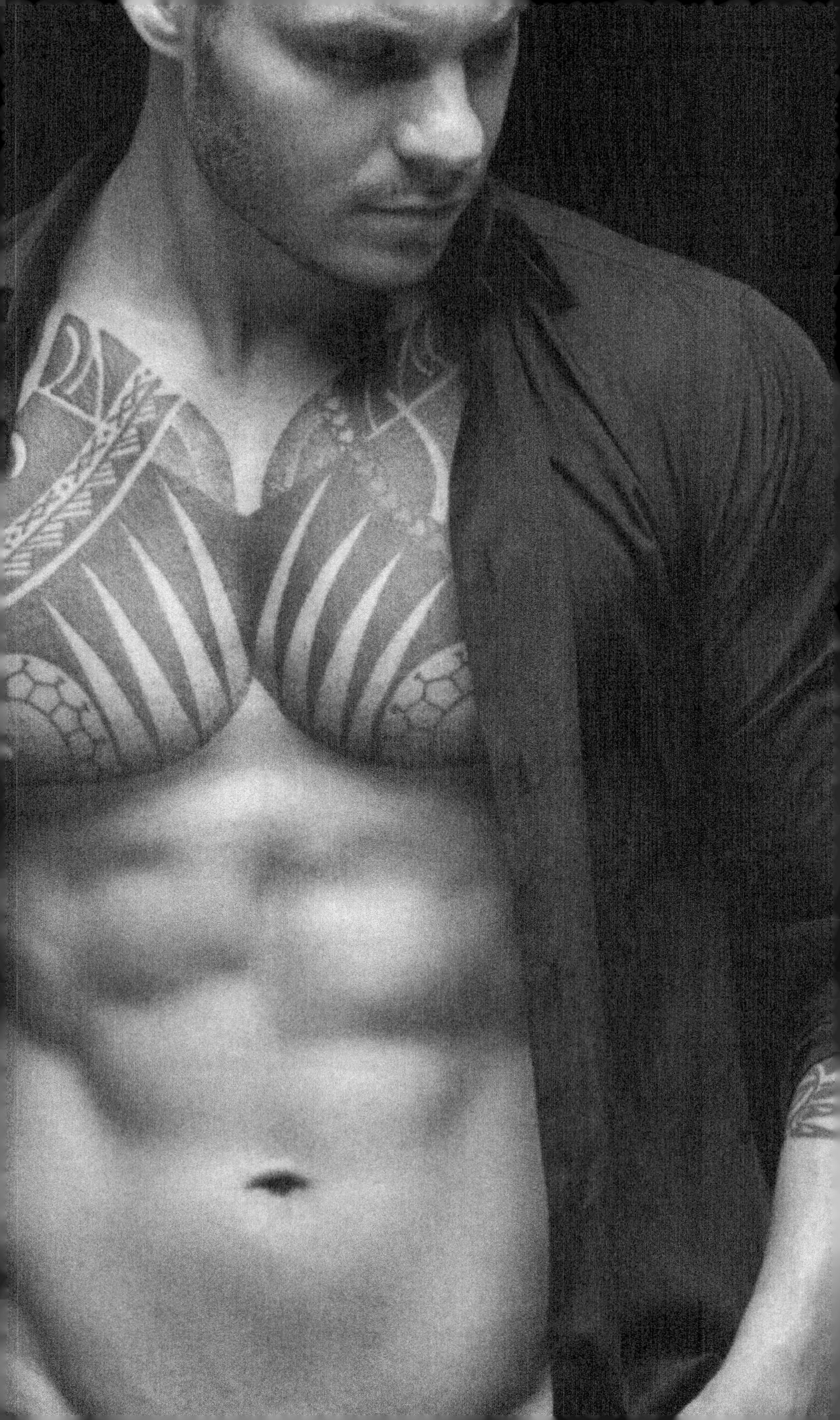

Chapter Twenty-Three

True

"The artists make their own schedules, True, but on the rare occasion there's a walk-in, some dick who wants to surprise his woman with an appointment as a gift, or one of those bachelorette party type things where it's a group project, you'll write it in here." Mace pointed down to the datebook spread out on the counter.

"That seems pretty simple," I answered with a tight smile.

"I assume you can figure out how to serve drinks without me having to show you. Fridge is stocked, but if you need to re-up, the shed in the back is where you'll find the cases of beer and shit. Paying clients getting tattoos only, no deadbeats, we clear?"

"Yes, I think so."

"Advice. Take some of your paycheck money and buy some more new clothes. Check around online and have Sal use her credit card, reimburse her with the cash. Can't have you walking around in tennis shoes wearing the same three pairs of jeans every week. The men will tip you more if you show some skin. Just putting it out there; I'll leave that up to you to decide."

It was my first day taking over for Angelica, and as luck would have it, Mace had volunteered to show me the ropes. I had to switch my hours to accommodate the busiest stream of clients for the shop. Corrine agreed to the later shift, and Sal eagerly gave up her chauffer duties. I was a little nervous at first but slowly got the hang of it. Plus, Kaden was around to give me a pep talk when I needed one. Of course, that was before he was ordered to *find some shit to do,* and I hadn't seen him since. The Mace who left us to visit his mother was not the same man who returned. He was short with everyone to the point of cruelty, or at the very least, overly brittle. No one was spared from his wrath, not even baby Kayla when he arrived late in the afternoon to drive us over to Mrs. LaFontaine's house.

He refused to hold her while I gathered the baby bag and other supplies she needed for the day. I had to put her carrier on the ground, where she somehow caught a glimpse of him and started to coo her little heart out. Her cries went ignored as if she were a nuisance to him. Unlike the last time, he drove like a bat out of hell, barely missing a stray dog as it tried to cross the street. He slammed on the breaks in front of the house and kept the motor running while he sat on his ass and watched me struggle with my arms full. He wouldn't even fucking look at her.

What type of asshole doesn't respond to a baby?

Acting like a prick to a bunch of adults was one thing, but when it came to my daughter, he had one more slip-up before I nut-punched his ass.

The training was pretty much over when one of the customers needed to have a word with Mace about his tattoo. He was so pleased with the artwork that he wanted to speak with the owner personally. The two men spoke animatedly—fist-pounding, back-slapping, profanity-laced words of mutual respect were exchanged, while all I could do was watch in awe.

Kaden appeared out of nowhere with a low whistle. "Better close your mouth, little momma, before you catch a dick in it...unless...that's the goal?"

"Be quiet, silly goof." I gasped, smacking him on the forehead.

"He really is pretty to look at, ain't he? All those muscles beneath that tight-ass shirt. I know for a fact he buys them a size smaller. And let's not forget about that dark wavy hair and five-o'clock shadow. I'm not ashamed to admit that my boy Mace has starred as the bottom to my top in several of my more erotic dreams."

I gave him a side glance.

"Does he know that?"

"Hell no! That secret is between me and my dick. Don't judge; it's complicated. Besides, imagine having to look your best buddy in the eye after a night of pounding the shit out of his asshole while listening to him scream out your name. I feel guilty just thinking about it."

He pretended to shiver.

"Sure, you do. Who wouldn't feel guilty after loving on all of that?" I tilted my head towards the offender in question.

"See, now I have a hard-on. I told you not to say anything." He reached down and adjusted his junk.

I couldn't help but laugh at his silliness, something I was sure Mace himself wouldn't find the least bit comical. I hadn't realized how stressed I'd been all day having to deal with Mr. Shitty Attitude until the pressure released from my chest while I continued to chuckle.

"Oh, hey, are we still on for tonight? Sal's going to pick up Kayla from Corrine's, and the place doesn't close until ten, which gives us about an hour, give or take," I asked, still giddy from his shenanigans.

I suddenly felt hot all over as if the thermostat had been

turned up to sweaty tits. Gone was the sense of euphoria brought on by the exchange of pleasantries between two friends. It'd been obliterated by a wave of arousal awakened inside me from an animalistic growl over my shoulder. My neck turned hot, my panties flooded with moisture, and I started to pant.

"On for WHAT?" Mace rumbled as he approached.

My heart pounded wildly in my chest. "Nothing. Kaden and I were…"

"You forgettin' something, *Nancy,* or are you still cock dumb from the other night?" He scowled.

"Mace, man, I wasn't going to put her in any danger," Kaden tried to interject.

"Shut the fuck up, Kaden. I decide what's dangerous and what isn't in my house."

He leaned in closer, inches from my face. "Got a man searching for you, woman. Or are you so eager to drop your guard and your drawers that you forgot about that? You trying to put someone else in a position to defend your ass for a second time? Not on my watch, sweetheart."

"Mace, it's not that serious. Calm the fuck down," Kaden urged.

"It *is* that fucking serious, Kaden. Pull your head out of your ass and start thinking with something besides your dick for once."

Nothing special.

Nothing special.

Mace had found us a place to stay, gave me a job, clothes, security, but right now, he was acting like a major prick, and I, for one, was sick of it. My husband hadn't managed to track me down in the weeks since I'd been living in Remington. My hope was that he finally gave up, went on about his life, and forgot about me. Mace wanted me to stay out of sight, I would do that if it meant he and Kaden would squash their beef and stop arguing over something so trivial. What we had planned wasn't worth all the hoopla, something he would've known had he asked before sounding off like an overbearing bull.

I turned my attention to Kaden. "Perhaps some other time when things aren't so...tense."

"Fuck that, don't let me stop you." Mace sounded smug and overly condescending. He snapped his fingers as if a new thought had occurred to him. "I'll tell you what, why don't we all go, make a field trip out of it. I'll bring the snacks and shit. My man Kaden can bring the sandwiches."

"Fuck off, Mace," Kaden countered, turning his back to walk away.

"We're going. End of," Mace clipped.

Guess that settles it.

The three of us piled into the monster truck after work and headed down the road. Since he had no idea where we were going or what the actual plan was, Kaden sat upfront and gave directions. When we pulled to a stop at the destination, Mace's mouth fell open in shock.

"The fuck is this?" he grumbled.

"The Sheraton hotel," Kaden snarked. "Room is booked, got plenty of rubbers and lube so we don't run out. If you think we're going to need more, tell me now so I can Instacart that shit."

The sign outside the massive building read *Hatch and Snatch, Grand Opening*. I was so excited I wanted to scream. I'd never seen anything so grand in scale.

I mentioned to Kaden, while we were setting up the new desk in the office, that it had always been my dream to try something dangerous like skydiving. He suggested ax throwing as an easy way to *get my tingle going*, without injuring anyone, namely myself. He saw an advertisement in the local newspaper, and *voilà*, here we were.

"I called ahead and booked a private room," Kaden stated, giving Mace a look that screamed he thought he was an asshole.

"This place is amazing, Kaden. Thank you so much for finding it." I beamed.

"Ain't no thang' but a chicken wang, little momma."

I was overwhelmed with gratitude, so much so, I had to turn my face away to hide the sudden tears that tried to break free. We walked to the entrance side by side, Mace noticeably quiet for once, probably trying to figure out how to remove his foot from his mouth. Served him right for being a dick.

"Y'all go on ahead. Reservation is under the alias Jack Hoff, for security and shit, 'cause I'm smart like that. I need to make a phone call," Kaden announced unexpectedly.

"Are you sure? We're happy to wait," I told him.

"Yep, might take a minute, and I want you to enjoy the full hour."

"Okay, then. See you inside."

Mace and I walked up to the counter, where a young girl wearing a T-shirt and jeans with the company logo greeted us with a smile.

"Welcome to Hatch and Snatch. How may I help you?"

"Reservation for Jack Hoff," Mace grunted.

The girl was taken aback but recovered quickly.

"Um…I'm sorry, Mr. Jackoff, but we don't take reservations. It's first come first serve. If you'll follow me, I'll get you set up with everything you'll need."

I made it about three steps before I dissolved into a laughing fit followed by an unflattering giggle snort that couldn't be helped. Only Kaden could manage to dump all over Mace while at the same time put emphasis on his rude behavior. The girl walked us towards the back of the building, where it opened up into closed-off lanes, similar to a bowling alley but with walls. At the end of the lane, there was a wooden-door-looking thing with a bullseye painted in the middle. It was private. There were hatchets in all different shapes and sizes lined up on a display case; there were even a few little knives that could've doubled as cutlery.

I was so excited I started to bounce in place.

Mace stood behind me like a dark shadow, unaffected.

"Where should we start?" I turned to ask.

He was quiet for a moment before he answered.

"I was a dick."

Whoa…I didn't see that one coming.

"Is that your way of apologizing, Mace? I must say, it could use a little work."

He answered my quip with another grunt.

"I never had any friends growing up, Mace, except for the one boy who wasn't around long enough for me to remember much about him. I had an old Barbie once with a missing leg and no clothes on, does that count?"

I looked to Mace to gauge his interest.

"Anyway…Kaden, Jerome, and Jagger are like those annoying brothers I always wished I had as a child. I hoped to gain a sister in Angelica, but I understand why she doesn't like me very much. What's there to like? I guess what I'm trying to say, Mace, is that when it's time for me to teach Kayla what it means to have a family, I'll tell her all about Masonry Ink and the friends I've come to care about."

"It's good to have friends, True. You deserve that. I thought for a minute that you and Kaden were more. I see now I was wrong."

He stepped closer and swiped a tear that had fallen from my eye. It was gentle, it was unexpected, and it was amazing. I wanted to lean into his touch, hold him to my heart so he could hear it wildly beating from the sound of his voice. An annoying timer dinged. Forty-five minutes left to throw, it warned. The spell was broken, and we were once again separated.

"Kaden must be sweet talkin' one of his women." Mace exhaled, taking a few steps back. "I say we start without him."

"Yes!" I fist-pumped. "I'm dying to try that big one."

I picked up the hatchet and giggled like a schoolgirl.

The heavy blade wasn't the only *big one* I wouldn't mind giving a try.

Only in my dreams.

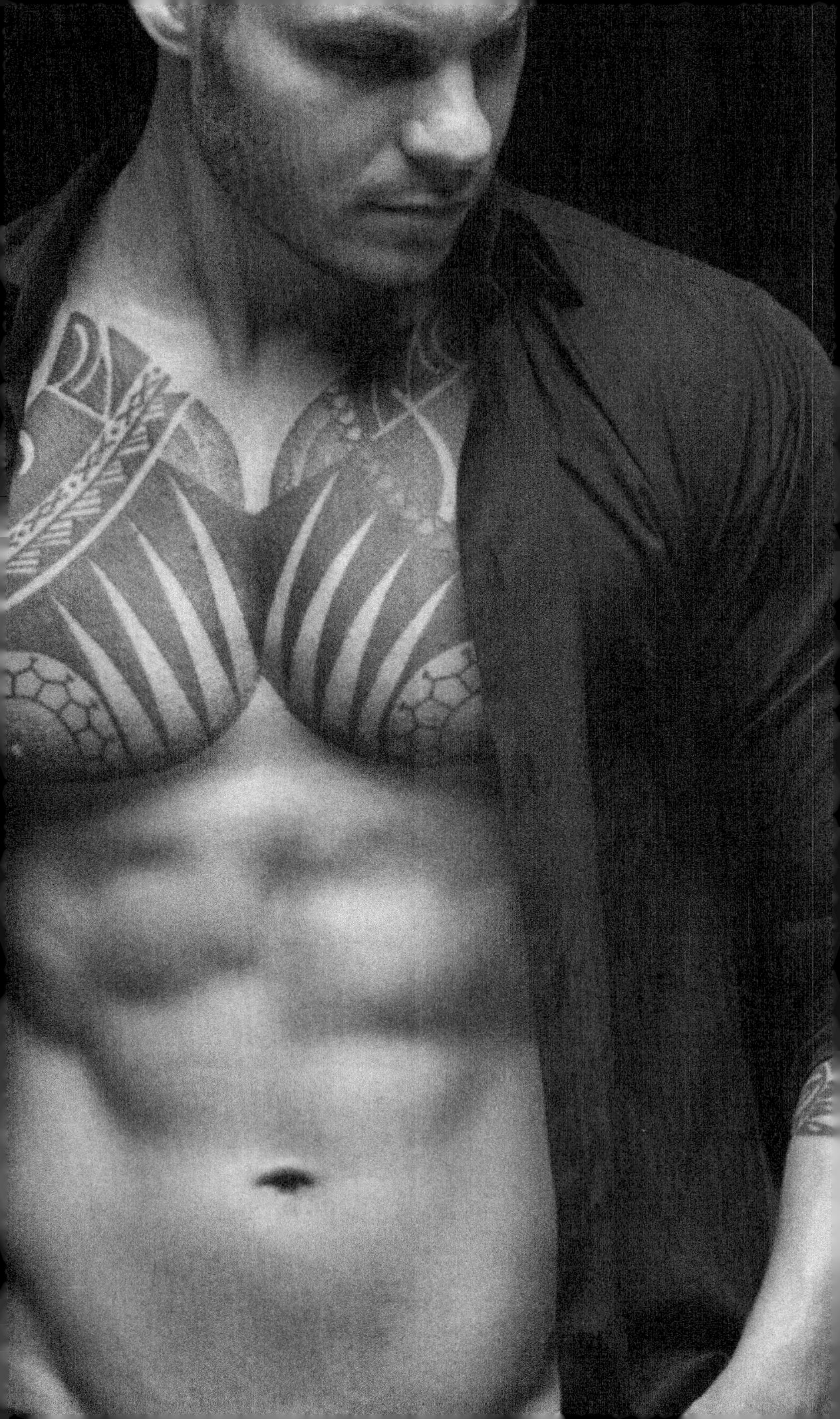

Chapter Twenty-Four

Mace

"Where the fuck did you disappear to, asshole? We waited almost twenty minutes for you to come inside before we realized you ghosted us. The fuck was that about?" I bitched at Kaden.

I was sitting in my office hours after I'd dropped True off at Sal's place.

"See... what had happened was, I felt this strong gravitational pull between my legs, sort of like a sting at first, then it got stronger as the sun hit it just right. Next thing I remember was turning over in my bed, staring into four sets of titties and a half-used bag of grapefruits siting on the dresser. I'm betting it was an alien abduction or something."

The bastard had a self-satisfied look on his face, wearing rumpled clothes, sporting a love bite the size of Denver on his chest. *Fuck's sake.* The collar around his shirt was damn near ripped off, which gave me a pretty good idea of how his evening went.

"Alien abduction, huh? Let's hope they stuck a probe in your ass and rewired your brain."

"Come to think of it, I do have this keen burning sensation back there. How thick is a probe? Is it bigger than an erect cock?"

Why me, Lord, why me?

I wasn't nearly as angry with Kaden for skipping out on the hatchet throwing as I made out. Honestly, it was the most fun I'd had in a very long time and definitely helped to lighten my grim mood. True was a natural, hitting the bullseye using both her left and right hand. Every time she squealed with excitement, one of the many bricks weighing me down seemed to lighten its burden by a fraction. Her smile and deep belly laughs were infectious, so much so, that when she mentioned that she wished Kaden were there to witness her prowess with an ax, I knew it came from a place of real friendship. That was a few hours ago. I went back inside the shop to go over the books when Kaden waltzed in, unbothered. It was late, and we were the only two people in the building.

"Did she have fun, or were you still acting like king prick the whole time?" Kaden asked, plopping his ass down in the chair in front of me.

"What do you think? I was king prick, of course."

"Yeah, figured that." He smirked, then suddenly got serious. "I'm told the most frightening time in lockdown are the weeks between parole and actual freedom. Waiting for those steel doors to finally open, wearing your civilian clothes, shackles removed. A lot can happen to a guy in a triple-max prison between now and then. Say the word, and I'll have the bids up before Jimmy cracks corn."

Of course, he knew about the parole hearing even though I never confirmed or denied it. I had the urge to tell him to do it, end that prick before his punk ass could even taste the open air. How easy it would be to make a simple call and wait for the sanctioned hit. I'd pay extra for the method and amount of suffering inflicted, but it wouldn't be by my hands, which was what I longed for the most.

"Leave it alone, Kaden. I'll handle it when the time comes." I pinned him down with a glare. "Your job is to take care of Masonry Ink and the people who rely on its presence to keep them safe. If anything happens to me..."

"It fucking won't." Fury twisted his lips.

I held up a hand.

"You're in charge if anything happens, Kaden, you feel me? Already sent the paperwork over to the lawyer to make it gospel."

"Fuck you." He kicked the front of my desk in a huff. "You think I don't know what you're feeling? Fuck you, man, just fuck your entire ass with a fat donkey dick."

"Kaden." I exhaled, rubbing at my temples. Getting his ass on board with this shit was pivotal to my peace of mind. "I need you to promise me that you'll look after my place."

"Go straight to hell, Mace," he seethed. "Not... fucking... happening."

Bling. Bling. Bling.

The silent alarm was triggered.

Kaden had implanted a chip in each of our phones that would tweet then vibrate in the case of a break-in. The rest of the crew would also receive the same alert unless it was called off by whomever arrived first, which, as you might expect, meant me since I lived upstairs. I'd never heard it put to the test before. That didn't happen in this neighborhood; the community knew not to fuck around here. This asshole was either stupid or didn't value his life. Either way, I was down to catch him up to speed.

Everywhere was dark in the front of the shop, the only light coming from the lamp atop my desk. I waved my hand above a secret panel that engaged the gun case hidden in the floor. I grabbed a gat and handed it to Kaden while I settled for my trusty twelve-gauge. From then on, we used visual signals to communicate with each other.

I motioned for Kaden to take the back while I opted for the front. I tipped closer to the entrance, back pressed flush against the wall, breathing controlled. Shadows of two individuals trying to jimmy the door were right there for the world to see. Motherfuckers were bold, I'd give them that. I wedged myself kitty corner to the doors opening. One foot inside, and it was over.

Click. Click.

The handle turned downward, shoulder on the glass, two count.

They were in.

"Don't. Fucking. Move." I pointed the barrel of the gauge to the leader's head. He raised his arms in surrender, revealing a leather-bound break-in kit he'd used to pick the lock. I unsnapped his holster and relieved him of his sidearm with one hand while patting him down with the other.

"Uh-uh...you flinch, and it's gonna be chitty chitty bang bang, fuck stain," I heard Kaden growl instructions to the second person, who was still partially outside. He'd come around from the back and was able to flank these fuckers without being noticed. He took the other cocksucker's gun then kicked him in the ass for good measure. I flicked on the overhead lights of the shop, never once lowering my weapon, and took one step back.

"Inside...slowly...and advice. Do. Not. Fuck. With. Me."

The glow of light revealed their particulars. Two men in shit-brown police uniforms, one older, the other younger, yet similar in facial features. So, a family of wet cunts, if I hazarded a guess. Tall in stature, physically fit but no match against me or Kaden even without our weapons. It was too dark to read the patches across their chests, but I had a hunch as to who they were and what they were after. *True.* I led them to the reception area and forced them to take a seat next to each other where I could look at them, study their eye movements, body language, and mannerisms. If they even thought about lying, I'd be slapping the shit outa them.

Kaden took up his post at my left.

"Should I call off the others?" he asked with a snarl.

"No, let them come. Might need 'em for the clean-up."

I said that last part loud enough for them to hear.

Two things stuck out to me at once.

The younger man was noticeably shaken up over having been caught. He was fidgety, flighty, looking to bolt the second he got a clear path to the door. I could smell pussy on him from a mile away, and its stench was rank.

The older fucker was different, indignant with self-righteous attitude, like he couldn't believe he let two tattoo artists best him at his own game. He had a calculating gleam in his eye, a killer's gleam from burying too many bodies. I'd know that look anywhere from time served in combat. His head was so far up his own ass, he had a skid mark for a mustache. I instantly homed in on him, the architect, my jaw flexed as I studied his face. I thought about shooting these two assholes and throwing them out back. Took effort to tamp that down. The motherfucker smirked as if he read my mind, and that shit set me off like a rocket.

"Breaking and entering is against the law. You pricks should know that being law enforcement and all, Captain Rich Boardman from Montana." I motioned with my chin to their stupid-ass uniforms, able to read the tags now that they were in the light. "Shame you skipped that part in cop school. Might've saved you some pain."

"We, uh…" the younger one started to speak.

"Shut the fuck up, Ryan. I'll do the talking around here. You keep your mouth shut, or you'll be sorry. Remember, I'm not only your superior officer, I'm your father, and you *will* follow my orders," the captain chastised.

Interesting.

Suspicions confirmed.

"Hindering an investigation could land you both in jail for a very long time," the old bastard threatened. "I'd suggest you think about that and lower your weapons so we can talk about this. My son and I are here on official business. You get in the way of that, and I'll see you're prosecuted to the full extent of the law."

"Yo, Mace, let me hit these fools while I beat my dick on their faces," Kaden bit out, ready to get messy. He sauntered over to the younger cop and smiled in his face. "Except this one. He's kinda cute. Might put 'im in a dress and fuck him in his tight little ass first. I bet you'd like that shit, wouldn't you, *Ryan?*"

The younger man's skin turned ashen as he looked to his father for help. If these motherfuckers didn't start talking, I'd give Kaden the go-ahead so I could watch them beg for their lives.

I waved him off for the time being.

"Unless you're investigatin' the cost of a new tattoo, you got no business fucking around my shop, late at night, in the dark. So, I'm gonna ask you one more time. What the fuck are you doing here?"

"Official...Police...Business," he snapped.

"That how you want to play this...Captain?" I leaned in, lifted my foot, and wedged it between his legs near his shriveled-up cock. "My story to the *local* police will be a whole lot easier to sell seeing as I'm the sole proprietor and a registered gun owner. I have the right to protect my property with deadly force if I feel threatened or happen to wake up to my shop being robbed in the dead of night by two unknown suspects. That is, once they find you both dressed in street clothes, holding unmarked guns, wearing the ski masks I happen to have lying around here somewhere. Pretty sure I'll be hailed as the hero in this particular scenario, Rich."

Before he could answer, the shop door burst open revealing a frazzled looking Jagger followed closely by my man Dread. Both were breathing heavily, evidence of their overexertion and surge of adrenalin visible by way of blotched skin and sweety foreheads. Armed with a crowbar and a fucking bat, of all things. I motioned for them to harness their beast and take position. Dread was new and not military or special forces trained. His education came from a bid in prison, but he was learning our ways through discipline. Now, it was four against two; the odds were in our favor. I returned my gaze back to the so-called man in charge daring him to dispute my claim. His continued defiance set my teeth on edge. I pulled the bolt back on my gauge and aimed it at the old fucker's head, tired of the bullshit.

"Say good night, cocksucker."

"Okay…alright!" He held up his hands and sighed. Defeated. "My daughter-in-law, True Boardman, took off and hasn't been seen for weeks. We tracked her whereabouts to Remington, which took some doing seeing as she's using a fake name. She's here, and I want her back. Now, where the fuck is she?"

"She your wife, Lieutenant Ryan Boardman?" I asked, reading his name badge.

"Yeah…yes, she is," he stuttered.

Yet, your old man is the one doing all the talking. Pussy.

"Well… Rich, the fuck makes you think she's hiding somewhere in my fucking shop? It's been my experience, a man who can't hold on to his bitch needs to figure out where he went wrong and reevaluate the weight of his cock, not go sneaking around uninvited."

He huffed out a cackling laugh, his face twisted into a knowing smirk.

"I know my daughter-in-law very well." His voice dripped. "This is exactly the type of place she would find herself lured into. Dirty, full of men willing to give her a little taste of home with just a flick of her pretty little eyelashes. Common, just like her."

The way he talked about True, as if she were some whore off the street looking for her next lay, made my blood boil. He was getting off on it, and his pussy-ass son just sat there like a piece of shit, not defending his woman against his father's denigrating words. I wanted to blast them both in the face with my shotgun and bury them in an unmarked grave. I took a step back and lowered my weapon, instructing the crew to do the same as I straightened. It was clear that these two motherfuckers had an agenda, one that would not be discovered with threats and intimidation.

Rich was too shrewd for that.

His son? Not so much.

It was his wife they were looking for, yet he never said a fucking word about it. If I pushed too hard, they would know that they were right and True was under my protection. I needed to dig deeper into this family, figure out what was really going on.

"Get the fuck out of here and do not ever come back," I ordered. "Don't know a True Boardman, slick. I suggest you take your asses back to wherever you came from and keep looking. I catch you sniffing around here again, blood will be spilled, believe that."

"We'll take that under advisement," old fuck said.

He snapped his fingers at his boy and rose from his seat to leave. Once they were gone, I flicked my chin to Jagger, and he took off behind them. I turned to Kaden, incensed.

"Get me everything you can on those two fuckers, especially the old man. He's as dirty as a ditch digger's dick. Need to know what we're dealing with."

"Roger that," he replied then paused. "Did you notice they never asked about the kid?"

I had noticed.

"Get me that info, Kaden."

I had the sinking feeling we'd be seeing them again.

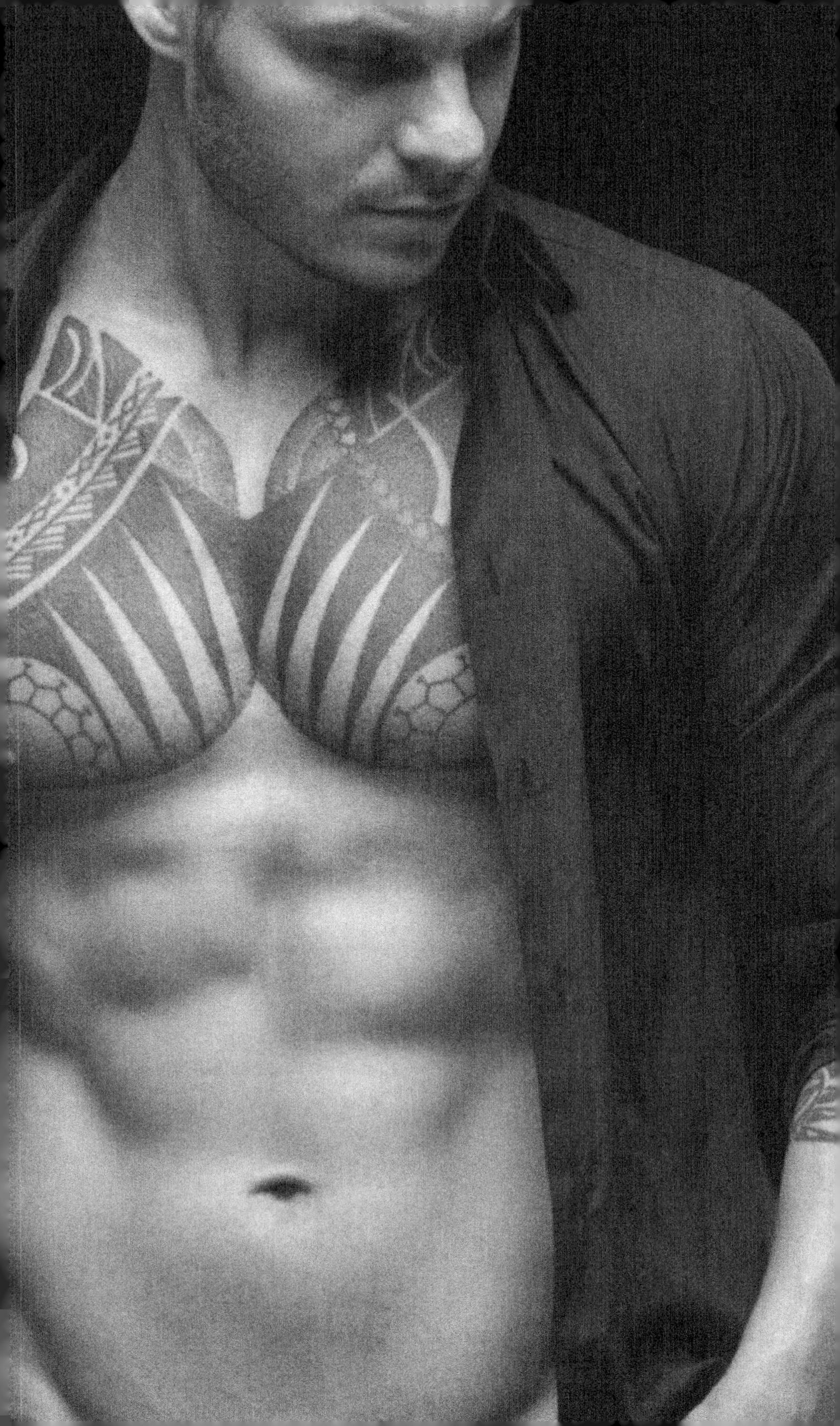

Chapter Twenty-Five

True

THROWING knives at an imaginary target for an hour turned out to be just what the doctor ordered. I was a little bummed that Kaden never showed up, but all in all, it was one of the best experiences of my life. I pictured *his* smarmy, grease-filled face and used it as my motivating force. By the time I was done, I'd killed that sick bastard with a hatchet, an ax, and a few of those pointy metal stars you see in old kung fu movies. Once I hit my stride, I added my mother's to the mix of faces I sought to eliminate. Every time I hit the bullseye, Mace puffed up in praise, folded his muscled arms over his chest, and blasted me with a smile so full, my heart swelled to the point where I thought it might burst.

I floated back to Sal's on a cloud of accomplishment, anxious to contribute to the days retelling of our notable events. I felt giddy with excitement and found it damn near impossible to keep from mentioning Mace's name at every opportunity. He'd made the experience so worthwhile that later, when it was time for bed, I closed my eyes to a beaming smile and a growly voice telling me that, *I did damn good.*

There was a light touch to my shoulder that startled me from a sound sleep. I squinted into the dimness of the room to see a hulking figure as it stood over my bed. Don't ask me how, but I knew who it was without the benefit of seeing his face. He had that effect from just being all that was him.

"Mace?" I wondered, still half asleep.

"Pack a bag for you and the kid. We need to hustle," he ordered.

"What's wrong? What's going on?"

"Not now. I'll explain on the way. Now move that ass, True."

I jackknifed to a seated position, whipped the hair from my face, and shook off the lingering effects of lethargy. Mace left me to it without another word, but I knew it had to be dire if he drove all this way in the middle of the night instead of calling.

I threw on the same clothes from earlier in the day and gathered as many supplies as I could. I heard spirited conversations going on throughout the house. Sal's voice rang out as she yelled at someone to get out and stop acting like a pervert. The commotion was enough that Kayla stirred in her crib, discharged a loud toot, then grunted her way through a stretch before falling back into a contented sleep. Not knowing the hows or the whys of it, I wrapped her in a blanket, careful not to disturb her any further. I hoisted my old backpack onto my shoulders and lifted the baby bag with my free hand, then struggled my way into the living room, where I heard more voices. The chatter came to a halt as the men from Masonry Ink regarded me affectionately before Kaden gentlemanly reached for the bags.

Mace made a grab for baby Kayla, his huge hands gently pulling her against his chest, where she sighed with contentedness. I felt my heart constrict at the sight, relieved that he was no longer ignoring her like he had during the week. I'm not ashamed to admit that I was jealous of my baby girl and would've traded places with her in a flash if it meant I, too, could be wrapped safely in his arms.

"I'm not going, Mace. This is fucking bullshit." Sal's screech broke through my stupor.

She wore stylish loungewear that doubled as pajamas, cool enough to sleep in and smart enough to wear outside for a quick supermarket run. She was none too happy about what was going on, and she was giving it to Mace using both barrels.

"It's not a request, Sal," he hissed to keep from yelling. "You're going to grab your shit, get in the car with Kaden, and shut the fuck up. You're going to let him protect you until I can figure some shit out, and I don't want to hear another word about it. End of!"

Baby Kayla stirred in his arms. He lifted her over his shoulder and patted her bottom until she settled. I was tempted to grab my camera phone and snap a photo, but I resisted considering the tension in the room. The entire crew from Masonry Ink was here, minus Angelica, of course. All wore the same grim expression on their faces while awkwardly standing on high alert, peeking out the window every few minutes, jaws clenched. I was concerned for my daughter's safety above all else. I reached out and touched Mace on the arm.

"Please tell me what's happening. I can't stand it anymore," I begged.

Indecision etched his features as his brow furrowed in reluctance. As our eyes met in the middle, I felt his worry, the pressure of his responsibility, and the subdued anger he was trying greatly to control while holding a baby.

He blew out a disgruntled breath.

"Got a visit from your husband at the shop. He was looking for you…"

Don't pass out.
Don't pass out.

"Was he alone?" I let out a desperate whimper. "Please, Mace, was he alone?"

He closed his eyes as if in prayer. "No. No, he wasn't alone."

I felt the blood drain from my face as I choked back a sob. That whooshing echoey sound that normally happens after a long day of swimming was the only warning before my knees gave out, my ass hitting the floor in an audible bump. All heads turned my way.

"True? Talk to me, beloved." *Sal.*

"I can't believe this is happening. I was so careful…so, so careful…" I wheezed. "If he finds me, I don't know what I'll do. He can't know about…ohmygod, he can't…"

"Look at me." I heard growled.

"Look at me!"

My vision cleared, and my ears perked to attention.

Mace.

He was close, down on his knees, a spitting distance away. He'd passed baby Kayla off to Sal sometime in the last minute, so there was no barrier between his heaving chest and mine. My insides were on fire, I doubled over, nearly falling flat on face it was that painful. I opened my mouth to speak, closed it, then opened it again to the sound of a tormented squall. Cold, so cold, an artic blast would've been welcomed instead of the frigid scorch of fear.

Rough, calloused hands gripped my forearms and delivered a solid shake then anchored me vertically from my folded position. The tremors in my limbs refused to subside, no matter how much I willed them to do so. Just when I was about to give in to the terror that haunted me, in the blink of an eye, it was all gone and I was home.

Strong muscles held me close while the scruff of a day-old beard tickled my neck.

The sound of an inhuman grumble drew my attention.

"I'll never let anything happen to you, True, believe that shit," Mace whispered in my ear.

"I'm scared, Mace, so fucking scared." I held on tightly.

"No, you're not. You're a real tough chick, remember? You carried a baby for nine months in your womb, nourished her from your body, and found a way to protect her by having a little bit of faith. I'm asking you to do it again, baby. Just have a little faith that I will safeguard your life and that of your daughter."

I pushed away to look into his eyes, to see the sincerity in them, or the lies like other men I knew so well. Leary of what I might find, I gasped in shock at the heat coming from a pair of hardened irises that belonged to a warrior.

"Promise me, Mace. Promise me, and I'll believe you," I pleaded.

He jerked as if I'd struck him. His brows creased in the middle, pained.

"I...I promise, True." He spoke so low that I barely heard him.

That was all I needed to exhale a breath I didn't realize I was holding and rise to my feet without his help. I would follow him anywhere he asked, without reluctance. He'd labeled me a *tough chick,* and for him, I would play that roll better than any other I'd performed before.

For him...for home.

We'd been on the road for a few hours. The sun was barely over the horizon in the distance. Baby Kayla slept soundly in the back seat of Mace's monster truck while I stared silently out the window, my thoughts ping-ponging back and forth between despair and longing. He'd found me and would try and take me back. Of that, I was sure.

I was angry, livid in fact, that for the first time in my life, I'd found a place in the world that resembled a home and *he* wanted to ruin it for me. Hadn't he taken enough over the years? I would give anything to make him disappear, to erase all the agony and hurt just so my little girl wouldn't have to learn about what a horrible person I really was. *He* made that hope impossible. Knowing him the way I did, he'd make sure the universe knew my secret, and it would hate me for it, more than I already hated myself.

"We're here," Mace announced from the driver's seat.

His gruff, overtired voice pulled me back to the present and the overly quiet cab of the truck. One look outside, and my body stiffened, my breath hitched.

"I don't understand, Mace. Why?" I wailed.

"Needed to get our heads straight, let the dust settle, and give Kaden enough time to get what I needed. Just got the word that we were golden, so here we are. You've been stuck inside your own head for hours. Didn't feel the need to fill you in."

"I can't believe we're right back where we started, at Masonry Ink. I thought…"

"What? That we were running away?" He turned his burley body towards me. "I don't run from a fight, baby. Never have, never will. You asked to stay in Remington, wanted better for your daughter. Has that changed?"

No, it hadn't.

I wanted it more now than ever. I had friends, I felt safe, and I never had to be what I was before. This was my home now, and I never wanted to leave it, but Mace needed to know who I really was, and it certainly wasn't the tough chick he claimed.

"The only thing that matters to me is Kayla. What I did…" I cleared the emotion from my throat. "Can I ask you a question, Mace?"

He nodded his head but didn't speak.

"Am I safe with you?"

"No," he answered without hesitation. "But...you'll be safe regardless."

My eyes landed on the backward-facing car seat that held my only reason for living, and I made a decision. *Please forgive me.*

"I hid my pregnancy from everyone for nine months. It wasn't hard. I carried small, mostly in my back, wore oversized shirts and pants to cover my tiny baby bump. No one knows I had a child except for the people at Masonry Ink, Sal, and Corrine. My husband, the man you met, has no idea that his wife gave birth to a child, only that I disappeared one day while he was at work."

Mace's brows pinched together.

He shook his head as if he couldn't believe what I said was real or I was making it up.

"He wasn't fucking you regular? How could he not know unless..." He scrubbed a hand down his face. "What sort of man doesn't lay hard pipe to his woman from sunup to sundown? The fuck?"

"Our intimacies were few and far between, and he preferred not to look me in the eyes. He wasn't very...attentive. Too busy with work, I suppose."

"That's why the all-points advisory never mentioned a baby," he surmised.

"Yes. I snuck out of the hospital a few hours after giving birth to Kayla and I felt she was healthy enough to travel. I registered under the alias, Nancy Jennings, before I needed to present identification or fill out paperwork. The loud screaming from labor pains helped with that."

"Why do I get the feeling there's more you're not telling me," he noted.

"Because there is."

"How far do you want to take this, True? Women say a lot of shit, but in hindsight..." He paused. "Any chance you'll want to go back to him, explain the situation, put your family back together, give it another shot?"

If he only knew the rest of the tale, he wouldn't ask that question.

"Ryan was never my family, Mace...and I'd die before I let *him* near my baby."

"Then that's all I really need to know. End of."

"You make it sound so simple." I smiled despite the subject.

"Nothing could be simpler, True."

Our heads were nearly pressed together in the front seat of that cab, so close, so warm, so...

I wanted to lean into him, feel his strong arms as he held me close while he blessed me with the heat of his masculine lips and tongue. I hadn't been kissed in ages, so long, I'd nearly forgotten how one taste could transport you to another dimension if bestowed by the right person. We stayed that way until Mace engaged the key fob to unlatch the door, indicating it was time to get out and face the real world. I didn't want to leave.

I wanted to stay right where I was. *Safe.*

Home.

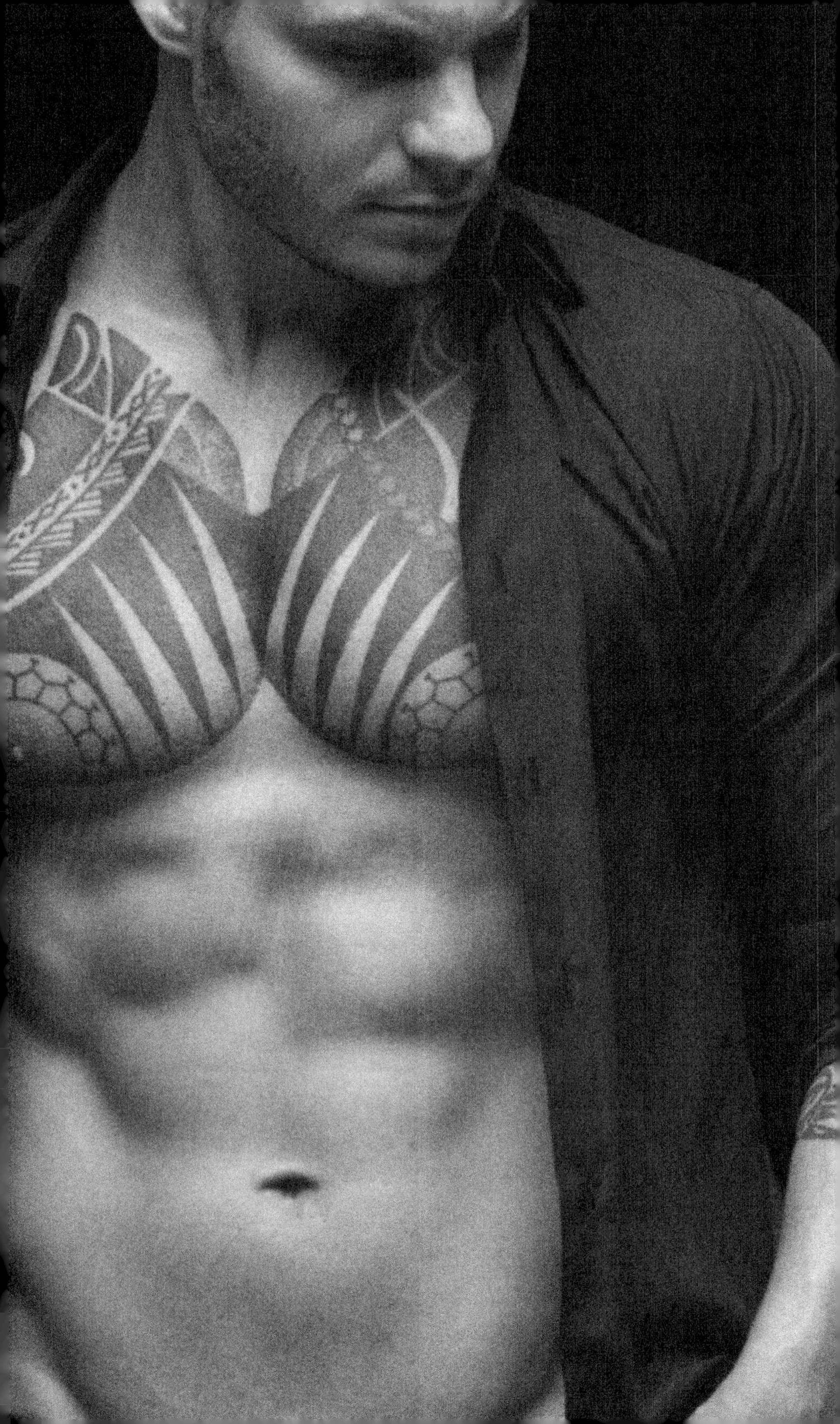

Chapter Twenty-Six

Mace

"What you got?" I glared at Kaden, who looked about ready to bust.

We were huddled inside my apartment, quietly talking in the kitchen while True and the kid slept in the spare bedroom. She needed time away from all the static, and since she didn't know the area well, it wasn't hard to drive around in one big circle. Her worried eyes, trembling hands, and wobbly bottom lip played on repeat in my mind whenever I allowed myself to think about her. How the fuck did a married woman hide her pregnancy for nine months without her husband noticing? If she were mine, I would've been inside her warm, slick pussy every chance I got. I would've had every inch of her body burned into my brain as if we were one. Junior Boardman was either batting for the other team or just plain ol' neglectful to have ignored such a fine piece.

I invited a vision of her lying naked in my bed showing off her baby bump just long enough for me to wonder then quickly shut that shit down. I promised to keep them safe, a vow I still wasn't comfortable having made. It hadn't worked out well the last time I gave my word to a woman, and this time, there was a kid involved. I couldn't risk that prick and his son coming back to Masonry Ink before we were ready to face off with them again. I'd sent Kaden off to work his magic, and he'd just returned with everything I'd need to take that bastard on headfirst.

"Far's I can tell, the husband's clean. Stupid, a sniveling little cunt, but clean," he replied, disappointingly. "But the chief? That motherfucker is into so much shit, I'm thinkin' about moving my ass to Montana, buy a buffalo or two, live the good life."

"Figured he was small-town dirty. Most of those inbred pigs usually are. It's genetic," Jagger added with a sneer.

"No, you're not following me," Kaden pointed out. "He's crooked as the day is long. Got his hands in everything from drug running, prostitution, money laundering, and not just local, Mace. He's connected. Hooked up with a crew running a string of mules over the Canadian border, stationed his boys on the USA side, intercepts, takes his cut off the top, all in cash. Uses it to buy real estate. Owns the house that True and his son shared before she took off, along with a few others, mostly of those in local power occupations."

"Fuck me. It's worse than I thought."

"Yeah," Jagger agreed. "Stood watch over those fuckers for hours. They hit a few spots around town, checked in with local PD, cased a few bars along the strip, then went back to their motel room and packed up. The chief left town without his boy. He's registered for another few days according to the manager."

"How's she doing?" Dread asked with a tilt of his chin towards the bedroom.

"Maintaining," I replied with a heavy sigh.

"I'm glad one of them is." Kaden laughed. "Goddamn Sal is a fucking ballbuster of the highest level. Took her to my place, ready to get settled, relaxed, and she went ape shit."

"That don't sound like Sal at all, dude," Jagger replied, confused.

"Okay, so, I might've suggested we put our heads together and come up with a way to pass the time while I made a few phone calls," Kaden said.

"That sounds surprisingly reasonable coming from you. So, what happened to make her go off?" Dread remarked, confused as the rest of us as to where this was going.

He turned away mumbling something inaudible, running a hand through his hair.

"Well? What the fuck happened?" I snapped.

He swung back around.

"Okay, so… what had happened was, I offered to give her head first, since I'm generous like that, then told her she could do me, but only from the back. That way, our heads would've been *together* for the rest of the night. Problem solved. She wouldn't go for it, not even the tip, said I was an asshole. I thought it was a damn good idea."

"Yeah, fucking brilliant." I breathed when he finished, 'cause what the fuck?

The silence behind his stupidity was the reset we needed to get back to business. Kaden would always be Kaden, and we'd learned to keep it pushing where he was concerned. If he thought his usual shenanigans were going to work on a woman like Sal, he had another thing coming. She was immune to the bullshit. Years of dealing with strangers' demands on her soul made her that way. Regardless, they'd have to get over it until this shit was handled.

"I'll talk with True about the husband, find out if she wants to engage the cunt, get him to back the fuck off so he and his daddy can go back to Cowtown. Until then, we operate business as usual inside Masonry Ink. Sal stays with Kaden. She gives you any shit, tell her I said she can talk to me about it. I'll keep

True and the kid here. No more going to Corrine's before we lock this shit down, understood?"

"What about Angelica? Any idea when she's coming back?" Jagger asked.

"No." I cut him a side eye. "She's fine where she is, and I don't need another headache."

He wanted to buck but thought better of it. We might be in crisis mode, but that didn't mean I wouldn't pause the action to get in his ass if he challenged me. I imagine it was hard on him, getting the cold shoulder from someone he claimed to care about, but he brought that on himself. He'd realize that eventually. I hoped by then it wouldn't be too late.

There was one more issue I needed to cover. Pragmatically, I knew it was for the best, strength in numbers and all that, but knowing what I knew, it was one of the hardest decisions I ever had to make. I faced Kaden, resolute yet heartbroken at the same time.

"Call him," I grumbled. "Get 'im back here. Tell him it's life or death, or I wouldn't…"

My words trailed off.

I ran a hand along my forehead, lost.

Kaden knew who I was referring to and the cost to my oath for asking such a favor. He acknowledged my request with a simple chin lift. The others remained quiet, oblivious to the silent conversation I was having with the only other person in the room who knew Dead Man's history and the real reason why he disappeared. We'd never shared, since it wasn't our story to tell. His reason for coming to Masonry Ink was as diverse as the rest of my crew. Once he received the call, he would come as asked, unconditionally. I prayed he would forgive me in the end.

Movement pulled my attention to the hallway leading to one of my bedrooms.

"Mace?" a soft voice called out.

True stepped into the light, staggered to a halt, her strides faltered.

"I'm sorry. Didn't mean to interrupt. I heard voices," she announced, taking in our little pow-wow with curious eyes. The kid wrapped in her arms made a cooing sound, and without a thought to what I was doing, I walked over and took her from her mother's comfort. She was all gums and squeals the second she realized it was me who had her. I lifted her up to my shoulder and patted her little bottom with the palm of my hand.

"We were just heading out, little momma," Jagger spoke for the group.

"Got clients waiting," Kaden followed up with a strange smirk.

"Later," came from Dread as they all left to head back to the shop.

True went about gathering the supplies to make a fresh bottle for her daughter. She'd asked me for something to rest in when we entered my apartment. She'd hastily forgotten to pack a nightgown. The sight of her in my T-shirt, the way it hung down to her knees, the mystery of what was beneath it, had my cock straining against my jeans the second she walked past. Her face was void of any makeup, and her hair was a rat's nest of wayward strands, but at that moment, she was the prettiest thing I ever saw. Holding the kid made that thought creepy as hell, so I lowered her off my shoulder, stared into her cerulean-blue eyes, and whispered, "Sorry, kid, it's a man thing. Better get used to it. Your mom is hot." That earned me another coo, which I took as forgiveness for being a perv. I lifted her back over my shoulder and watched her mother now that my erection was gone.

True yawned, not bothering with covering her mouth, and gave her ass a little scratch on the cheek like I'd seen a million times before during my military days. In a word, she was cute as hell. With her back to me and the kid, she called out while busying herself with her task.

"Did I hear you tell the guys that we were going to be staying here with you instead of going back to Sal's?"

"For now, yes," I told her, handing back the kid once the bottle was made.

The kid gluttonously sucked down every drop, belched like a grown man, then lulled herself into an adorable milk coma. I watched with rapt attention as her mother laid her on the couch and arranged a few throw pillows around as some sort of mock barrier. The kid was too young to roll over, so it really was a waste of effort, but who was I to judge?

"She's out for the count. Guess we're both off our usual schedules. What time is it anyway?"

"A little after six in the evening," I told her.

She nodded once and advanced toward me still standing in the kitchen. She gathered the empty coffee cups scattered around the island and started to rinse them out in the sink. The way her ass jiggled was a sight to behold, but the slump in her shoulders made me anxious. Something was on her mind, and I had a pretty good idea what that was.

"Staying here going to be a problem for you, True?" I stepped closer, needing to see her reaction to my question.

"No." She shut off the water and reached for a paper towel to dry her hands. "It's just that…your woman might not like the idea of another female in her man's space. I know I wouldn't." She laughed nervously.

"We back to talking about my dick again? Told you before, no wife, no girlfriends."

"What? No…I just assumed since you're, you know, and your place is so neat and orderly, it has a *woman's* touch. I guess I was a little surprised, is all."

I wasn't sure why, and I'd probably beat myself up over it later, but I invaded her space, enjoying the way her cheeks pinkened at my closeness. Maybe it was her bare legs that ended at her tiny feet, or the fact that she was wearing my clothes that kicked in my primal instincts, or better yet, maybe I just wanted to.

"I like my things in their proper place, True. Dishes in the rack, shoes by the door, women on their knees while they choke on my cock, that sort of thing."

Her eyes were as big as saucers by the time I finished my spiel. Her sharp intake of breath, the rise and fall of her chest, and the way she gulped back a moan spurred me on.

"And for the record, I don't fuck here. I prefer to have my fun on neutral ground."

"That's…good to know," she whispered.

My hand rose of its own accord, lightly touching a strand of her golden hair before tucking it behind her ear. I watched her lean into my touch as my chest grumbled in satisfaction. I growled, so close to picking her up and slamming her against the countertop, exposing her pussy, which guaranteed, was soaking wet with arousal. I just barely stopped myself, took three steps back, and walked away. Doing that was harder than the current state of my dick. It was going to be a long couple of days.

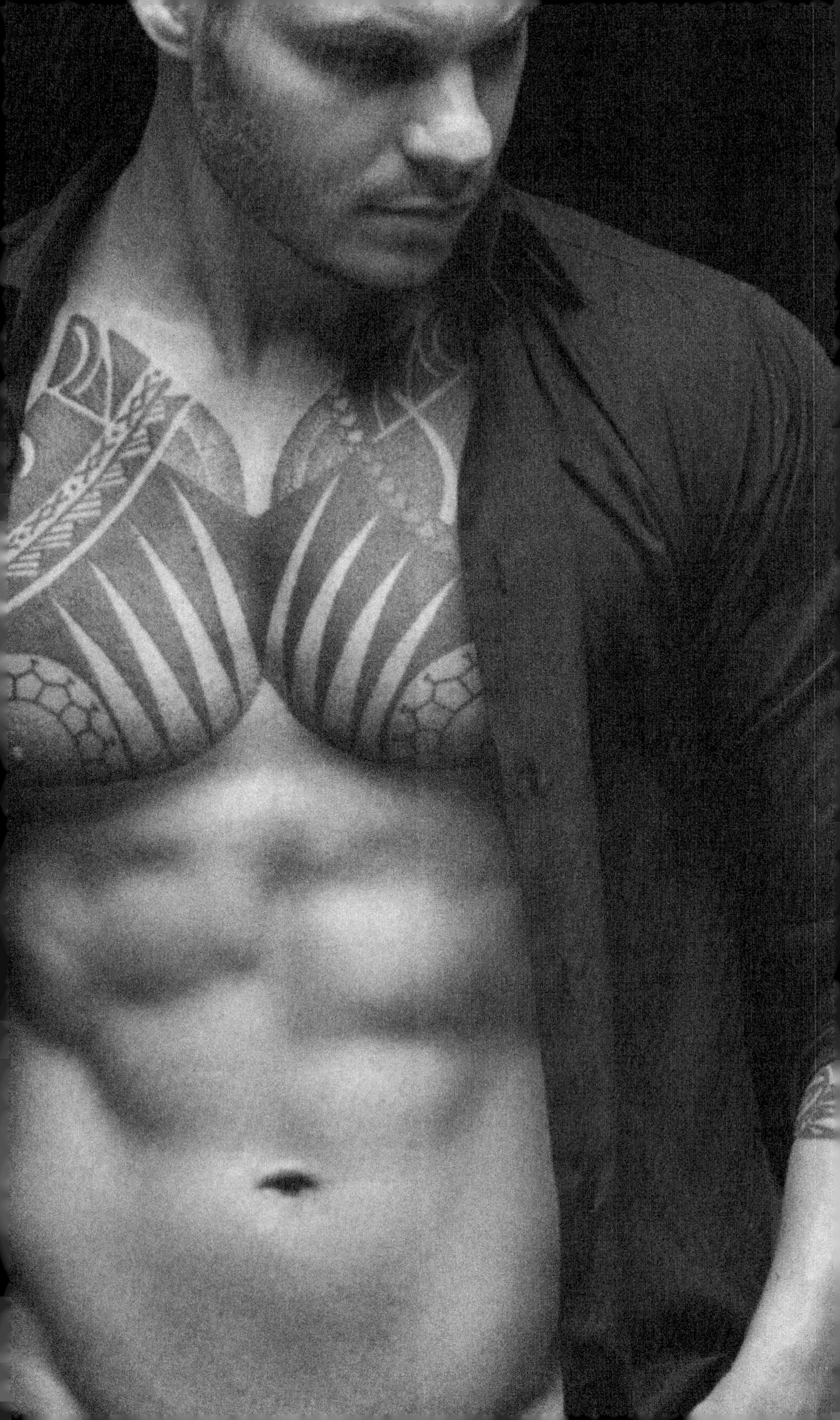

Chapter Twenty-Seven

True

"I swear to God, beloved, I'm going to kill this motherfucker with a letter opener if I don't get out of here soon, straight facts. You better come bail my ass out of fucking jail."

"Oh, Sal, it can't be that bad." I giggled into the receiver.

"Not that bad!" she screeched. "Last night, I was in the spare room, having just told him not even ten minutes before that I didn't want to play topless Jenga with him, when all of a sudden, I was psychologically accosted and forced into auditory range of a live fucking porno movie!"

"Oh my..."

"Picture this, if you can. The doorbell rang, so I braced, because I knew there was about to be some shit. Two sets of high-pitched cackles followed by loud-as-hell rock music started blaring from the living room, so I thought okay, cool, he invited a few friends over to...I didn't know what, but it wasn't what I expected. Now keep in mind, I'm no prude, not after my previous life choices, but anyway, this motherfucker? When I say it was a complete shit show, I mean it was a complete shit show."

"Packed house, huh?" I smiled, invested in her story.

"Yeah, packed with a pair of willing assholes! I'd just started to get used to the ear-splitting head-banging music when without warning, I heard Kaden scream, *'Squeal like a pig, squeal like a pig,'* and those bitches actually started to do it! For the next hour, all I fucking heard was *oink, oink, snort, squeee*...I damn near had a heart attack. What self-respecting bitch wants to bovine fuck, for shit's sake? I mean, I've role played, but this shit was insane."

"Wow...that is pretty traumatic, Sal. Then what happened?"

"As if that wasn't bad enough, between all the ass slapping, slurping noises, and *hee-haws*, he must've decided that farm animals weren't doing the job, so he started groaning, *'Show me the money, show me the money,'* to which them skanks starting chanting, *'Show you the money, show you the money.'* When I say I'm exhausted, I mean borderline delirious. I had to call off work today just to get some damn sleep."

By the time she finished her little diatribe, I was in stitches. The poor woman was clearly at her wit's end, and there I was, doubled over in a fit of laughter. We'd been keeping in touch via telephone over the last couple of days since Mace forbade us from returning to her house until further notice. She, at least, was allowed to go to work, while I was stuck staring at the four walls all day with only baby Kayla to keep me company.

"Hopefully, this will all be over soon. I really miss you, Sal."

"Right back atcha, beloved, and of course, I miss my little banana pudding, coconut swirl, butter bean brickle. Give her a big kiss for me and tell her that her Aunt Sal can't wait to squeeze her fat cheeks and suck on her little toes again."

"I will. Call me back tomorrow, unless you go over the deep end and commit homicide, in which case I'll see you at your arraignment."

"From your lips, little momma, from your lips."

We reluctantly said our goodbyes and hung up.

I busied myself with tidying up the place even though it was cleaner than any bachelor pad had a right to be. Talk about anal retentive? Even his underwear drawer was neatly color-coded. I should know; I looked through it this morning because I couldn't help myself. I wanted to know more about the man, and what better place to start than with his unmentionables? Who knew silk could be such a fucking turn-on? My creepy behavior lasted only a short while until I found something else to occupy my time and attention.

Mace had a full pantry stocked with all sorts of organic items perfect for a hearty meal. The first night we stayed at his place, I threw together some dinner then took it upon myself to set aside a plate even though he wouldn't be home until the shop closed in the wee hours of the morning. I placed a sticky note on top of the foil that read, '*Eat me,*' and was surprised the following morning when I found the empty in the dishwasher.

Giddy with pleasure, I repeated the process for the second night, only this time, the note read, '*Consume me*,' and as with the previous meal, the empty was cleaned and put away. Tonight, I made Salisbury steak with mushrooms, grilled asparagus, and mashed potatoes, everything a growing boy needed, in my opinion. I fed Kayla her last bottle for the night before putting her down. She was out before her head hit the mattress. My plan was to get up in a few hours and have it warmed by the time Mace arrived, but I must've fallen asleep on the couch. The next thing I remembered was being lifted in the air by a pair of strong arms and carried to my room. *Home.*

I startled a bit but settled into his solid embrace, burrowing my face into his shoulder. He smelled like hard-working man and sex, or better still, a man who knew how to work hard at having sex. Luckily, I was wearing a pair of yoga pants I'd stolen from Sal along with Mace's oversized T-shirt, or I might've been embarrassed. His hands under my legs were way too close to the promised land for my liking, especially since I was sure he could smell my arousal. I didn't recall ever feeling that turned on, but I could certainly get used to it.

"Hmm, wait, I want to watch you eat," I groaned sleepily.

"It's late, or early, depending on how you look at it, and you need sleep," he grumped, still walking. I jerked in his arms.

"I'm really not tired anymore, Mace. Please, just a little while."

He paused for a moment, turned us around, stomped back the other way, and deposited my ass at the kitchen table with little fanfare. He looked tired. Sexily disheveled but tired all the same. His shoulders were bunched to his cheekbones with tension, and he could hardly lift his feet to walk across the tiled floor. I sprung from my chair and stopped him in his tracks.

"Sit down before you fall down, Mace. I'll warm up your plate," I ordered.

"No need. Got this."

"Yeah, I can see that," I chided. "Sit."

He flopped down while I got busy.

My desire to please him kicked into full gear. I went about setting out the silverware, grabbed a bottle of water and a beer not knowing which one he preferred, warmed the steak and potatoes, and presented it for his enjoyment. I took the seat opposite him and watched with rapt attention as he lowered his head, sniffed the beefy aroma in the air, and hummed with satisfaction. He ate all the sautéed asparagus, the mushrooms, and one bite of the meat before shoving his plate away. He unscrewed the cap from the water and took three huge gulps, wiped his mouth with the napkin, and threw it down on top of the half-finished meal.

Maybe he didn't like it.

"Not hungry tonight?" I asked.

"Can't have the pot bigger than the handle, babe. Two nights in a row, eating like this? I won't be able to see my dick by the time I'm fifty, and I happen to like the look of my dick. It's big, long, and sparkles in the sunlight."

He flashed a cheeky grin my way, and I nearly melted on the spot.

"I'll try and remember that for tomorrow night," I remarked, clearing away the dishes.

"Won't be a tomorrow night," he answered. "Your old man checked out of the hotel he was staying at and took off towards home. Unless he decides to double back, which I can't see why he would, he should be back in Montana before long, licking his wounds, searching for you elsewhere."

"Oh? That's good. I'm sure Sal will be happy to get away from Kaden and his antics."

I tried and failed to keep the disappointment out of my tone. Truthfully, I wasn't convinced that leaving this sanctuary was what was best for Kayla or myself. I felt a sense of ease and comfort I'd never felt before, and that included my years living with Ryan before the trouble started. I grabbed a dish towel and wiped down the already clean counter in an attempt to distract myself from the burning sensation inside my nostrils. I remembered what happened the last time Mace caught me crying, and I didn't have the bandwidth to go through that with him again.

My spine tingled as the hair on my shoulder was moved out of the way to make room for the soft pads of tender fingertips. I shivered but refused to turn around for fear I was imagining the whole thing. When he spoke, he was so close, so solid, I wanted to lean back into his chest, if only for a moment.

You're nothing special, I reminded myself.

His words had hurt me so much, and he didn't even know it.

"If you were mine, I would have never let you go," he rumbled against my back. "I'm not what you think I am, True. I see it all over your face. I could fuck you three ways from Sunday right now and walk away a happy man, but you'd want more from me, wouldn't you? A commitment, a ring, a white picket fence? Let me save you the suspense, tough chick. I'll never get married, have children, or live happily. My life was meant for other, more pressing things. That's not to say I'm not tempted, because I am, baby, painfully so. Maybe if things hadn't happened the way they did..."

I finally turned in the small space between the sink and his upper body.

"What things, Mace? What aren't you saying?" I asked.

He shook his head.

Denied. *So be it.*

"I know all too well the impulses of evil men, Mace," I whispered. The nearness of his lips invited me to taste, to nip, and savor. "They lack the imagination to seduce their prey, and they claim to be different from the last, but in reality, they are far worse. I fear them most when I'm awake. They are your typical doctors, lawyers, and humble civil servants to everyone else, but to me, they are pure evil. Don't assume to know what it is I want, Mace Fox. The answer might surprise you."

I set him straight on his basic assertion that my goal was to find another husband. That wasn't what I needed from him. If this was to be our last night together, then I had nothing to lose by taking a risk.

"Real tough chick," he growled. "So, tell me, then, True. What is it that you really want?"

I want you, Mace Fox.

It was right on the tip of my tongue.

"I want something of my own choosing." I leaned in, impossibly close. "A kiss."

"And what if I can't stop at just one?" he groaned.

"What if..."

He silenced me with his mouth, sure and steady. I yielded to his need and bested him with some of my own. And in that moment, in his freakishly clean kitchen, I chose this man of my own free will, and it was the second best feeling in the world next to becoming a mother.

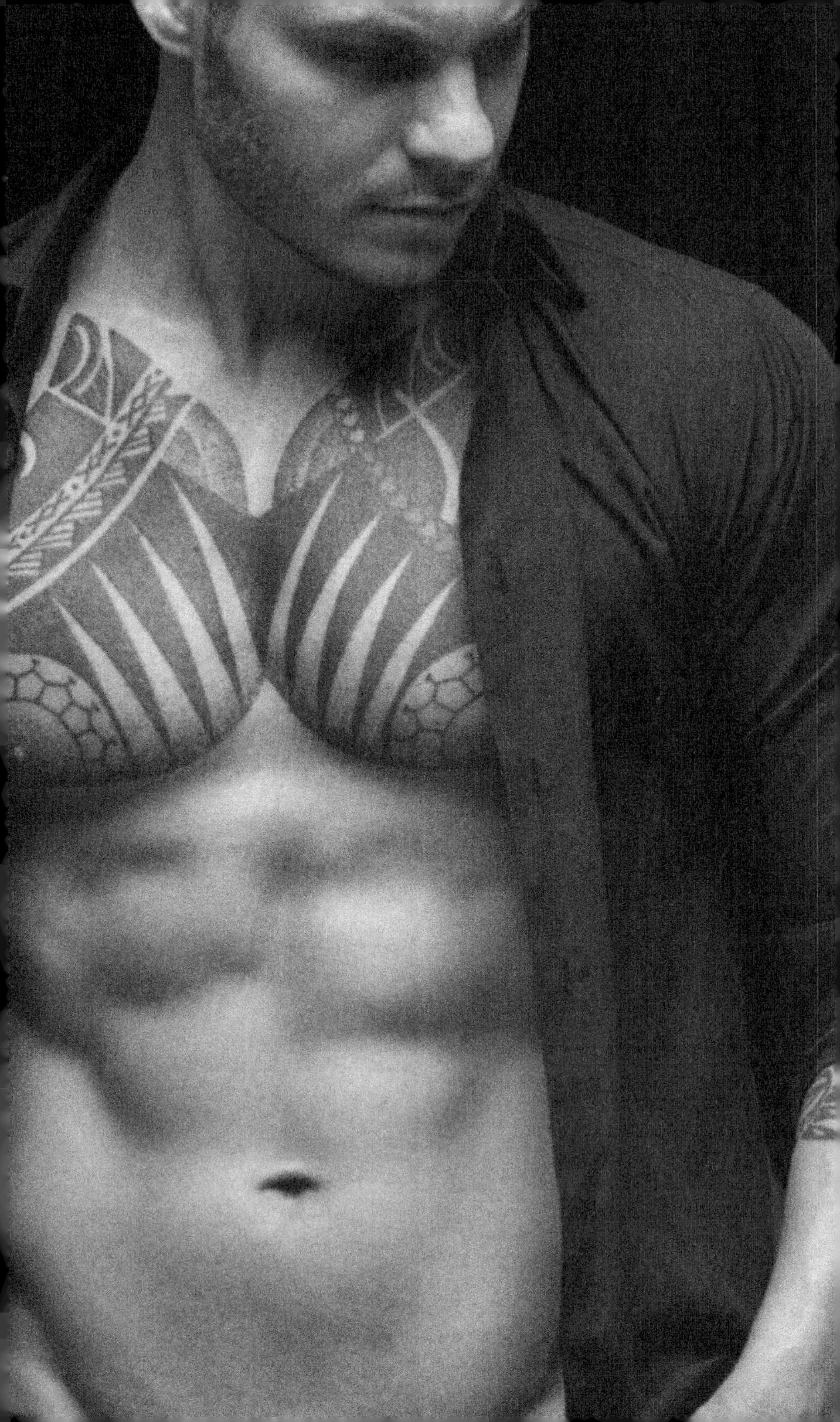

Chapter Twenty-Eight

Mace

My cock hardened beneath the black satin sheet strewn over my waist as I wavered between wakefulness and sleep. The memory of the night before was battling it out with The Sandman, and his bitch ass wasn't putting up much of a fight. Behind closed eyelids, I saw everything as it happened, down to the very second. I knew there was no turning back. All it took was a simple kiss, an emphatic plea for more, and a swallowed moan to obliterate all my misgivings. I blew out a shaky breath, resolved to let the vision take me where I wanted to go in my subconscious. Back to her, burning up from the inside out, where fairies danced to the sounds of the ocean...

True had hooked her leg over my thigh and rubbed her warm center against the front of my jeans. I looked into her dazed and unfocused eyes as she chased her pleasure like a starving hound let loose on an unsuspecting fox. I broke away from her sensual lips, swollen and puffy from our mutual assault. She was just as hungry, if not more so, than I was to take things to the next level.

She was so soft and pliable, my cock ached at the thought of bending her to my needs, twisting her to relieve my ever-present frustrations, pounding her sweet pussy until we were both spent and sated. I should've stopped, forced her to leave and never look back, but she felt so damn good that I couldn't deny my thirst anymore.

"Don't scream, or you'll wake the kid and ruin our fun," I told her, lapping my tongue along the seam of her lips before placing soft pecks on the corners of her mouth.

"Mmm, yes, fun. I like fun. Please don't stop at one, Mace," she mewled.

"Be sure, True, no games," I warned for the last time.

"Please Mace, I need this," she begged.

As much as I loved control when it came to fucking, I was struck powerless by her ravenous hunger and eagerness to skip the foreplay. Every touch was a wonder, as if she expected something from me that never came. I gentled my ministrations and watched as her pupils dilated and her nipples peaked to hard pebbles. She was damn beautiful like this, and I couldn't wait to see what she looked like when she came. She fumbled with the zipper on my jeans, grunting in frustration when she couldn't work the snap. I steadied her hand with one of my own. Her shoulders sagged in defeat with questions in her glare.

"Not fucking you on the kitchen floor, True," I growled.

"I'm sorry," she responded, her voice growing small. "I haven't done this in a long time, Mace, this being involved in the act itself part, not this way."

"How's that?" I asked, brusquely.

I took a step back and forced my nerves to steady.

Her body language was off, telling.

"I haven't wanted to touch a man in so long...I don't know where to start...please."

Her voice trailed off as she begged with her eyes for understanding. She wanted to have me, but at the same time, she didn't trust her own desire, which meant fucking wasn't something she enjoyed but rather endured. It made me want to stick my foot in her husband's ass for not worshiping her body on a regular basis, which was his duty as her man. It also meant that he took before she was ready to give, a fact that made him unsuitable to call himself a *man*, more like a low-class cunt who didn't deserve to sample such sweetness. If I ever saw him again, I'd be sure to tell him that to his face.

True needed the freedom to let go, to ride the wild with abandon on her own terms, something I was equipped to help her through. I led her to the living room, grabbed her by the hand, and pulled her over to the couch. Once I was seated, I positioned her in front of me with a turn of her hips without saying a word. She looked so lost yet hopeful at the same time. Tonight, I would allow her to take what she wanted, however much she wanted. I stretched my arms wide over the backrest, spread my legs apart, and presented myself to her.

"Clear your mind, True," I told her. "I'm all yours, sweetheart, yours to command, yours to conquer, yours to fuck. I won't touch you, not unless you ask me to. I can see that's not what you need from me. Tell me what you crave, tell me what you want me to do, and I'll obey."

She took a noticeable deep breath and stared at me like I was the biggest present under the Christmas tree stamped with her name on it. I smirked at her indecision, could see her fidgeting, not sure where she wanted to start, or if she could really do this after all. The war she fought against herself waged on until lust finally won out. Her eyes sparked to life as she licked her lips and prepared to give me an order.

"Take your shirt off, Mace. I want to see your skin," she asked, barely above a whisper. "You can't...I ...don't move your arms when you're finished. Put them back behind your head."

I relieved myself of the Henley I was wearing. My pectoral muscles strained and jumped of their own accord. There was an audible intake of breath as she panted, the sight of me making her pussy weep. I felt like a fucking god in that moment of being looked upon as if I were a meal. She shuffled closer between my knees, yet I refused to move. It was her time to shine.

"So beautiful, so strong," she said in awe.

"Like what you see? Come closer." I spread my knees wider.

She leaned forward. Her tiny fingers trailed along my shoulder blade, down my arm, over the freshly made scar along my ribs, until they circled the waistband of my jeans. Without me prompting her, she crawled onto my lap. I immediately felt the wetness coming from her pussy against the barrier of her thin yoga pants. I moaned, a deep rumble that came out of nowhere as I watched her settle her weight on my hardened cock.

"You healed up nicely, Mr. Fox. You had me worried there for a second. Scars are a symbol of masculinity and valor, did you know that? It means you survived something tragic, and what could be more perfect than imperfection?"

"Blowjobs? They're pretty fucking perfect," I joked.

She made a humming noise, distracted by her ministrations along my torso.

"Would you think it was weird if I said I wanted to cut open your chest and bury myself inside it for a few hours?"

"Not weird, though it would be hard for me to carry around the extra weight," I answered through a lump in my throat.

She giggled, adding more pressure to my already throbbing cock. She leaned in and took my mouth in a searing kiss with the perfect amount of tongue. Her blonde hair tickled my nose. Its fruity scent made me want to gyrate my hips, or better still, rip off her clothes and slide my dick along her dripping slit. Sharp nails scratched along the hairs of my chest with the promise of more pain. We moaned in unison.

"You are so irresistible, Mace Fox," she mewled.

"So, stop resisting, woman. My dick ain't gonna get much harder," I told her.

True rocked her hips against my jean-clad hard-on. I'd admit I was about ready to bust when she moaned deep in her throat and kissed along my jawline. Soft at first, then rougher as she gained momentum. Watching her work even though we were fully clothed was the biggest turn-on imaginable. She moaned huskily, a good sign that she was getting off on what she was doing. She yelped, then attacked me, and still, I didn't move my arms.

"Are you right- or left-handed, Mace?" she asked.

"Right, why?"

"I want you to touch me, but only with your left hand," she requested.

Fucking finally. Little did she know, the fingers on my off hand were as nimble as those on my right, especially where pussy was concerned, but if she needed that false sense of security in order to let go, I was all for it.

I went straight for the land of milk and honey. I slipped my fingers beneath the waistband of her yoga pants and found her clit poking out from between her folds, begging for attention. She spread wider, soaking my fingers with her slick cream, fucking my digits like her life depended on it. I watched for her reactions as I applied more pressure, adding then taking it away, denying her what she needed to come until her movements became frenzied. Her pussy chased after the target of her pleasure. Being the dirty bastard that I am, I gratified her hunger with barely a feathery touch. I smirked at her obvious frustration. She damn near pulled her hair from the root as she considered her options. I should've felt guilty for pushing her limits, but I didn't. I kept my promise not to touch her as she asked. Since this was her doing, it was up to her to fix it.

She stood from my lap, flustered.

"What's wrong, baby? I'm following your instructions. Not

getting what you need?" I asked, my tone full of amusement, but there was nothing funny about this whole scenario.

"I don't know, yes, no, maybe..." she cried, worked up.

I was used to women asking for what they wanted in a fuck. Pull my hair, spank my ass, cum down my throat, they owned that shit. They knew what made them feel good, and they demanded nothing less. Married or not, this woman was a novice and needed to be shown the ways of sexual gratification.

"Back up a little, baby, watch," I ordered.

I made a show of sticking the fingers I'd used on her clit by shoving them in my mouth and sucking off the juices she'd left behind. *Sweet.* Her breath caught and her nipples hardened beneath her shirt. Now that I had room to maneuver, I reached inside my jeans pocket and pulled out my wallet. The condom I kept inside was easy to find. Her eyes lingered on my chest until I lowered my pants and freed my cock. I was so hard, it bobbed up and down as if to say hello, hitting my bellybutton, calling to her. By the time I removed the rest of my clothing, she was practically foaming at the mouth. Her eyes were as big as the hubcaps on my truck, eager, wonton.

"You wanna suck it or fuck it? Choice is yours," I offered her.

"Fuck it," she said quietly.

"Can't hear you, tough chick. Say it like you mean it, woman."

"Fuck it, Mace. I want to fuck it." *Yeah, that's what I'm talking about.*

I suited up, got rid of the wrapper, and invited her back in. My arms, as requested, were back on the headrest of the couch where she wanted them to be. I might not have been able to touch her, but my mouth worked just fine, and I planned on using it.

"Please, Mace, I ache all over," she whined.

"Take off your pants, True. I want to see that wet pussy dripping for me."

She took them off, and I nearly choked on my own spit. Her clean-shaven cunt was magnificent to look at, all swollen and ready for my cock. I wanted to taste her juices on my tongue, savor the sweet cream as she exploded on my palate. Time wouldn't allow for such exploration. We were on a couch, not in a bed; plus, I didn't think she could last much longer.

"Now, lose the shirt...slowly."

I reached down and palmed my balls, squeezing, twisting, needing to relieve some of the pressure before I blew my load and embarrassed myself. She hesitated, but only for a moment.

"I, uh...recently stopped breastfeeding, so there's no need to worry about getting squirted on." She sheepishly turned her face away.

"Oh, baby, I'm sure your pussy will be happy to take over that responsibility tonight."

She regarded me for a brief moment then reached down, grabbed the hem of my T-shirt, and pulled it over her head in a whoosh. *Sweet fuck.*

This woman's breasts were a goddamn work of art. Pert pink nipples I would've given anything to put my mouth on while I worked her over with my thumb in her asshole. True would've loved that feeling of fullness, the coaxing of her pleasure from that forbidden area, if only I were allowed to touch. Apples to oranges, I was definitely a tit man to the core—big, small, fake, real, I didn't give a fuck. Shame I'd have to settle for watching them bouncing in my face. I'd much rather slide my dick in the middle of them until I nutted all over her face. Shit just didn't seem fair. Such beautiful globes should be worshiped, but I'd take what I could get.

"Climb onboard and take it for a spin," I groaned. "It's waiting for you."

"All for me? I..." She touched her fingers to her lips.

"Don't think, True. Take your fill."

She straddled my waist. Her small hands held on to my shoulders for support as we made eye contact. Her knees hugged my hips, but she didn't immediately jump on. She looked so goddamn beautiful, if only she knew just how much.

"Rub the head of my cock on your clit, True. Make it nice and slick for me, baby."

She grabbed hold of my dick, lined it up with her slit, and slowly, tortuously eased back and forth against the latex of the rubber. Before long, her juices started to flow, making slopping noises the longer she stroked, until her final pass when she placed me at the entrance of her warm heat. We moaned in unison. Up and down, our mouths inches away from one another's, she guided me inward painstakingly slowly, all the way to the root until her sweet ass rested on my balls. I sucked in a deep breath, giving her time to adjust to my size. She leaned forward, pressed her forehead against mine, and lazily started to ride.

"Like that?" I hiss. "You like that, baby?"

"Hmmm, yes, so good," she moaned.

"If I had my way, I'd slap your sweet ass, light it up, and make your pussy burn for my cock. Would you like that? You'd like that, wouldn't you, True? My handprint on your ass, heat shooting up your spine making that clit tingle?"

"Yes, Mace, I would like that."

"Your pussy feels like heaven, True, pure fucking heaven on earth."

"You feel good, too, so fucking good, I never want to stop."

My dirty words spurred her into action.

Her head flew back, causing her silken hair to tickle my thighs. She gripped my shoulders as she lifted her hips up and down my shaft. Faster and faster she went, riding me like a kid on a seesaw during recess. Reaching for it, I thrust upward with each pass until we worked in tandem towards the finish line.

"That's right, baby, fuck me harder," I urged. "Get yourself there, True, play with your clit."

"My choice. All for me," she wailed.

"Fuck... that's good, baby. Fuck yourself with my cock."

She reached down between us and rubbed at her hardened nub, chanting how good it felt. My ass cheeks clenched to keep up with her assault. The moans coming from the two of us were carnal. I worried the noise would wake the kid if we went on much longer. One final drawn-out grunt as my cock hit her sweet spot, and she flew over the edge, screaming my name. The second her muscles clamped down on my shaft, my balls tightened and I, too, went off like a rocket, filling the rubber with my warm seed. I was normally pretty good with aftercare—spooning, rubbing, holding—but with True, she'd touched her forehead to mine, taken a deep breath, and dismounted my cock without the courtesy of giving it a kiss for showing her a good time.

The flashback of her warm, wet cunt was enough that I nearly climaxed from the feel of the silk sheet against my shaft. This train of thought was not helping the cause. Another hour and a firm tongue lashing to the Sandman for giving up so easily, and I finally settled long enough to doze off.

Click.

"Wake your bitch ass up." I heard the release of the chamber and felt a gun barrel against my head. "Sleepy time's over, motherfucker. Gettin' sloppy, Mace."

I tapped my nine along his ball sack without removing the arm that was slug over my eyes. "Same could be said for you, Dead. Downwind, you smell like cheap hotel soap, dusty road, and day-old cunt. Clocked your ass before you hit the fucking landing, asshole. Took you long enough to get here. Thought I was going to have to come and get you."

"Been busy, fucker," he snapped as he backed away slowly. "Get dressed, meet me out front."

It was pitch-black outside, around four in the morning, if I had to guess. I threw on some sweats and made my way to the living room, where I found the brooding big man leaning up against the picture window, looking out. I didn't need to announce my arrival. He knew I was there, always. Silent as the grave but deadly as sin, he was not a man to be fucked with unless you were ready to die a slow, painful death. Dead Man hadn't changed much in all the years since I'd known him. Cropped military-style haircut, a perpetual scowl on his face, five-o'clock shadow, and dressed in black from head to toe. He was a man of few words, but when he spoke, you'd best listen to what he had to say.

I grabbed a glass of water and took a seat. My eyes immediately shifted to the spot where True and I got down and dirty. I swallowed a moan that threatened to break free. That would not have been a good look with just the two of us dudes in the room. He was handsome and all, but my preference was squarely for the ladies.

"Where you coming in from, Dead?" I asked.

"West, by way of Sorenson, Montana," he griped without turning around. "Over the river and through the woods, back to the homestead."

Fuck me.

I was not expecting that.

I couldn't tell if he was deep in thought or if he was angry with me for summoning him back to Remington on such short notice. Either way, pushing him wouldn't end well. He'd only lock up tighter than a vice if I tried to engage him before he was ready. The firm set of his shoulders, the veins popping in his muscled neck, the subtle fidgeting of his fingers against his thighs were all tell-tale signs that he was barely holding on, and all I could do was wait him out.

"She know about me, our history?" he finally asked after a few minutes.

"She doesn't know shit about fuck, Dead," I assured him. "Not my place to tell her, and you damn well know that's not how we roll. Your business. I'm sure you'll handle it at your own pace, when the time is right."

He shook his head as if to clear it, convinced that his secret was safe, at least for now. He ran a hand over his scruffy beard and visibly relaxed enough to rotate his large frame away from the glass and took a seat in the opposite chair. He reined himself back in and was staring at me with his usual glower of emotional blankness I'd come to know as his resting murder face.

"Hurt my soul to recall you, Dead. Hope you know that."

"Done. Over," he grumbled. "Would've come back anyway," he replied.

"Why is that?" I asked.

His empty darkened eyes flared to life with a fiery spark. "For the sake of the child… and her *mother*," he said the word *mother* as if it left a bitter taste in his mouth.

It pissed me all the way the fuck off.

"She's a good woman, Dead, dealt a bad hand, trying to make the best of it. She doesn't need you shittin' all over her progress for reasons she knows nothing about."

He reared back as if I'd punched him in the gut, eyes narrowed into slits, brows drawn together.

"You fucking her, Mace? That what this is?" he accused.

I wanted to lie.

I should have lied.

"No," I clapped back. "I made it possible for her to fuck me. It wasn't smart considering everything that's going on, but it is what it is. I take all the blame."

I wasn't trying to brag about another one of my many

conquests or rub his nose in it. Dead was smart enough to smell it on me if I were being less than honest about my dealings with True. Most times, he was better at reading people than even I was, and that was saying something. He shook it off, clearly more interested in discussing something other than my sex life. *Thank fuck.*

"Didn't take long to get the lowdown on both the Boardmans and some seriously fucked-up shit rumored to be happening around Sorenson before I got the call from Kaden. You sure you want to hear this?" He sat forward balancing his elbows on his knees and waited for me to answer.

"Know all I need to know about that king shit cop. What else you got?"

He exhaled long and hard as if telling me the details would cause him physical pain and he'd rather have his cock removed with a pair of plyers than to be the bearer of bad news. It was so unlike him I braced for the blow.

"True was the pig's station whore, Mace, passed around from man to man like a fucking bong." He shuddered in disgust. "Never said no, apparently, was really popular with the fellas from what I understand."

"Come again?" Surely, I'd heard him wrong.

There's no fucking way.

"Not sure how her husband convinced her to take part in that shit. Word on the street was that he was a little light in the cock and barely paid attention to his wife. Went on for years, long enough for her to develop that reputation, walk around with it painted across her back, and he never did fuck all to stop it."

My chest refused to expand.

That motherfucker.

The woman who fucked my brains out the night before wasn't a diehard pro, nor had she used her sexuality in a way that was indicative of someone familiar with a man's desires. She was unsure of where to touch, how to caress, where to position my cock to make herself feel good. When she came, it shocked the shit out of her. Never heard a woman yell so loud in my life. Then I felt her tears as they streamed down my arm, which wasn't exactly the happy ending I was hoping for. At the time, I wasn't in the position to question it, nor did I want to. She had her reasons, and I needed to separate the act from the woman if I wanted to remain impartial. Our fuck wasn't meant to be a love connection, so why did I feel so wrecked?

"Doesn't change anything, Dead. She's still under my protection. So's the kid." I exclaimed, and I meant every word. "She hid the kid, never told anyone she was pregnant. Could be the reason for the runner."

"Hid the kid? How the fuck do you not know your bitch is pregnant?" he balked.

"Don't know. Guess Junior Boardman wasn't getting the job done in the bedroom."

"Bet she learned how to trick from her whore of a mother," he raged.

The insult chapped my ass.

"That gonna be a problem for you? Seeing her at the shop every day till we deal with this threat? I'll understand if you need to make yourself scarce."

He gave a noncommittal grunt, which meant he'd be sticking around for my sake. The rest would have to wait its turn in the cocked-up line with the rest of the bullshit.

"Kaden told me that fuckstick is getting released soon." His subject change surprised me.

"Yeah, good behavior or some shit. My mother is having a hard time over it."

"Want me to take care of it? Quiet, no witnesses, closed casket," he offered, and I had no doubt that he would, but this was my fight.

"No," I replied brusquely. "He's mine, not your problem to handle, Dead."

"Fair enough." He sighed. "But the offers still stands if you want it."

After a short beat, he stood up and walked out the door without another word, and that was Dead Man in a nutshell. Perfectly unbothered that he'd offered to kill a man at my say-so while at the same time incapable of facing the demons of his own past. Killing came easy to those missing a heart. Wouldn't be long before I put that theory to the test.

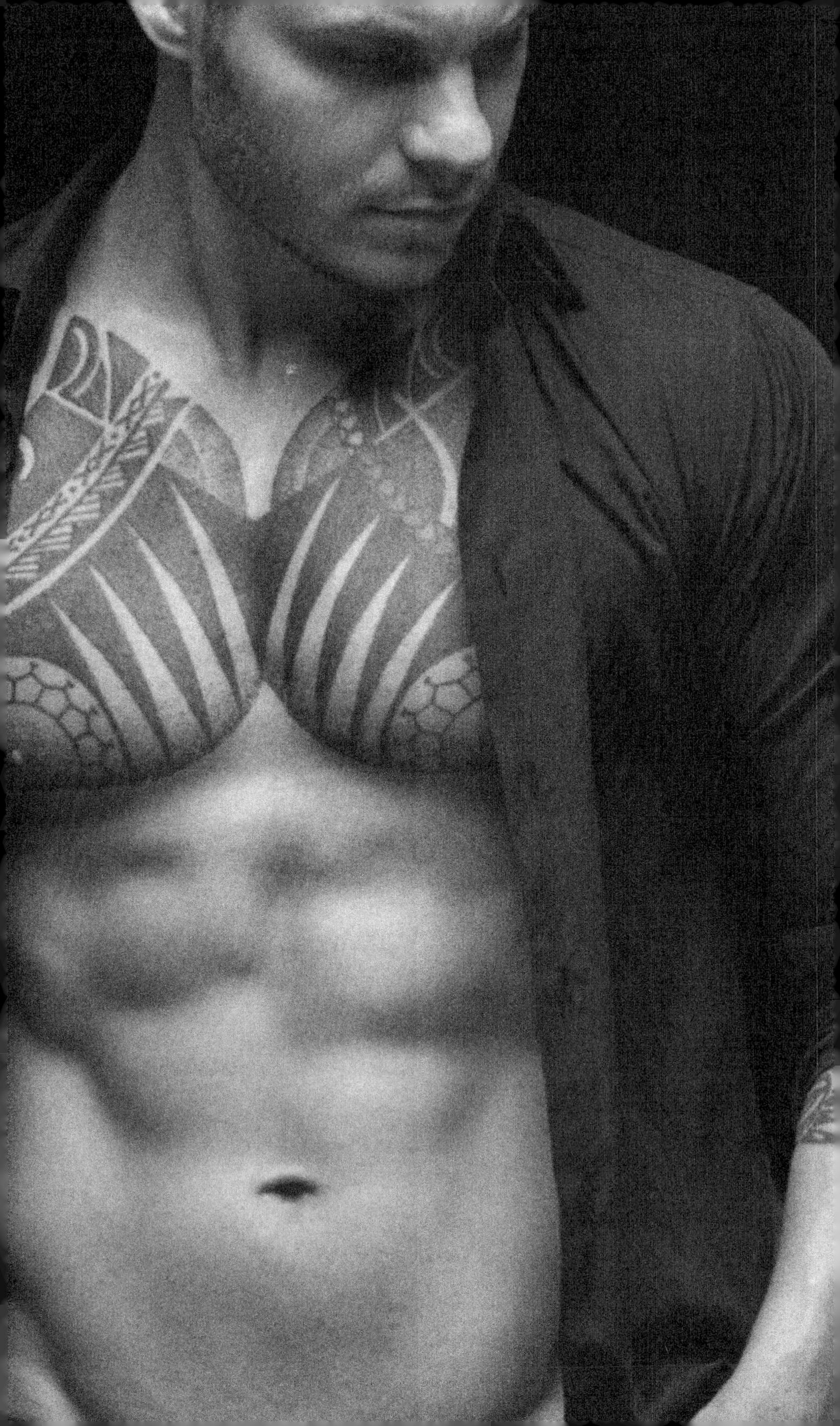

Chapter Twenty-Nine

True

Mace drove us back to Sal's the morning after I allowed myself to partake in all that was him. Packing up our things and leaving his place was an emotional experience that troubled me more than it should've. He'd made his position clear on more than one occasion. I wasn't his wife, his apartment wasn't my home, and he wasn't interested in furnishing the details of the women with whom he stuck his dick into. I knew all of that going in, but for the few days we were there, it felt so incredibly right. As if I was needed and by his side was where I *belonged*.

The whole ride over, I wanted to scream, '*Stop! Take us back!*' but couldn't work up the nerve. There was a noticeable shift in the air around us, from friends to *other*, depending on how I chose to look at it. We didn't talk about our night together, and I wondered if he saw me differently than he previously had. Was I still a damsel in distress, a real tough chick, or just your run-of-the-mill street whore minus the exchange of money? Theatrical, I know, but deciding to fuck your boss deserved a little melodrama. How else was I supposed to convince myself that what we shared was real and it actually happened?

Taking care of the sexy caveman filled my heart with so much joy. Waiting up late for his return, cooking his meals, listening to him talk about his day was a routine I could've easily gotten used to given the chance. Leaving it all behind was pure agony. Even baby Kayla felt the effects of Mace's absence. She cried her little eyes out for hours. It took both Sal and me rocking her in shifts before she finally settled. It wasn't until the house was quiet and everyone was sound asleep that I, myself, succumbed to the misery and shed a few tears. Did he miss us as much as we missed him? Was he sobbing over the loss of us, or was he happy to be rid of another pain in his ass? There was no use in dwelling on the what-ifs, so I pulled up my big girl panties and counted sheep until it was time to face him again.

The following day, I resumed my regularly scheduled pre-Ryan appearance routine, but with a little twist. I asked Sal to drop me off at Masonry Ink on her way to work instead of waiting for Mace to pick me up in the afternoon. When we stopped out front, I sent him a text letting him know that I'd already arrived and he was relieved of his chauffeur duties. It was a chicken move, I'd admit that, but on the flip side of the coin, I wasn't ready to face my boss, so sue me. It also meant that my workday would last around twelve hours since I was still filling in for Angelica as a server. *What the hell am I thinking?*

Kaden was already there, per usual. I sighed with relief when he approached me from the back of the shop. It meant I wasn't alone. Weirdly enough, he was eating a bowl of cereal laughing to himself, winking at me for no reason. *Strange.* His laid-back demeanor set my mind at ease even though Mace had assured me that *he* was gone and that I was safe. I believed him for the most part. Ironically enough, *he* wasn't the person who took center stage in my thoughts.

I committed myself to keeping up appearances and carrying

on as if nothing had happened. By the time Mace made it into the office, I was pretty down about the whole thing. He kept his distance for most of the day, which was to be expected, but it still hurt like a mother. Each time I looked in his direction, I wanted to pounce on him and ride him like a bucking stallion again, but I held back. The man certainly didn't make it easy on my hormones, that's for damn sure.

He wore a pair of dark jeans that hugged his rock-hard ass like a glove, and oh, what an ass it was. *Tasty.* A black button-down shirt left open at the neck with the sleeves pushed up to the elbows. His colorful tattoos were on full display, and black Timberland boots had him looking like a badass. My center grew damp just thinking about our time together and how I got to touch all that wonderful skin. I vividly remembered how his fingers looked, covered in ink, bold against pale, tweaking and flicking my clit until I thought my head would explode.

Mace somehow knew how difficult it was for me to let myself go and simply enjoy. He'd talked me through it, and I'd felt alive for the first time in many years, without fear or shame, my soul ignited in the wonderful workings of two bodies united. My orgasm ripped through me and caused a domino effect of emotions to surface I'd long ago buried beneath a stone slab that was once my heart. I felt the tears of relief as they saturated my cheeks until I forced them away. I wasn't being held down while my body was invaded. I wasn't forced to take what I never wanted to begin with. I wasn't being used as a plaything, all in the name of family loyalty.

Mace allowed me to call the shots, and call them I did.

It was over now, and things were back to normal between the two of us. He spent his time and energy looking after his business and friends while I sat around and considered my life choices. Somehow, things were clearer in my mind's eye, more tragic in some ways yet liberating at the same time. My night with Mace showed me that I *was* a real tough chick, that I was worthy of pleasure from a man of my own choosing, that I might be a little broken but not completely shattered. I wanted more of what he had given me. I wanted it all. And most importantly, I wanted him.

I reached for another stack of invoices and got back to work. It was too early for the drinking customers, so why not keep myself busy? The only bright spot in my morning was watching how excited Kayla was to see Corrine and Sal after being separated from them for a short while. They each took turns inundating her with hugs and kisses, to which she squealed with excitement at all the attention. The surrogate aunty and grandma loved my baby girl, and she loved them back. They were our family now. It felt amazing to say that, and I wouldn't give them up for the world.

A commotion in the shop caught my attention, but I chalked it up to a regular day at Masonry Ink and its string of offbeat customers. The door swung open, and I expected it to be Mace, so I didn't bother lifting my head until I heard a low growl coming from somewhere above me.

"We got trouble. Come with me," a man ordered angrily.

I jumped with a start and locked eyes with the most menacing individual I'd ever seen up close. He was what I could only describe as sexily dark. Dark hair, dark eyes, dark clothes, shadowed by a dark cloud that followed him inside the office and hovered over his buzzed-cut head. Dude was intense, like Attila the Hun intense. His scowl deepened when I hadn't immediately moved at his command. He was a stranger to me, yet something familiar about him touched my senses, a strong case of déjà vu. Perhaps it was his alpha male vibe similar to the others here at Masonry Ink. Regardless, I wasn't budging an inch until I knew what the fuck was going on.

"What? Who are you? What's happening out there?" I shrieked.

"Woman." His nostrils flared. "Move that ass before I *make* you move it."

I jumped from my seat, ready to bolt out the door, when he grabbed my upper arm in a death grip and dragged me towards Mace's desk. It wasn't painful as much as it was unyielding for someone of my size and stature.

"Please tell me..."

"Quiet, no talking," he demanded.

"I want to see Mace," I begged, dragging my feet across the floor.

This motherfucker is doing too much.

How dare he manhandle me.

"Shut the fuck up and MOVE!" he hissed.

The commotion was getting closer, but before I could scream, fight back, or knee the fool in the junk, he waved his free hand over the side of the desk, and a panel opened along the wall that revealed a hidden crawl space door.

Whoa, where did that come from?

It was wooden, tall enough for me to walk into without bending over, not so for the asshole growling like a bear. He tossed me inside and lowered himself into the hole just as the office door burst open and uniformed men filled the room. He pressed another button, cloaking us in darkness before we could be seen.

"What's happening?" I whispered to the hulking man.

He'd already let go of my arm, as if my skin had burned him or something, and was leaning against the opposite wall of the enclosure. It was big enough for the two of us to temporarily coexist without having to invade each other's personal space. At my wit's end, I snapped.

"Tell me what the fuck is going on right the fuck now, asshole, or I swear I'll remove your scrotum with my teeth!" I screamed, surprised that the enclosure was apparently soundproof as well as secret.

The absence of light meant using a bit of my imagination to picture his response after my hysterical outburst. His manner made that pretty easy. His head snapped my way as he took in my insult, puffs of fire shot from his eyes, and there was a string of drool dripping from the corner of his mouth. Fileting my liver like some sinister cartoon villain was definitely in this guy's wheelhouse. He probably kept a few stacked in mason jars around his house as souvenirs. I shuddered at the thought.

"Fucking pigs came to take Mace," he snapped.

"Pigs?" I blanched. "What pigs? What do they want with Mace?"

I heard his feet shuffle.

He'd moved closer. The air around us vibrated with barely contained rage and emotion.

"Feds executed a warrant for his arrest on kidnapping charges."

"Kidnapping?" I choked in surprise. "Kidnapping who?"

Warm breath fanned across my face. "You, woman. He kidnapped you."

What the fuck?

"No, that's absurd!" I screeched. "He's done no such thing! How could they think he kidnapped me when it's just the opposite? He's my savior, not my jailor."

"Tell that to your cunt of a husband and his dickface father."

My heart sank all the way to my knees. This was all my fault. I never should've come here and disrupted their lives. My eyes prickled behind closed lids, and I stifled a sob that threatened to escape my trembling lips. I'd finally found what I'd been looking for my entire life, and *he* wanted to take it all away, as if he hadn't taken enough from me already. I shook my head *no* over and over. So close. I was almost there, almost home. The sadness filled my soul with grief until I couldn't take it any longer. Anger slapped me on the back of the head like a hammer as I steeled my spine, ready for battle.

I would not let him win this time.

Kayla deserved better.

"Tell me your name," I demanded with a low hiss.

"Dead Man," he grunted. *It suits him perfectly.*

"Well...Dead Man." I blew out a heavy breath. "You have thirty seconds to let me out of this panic room. I'm not asking you. I'm telling you. And mark my words, if you don't listen, you, sir, are going to rue the day you were born. Mace calls me a real tough chick. Want to find out how tough I really am? Try me."

His low growl was a warning, but I gave less than that first fuck.

Mace needed me.

"You can't help him, woman. He ordered me to hide you until this shit was over, and that's exactly what I'm going to do. Shut the fuck up and deal with it."

I advanced into the blackened space not knowing how close I was to the hulking man, if at all. I could've been talking to his ball sack for all I knew, but there was a point that needed to be made, and I was determined to make it.

"No deal, fuckface. I want out of here...NOW! Unless you want your eyes scratched out."

"Don't care what you want, woman. This ain't about you."

"That's right; it's not about me. It's about Mace being wrongfully accused. He needs me, and I'm going to help him. Now, get out of my way."

"That's rich coming from a bitch like you. Snake in the grass little cunt who'll stick it in your ass the moment you turn your back. You know fuck all about loyalty, respect, or virtue. You must really want to orphan that kid of yours. A donkey would make a better mother."

"You don't know me, asshole. If you did, you'd know I was loyal to Mace!"

"We'll see about that."

I prepared myself to go Hong Kong Phooey on his ass if he didn't comply with my wishes. To my delight and astonishment, I heard a loud click just before the panel opened, flooding the space with light. I didn't wait for instructions or reprimands. I took off running towards the front of the shop at full speed in time to witness Mace being hauled towards the door in handcuffs.

The others—Kaden, Jagger, and Jerome—were on their knees with their hands behind their heads being guarded by armed FBI agents. They spotted me right away, and I could see the word *fuck* as it formed across Kaden's lips.

I never stopped running.

Never stopped praying.

"STOP!" I screamed, skidding to a halt.

All eyes turned to me, shocked, appalled, stunned stupid, you name it, I watched it. One of the officers turned his gun towards me, aimed that thing right at my head, which caused Mace to struggle against his hold. I threw my hands up in surrender.

"I believe I'm who you're looking for, officer. My name is True Boardman, and I have not been kidnapped! You are making a big mistake, and you need to let him go...Now."

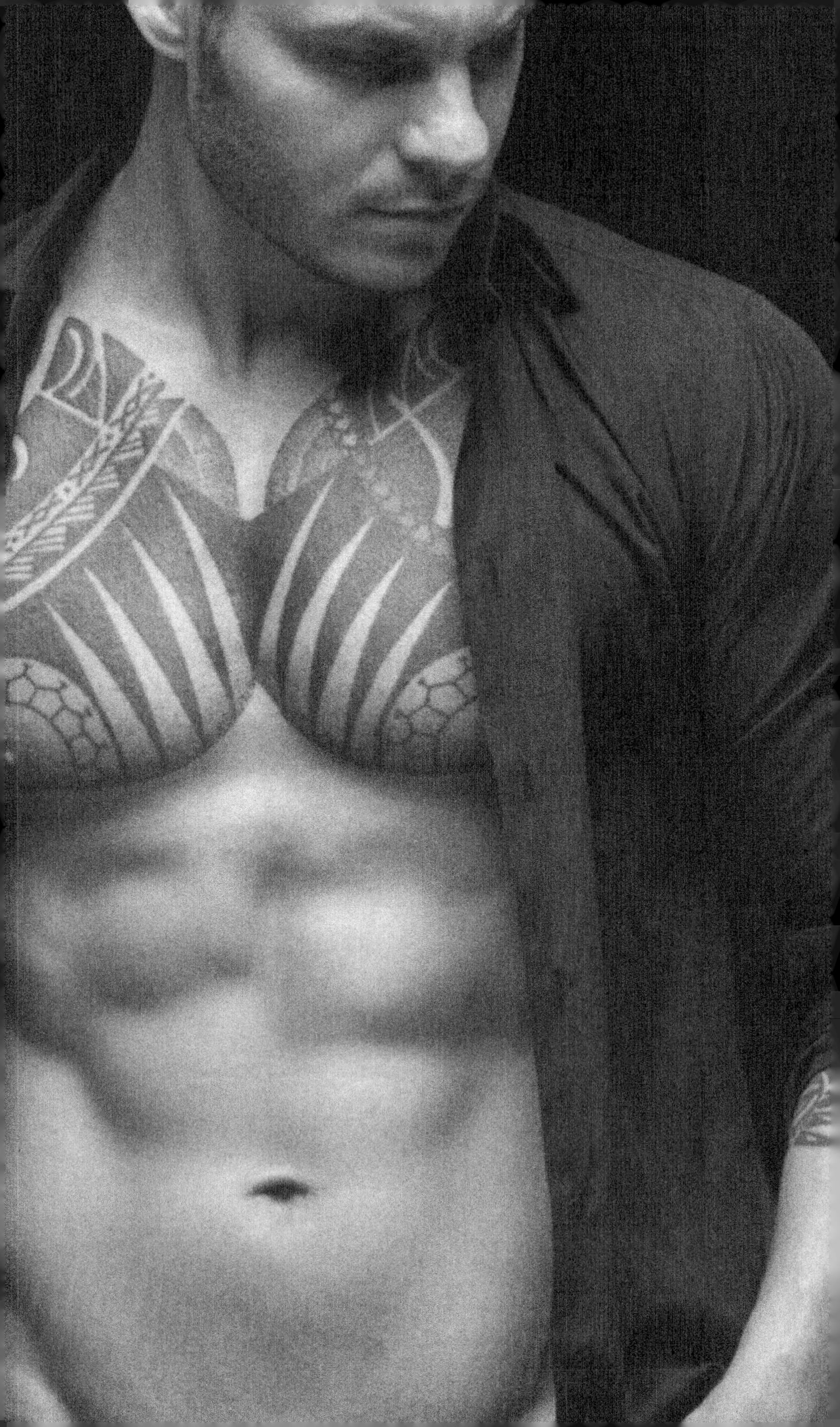

Chapter Thirty

Mace

"I was hiding under the desk when you all busted through the door. I heard a noise from inside the office and panicked. I didn't know what to do," she lied, convincingly.

Her animated words broke through my haze of unsettled nerves.

"That would explain why my men didn't see you when they swept the room. It doesn't, however, explain why your husband put out a missing person's report and named Mace Fox as a person of interest in your kidnapping," the special agent continued to grill.

"Mr. Fox is a fine upstanding citizen of Remington Township, sir. I assure you he's done no such thing, and I would appreciate it if you would refrain from sullying his name."

"All the same, Mrs. Boardman, I need answers."

Clearly, the prick was annoyed that his men were shit at their jobs, or so he thought. I had that panic room installed when I bought this place years ago, and only my most trusted friends knew where it was or had access to the control panels. Dead Man had a lot of explaining to do, starting with why she wasn't locked away like I ordered and was giving a statement to the goddamn FBI about her whereabouts over the last few weeks.

Treated like scum in my own place of business? Hell no. That colossal prick, Rich Boardman, was going to pay for this, and I did mean fucking soon. When I got my hands on that shit stain, I was going to fracture his cock with a crowbar, stomp it in the ground with my boot, then scrape it up with a stick and make him swallow it. He'd sicced those pigs on me using some bullshit story about kidnapping. I expected better from that smarmy cunt. A slippery, bitch-ass tactic from someone supposedly connected. The list of shit that needed taken care of before that bastard Chad Jensen was released from prison was getting longer by the day.

I could shoulder this sort of heat, but having to bear witness to how this bullshit raid affected my men had me worked up to the point of stroking out. Dread had finally been released from his chains, but because of me, he was right back in them. His skin had turned ghostly white, eyes empty and vacant. That shit fucking broke me. My muscles tensed from the rage I felt. I had to call on Jesus and all the Apostles to keep myself from breaking heads.

Breathe easy.
Calm.

Jagger's chest had distended to twice its normal size as he hunkered off to the side with the rest of my crew watching helplessly. His body language screamed fight instead of flight, and his icy stare was ominous. I knew from experience that this was how he prepared himself to take on the most savage of men with just his bare hands. The deadliest first step I ever saw in the ring belonged to that man, right before he broke his opponent's jaw. Given half a chance, he'd decimate at least three of those FBI pussies before they took him out in a hail of bullets. I wouldn't allow that to happen, not to him or any one of them.

Breathe easy.
Calm.
Dead crouched alone, still as a granite statue carved by the hands of a stone mason's stroke. His dark presence took up most of the space we were regulated to while heat pored off him in waves. I could hear guttural noises coming from his deepest reflections of despair. Calling him back here wasn't worth seeing him like that, shattered and broken. I would carry the weight of his agony for the rest of my days.
Breathe easy.
Calm.
Kaden wouldn't be Kaden if he wasn't acting a fool, bouncing around like a jack rabbit twenty-four hours a day, except now the opposite was happening. His movements were restricted to a small square between muscles and guns. Too far, and he'd get killed, only I knew he was already in the midst of dying. The longer he remained in one place, the closer his pangs of conscience were eating him alive. He wasn't anywhere near ready to face that black hole and survive its wreckage.

"Settle," I ordered, sensing his fragile state.

"I feel like tearing the fucking room up, Mace," he answered in a strangled tone.

"Settle the fuck down, Kaden. NOW!"

He kept bouncing around on his knees but was stable for the time being. True continued to fast talk her way out of the colossal mess she'd put us in by keeping secrets.

"Are you married, Agent Banks?" she asked with a hand on her hip.

"Divorced," he replied.

"Then you, of all people, should understand that relationships are complicated, made more so when one of the two parties is no longer interested in being hitched to the other. He knows how the system works, and unfortunately, what you see before you are the results of clever planning."

297

"So, you're saying this is some sort of domestic dispute, Mrs. Boardman?" he snapped. "My officers are not paid to act as private security to wrangle wayward wives of fellow law enforcement officials! I'll be filing a formal complaint with my superiors. In the meantime, I suggest you work out your difficulties with your soon-to-be ex-husband so this sort of thing never happens again."

"I couldn't agree more, Agent Banks. I'll be filing for divorce as soon as humanly possible," she assured him. 'I'll also be contacting the Attorney General and reporting this complete overreach of power. Someone could've been hurt. It's not fair to me or anyone else involved, including yourselves."

"Well...good." He snapped his fingers. "Put your guns away and release these men."

He leveled me with a hard stare. "My apologies for the inconvenience, Mr. Fox. I hope you can forgive our intrusion. We were just following up on a lawful complaint. Won't happen again."

"Yeah, whatever, motherfucker, suck my dick."

I rubbed circles around my wrists to ease the burn of the abrasions left behind by the metal. I fucking hated being placed in handcuffs. That shit was not at all cool like it looked in the movies.

"Well...we'll be going now." He snapped his fingers a second time with a huff, rallied his men, and shouldered his way out the door without looking back.

My guys scampered off in different directions in search of what they needed to see them past this obtrusion into their safe space. Pussy, booze, fists, blood, all distinct balms for the same corrosive ailment. A personal trait they all had in common was the need for control. Take that away, and you're left with a bunch of ticking time bombs until their narrow compasses realigned. I wanted to go after them, access their humanity before setting them loose on the community. They were all dangerous men, and if provoked, they could cause some real damage, but I had to trust their principled sense of restraint. I wouldn't always be around to save them, and it was time they learned on their own how to function without a leader.

I locked the door and set the alarm even though it was early into normal business hours. My regulars were going to be pissed, but fuck it. Life's a bitch. I was reminded once again that a woman in my charge took it upon herself to defy my wishes against her own safety and those of my men, all to make a grand entrance and save the fucking day. I hoped she was proud of herself. If one of those cops had an itchy trigger finger, things could have gone south really quick, and it would've been all her fucking fault. *Willful disobedience.*

I was fresh out of fucks to give.

"Mace?" she called out.

"Text Sal. Have her come get you," I lashed out. "You're done here."

"Please, I'm so sorry this happened. I had no idea that Ryan would go to such lengths to get me back. I want to junk punch him for being such as asshole, I assure you. You didn't deserve this. None of you did. I just hope you can forgive me," she pleaded.

I ignored her and kept on task.

Now wouldn't be a good time to engage me in conversation. With the way my anger was churning below the surface, I was libel to do something I'd regret. True didn't seem to take the hint, though. She followed me around like a lost puppy, picking up items that had been wrecked when the FBI broke through the front door. The longer she stayed, the more pissed I became, until I was two seconds from wringing her skinny-ass neck.

I wanted her gone, one way or another, and I knew just how to make her take off. I stepped into her space and slammed the box she'd been holding to the ground, stunning her into silence.

"The fuck you mean you didn't know he would go to such

lengths to get you back, True? You can't be that naïve, not with the way you took my cock in your tight little pussy. You knew he was a simp for that ass, and this whole thing was your way of getting even."

It was a low blow, but I kept at her.

"Or maybe you *have* learned a thing or two from your mother, like using your pussy to push that bitch husband of yours to the brink of insanity. The way I hear it, you were the grand marshal of free snatch in that Podunk town you came from. That really why you ran, True? Got tired of giving it away for free?"

"What?" She blanched. "Who told you..."

The shock of my accusation hit the mark I was aiming for.

"A second-generation whore is what you are, True, and your daughter will take up that torch as soon as she's old enough to spread her fucking legs, same as her momma."

"How fucking dare you, Mace Fox! I never lied about my situation!"

"Woman, you wouldn't know the truth if it ran up and punched you in the tits. Now, get the fuck out of my shop. Done with this shit. End of."

She scoffed in my face. "Not to sound cliché, Mace, but you can't handle the truth."

"Well, take it with you on your way out of town. I don't ever want to see you again. All you had to do was wait for me. How fucking hard would it have been for you to follow orders, huh? So busy trying to do things on your own, meeting up with that asshole all alone cost you your fucking life, Maya. You died because you didn't think!"

"Who's Maya? Mace, you're talking crazy..."

"GET THE FUCK OUT!" I roared. "You're nothing to me, and neither is the kid."

She stumbled backwards as if I'd struck her, but she wasn't giving up.

Her face twisted into a sneer.

"Never took you for a hypocrite, Mace," she snapped. "'Cause that's what *you* do, right? Play the part of hero with all your self-righteous talk of not wanting anything in return, but that's not really what happens, is it? You think because we fucked, you have the right to talk down to me? Well, let me tell you something, mister. Your insults are amateur hour at best. Try and do better. Being compared to my mother, called a whore, I've heard it all before, many times, and trust me when I tell you, the sting only hurts for a little while."

"Your lips are moving, but you aren't saying shit, woman. When the fuck are you bitches going to learn to keep your mouth shut and follow fucking instructions? What's so fucking hard about doing what you're told? My men were made to suffer because of your bullshit, True, and that…I will not stand for, you feel me?"

"I'll get them to back off, Mace. Tomorrow, I'll go down to the station and make a statement to the police that I wasn't kidnapped. What else do you want me to do?" she cried.

"Done with this shit." I turned. "Call your husband, tell him you made a mistake and you're ready to go back home. He'll take you back, no problem."

"This isn't about him, Mace; you don't understand. I can never go back. Sorensen was never my home. Just listen to me for one second!" she shouted.

"See yourself out. Got no place for you here anymore."

I'd already waisted too much time on this woman, allowed her to distract me when I should've been shoring up my plans, making certain my boys would be looked after once I was gone. Her watery eyes did nothing but incense me more than I was already. Her cheeks had reddened to an unnatural shade from all the yelling, just before she seemed to come to grips with being cancelled. I didn't make it two steps before I heard the bitter voice of a woman brought low. I thought she was still talking to me, but it was as if she'd forgotten I was even in the room.

"I made a promise to find you a place to belong, baby girl," she whispered on a head shake. "I tried so hard. Please believe me, I tried my best, but it wasn't good enough."

I paused, unable to continue with my exit strategy. The pain I saw in her expression was heart stopping. She made her way over to the window seat and fell into it, still distracted, still muttering absently to herself. She turned her face away to hide the silent tears as she wept all alone with nothing but her own arms to give her solace. I imagined it was something she executed often because she was *forced* to self-sooth and not because she preferred it that way. Watching her soundless torment affected me more than it should've, like a punch to the chest. I realized I'd become that which I despised the most. Should I expect retribution? An ass whooping? Death? Maya always said I was her hero, but what would she think of me now? I was nothing but a goddamn coward.

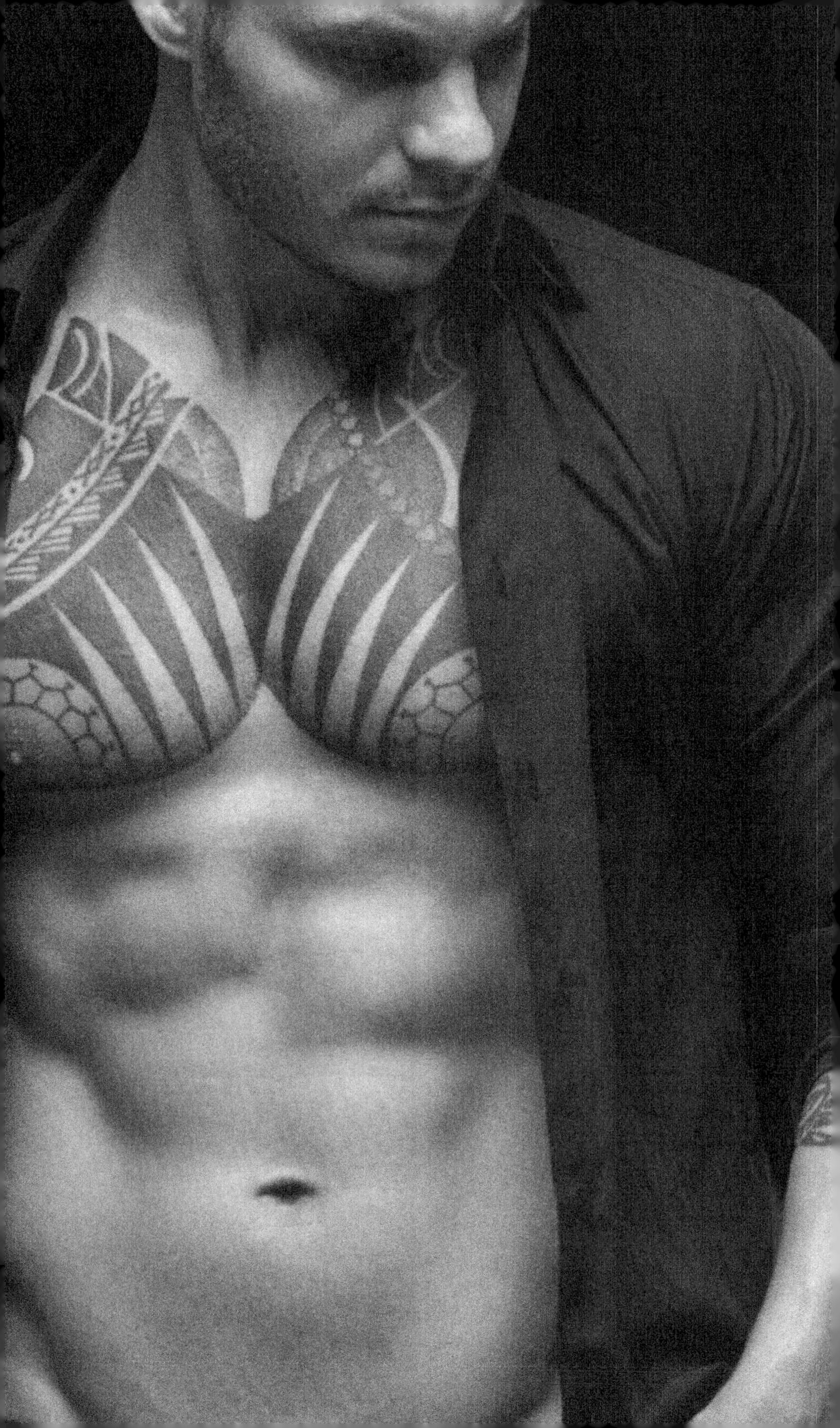

Chapter Thirty-One

True

I FELT a hand lightly tap on my shoulder, but I refused to turn around. It could only be one other person, and I was done getting verbally pistol-whipped. Things could've ended so much worse if I hadn't intervened in time to put a stop to Mace's eventual arrest. He'd long ago told me that he was responsible for the safety of everyone at Masonry Ink, and I'd nearly jeopardized his freedom because of the lies I'd told. If only I had confided in them sooner, confessed my sins and left them all in peace. None of this would've ever happened. I knew full well what *he* was capable of, yet I did nothing to warn them. Guilt weighed me down like cinderblocks tied around my neck. One push into the deepest part of an ocean, and I'd surely drown.

It was all out there now, or more to the point, *his* version of what happened in Sorensen over the last five years. Can't say I was surprised to learn that I had been painted as the town whore. He was the law after all; he could make up whatever lie he wanted, and people would believe it. I never expected Mace to be one of those gullible enough to fall for his bullshit. Everything I'd promised my baby girl went balls up, which was exactly what *he* promised would happen. To serve and protect was a fucking joke. *He* set his thin blue line brothers on Masonry Ink, and it cost me my job, my friends, and my newfound family.

He'd finally won.

I had nothing left to give.

"If you'll forward my final pay to Sal, I'll collect Kayla, and we'll be on our way, Mace. I want to thank you for everything you did for us, your kindness...well, you know the rest."

I wiped away the tears and prepared to leave, hauling my shattered spirit along with me. I was tempted to ask for a sendoff fuck in lieu of my final pay, but somehow, I didn't think he'd go for it. *Pity. It would've been epic.*

"Where will you go?" he asked, calmer now that he'd had time to cool down.

"We'll head north, I suppose. I'm a professional bookkeeper now. Shouldn't be too hard finding another job. I'll just use you as a reference," I half-joked

I felt him sit beside me on the window seat in front of the shop. His heat warmed my tired bones and lulled me into a sense of peace. After everything I'd done, this exceptional man was still trying to save me. I folded my hands over my lap and cleared my throat of its sadness.

"I was a cunt for spewing that garbage at you, True. Shit was uncalled for. There's only one asshole to blame, and his time of feeling himself is drawing to a close."

He sounded so sure, but Mace didn't know *him* like I did. *He* was rotten to the core.

"There'll be no need for retaliation once I leave. Like you said, I'll take the bullshit with me." I glanced over my shoulder and gave him a shaky smile.

"You're not leaving, and neither is the kid. You belong here now, True, and I'm sorry for everything I said. Please stay. I want you to."

My heart warmed at his honest plea, but my mind was made up.

"Let me go, Mace. I'm not worth the trouble, can't you see that? I lied about everything and tricked you into believing I was some fallen angel when really, I'm just your average run-of-the-mill Jezebel. As you said, just like my momma."

He glanced my way, threw his head back, and laughed his ass off. Thick and hardy from his whole chest, causing the seat to vibrate. Such a great sound, but what the hell?

"Hardly a Jezebel, but nice try though," he said through residual chuckles. "I knew who you were the day you walked into my shop, True. Knew it then, know it now. I fucked up, said the wrong shit, especially about the kid. No excuse, but I've had a lot on my mind, and the raid didn't help. Do you forgive me?"

I took the bait and swiveled around. The second Mace's beautiful face came into view, it stole my breath and caused an involuntary shiver. I could stare into his eyes for all eternity and marvel at the intensity nestled in truth. How could that be? Why would anyone take on such a burden?

"You knew, and you just sat there and let me lie to your face without saying anything?"

His lip curled up into a sexy smirk.

"And what exactly did you lie about, huh? Your name?" He shot me a challenging look.

"Well. Yes and…"

Mace raised one of his eyebrows in expectation as I thought about his question. Was that really the only thing I had lied about? Surely, there was more. It felt like more, a tractor trailer's full load of more. I shook the fog from my head.

"I still don't understand any of this, Mace."

"Let me show you." He stood up, reached out a hand, and waited for me to take it.

What did I have to lose?

"Okay."

We walked together through Masonry Ink while Mace pointed out the locations of the various hidden cameras, sensor strips, and closed-circuit televisions used for facial detection. By the time we reached the office, my mind was blown for the second time as he revealed a hidden compartment under his desk. The room darkened, and every flat surface was filled with computer monitors of all different sizes. I'd been in that office for weeks and would've never known such things existed if not for this moment. To say I was awestruck was an understatement.

"Why would an owner of a tattoo shop need all this high-tech equipment? This is more than just personal security, Mace; this is some *Bourne Identity* shit." I cocked my head to the side.

"You could say that," he preened, clearly proud of his toys.

I turned around in a circle to get a better look. "And that makes you more than just a business owner with a crew of talented artists, doesn't it?"

"Damn right, it does. Impressed?"

"Totally," I responded. "Does that also explain why Dead Man is here when he hasn't been this whole time? I would say he's the muscle of the outfit, but have you seen Jagger?"

"You, of all people, should know who has the biggest muscle, sweetheart, and it's always been a question of size versus skill, for sure." He smirked.

Shit, he has me there.

Something dawned on me at that point. I snapped my fingers with recognition. "The invoices, the strange visitors, the secret meetings, the knife wound…"

He folded his arms over his brawny chest, nostrils flared in anger.

"The average person doesn't always get the benefit of the doubt, True. You saw that today with your own eyes. Our lives, our histories, our skills, all different, with *one* unifying factor. The notion of fairness. Therefore, we are sometimes called upon to give aid to those who are marginalized or made to feel inconsequential simply for being weaker. We help out the best way we know how, the only way when dealing with scum."

"Hmmm." My brows shot to my hairline. "The angry old man?"

"Dickhead landlord wouldn't fix his fucking stove. Nearly starved till someone pointed him in my direction. Cops were no help. It's a civil matter, they told him. He lives alone with no living family to take his back, so we did."

"And now?"

Mace almost looked sheepish before he answered.

Almost.

"Made a pork roast for Sunday dinner, mashed potatoes on the side with fresh cut green beans. Landlord turned out to be flexible when push came to shove. Just needed the right...incentive."

I wondered who did the pushing and the shoving and if there was an open window involved.

"The black woman with the bible?" I wondered.

"Has a grandson. Best damn shooting guard at Remington High School. Kid is going places. Local gang wants him in that life instead, started applying pressure for him to join up. Know the president of that crew, had a few run-ins with them before, so I paid him a visit, cashed in a favor. The kid received his first scholarship offer from Georgetown University, full ride."

I exhaled a breath of relief I hadn't realized I'd been holding. I was invested in the outcome of these stories, the triumph of good over evil, told by a man who had nothing to gain and everything to lose. My heart beat faster, and I hesitated in going there, but I needed to know.

"There was a young boy who came to the shop as well, Mace. What happened to him?"

"No." He shook his head. "He's off limits."

He said no more on the subject.

There were no smiles or inuendoes of violence that led to a

happy ending for the boy. Instead, Mace appeared to wither before my eyes, the weight of the events from the evening finally taking its toll on the hard-as-nails warrior. I pictured the other men and considered their roles, their personalities, their grit, and clear as plate glass, I knew what this was all about. I crossed the room and stepped into his space. His eyes were downcast. I needed to see them. I studied him closely. Up and down, I took in the man before me.

"You couldn't protect us from this...intrusion. You're accustomed to being in control all the time and were made to feel powerless in your own domain." I ventured into his comfort zone, uncertain. He flinched but didn't react.

I continued to scrutinize.

"No, that's not it at all. It's too simple, lacks depth. There must be more. Your anger was directed at me, and rightly so, but to be intentionally cruel when all you've ever shown me, or anyone, is kindness...I wonder..."

I noticed the slight tick of his jaw, his taut shoulders, and rigid posture. I was treading on dangerous ground, but he opened the door by showing me his secrets. If he'd known who I was since the day I arrived, then he must know the rumors about me were false, yet he used them as a shield to push me away. But why?

"Am I safe with you?"

"No," he always replied. *"But...you'll be safe regardless."*

He stared off in no particular direction.

"Some buddies of mine found themselves in a situation where they needed protection for their women. We were supposed to get them out of town for the night, keep them out of harm's way until we received word that it was safe to return to Remington."

Mace personified the label of *white knight* and would've embraced the role of protector to the highest degree. Whatever happened must've caused him great pain, or he wouldn't have bothered to bring it up at this juncture. I paid particular attention as his tone shifted to one of anger and something else I couldn't quite make out.

"One of them, Ashley, played like she needed to use the bathroom, so we pulled over at a rest stop just outside of town. She was special to me, someone I considered as more than a friend, almost like a sister. I let my guard down, and she played me for a bitch, picked the keys from my pocket and hauled their asses right into the fucking lion's den. They could've been killed on my watch! My men could've been killed. I could've lost another person I cared about..."

As his voice trailed off, I put it all together in terms I understood. "Parts of a whole and filled with responsibility, hero to the forgotten ones," I speculated. "It's not about the ones you've helped; it's about the ones you couldn't help, isn't it? Or better yet, a specific someone."

"Don't," he growled. "Stay the fuck in your lane, True."

"Oh, Mace." I reached out a hand and cupped his hard jawline. "You can't save us all. It's a weight of responsibility too heavy to carry despite having shoulders made from tempered stone."

I stood on my tippy-toes and pressed my lips against his firm yet gentle ones. He resisted my attempt at comfort, folding his muscled arms over his chest to create distance between us.

"Last time, I *allowed* you to take from me what you needed, True. Tonight, the way I feel, my men out in the streets doing fuck knows what, barely holding it together, I'm telling you now, woman, call Sal and walk away. You do this, and I'm going to fuck you... *hard*."

I knew he was leaving a lot of stuff out. He'd called me Maya and said I'd died because I didn't think. Who was she to him, and why was he so angry with her? The window of opportunity to find that out had closed. Any illusions I had about home were shattered the second I'd witnessed Mace's vulnerability. It wasn't where you were from or a brick structure with Godawful furnishings inside. Home was where you belonged, and there was no place I'd rather be than right here with him. Mace was my home.

"Come." I held out my hand. "Let me lighten your burden."

He took it and led me upstairs.

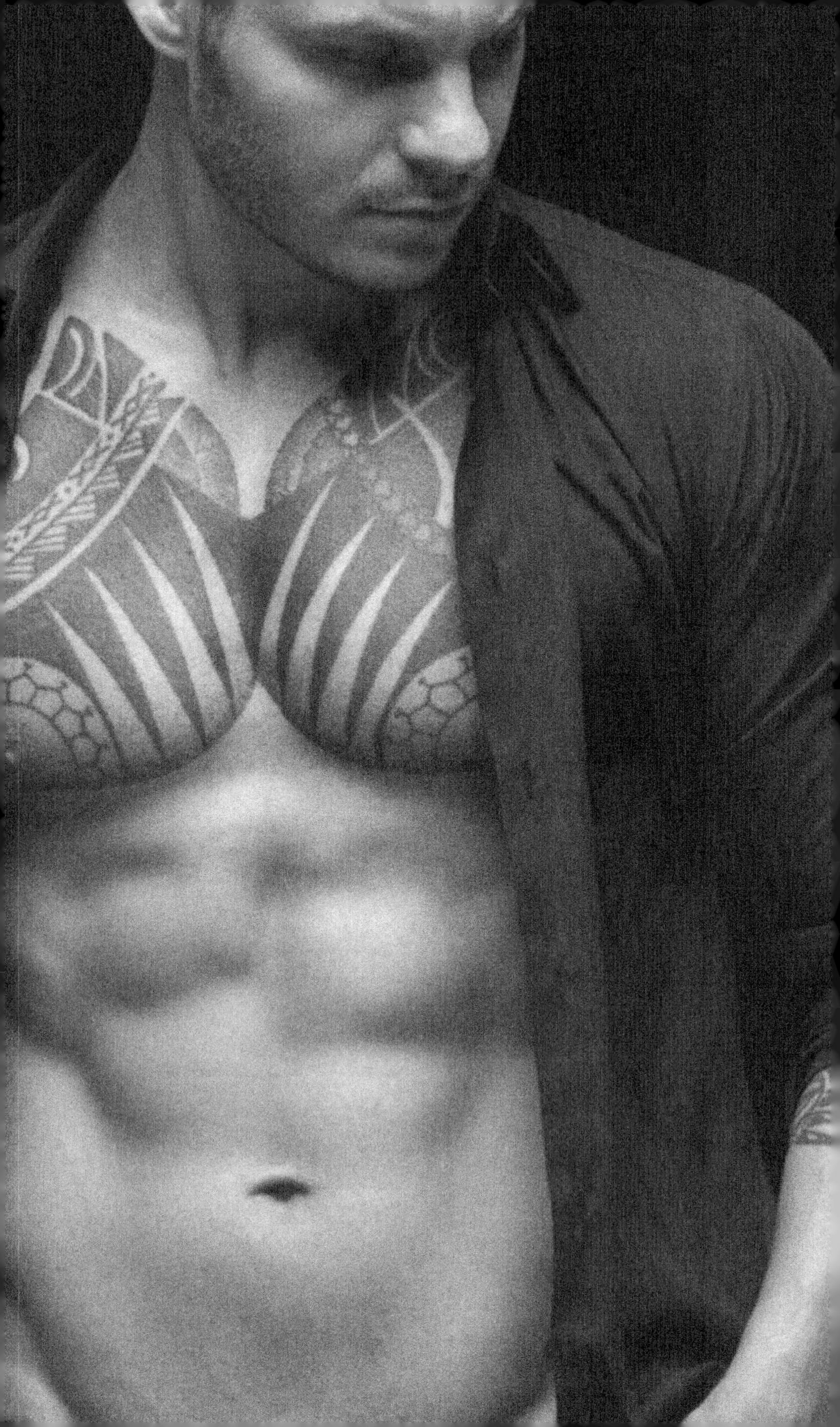

Chapter Thirty-Two

Mace

EVERY SOLDIER THINKS about his own death.

Watching many of his brothers in arms fall to the enemy had a tendency to fuck with one's psyche that way. Once I became a civilian, Maya's murder was the catalyst that sealed my fate, right down to the exact date, time, and location. Confirmation that that cocksucker was being released from prison was the marching orders I'd been waiting for, and now, I was going to die. The moment of truth was liberating in a morbid kind of way; it also put things into perspective. True's pussy would be the last one I'd ever get to sample in this lifespan, and the thought of that thrilled me beyond belief. I couldn't have imagined a better send-off.

I sent a quick text to Sal asking her to pick the kid up from Corrine's. Her mother was going to be too busy stuffing her mouth for the next few hours. Sal's replied thumbs-up emoji had a visceral effect on my cock, sending it into a state of hardness I wasn't prepared to accommodate just yet. We had all night. I followed her to the rear of the shop, up the back steps to my apartment, and into my bedroom. Her gait was steady and sure, like she was the one in control of this situation and I was her simp of a fuckboy husband. I stifled a laugh thinking of all the ways I planned on making her beg for my cock before I gave in to my savage desires and took her the way I needed. She looked around nervously before letting go of my hand, turning around to face me.

"Do you want to…um…get undressed and um…lie down on the bed?" she asked. "You can, you know, and then I can, maybe after, do something to make you feel good."

That time, I did laugh out loud.

I reached out and cupped her cheek. Her breath caught as she gasped.

"Sweet, sweet True. Fucking should always be a marathon, not a sprint. There's nothing else in the world I'd rather do than to watch you get undressed for me." She bit down on her full bottom lip, unsure yet resolved to obey my command.

"Okay, sure, I just need to use the restroom first."

She scampered off to do her business. All the while, I imagined her talking to herself in the mirror, hyping herself up in the reflection. In many ways, she was more like an untouched virgin than a married woman with a child. Our first sexual encounter proved as much. The idea made me want to strangle her husband all over again. What the hell was he doing with her all those years if he wasn't fucking the shit out of her? Thoughts of her previous life had no place here, and I quickly squashed them. It was our night, no one else's.

I took a seat in the corner of my bedroom where I kept a small leather accent chair. I was far enough away from the bed that when she returned, my presence wouldn't spook her more than she already was. The anticipation was making me antsy; we had that much in common, but for vastly different reasons.

Finding a willing body to suit my needs had never been a problem. Hell, I could leave right now and be knee deep inside some pussy before True came out of the bathroom. Deep down, I knew I wanted it to be her. She was kind to a fault, tough when she had to be, yet soft and pliable in all the right places. My perfect match? Maybe. If only I hadn't promised another that I would avenge their death. My principles wouldn't allow me to consider anything else where my sister was concerned. Tonight, I was going to ride her pussy rough, bask in its glory, then prepare for the only guaranteed part of life. *Death.*

I heard the patter of tiny bare feet and steadied my breathing. True stood in the doorway cloaked in darkness, her golden hair shielding her lovely face, completely naked. How the fuck did I get so damn lucky?

"I, um…ditched the clothes," she said shyly. "Don't think I'll be needing them."

I adjusted my hardened cock. Didn't even try to hide it.

"You look beautiful, True, a vision to fucking gaze upon."

I could feel the heat from her blush clear across the room.

"Come to me, baby, slowly," I commanded, my throat tight with lust.

I spread my legs to accommodate the growing girth, sat back, and enjoyed the show. With each step she took in my direction, I removed an article of my own clothing. First step, the shirt, second, socks and boots, third, the pants, and finally, when she was mere inches away, I disposed of my underwear. She tried her best not to look at my dick, but it was pointing right at her. She wanted to appear unaffected, but I could tell she was seconds away from fingering herself.

"You didn't get to see them the other night, but I have a few stretch marks from having the baby," she fretted. "I hope you don't mind."

This woman broke my heart and ignited my baser instincts

all at the same time. Her comment turned me into a snarling, growling barbarian ready to drag my knuckles along the floor. How could she not know how goddamn beautiful she was standing in front of me? Fuck a stretch mark. I stroked my dick a few times and watched as her eyes widened.

"Does it look like we mind?" I smirked.

"It certainly doesn't." She smiled.

I wanted this woman breathless, starved, and begging for my cock instead of beating herself up over trivial bullshit that made me no never mind. There wasn't a man on this earth who would turn down a good piece of pussy because the polish on a woman's toes didn't match the color on her fingernails. Shit was whacked.

She wanted to know how I really felt? I planned on showing her in great detail, so there'd be no mistaking my desire, stretch marks be damned. But first things first.

"May I have your permission to touch you tonight, True? I need to feel all of you."

"God, yes." She exhaled a relaxed breath. "You have my permission, Mace."

"Good, baby, that's good. Now, indulge me by sitting on the edge of the bed and spreading your sexy thighs so I can see your wet pussy."

She turned around, flashed me a wicked smile over her shoulder, and sat demurely on the corner of the mattress. It took her a minute to open her legs, but when she did, I nearly doubled over in hunger. Above her head, the ceiling fan was set to low, which created a light breeze and made her look as if she were in a photoshoot. Her blonde hair whipping around her face, she looked like a celestial being, primed and eager to be fucked.

I stood from the chair, still tugging my cock, and made my way over to her. She licked her lips in anticipation, but she wasn't near ready for me just yet. I got close, not enough to touch but enough for her to feel my body heat and react to it. She moved about the silk sheets, fidgeting, wondering what I was going to do to her. I waited for the visible signs of her arousal. As I circled the front of the bed, I noticed her small hand moving downward towards her engorged clit, ready to relieve some of the pressure.

"I wouldn't do that if I were you," I warned, leaning in towards her mouth. "If you make yourself come, you'll ruin it for my tongue, sweetheart."

She blushed even harder, if that were at all possible.

"Please, Mace, I ache all over," she whined.

"Patience, tough chick. It'll be worth your while, I swear it."

I took my index finger and lightly trailed it along the column of her neck, down her shoulder, then over the swells of her lovely breasts. I heard a gasp, then a sigh, and I knew I had her right where I wanted her. Now all I had to do was fire her up and watch her go off like an old '57 Chevy.

"You look so beautiful sitting there waiting for me to fuck you, I can't decide where to start. Should I bend you over and eat your asshole, or would you prefer I lick your cunt *and* finger your asshole at the same time? Hmmm, decisions, decisions."

She opened her mouth to respond, but I stopped her with a firm twist to her nipple. She moaned shamelessly as she bit down on her bottom lip. It was sexy as fuck to see her react that way to the slightest bit of pain. I leaned in and took one of her puckered nipples in my mouth. True's eyes rolled to the back of her head as I savored her sweet flesh knowing it would be my last. I alternated between each breast, lavishing them both with attention, nipping, biting, enjoying the feel of them in the palms of my hands. We were both panting like feral dogs by the time I reached for her clit and rubbed it firmly between my fingers. She screamed out my name, overcome with lust.

"Ohmygod Mace, so good, keep doing that," she moaned.

"You like that? You like the way I play with your sweet pussy, True? Tell me."

"I can't, going to ...ugh, I'm going to come."

I lightened the pressure on the bundle of nerves, enough to send her over the edge but not enough to render her useless for the next few hours. I needed her alert, invigorated, and her pussy weary but not worn out when the time came to take my cock. As soon as her orgasm hit, I was on her. I dropped to my knees on the carpeted floor, gripped her thighs, and with a tug, I shimmied her waist to the edge of the bed. Perfect. Right where I wanted her.

I dove in headfirst. My tongue lapped at the bitter cream leaking from her hole till it was all gone. I alternated between flicking the tip of my tongue and flattening it over the bud. Before long, we'd created a rhythm. Her hips moved in a circle as she chased her pleasure, her ass no longer on the mattress but in the air. My lips latched on to her swollen clit. My assault felt relentless. I was determined to make her scream so loud that the neighborhood would know my name. I took her to the brink, backed off, then straight to the edge again without mercy until her knees squeezed my ears like a vice. I knew she was close, but selfishly, I wanted her to come on my cock, not in my mouth. I pulled back, releasing her clit with a pop.

"Ohmigod, Mace, I was so close. You're driving me insane," she mewed.

"Prepare, woman, the best is yet to come," I told her.

"Hurry, please, I think I might die if you don't fuck me."

The nightstand where I kept my stash of rubbers was open, so I grabbed one, suited up, and returned to her trembling thighs. She'd offered to ease the load I carried, and she was about to get her wish, starting with the contents of my ball sack when I shot deep.

True hooked her feet around my ass, drawing me in as I leaned over, inches from her face. Our eyes made promises we wouldn't dare say out loud for fear of revealing too much. I slid into her folds relishing the warmth of her wet heat. The pleasure sent a shock wave through my asshole all the way up to the top of my head.

"Your pussy feels amazing, True. Need to take you hard, baby." I peppered kisses along the column of her neck, clasped her hands in mine, and raised them over her head, anchoring her in place. I was balls deep and loved the way her titties bounced up and down with each stroke.

"I'm so close already, Mace. All that teasing was too much," she whimpered.

"Wait for me, True. Don't you dare come yet." I backed off a little, giving her a chance to catch her breath. I rotated my hips in a circular motion until she was right there with me, swirling as one attached unit in the throngs of passion.

"So fucking good, Mace. I'm not going to last long," she warned.

"Then take all of my cock, baby, take it all." I surged back inside to the root, deeper, harder.

"Yes!" she yelled, and that spurred me on even more.

"You like that dick, don't you, baby. You like that shit. You love the way I fuck, don't you?"

"So good, don't stop."

It wasn't long before she was raking her fingernails down my back, chanting in tongues for more, until her back lurched off the bed and she came with a scream. True felt like heaven beneath me, and when I shot off, I shot hard. My teeth sank into the meat of her neck that would surely leave a mark. I collapsed on top of her sweat-soaked chest. My head found the perfect nook between her breasts. Her heartbeat was steady and reassuring, along with her sighs of contentment. Tentative fingers massaged my scalp, damn near putting me to sleep, but I wasn't near done with her yet. It felt amazingly comforting and rueful at the same time, knowing that before long, she'd be mourning my death with the rest of my crew.

Over the next few hours, True fulfilled her promise to ease my suffering again and again. I never suspected that being with her would change the path I was set upon nine years ago. Choosing would take all my courage, but there was one more thing I needed to ask of her.

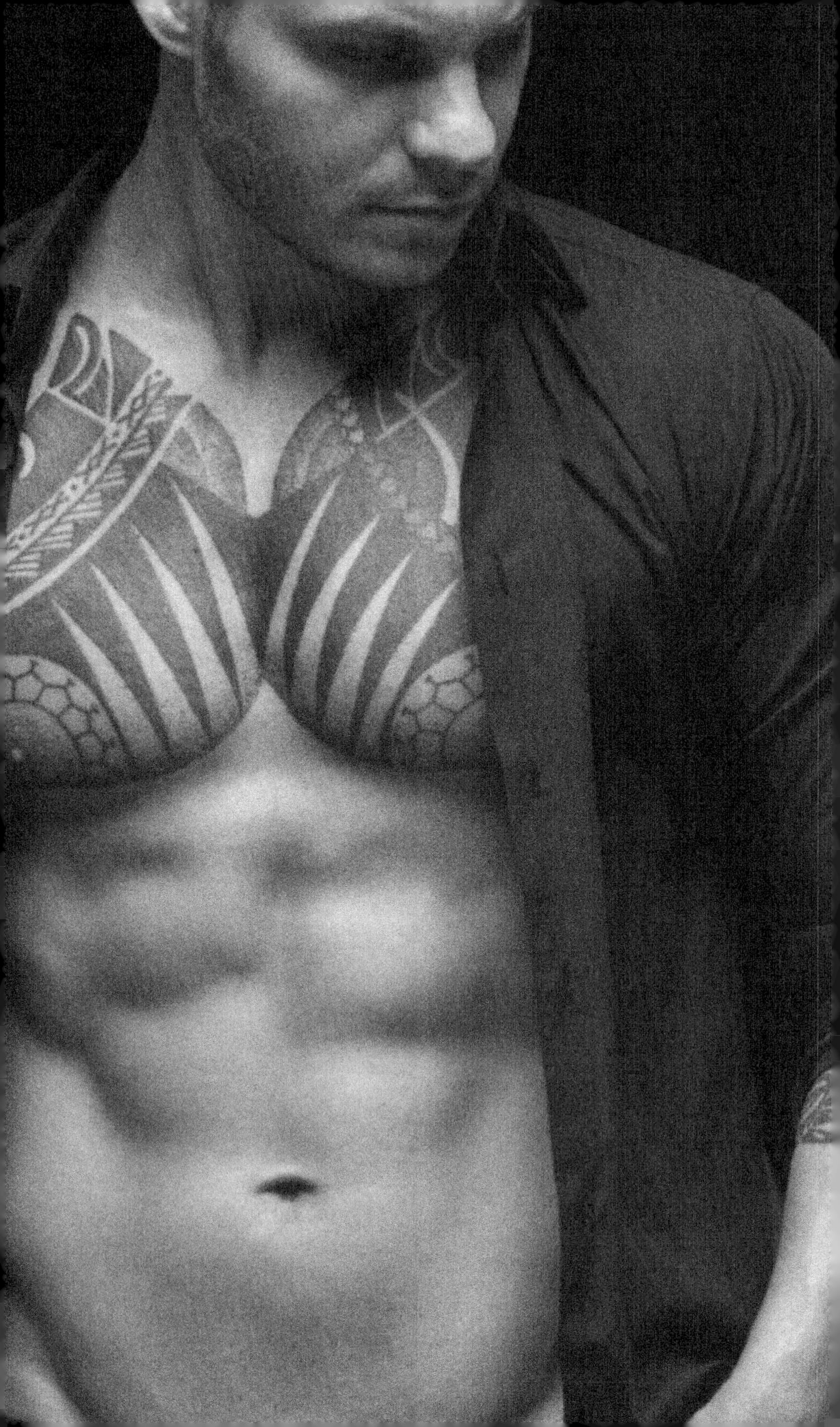

Chapter Thirty-Three

True

The ride out of town was unexpected.

Awkward, uncomfortable, and mostly silent except for Kayla's cooing that filled the cab from the back seat. Mace sat stoically behind the wheel deep in his own head, where no one could reach him, an occasional sigh the only recognition that he was aware of his surroundings. I still wasn't quite sure why he'd invited us along on this trip but decided it was in my best interest not to read too much into it. Sal thought it was a step in the right direction or some sort of a cosmic intervention when I told her about our plans. I conveniently left out the evening's little fuck-fest or how the request came out of the blue once it was over. Sal liked to play the tough street girl act, but deep down, she believed in romance, soul mates, and all that other bullshit. I allowed her fantastical rants of Mace and me someday living in wedded bliss as the king and queen of the tattoo world. Who was I to break her little dreamer girl heart?

Our night of unbridled passion was too fresh, both mentally and physically, to think of such foolishness. The bruises on my wrists, neck, and shoulders proved that. I'd be lying if I said I wasn't filled with joy at the prospect of them sticking around a while longer. It felt like a brand, a claim, from the mightiest hero on the planet, and let's be real, who wouldn't want to belong to a man like Mace Fox?

I felt that unmistakable tingle of arousal between my legs every time I glanced his way. So many things needed to be said, but to what end? In the eyes of the law, I was still a married woman, and Mace was pretty clear about his stance on women and relationships. Just as well, I suppose. I was falling hard for this man, but the woman he thought he knew, that real tough chick? She wasn't nearly as impressive as he made her out to be.

We came to a full stop in front of a lovely colonial-style home with a fenced-in yard that looked straight out of a magazine. The view took my breath away, along with a vision of a young Mace running around playing cops and robbers on the beautiful lawn. I undid my safety belt and stepped out of the car. At the same time, the front door flew open revealing a middle-aged woman with a huge smile on her face. She was absolutely stunning in her mom jeans, plain purple T-shirt, and comfortable Vans sneakers. Not too tall or too short, she was just right, and the spitting image of her handsome son. I self-consciously did that thing where you feel around your head for fly-aways, your lips for cookie crumbs, and your breath in case you needed a mint. She bounced down the walkway with her arms wide open heading straight for me.

"Welcome, it's so nice to finally meet you." She hugged me close as only a real mom could. Fucking hell, she even smelt like a real mom, all warm baked bread and flowers. I could've died in her arms and been completely happy about it.

"Ma, True, True, Ma!" Mace shouted by way of introductions.

"Hello, Mrs. Fox…"

"Oh, please, call me Belinda." She took a step back still

holding me by the arms, giving me the once-over. "Angelica was right. You are a pretty little thing."

I blushed clear down to my toes at her compliment.

"Thank you, Belinda."

"Hey, son!" she yelled, waving excitedly.

"Beautiful mother of mine, you look great," Mace greeted his mother while he leaned into the back seat of the truck, grabbing the car seat.

He didn't seem the least bit surprised by his mother's behavior towards a complete stranger, so I took that as a good sign. I went to try and grab Kayla from him, but Belinda led me in the opposite direction.

"Don't worry about them. Come inside," she spoke. "He'll bring her in when he's ready, and it will give us some time to get to know one another a little better."

"Um...sure."

One quick peek behind me, and I saw that Mace indeed had it covered. Belinda looped her arm through mine and led us both inside. The second I hit the doorway, I felt overwhelmed to the point of tears. Photographs graced the walls everywhere, some old, some newer, each one more special than the last. This was what it meant to be a family, to have a home, and to be loved by those you held dearest. They began to blur and blend together through my misty eyes, so I breathed through my nose in hopes of calming my shit.

"I've got fresh coffee made in the kitchen, True. Angelica should be down shortly." She nudged me gently. "Come, it's just this way."

If she noticed my little freak-out, she never mentioned it, thank goodness. First impressions and all that. The kitchen was ginormous, just like the rest of the house, with modern appliances, a built-in island, and a huge bay window overlooking an expanse of yard with colorful flowers. Belinda offered me a seat, and I gladly accepted her hospitality.

"You have a beautiful home, Belinda," I said to her back as she prepared the coffee.

"Why, thank you, dear. Mace's father dabbled in carpentry when he wasn't being a big pain in my ass. He built that island the year before..."

Her hand went to her mouth. She leaned over the sink and suddenly stopped speaking. I wondered, and not for the first time, what the hell was taking Mace so long to come inside with Kayla. When her shoulders started to shake, I became concerned and approached her with caution.

"Belinda?" I reached for her hand.

She turned with unshed tears in her eyes. "He used to do that with his little sister, Maya...I'd nearly forgotten about that. The years have stolen my memories."

I followed her line of sight through the glass window into the backyard and froze. Mace was sitting on a swing set with Kayla in his arms while his long legs glided them gently into the breeze. I dissolved into a pile of goo watching my baby girl soak in all the love and affection from the only man she'd ever known. Something Belinda said struck me then, and I gasped. *Maya.* I knew that name. Mace called me that during our argument.

"Mace has a sister?" I asked.

She stood to her full height and steeled her shoulders.

"Not anymore." She exhaled a long cleansing breath. "She was taken from us all in the most tragic of ways. She was our center of gravity, True, and when she was stolen from us, we all seemed to topple over, especially her big brother."

"I'm so sorry, Belinda. I didn't know." My gaze shifted downward.

"Mace never told you?" she asked.

"No, he never did," I whispered back.

Our conversation was cut short by footsteps as they

approached from somewhere behind us. I heard a sharp inhale followed by a concerned screech.

"Momma?" Angelica approached. "What's going on?"

She looked between the two of us, with our misty eyes and grim expressions.

"You bitch!" she yelled while hurrying over to Belinda's side. "What the fuck have you done to her?" I was taken aback by her accusation as her harsh words caused a grimace to appear on my face. Belinda stepped in before I got the chance to defend myself.

"I know the daughter I raised did not just curse in my house," she reprimanded.

"But, Momma, she…"

"No, ma'am, apologize right this instant, Angelica. You're not too old for me to go outside and grab a switch," she demanded with her hands on her hips.

"I'm sorry, Momma."

"Not to me, young lady, to our guest," she chastised firmly.

She huffed and puffed like an adolescent child before finally giving in. "Sorry, True."

"No worries," I replied. "I'm going to go outside and check on the baby."

I left the two women in the kitchen and walked out the sliding backdoor into the yard. The closer I got to the swing set, the more my ears perked up. I noticed that Mace was actually singing to my sleeping baby over his shoulder. My stomach did that galloping horse thing 'cause holy shit! Was there anything sexier than a tattooed badass holding a baby while singing? I committed the scene to my memory bank for later, sat down next to them on the empty curve of plastic, and held on tightly to the chains.

"I think your baritone voice must've put her to sleep, Mace. Want me to take her?" I asked.

"Nah." He sighed. "She smells good, like fresh laundry and sunshine. I miss that smell."

I stuck out my legs in front of me and let gravity take its course. It was so peaceful out there, the light breeze, the smell of flowers, the melodic chirping of the playful birds. I wished I could say that being out here brought back memories from my childhood that involved my mother taking me to play in the park after a lovely picnic lunch. That would've required her to act like she gave a shit, which clearly, she never did. Her only orders were to keep quiet while she entertained her *friend,* or else. You need a license to own a pet. I would argue that the same should apply for having a child.

My swinging slowed to a stop as I observed man and baby.

"Your mother is a lovely woman, Mace. You definitely lucked out in that department."

"She's the best *everything* and more than I deserve." He smiled proudly.

"I didn't realize that she and Angelica were so close," I asked, hesitantly.

"Raised her from the time she was eleven," he replied. "She's the only mother she knows."

That certainly explained why she and Mace were so tight, their bond reminiscent of brother and sister. Yet there was another, one he never spoke about even after our intimacies. I started to feel some type of way that he never confided in me. It was wrong to assume we had that type of relationship. Sure, we fucked, but I thought we were also friends. *Don't be a hypocrite, True. You're also keeping secrets.*

Still, I wanted to express my condolences without sounding like a spurned lover.

I looked over at the second swing. "I'm sorry for your loss, Mace."

He stiffened, which caused Kayla to stir in her sleep before he settled her with a few pats to her bottom. After a few minutes, he still hadn't replied, so I kept going.

"How did she die?" I asked, my voice growing small.

"We should probably get this little one inside." He stood up still holding the baby.

I was incensed.

He completely ignored my question.

"Why did you ask us to come here with you, Mace? You had to know that I would find out about your sister's death. If you planned on keeping it a secret, perhaps you should've come alone and saved yourself the trouble."

"Not a secret, True, just something I don't like to talk about...with anyone," he hissed.

I could understand that...and yet.

"That doesn't explain why you asked us here, Mace, or why you never told me about her. Is she the real reason why you blew a gasket after the FBI raid? Was she the person you lost and why you called me by her name? Talk to me, please."

I heard him expel a long-suffering breath before turning to face me. His posture was stiff, but there was a pleading in his gaze, something that screamed remorse or regret; I couldn't tell which. Sorrow engulfed me, so much so, I reached out and touched his hand, willing him to trust me. My heart shattered when he pulled away.

"My mother deserves to see this in her lifetime, True. I owe her that much."

"See what, Mace?" My brows pinched in confusion.

"Me, happy, with a child I've grown to care about, a woman like you who'd make any man proud to call her his wife. She'll never have this...fitting ending. There isn't enough time. I asked you here because you are the only woman that's ever come close to claiming that part of me. Please, let me have this...for her."

Belinda looked perfectly healthy to me, but I could've been wrong.

"If your mom is sick, I can understand..."

"She's not sick, True, just...please, I'm asking. No more questions. Either you're with me, or I'll walk back in there, tell her we can't stay, and drive our asses back to Remington. It's important to me that I do this now while there's still..." His words trailed off, and his gaze became unfocused.

I held my breath. "Are *you* sick, Mace?"

"No, True, I'm not sick," he stated plainly.

"But you're not telling me everything I need to know."

"Well...neither have you." He cut his eyes knowingly.

And there it is...Checkmate.

How could I deny him such a simple request even though it didn't make a lick of sense? Mace was a sexually competent, successful, charming, and protective man. He could have any woman he wanted if marriage was his goal. Pretending that he was mine was the easiest thing in the world. I already thought of him as such, but what would happen to me when the show was over? Would I be able to give him back?

"I'll do it, Mace, for you. I owe you that much and more."

He exhaled a sigh of relief, stepped into my space, and embraced me so firmly I felt like crying. If I had my wish, we would've stayed like that forever, the three of us. A family.

My chest ached for the fantasy to become a reality. *If only...*

"Thank you, True," he said quietly while planting a kiss on the top of my head. "And for the record...last night was more than just a fuck. It meant more to me than you'll ever know."

Right back atcha, buddy.

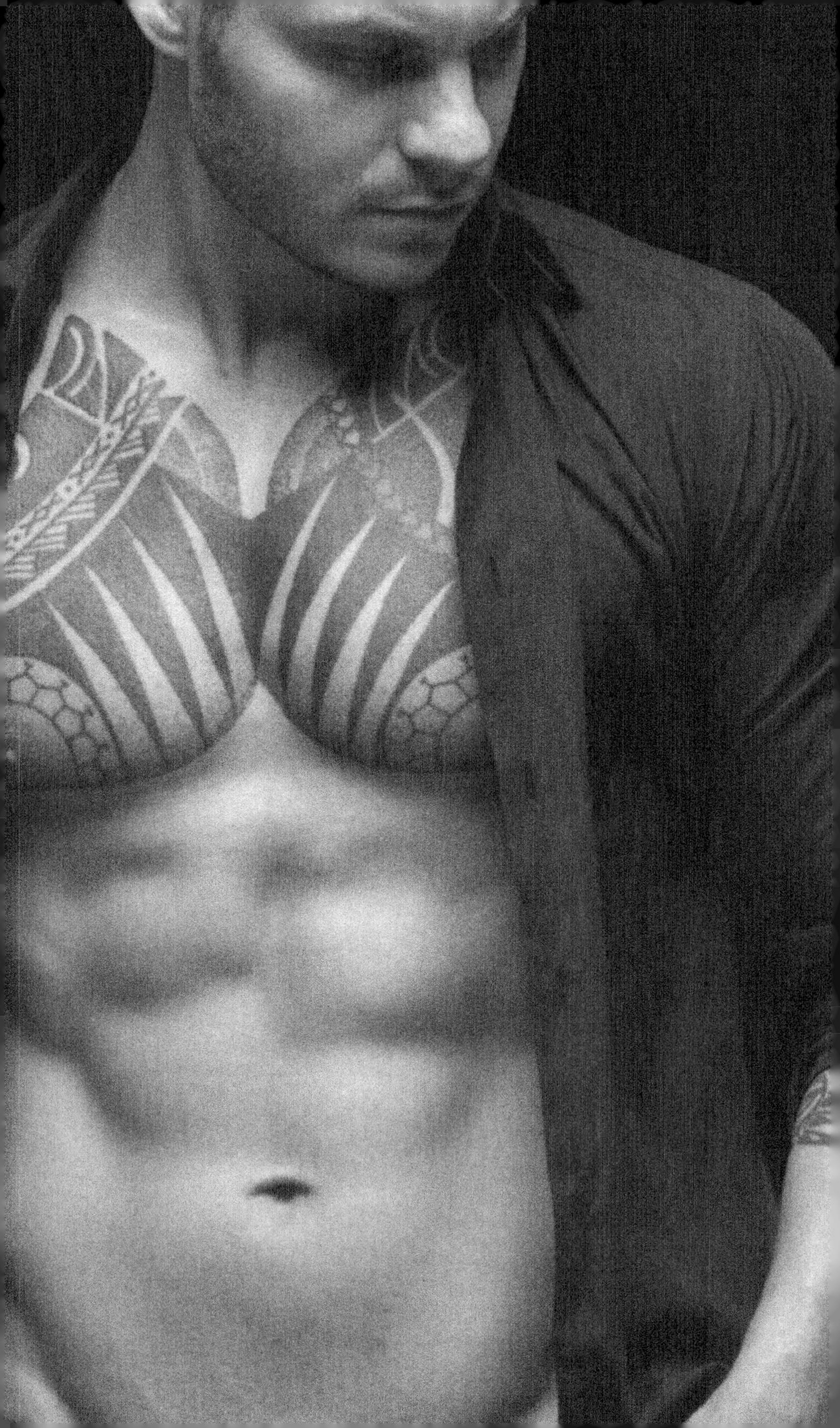

Chapter Thirty-Four

Mace

My Glock sat freshly cleaned on the passenger seat beside me. Loaded with fifteen rounds in the clip and one in the chamber, I aimed to use them all before anyone would notice. Two hours to the prison in time for processing set my arrival right before daybreak. The road ahead was lonely, filled with regret, second thoughts, and what ifs, but I steadied my resolve and kept pushing forward. I was prepared to wait all day if need be. As long as I was stationed at the gate to intercept that rancid cunt when he took his first steps into freedom. Before I pulled the trigger, he'd know my name and that I was sent by my sister to avenge her death. Thinking about it bought a smile to my face, and I felt my dick harden with exhilaration.

I stared out the window at the passing scenery, looking yet not *seeing* a damn thing. My mind was in a contest of strength thanks to a tough chick and her tiny baby girl who'd stormed into my life and made me question the bitter conflict of having a future. Sacrificing myself over a vow made nine years prior wasn't an easy thing to explain unless you had been there to witness the pain firsthand. She'd tried her best, but I wouldn't be swayed, no matter how much I wished things could be different. I hadn't factored in a means of escape, so the tower snipers should have a clear line of sight once he was lying on the ground covered in his own blood. With luck, they'd aim for my head. One shot, one kill. Clean and easy. My stomach muscles tightened when I heard that familiar whisper in my ear, only this time, it wasn't Maya's pleading for me to save her that assaulted my senses; it was True's voice as she begged me to reconsider.

She looked so beautifully sad when I dropped her back at Sal's after we returned to Remington. We held hands the entire way, never saying a word, simply touching one another to keep us both anchored against the inevitable. One small wave and a lone tear from her baby blues were the extent of our goodbye. We'd said all that needed to be said the night before, using our anatomy to convey our feelings. Watching her slip away carrying the kid nearly broke me. I wanted them both in my arms where they belonged, where they were safe, but my wants and needs were put on the back burner long ago. For better or for worse, I had to see it through.

It seemed my selfish behavior was limitless as long as I ascribed it to a piece of my revenge plan, last days on earth and all that. It wasn't my intention to bring them along with me to my childhood home. That little lightbulb moment came courtesy of a long night of sticking my dick inside her sweet pussy and my reluctance to let her go. I'd meant it when I told her that she was the only woman who'd ever gotten close. She fit me. Her gorgeous smile, her laughter, and her tender heart. She deserved to have candlelit dinners, long walks on the beach, and a strong man who stood by her side through anything. Most of all, she deserved the home she so desperately wanted, so in a way, our visit gave her a taste of what she'd been missing and a glimpse into the brilliant future I'd never have.

You could give her that, Mace. Just turn around.

My father told me once that when a man died, he carried his fondest memories on the journey to the pearly gates of heaven. The last few days I spent visiting with my mom, reminiscing about the good old days, laughing and joking, were filled with such mementos.

My mother transformed into grandma mode so easily, as if it were the most natural thing in the world. She laughed with her full belly while she played for hours on the living room floor with baby Kayla, completely taking over. She conversed with True as if she'd known her for years and not just a few hours. The two babbled on and on about breast feeding, the trials and tribulations of potty training, and of course, our potential for marriage once I was ready to settle down. True, to her credit, did what I asked and left things vague, but I could tell the rouse made her uncomfortable as hell. The longer it went on, the more I realized that the subterfuge wasn't only for my mother's sake; it was for mine as well. I felt like a proud husband, a doting father, and a loving son, all while wearing a fake-ass smile on my face to mask the grief.

The biggest surprise was Angelica's change in mood after she was forced to hold the kid for the first time. Prior to that, she'd been snarky towards True, deliberately short, and a raging bitch when she thought no one was looking. That went on until Kayla started to cry and my mother handed her off to the little brat to make a bottle. One toothless smile later, and she was hooked faster than a bass could swim upstream. I could've died happy watching her play peek-a-boo, make kissy sounds, and sneaking whiffs of that intoxicating baby smell, if it were not for the anguish that ensued.

I'd long ago come to terms with my role as big brother slash observer where Angelica was concerned. She'd been in love with Jagger since the first day they met, age difference be damned. It saddened me knowing that she'd never open herself up enough to accept physical love from any man and that she thought herself doomed to be alone forever because of it. My protective instincts weren't happy about that; they thought I should swoop in, fuck some shit up, and force Angelica to get over her past and commit to living her life to the fullest. My rational side knew it wasn't my place. *She* had to be the one to put an end to the horrors of her earlier years. I wouldn't be around to finally see her soar, but I had to believe she'd make it through. *She had to.*

By the second day of pretending, True was done with the fuck shit. She barely spoke except to say yes or no when asked a question. I played it off to my mother as fatigue, but she had to know I was full of shit. The change was that drastic, and I was less than passionate with the lie. Things had gone quiet once Momma, Angelica, and Kayla turned in for the night. True and I were both too anxious and somehow found ourselves back out on the swing set, the day having taken its toll. The mood between us was stifling, and I could tell she was trying her best to reel in her emotions, but like any simmering pot, it's bound to boil over at some point.

"Belinda is a kind and caring woman," she hissed under her breath. "Too bad she raised a heartless bastard for a son. How can you continue to deceive her like this?"

"It's what she asked for, True. Don't speak on things you know nothing about." My temper sparked.

"Then tell me, Mace, for Christ sakes, tell me something because *this*, whatever it is you're doing, is cruel, and I can't be a part of it anymore. I feel like shit for lying to that woman, and damnit, I deserve an answer."

She jumped from her swing and stormed towards the house.

I froze her in place with the truth.

"My little sister was murdered by her high school boyfriend when she was seventeen, True, and when that motherfucker is released from prison, I'm going to kill him. Don't give two fucks who's around or getting my ass clapped in the process. That fucker is dead."

Her stride faltered as she slowly turned to face me again, eyebrows furrowed.

"Ohmygod, Mace, I'm so sorry. I didn't know." She sighed. "I can't imagine what it feels like to lose a child, especially in that way. If anything were to happen to Kayla, I'd... Wait, you said you were going to kill him? When? How?"

"Two days from now, and you're the only one I've told. My crew will be pissed, but they'll be safe, which is the only thing that matters. I've left a letter explaining to them the shit that's going down. Should be delivered certified the morning of that fuckhead's release."

"But...but..." she sputtered.

My eyes narrowed. "NO! You wanted to know. Now you do. Don't need you telling me how killing is wrong in the eyes of the law. This is God's law! An eye for a fucking eye. End of."

"Jesus, poor Belinda...and you, Mace, I don't know what to say."

She reached out for something to hold on to before her ass hit the ground with a thud. I started towards her without thinking despite the fact that she tried to wave me off. She looked to the sky for help, the color drained from her face. I squatted down to eye level against the thick grass and braced for the disdain that was sure to follow, the threats to turn me in to the cops, maybe even regret for allowing me to fuck her. What came instead were tears of understanding mixed with a look of complete devastation.

"You bought us here so you could say goodbye to them, didn't you, Mace? You've already got it in your mind that you're never coming back. Shit, the other night was a deathbed fuck. How could I not have felt it? The tenderness in your movements was so..."

She turned her face away, blushing.

"You've made the last few weeks...some of the happiest of

my life, True. I'll treasure them long after this thing is over. You certainly are one of my biggest regrets."

She threw her arms around my neck and hugged me with all her strength. Her face buried in my neck, and I felt the wetness coming from her tears. We held on, neither one of us ready to face the reality that these were a few of our last moments together.

"I'm not going to try and convince you to change your mind, Mace. I know the type of man you are, and this *pursuit* somehow all makes sense to me now. The way you are with the other guys, Angelica, the strangers you choose to help. You're a stubborn bastard, Mace Fox. Once you set your mind to something, the rest of us are screwed. It was how you persuaded me to stay in Remington, by not taking no for an answer. I just..."

"You just what?"

She pushed away and stared into my eyes. "If we had more time, there are so many things I wanted to share with you, so many hopes and dreams. Would you have listened to them?"

This woman was breaking my heart.

I cupped her cheek in my hand, rubbing my thumb along her bottom lip.

"Every damn day of my life, but it's not too late, True. Tell me now."

For the next hour, we sat face to face on the cool grass and shot the shit about everything and nothing. I learned so many small details about her life in Montana. She, in turn, laughed at most of mine. We touched often and with purpose—a stray hair, a phantom piece of lint, skin on skin until my fingers ached for more. When we could barely hold our eyes open, I took her to the quietest most remote place in the house so I could be alone with her for one more night.

The last night of my life.

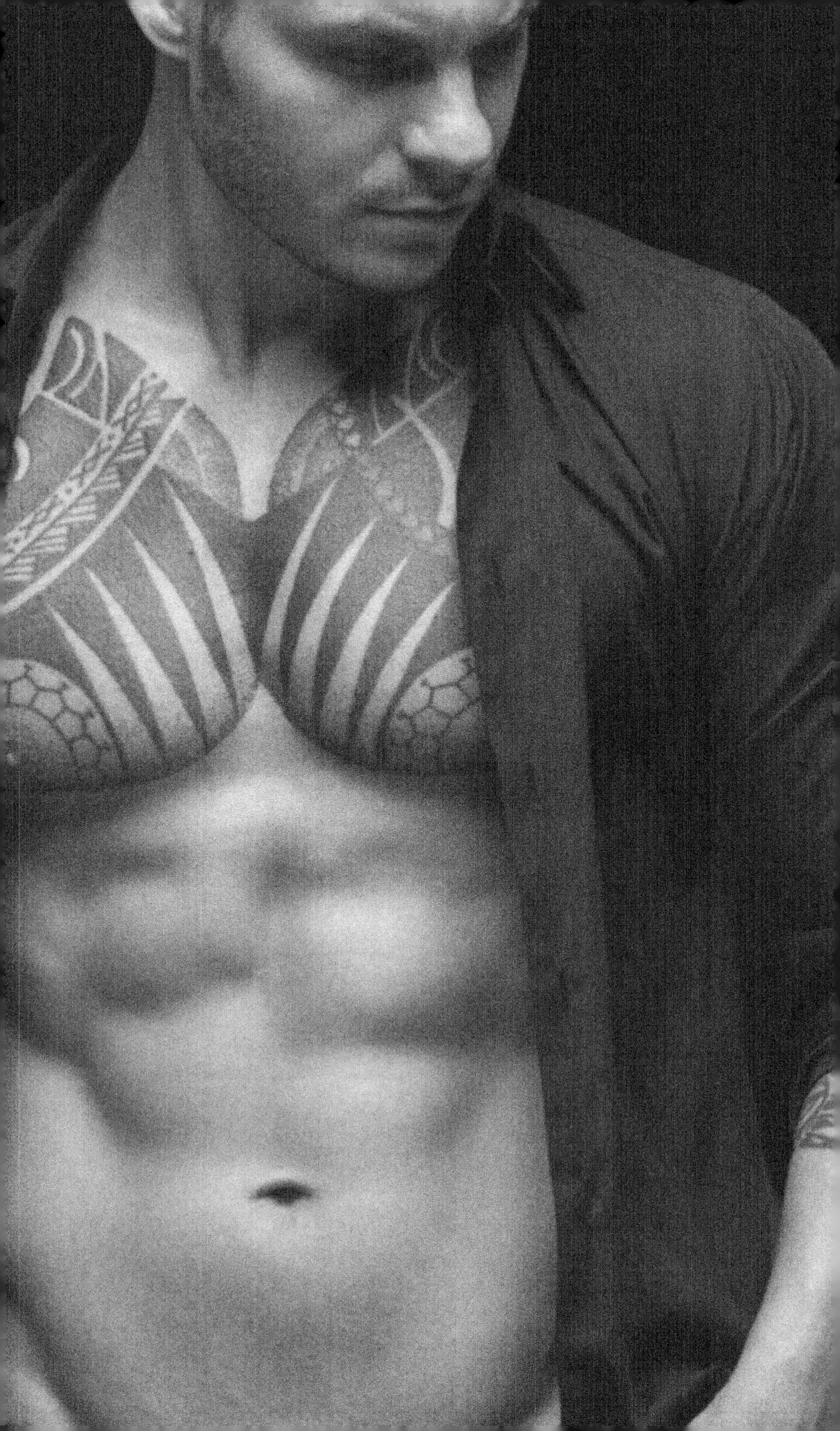

Chapter Thirty-Five

True

"What is this room, Mace?" I asked, turning in a circle to take it all in.

The walls were lined with woodworking tools, chisels of various sizes, handsaws, and mallets. I could see where Mace got his penchant for organization. Everything was so neat, it hardly looked used.

"My father's work area slash mancave. It's nearly soundproof with noise-cancelling insulation 'cause my mother complained about the ruckus, lucky for you." He smirked.

"Yeah, lucky for *us*," I replied.

The fatigue I felt lying out on the grass disappeared the moment I laid eyes on the king-sized bed perched in the corner. I knew how we ended up here, alone, ready to rip each other to shreds. It was the touching, the intimacy, and the grief of knowing how things were destined to end. The thought of never seeing him again, hearing his voice, or feeling his presence when he walked into a room shattered my heart into a million tiny pieces. He might have been willing to give up the fight, but I wasn't. I had to make him see that there was another way, another choice to be made. All he had to do was reach for it.

I spoke through the painful feeling in my chest. "Have you considered what will happen to the crew at Masonry Ink? It's no secret that they think of you as their leader, Mace. They'll be lost without you."

He visibly flinched before recovering quickly.

"Made arrangements to have the shop turned over to Kaden. He'll be in charge going forward. The rest of my assets will be divided up amongst the rest of the crew with a large stipend set aside for my mother's care if or when she might need it."

"So, that's it, then? You've got all your bases covered."

"I told you I did. This didn't happen yesterday, True. It's been in the works for years."

"I see that now." I licked my dry lips, grief-stricken.

Mace was like a brick wall, solid in his belief, immobile. If he wouldn't change his mind for the people he loved more than anything, I didn't stand a chance in hell of getting him to back down. I surrendered to the misery. My shoulders slumped in defeat, and I started to feel lightheaded. He stood off to the side, watching me wearily. His eyes told the story of a man barely hanging on. He could have chosen anyone to spend this night with, yet here I was, giving him shit when I should've been trying to comfort him. I walked over to him, slowly and with a purpose. I needed him to feel my next words as I said them.

"And what about me, Mace? What should *I* do without you?" I whispered. His nostrils flared at my closeness. I reached down, took his hand, and placed it over my heart. It beat so wildly I was sure he felt it.

"Kaden will protect you, True, get you away from that cunt you call a husband. Once he's out of the picture, I'm sure he wouldn't mind if you stuck around the shop, kept working."

He wasn't getting me.

I had to try harder.

"What if I don't want him to protect me?" My lips were a hairsbreadth away from his. "He's not my home, Mace. You are. What if... I only want you?"

He answered by attacking my mouth with his own. I wrapped my arms around his neck and went along for the ride. I didn't shy away from his touch; instead, I sought it out with vigor. Our tongues danced to their own rhythm, slow at first, then firmer, more ravenous. We nipped and sucked through the exchange of spit, mauling each other's faces like desperate teenagers. I couldn't get close enough, which frustrated the hell out of me. I was reminded of the night I told him that I wanted to rip open his chest and live in it for a time. Heat rose from my belly, singed the peaks of my nipples, then descended back down until it lit up my pussy from lips to hole. I broke away panting as if I'd run a marathon. I needed to feel him inside me, or I might literally die from longing.

I took a step back and looked upon his beautifully flushed face and closed my eyes. I'd remember him just as he was tonight—hungry, virile, and masculine. He was my hero and deserved a hero's farewell. Over the next few minutes, we acted out of instinct and without the exchange of words. I removed my shirt. He, in turn, removed his. The rest of our clothing soon followed until we stood naked, inches from one another, waiting. I was the one who finally broke the silence.

"I won't ask for the impossible, Mace. It's too late for that. If I were faced with the same set of circumstances..." I shook my head, refusing to even think about it. "The most remarkable word in the English language to me isn't love; it's *home*. If this is to be our last night together, then I beg you, Mace, choose home."

His eyes flashed with hunger.

We came together like a magnetic force, having met somewhere in the middle. I reached for the back of his neck and drew his lips to mine. I sucked on his tongue as if it were a lollipop, causing us both to groan in unison. The feel of my naked breasts rubbing against his chest hair ignited a passion deep within my soul that would only ever be quenched by the man in my arms. I wanted to do filthy shit to him so he'd remember me in the afterlife and visit me in my dreams. I'd never been a believer of witchcraft, but for him, I'd certainly give it a try.

"I'm going to fuck you so hard, True, that you'll be ruined for any man who follows." He moaned against my ear right before I felt a sharp bite to the tendon on my shoulder. I screamed out. My legs nearly gave way it was that intense.

"I'm already there, Mace. Gone for you," I whimpered.

I hiked my leg around his hip as he leaned into me, kissing down the column of my neck until he latched on to one of nipples. I thanked the Lord above that the room was relatively soundproof on account of the noises coming from my mouth. I could smell my arousal as it perfumed the air around us. I might've been embarrassed if it weren't for the stream of wetness I felt on my inner thigh, courtesy of Mace's pre-cum dripping down my leg. He was just as turned on as I was, if not more. With great effort, I maneuvered us over to the edge of the bed and gave him a purposeful shove. He landed on his ass and scooted over to the middle with a smirk, not knowing that my next move would wipe it clear off his face. I lay on top of him, belly to belly, and slid downward between the tree trunks he called legs.

My lips attached themselves to that lovely V along his hips before he could blink, but I didn't stop there. My tongue had its own ideas, licking down towards his hard cock. He tasted like sin and power all wrapped up into one delicious morsel. His hips bucked when I blew a warm breath against his cockhead. He expected to feel my mouth, but not yet.

"The fuck, True. Are you going to suck my cock or tease it all night?" He groaned, trying his damnedest to shove it in my face.

"Patience is a virtue, Mace. Haven't you ever heard that before?" I teased.

"Not right now, it's not," he complained.

I couldn't help the smile that spread across my face. The idea that I was driving a man crazy with my sexual skill was surreal. Not too long ago, I would've been curled up in a protective ball at the very thought of being intimate. Tonight, all I wanted to do was let go and lose myself to the point of depravity.

"Lift your knees to your chest, Mace, and hold them there," I ordered.

"What are you..."

He didn't raise them all the way, but it was enough for my face to fit between his ass cheeks. I sat back on my hunches, spat towards the target, lengthened my tongue, and licked along the seam of his crack, stopping only to circle the rim of his forbidden hole. He moaned long and deep from the back of his throat, and only then did he raise his knees all the way to his chest. That was my cue to let the freak out and go to town. I licked his ass with abandon, using the peak of my tongue to penetrate his puckered entrance, slipping it inside as far as it would go. I rubbed my hands along the backs of his thighs while I swirled my tongue around his opening. It wasn't enough to simply hear him moan; I wanted to hear him scream with rabid hunger. Time stopped as bursts of light flashed behind my eyelids, egging me on. Since his ball sack was lying on my forehead, I concluded that it needed some attention also. I abandoned his rear, sucked them into my mouth, hollowing it out, and gurgled deep in the back of my throat to create a vibration. The groan that followed was exactly what I wanted to hear. I could've pleasured him all night and not given that first fuck about my own release. Mace was far more generous in his way of thinking. To my delight, he twisted his hips, reached down, and picked me up as if I weighed nothing. I yelped in surprise as

I was dangled in the air like a Thanksgiving turkey right before it's submerged in hot oil and deep fried.

"Mace...what the fu..."

"Good work, tough chick. Now, it's my turn," he taunted.

I was lowered down to the warmest set of lips I'd ever felt. He kissed my pussy with a loud smack and went to work. Mace was better skilled with his tongue than I was, so it took him less than a minute to snatch my soul and send me over the edge into a screaming orgasm. My legs shook so badly, it was hard to catch my breath. I thought I was having a seizure he was just that good. He pretty much threw me down onto the mattress so I could recover as he reached for his pants to retrieve a condom. I stole glances at his glorious nakedness through heavy lashes. God, he was without a doubt the sexiest man alive in my book. He caught me checking him out, not knowing I was seconds away from bawling my eyes out.

He approached the bed like a panther ready to strike.

"Do you know how beautiful you look when you come, True?" he whispered.

"It's you who's beautiful, Mace. You're like a dream in a world full of nightmares."

He put one knee onto the bed and crawled forward. I spread my legs wider, anxious to receive him where I needed him the most. He settled his weight on top of me, and I gasped. The silky feel of his shaft wrapped in steel pressed against my inner thigh was my kryptonite.

"Now let's see how you look coming around my cock, tough chick."

I moaned shamelessly as he entered me slowly, deliberately, savoring the moment.

"Ahhh...Mace, too much, I can't..."

"Take me, True, take all of me." He pumped his hips. "Pussy shouldn't feel this fucking good, woman. I want to fuck you until I feel that tight cunt of yours clenching around my cock."

"Only for you, Mace, only for you. *Forever,*" I muttered quietly.

"I could die between your legs a happy man, True, so fucking pretty."

We held each other's eyes, watching through every dip and surge of his powerful thrusts. I would never be with him like this again, safe beneath his massive muscles, wanted and cherished. *Home.* We fucked for hours, made love at daybreak, and held on to what little time we had left locked away in his father's workshop. Who would've guessed that Mace Fox was a cuddler? Or perhaps it was his way of letting me go. Not once had I shied away from his touch; instead, I sought it out. I stroked his hair while his head rested on my stomach. We were both sated and spent, dreading the hour of our departure. As the sun rose higher and higher, I knew it was almost time to leave. This was my last chance, my last-ditch effort to sway his intent to kill.

His breaths were even, calm, and I assumed he was asleep.

"Choose home, Mace, we need you," I whispered.

God, I prayed he was listening.

Sal and I were on our way to work as per usual, except I knew today was no ordinary day. Mace wouldn't be arriving at the shop, late or otherwise, he wouldn't grump and grouch until he drank his second cup of coffee, nor would he be taking any meetings with the community who so desperately needed him. He'd set out on a suicide mission to fulfill a promise made years ago from a place of anguish, and I was powerless to stop him.

I'd hardly slept the night before knowing that I was the only one who knew about his plans. I stared at the ceiling in my bedroom consumed with guilt at being a party to his deception, the moral obligation to tell the authorities, and the sorrow of fearing that I could've done more to change his mind. In truth.

Words were often hollow when delivered from a place of ignorance. I knew he loved his sister with all his heart, that he was a hero to the masses, stubborn and brave. He hadn't come to this decision lightly. What did I know of that type of devotion to another person? My own husband gave me away without a care in the world as to how it would affect our future. I chose instead to let my body do the talking. It begged and pleaded in earnest for Mace to choose life, to choose home with me and Kayla. In the end, it wasn't enough.

"I'm surprised you didn't hear me chanting from across the hall." Sal chuckled from the driver's seat. "The shit was intense, True."

"No, sorry, I didn't..." *What is she saying?*

"It was so vivid, like I was actually there in the mist with my ass hanging out."

Sal had been trying to tell me about a weird dream she had, but damn if I was listening. I was so distracted that I only caught bits and pieces, something about déjà vu or a bad omen of some sort. Apparently, there was a barking dog, loud at first, then fainter the closer she got to the animal, and somehow, that meant bad shit was coming. Then there was something about her big toe tingling, but I was too far inside my own head to make sense of it. All I could concentrate on was Mace. My nails were bitten down to the quick hours ago. I rubbed at the spot in my chest where the ache was coming from, a hollow pounding so deep, I felt it roaring through my ears.

He is probably at the prison already.
Is it over?

"The cat and the cow were married the next day."

"Hmm, that's cool," I responded absently. "I'm sure they'll be happy."

"You haven't heard a word I've said, beloved. Still not ready to talk about what happened on your trip? You seem pretty upset. I'm always here for you, girl. Unburden yourself."

She'd asked me earlier if I wanted to share, and I vehemently replied no. It wasn't my story to tell. Besides, I could never give it enough justice for her to understand its magnitude. Mace and I had shared so much in so little time, lying out on the cool grass near the swing set that meant so much to him. Whoever said it was better to have loved and lost was a dick of epic proportions, for I had no doubt in my mind that I was truly and irrevocably in love with Mace Fox. He was my home, forever, alive or dead. He was what I'd been searching for, and I took comfort in knowing that I no longer had to imagine what that felt like.

"I'm fine, Sal. Let's just get to Masonry Ink." My throat constricted, thick with worry.

Please be okay, Mace.

Please come back.

I could tell she wanted to say more but thankfully let it go and continued on with her jabbering. It wasn't long before I tuned her out again. My thoughts quickly returned to more pleasant memories. I smiled to myself through watery eyes remembering what it was like being locked inside that workshop with no one to hear us. It didn't matter that I never told him the origin of Kayla's conception or the horrors I'd faced living in Montana over the last five years. He wanted his real tough chick for the last hours of his life, and I was more than happy to serve him. If only tragedy hadn't struck his family, forcing him to make that vow of retribution. He would've made an excellent husband and father, better than I deserved but desired nonetheless. Hot tears sprang in my eyes, and I quickly wiped them away before Sal caught wind of my distress. The lump in my throat that had been hanging around for the last two days wouldn't go down, no matter how hard I swallowed.

He's not dead, True.

He'll come back.

"I, um…forgot to tell you something," Sal hedged.

It was hard, but I finally gave her my full attention.

"Oh yeah? What's that?" I replied.

"Kaden." She exhaled. "He came to see me the night of the FBI raid at Masonry Ink. He told me what happened, how they thought you had been kidnapped and that Mace was about to be arrested until you called off the dogs! Holy shit, beloved, that must've been crazy scary."

"It was extreme, and I'm sorry we didn't get a chance to talk about it before I left town. Everything happened so fast I..."

Beep. Beep. Beep.

"The sign says STOP, not die! Why isn't this motherfucker moving?" Sal yelled.

"What? Where?" I rubbed my temples, the noise too much on too little sleep.

She blew the horn a second time, flailed her arms around indicating the car that'd been sitting idle for far too long. She finally gave up and decided to go around, and that's when I noticed another car headed straight for us.

"Sal, look out!" I screamed, but it was too late.

A large black SUV careened into the driver's side door at full speed. Glass shattered through the air, landing on our laps. The metal frame smashed inward, slinging Sal violently against the steering column before flinging her backwards against the seat. It was a miracle we hadn't toppled over. If it weren't for the car still sitting at the stop sign, we probably would've. My ears echoed and rang through a haze. I heard Sal groaning in pain, but she sounded so far away. I turned ever so gently and could see a large gash on her forehead. The blood flowed crimson down her beautiful face. Her lip was busted, and speckles of glass gleamed along her cheeks. She'd taken the brunt of the impact. Her arm was twisted in an abnormally lopsided position, and she was pinned between the crushed metal of the door.

"Sal, can you hear me?" I mumbled through a sharp pain.

No answer.

"Sal? Sal, can you hear me? Please answer me."

He or she better have a damn good explanation for when the cops arrived. There was no fucking way they hadn't seen us before the crash. Idiot driver was probably using their cell phone and was distracted by the latest Internet gossip. I flexed my fingers to see if they still worked, extended my legs, relieved that nothing felt broken, then twisted my neck from side to side. That probably wasn't a good idea, but fuck it. I was a little banged up, but my only concern was getting to Sal. Surely by now, someone, a bystander perhaps, heard the commotion and called for an ambulance. Any minute, I should hear the sirens coming to our rescue. *Please hurry.*

"Grab the fucking crowbar. Gotta pry this door open."

Wait, someone was out there, maybe the driver from the other car.

"Help! My friend needs to get to the hospital!" I yelled, voice trembling.

I tried to remove my seat belt, but I couldn't get my fingers to work properly. They were stiff, shaking, and filled with shards of glass. The billowing steam coming from the other car's radiator distracted me enough that it was hard to gather my bearings. The Good Samaritan, other driver, or whoever the fuck he was, leaned down and peered into the passenger seat, where I was sitting. The door violently yanked open from its hinges, and my world came to a screeching halt.

"Noooo!" I cried out weakly while trying to move out of his reach.

"Don't fight, True. I'm getting you out."

"Why, Ryan? How could you do this?" I shoved his hand away.

"Grab the bitch and let's go. Cops are on the way, and I'm not getting caught because your stupid ass panicked and jammed on the fucking gas," a voice I didn't recognize growled from somewhere behind my soon-to-be ex-husband.

"Fuck off! I got this!" Ryan yelled back.

He used his utility knife to cut the seat belt, snatched me up from under my armpits, and dragged me out the car along the pavement. I fought against his hold, groaning, praying. My body ached from being tossed around, but I wouldn't let that stop me. I felt the sting in my nose and the hot tears that sprang from my eyes and rolled unchecked down my cheeks.

Push, pull. I wobbled and stumbled.

"Please don't do this, Ryan. You don't understand," I pleaded.

He shook me by the shoulders.

"I understand you up and disappeared, True!" he yelled, spittle flying in my face. "I understand you gave up on our family to whore around with a bunch of tattooed pricks who don't give a damn about you. I understand that you left me all alone and made a fool out of me!"

"I had a reason, Ryan, please…"

"Yo. What the fuck is all this domestic bullshit? Let's get the fuck out of here." My husband's partner yelled as he paced back and forth. He wasn't a member of the Sorensen police force, that much I knew. He was dirty looking with unkempt hair, stained and yellowing teeth, and he sported a leather vest with patches on it.

My eyes frantically searched the car for any sign that Sal was still alive. She wasn't moving, and I could no longer hear her groaning from the driver's side. I lunged for her only to be stopped in my tracks for a second time by a smelly cloth that was placed over my nose and mouth. Everything went black as my scream was muffled.

"Where were you, Mace?"

"I needed you."

"You promised."

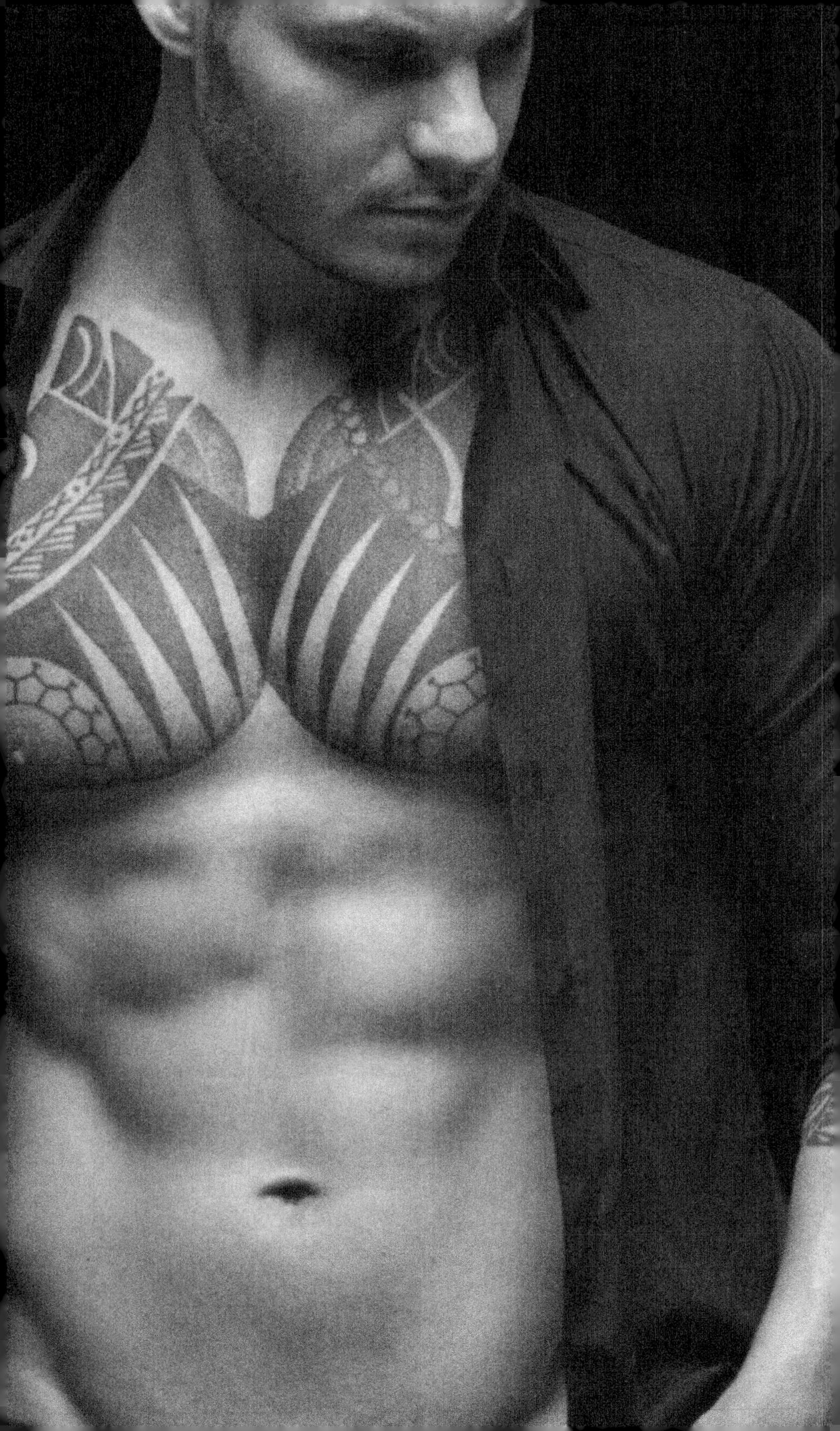

Chapter Thirty-Six

Mace

SAYING GOODBYE TO MY FAMILY, knowing it would be my last, was a feeling worse than death. It was as if my mother knew somehow, sensed it. She hugged me longer than usual, squeezed my middle impossibly tight, and touched every part of my face with her fingertips. Her eyes searched my own as she committed it all to memory, deep and meaningful, straight into the dark pits of my soul. When she stepped away, it was with a tight nod of determination that screamed, *'I'm on your side.'* She begged True to visit often, with or without me, and wouldn't let up until she promised to do so. Once Kayla was strapped in her car seat, she leaned over and whispered that she was part of our family now, that she was her grandma regardless of blood ties. The trip back to Remington was a somber affair that fucked me up more than I cared to admit, but I'd done what I set out to do and could rest easy knowing that my first love had gotten her wish to see me as a family man.

The perimeter's high walls appeared over the hilltop. My chest expanded with excitement. This was it, the day I'd been waiting for. My cell phone lit up in the cup holder. *Private number,* it read, so I ignored it. It rang a second time. *Ignored.* Then a third. *Ignored.* A fourth. Until the fifth made me snatch it up and bark at the solicitor.

"Fuck off! I don't need car insurance, I'm fine with my extended warranty, and I'm not donating to save the fucking whales. Get fucked, asshole."

Heavy breathing came through the Bluetooth, then laughter. Sinister and arrogant.

"I would give my left nut to see your fucking face right now." The voice sharpened. "Surprised to hear from me? You shouldn't be. It was inevitable once I knew for sure you had my daughter-in-law in your dirty little hands."

Fucking Papa Boardman.

I swerved to avoid hiding the median as I took the exit towards the prison too fast. The motherfucker's timing couldn't have been any worse if he'd tried. As things were, I didn't have the patience to spar with this prick, not when the walls were in view.

"Fuck do you want, Boardman? You're like that little piece of shit that continues to float round the toilet after you flush. You tried to break in, and that didn't work. Tried to call the Feds; that didn't work. What is this a last-ditch effort to be a pain in my fucking ass?"

"Macho to the end, I see." He snickered. "You fuck her yet, son? Pussy so sweet, nothing like it. The harder you slam into it, the wetter it gets till' she's soaked clean through the sheets. I taste that cunt every chance I get, even let a few of my deputies in on the action. Ryan never knew what to do with a fine piece like that. Shame he couldn't keep her in line the way I did his mother. All she needed was the right incentive, and she was butter in my hands."

My jaw locked tight.

"I'm not your fucking son, dick weasel! *Your* son is a spineless bitch who'd rather take it up the ass than protect his woman from the likes of you. Fucking pathetic, if you ask me, having to force a woman to suck your shriveled up prick, 'cause let's be honest, you couldn't pull a woman like True on your best day, motherfucker."

"Forced? Is that what she told you? She begged, son, oh, how she begged." He grunted. "Little bitch knew what side her bread was buttered. Just like her momma, that one. Gold-digging whores would've strung my son along for years if I hadn't intervened. I showed him how a real man handles his bitch. They're like children and need discipline."

Jesus, True, why didn't you tell me?

Choose home, Mace.

Choose home.

My voice shook with rage. I gripped the steering wheel so tightly my knuckles split. "She's out of your reach, cocksucker, so you and your spawn can crawl back into your hole and rot."

Silence.

"Wrong again, son. She's right where I knew she would be, same as the rest of them. How's it feel, Fox, knowing you couldn't stop me from taking back what's mine, right from under your sissified nose?" He cackled into the receiver.

"You're a fucking dead man, Boardman, you hear! When I get through with you, they'll need your dental records to identify what's left of your body."

The asshole snorted. "Thanks for keeping it warm for me, son. I'll take over now."

The line dropped.

"SONOFABITCH!"

Fuck! Not now, not when I was this close. The prison was right there; I could see it. My Glock gleamed in the light of the rising sun next to me on the seat. *Get on,* it taunted me. I hesitated for a second. Could I really give this up for her? For them?

"Where were you, Mace?"

"I needed you."

"You promised."

I flipped a bitch in the middle of the road and took off back towards Remington. Every call I made went straight to voicemail. Fuck! Why wasn't anyone answering? The tires spun on my truck as I stomped on the accelerator praying that I made it in time.

I'll never be on the wrong side of the clock again.

I slammed my fist against the steering wheel hoping it would tamp down the anger I felt. Boardman's demented ass was out there making credible threats, and my woman and her kid were all alone thinking I was dead. *Mine.* The realization that I'd claimed them slapped me across the face, lighting me up inside. *Mine.* The shit that fucker said to me played over and over in my head. Every mile marker I crossed was a jab, every small town a dagger. I drove at breakneck speed, pushing the horsepower as far as it would go without blowing the engine. *Mine.* I'd die before I let that fucker take them away from me.

True's sweet ass had a tanning coming for allowing me to believe she was station house pussy when in fact, it was her own father-in-law who'd been abusing her. How long had she suffered in silence before her only recourse was to run? Worst yet, I'd victim blamed her, fell for the rumors likely started by that piece of shit himself, and the thought of it made me sick to my stomach. My heart wept for what that motherfucker must've put her through. I knew now why she hid the fact that she was pregnant and why her bitch of a husband never noticed her body's changes. Yeah, she had a lot of explaining to do, but only *after* she was safe. True had gotten in there somehow, between barging into my shop uninvited and saying goodbye after a long night of passion. She'd captured my heart and released my soul from its burden. She just had to hold on for a little longer.

The normally three-hour trip back to Remington was shaved to just over two. I slammed on the breaks in front of the shopping plaza, narrowly avoiding a dark sedan as it sped away from the curb. A flash of light in my peripheral caught my eye as something ricocheted off its back bumper, followed by round of *pop, pop, pop.* Kaden was running from inside Masonry Ink at full speed, dragging his left arm while blasting away with the gun held in the other.

Didn't matter who or what, I jumped out the truck with my piece and emptied the clip into the back of the car right alongside him. A bullet hit the rear window and busted the glass out right when those fuckers sped past the red light. They took the road headed out of town on two wheels concealed by a cloud of dusty smoke. I saw old man Foster, who owned the candy shop, trying to usher his wife and Ashley Benjamin inside away from the danger. The last thing they needed was to recover from another fucking shootout. They never quite got over the death of Buck Calhoun, who was murdered in their establishment not long ago. I felt a twinge of guilt putting them through more shit, but I had to let that go.

Gasping for air, I turned my attention back to Kaden and lunged towards his shooting hand. He was still pointing his gun in the direction that the car took off, gritting his teeth.

"The fuck happened? Talk to me!" I yelled.

"We got hit." He spat on the ground. "Motherfuckers walked in and started spraying. Didn't say dick, just blasted. By the time the metal detectors went off, it was too fucking late. One tall goofy-looking piece of shit, the other a short, fat, bowlegged chump carrying a shotgun."

Boardman.

I grabbed him by the shoulders, causing him to wince.

"In broad fucking daylight? It's barely past eight in the morning."

Kaden's eyes narrowed to slits. "Bastards were surprised we had weapons. Heard one of them yelling to his partner, something about a double-cross and a rally point. Couldn't make out anything else." He looked me up and down. "Thought you had business to see too, Mace. It's what your bullshit letter said. Why're you back so soon?"

"You hurt?" I asked, ignoring his question.

"Just a graze, but Jagger took one to the chest. Ambulance is on its way. We gotta move."

Fuck me.

Fuck me.

We ran together towards the shop. The smell of fresh gun powder still permeated the air and burned the insides of my nostrils. Metal mixed with blood that reminded me of my time on the battlefield as a marine. Bullet holes littered the walls, the chairs. Even the goddamn ceiling took a beating. True was nowhere to be found even though her shift started a few minutes ago. I was close to completely losing my shit when I spotted Jagger lying on the floor with Dread, who was seconds away from falling to pieces, applying pressure to his wound with a stack of towels. The two started out as enemies; now they were brothers, clinging to one another as a matter of necessity. Dead Man stood with one leg on either side of his prone body, sporting a blade in each hand in case anyone tried to get close. He had the look of the devil in his eyes, and I knew better than to approach, not if I wanted to keep breathing.

"Dead!" I yelled. "Stand the fuck down." *Nothing.*

I tried again, this time with more base in my voice.

"Dead, you need to reel it the fuck in, brother, so I can see to Jagger before he bleeds the fuck out." He bared his teeth but still wouldn't move.

This could end badly.

If the cops came in here right about now, they'd surely see him as a threat and shoot on sight. If I couldn't talk him down, we'd be looking at not one, but two potential deaths. Jagger was a tough motherfucker, but he was gut shot and fading fast.

"Dead, for fuck's sake, man, snap out of it," Kaden tried and failed.

The only thing I could think to do was tackle his ass and pray the crazy bastard missed my vital organs when he shanked the shit out of me. Jagger's sudden movement stopped my ministrations. His bloody hand reached out and grabbed hold of Dead's ankle, breaking the spell. I breathed a sigh of relief, grateful that I didn't have to resort to kamikaze tactics to get his attention. He sheathed his blades, leaned down close to Jagger's mouth, and listened as the big man said something that only he could hear right before the paramedics rushed in. They got right to work applying a pressure dressing before hooking him up to a cardiac monitor and IVs.

"You'd better call Angelica. Get her ass back here pronto," Kaden said, watching closely as the medics worked to stabilize Jagger before transport.

"What about True? Where is she?" I asked while reaching for my phone.

When I pulled it out of my pocket, I realized it was vibrating with a call. I answered with a snarl, intent on getting whoever it was the fuck off as fast as possible. Angelica needed to be told what happened to Jagger. She was three hours away, and a lot could happen in that time. She'd never forgive herself if she wasn't here in case it did. I didn't even bother to check the caller ID.

"I can't talk right now…"

"Oh, Mace, thank God. This is Corrine," she cried. "Sal's been in a terrible car accident. I don't know…it's real bad, Mace, really bad. She was on her way to work and never made it. True had to have been with her, but she wasn't in the car. Mace…I'm afraid she's missing. I tried calling her cell, but there was no answer. It went straight to voicemail. She'd never abandon the baby like this. Something's wrong, I can feel it."

"Motherfucker!" I growled. "When?"

"This morning, about a half an hour ago. I'm on my way to the hospital now," she replied.

"The kid?"

"Safe with me, missing her momma," she answered.

"What?" Kaden snapped.

I held up my hand, slowing his advance.

"Meet you there...and Corrine?" I paused. "Guard the kid with your life."

I hung up the phone, took a few deep breaths, and faced the manic blond.

A hush of silence filled the chaotic scene. My ears echoed as someone spoke to me, but I couldn't hear a fucking thing. I kept thinking this was all my fault...again, another innocent lost because of my selfish actions. I wasn't where I should've been. If I had, none of this would've ever happened. I chose to kill a man who undoubtably deserved to die, but at what cost? True's life was worth more than that asshole's would ever be.

Boardman had no idea who he fucked with or what I was capable of if provoked. And make no mistake, that motherfucker had definitely called forth the savage inside me. For my family, my *entire* family, I'd give my life over to the highest power known to man, but for the people I loved, I'd relinquish my soul to the devil himself.

I waited until the medics had Jagger strapped to the gurney before rallying the crew. His IV fluids were running wide open. He barely held on to consciousness but was still battling. I led them to the door, slipped the lock in place, and posted the closed sign. A crowd was beginning to assemble outside, police tape cordoned off the building, and any minute now, they were going to want a statement. The crew was anxious to get going.

"That was Corrine on the phone," I began, cautious. "Sal's been in an accident. It's bad."

"The fuck?" Kaden shouted, shouldering past me. "Move the

fuck out of my way, Mace. I need to get to my wom— I need to get to Sal."

He tried to barrel his way out the door, but I stopped him with my next words.

"It was Boardman," I announced.

He turned his head sharply. "The pussy-face husband?"

"No," I replied. "It's been the old man all along. We knew he was dirty. Turns out he's a different breed of animal and needs to be put down."

Kaden's eyebrows shot to his hairline just before he started to laugh maniacally. This behavior would seem strange to an outsider looking in. I, on the other hand, knew what this action symbolized, and so did the rest of the crew. He was enraged, and this was the only warning you were going to get before he snapped your neck. He bounced around on one foot with a sardonic lopsided grin on his face, the bullet wound forgotten.

"When I get my hands on that guy, I swear to fucking Christ, I'm going to fuck him in his ear, stick a hot poker up his dick slit. Whew, Lord! ..." He howled. "I'm going to toe tag that motherfucker, if it's the last thing I do."

"There's more," I interrupted.

"Speak," Dead growled, his timbre menacing.

"They got True. Don't ask me how I know; I just do. Corrine said that Sal was the only one in the car when it was hit, and we all know they ride to work together every morning. Plus...the bastard called me, made threats he was coming after her...after me. Hauled ass back to Remington but..."

"Let him have the bitch!" Dead sneered. "What are we talking about this shit for? Jagger and Sal need us now. What the fuck do I care some skank whore got what was coming to her?"

I advanced into his space so fast I barely felt my legs moving. I grabbed him by his shirt collar, not caring that first fuck that he still had his blades. "She's been through a lot, Dead, more than I can say, and all of it fucked. That shit you heard about her back in Sorensen? All bullshit. None of it is legit. She fought like hell to give her child a home, and goddammit, she's going to have it!"

Dead lifted his chin in response. He got me. They all did. She was mine.

"I...I...can't go back to prison, Mace, but if you need me... I'm ready to roll," Dread offered.

"Fuck yeah! Let's rock," Kaden roared.

I stared at the three of them. They were my family, my home. Goddamn, True, this was what you meant all along, and I was too fucking blind to see it.

Choose home, Mace.

A bang at the door let me know that my time had run out.

"Get to the hospital. Make sure Jagger and Sal are treated as a high priority," I ordered.

"Tell the cops you don't know nothing, didn't see nothing, and you won't be making any statements without a lawyer present. I'm going out the back. Keep me posted. I want to know everything that's happening down at that hospital."

"Coming with you," Dead demanded. "Please..."

Bang, bang, bang.

"You sure? It's going to get messy."

"I owe it... to the kid," he uttered.

"Roger that."

We took off on a sprint towards the back of the shop. I stopped when I heard Kaden call out my name and turned to face him. He smiled, this one warm and caring before it turned deadly.

"Glad you came back, brother," he spoke. "Now go smoke that fool and bring our girl home."

"Fucking right, I will!"

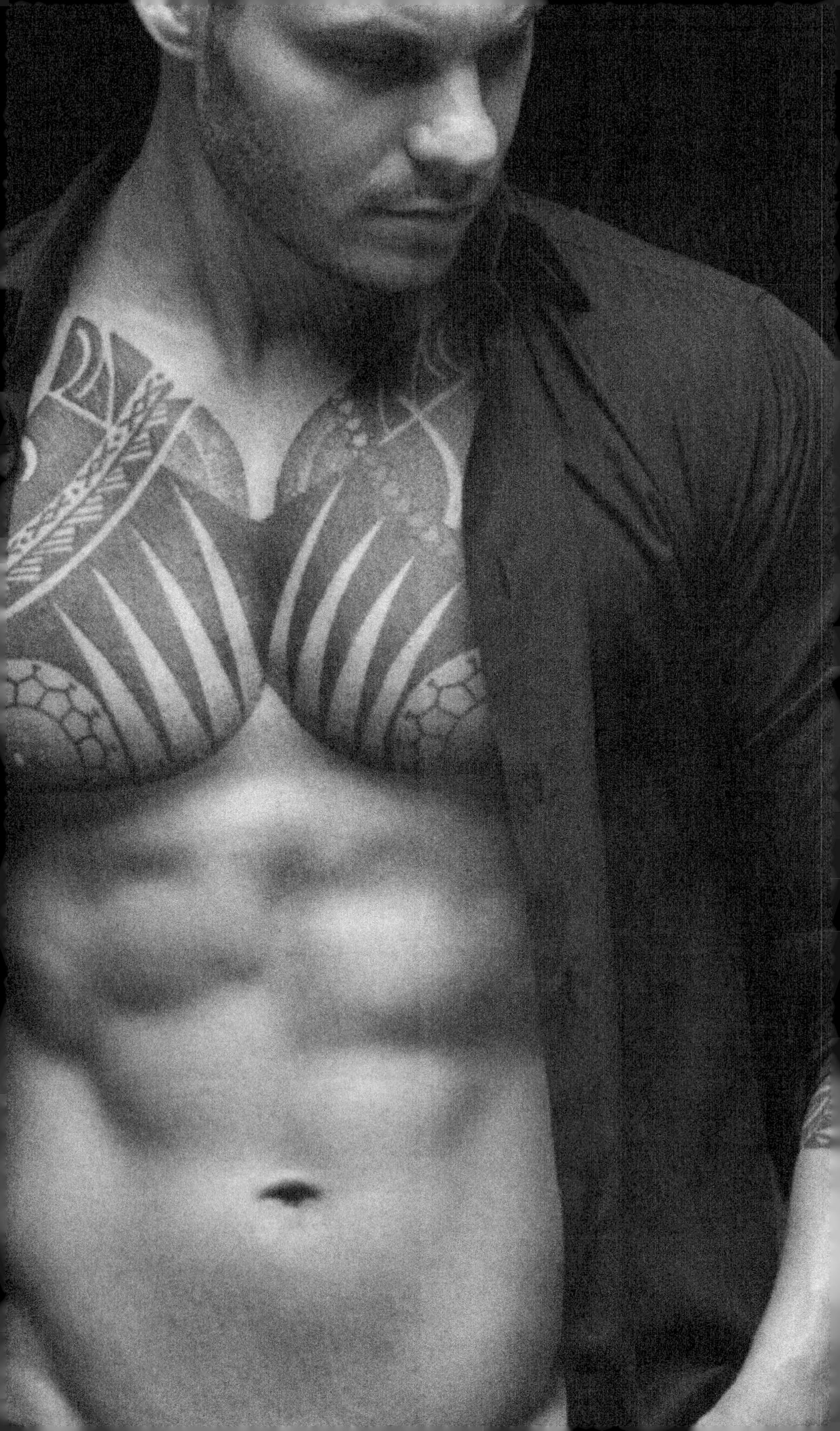

Chapter Thirty-Seven

True

THE GANG WAS ALL HERE, and I meant that literally as well as figuratively. I awoke some time ago to my *husband* dragging me inside a dilapidated cabin set far back in the woods surrounded by junked-out cars and tall weeds. The place reeked of piss, stale beer, smoldering marijuana, and rotten tuna from recently performed sex acts within its walls. I gagged on my own spit while managing not to projectile vomit all over the dusty wooden floor. Not that they would have noticed; might've even been an improvement. The men who I assumed owned this heap were all milling around shooting me dirty looks as they talked amongst themselves. No help would come from them, that much was certain. My body ached all over from the crash, and I was desperate for news about Sal. Ryan had given me a drink of water but refused to answer any of my questions, damn him.

None of this made any sense.

Ryan was a sheriff from Montana, so how the fuck did he get involved with a bunch of outlaws from Virginia? I'd watched enough movies to know these guys were in some sort of one-percenter biker gang. They wore matching leather vests, rode Harley Davidson bikes, and used terms like *brother*, *old lady*, and *tar snake*. They spoke brashly all around me, accused Ryan and his father of flipping the script and owing them more than the agreed-upon percentage for dealing with runaway bitch problems—their words, not mine. He assured them that all would be made right once his father arrived. I never thought my husband had it in him to surround himself with hardened criminals, but there he was, making nice with these goons as if we were attending a neighborhood barbeque, dressed in his state uniform no less. *Ugh.*

I missed my baby girl something awful and longed to hold her in my arms again. My only saving grace was knowing that she was with Corrine, who'd never let anything happen to her. I had to be strong and think of a way to get myself out of this mess. *A real tough chick.*

Mace would know what to do if he were here, but he wasn't. By now, he was dead, shot by prison guards after he killed the man who'd murdered his sister. Selfishly, I wondered if his last thoughts were of us and everything we'd shared. Did he call out my name when he took his last breath, or did he die alone, untroubled in his righteousness?

I pressed my lips together to stifle the sob that threatened to escape. If I allowed myself to go down that road, I'd get lost in a sea of sorrow and despair. Kayla was counting on me and took precedence over my broken heart. There would be time enough to mourn once I was out of here and away from my husband.

I had to try and talk some sense into Ryan before his father arrived. For whatever reason, he wasn't around and hadn't been all morning. Experience taught me that I needed to use his absence to my advantage. He wasn't a sane man and held too much influence over his grown son to ever be denied his say. I prayed that this time, my husband would listen.

"Ryan," I called out, getting his attention.

He stepped around one of the bikers and shot me a heated look.

"What is it, True? Fucking busy here."

"I, uh...need to use the bathroom...please."

He let out a harsh breath, stomped across the room, and snatched me up from my seated position. His fingers dug into the meaty flesh of my upper arm, causing me to wince in pain. Once we were finally alone, I drew back my arm from his grasp and faced him with a scowl.

"Is this your plan, Ryan, to keep me here against my will? How could you do this?" I snapped.

"Easily! Or have you forgotten that you're my wife?"

"Wife?" I scoffed. "I haven't been your wife in years, Ryan. Are you insane?"

His lips formed a hard line.

Deny, deny, deny. It was his father's way.

"We just hit a rough patch, True, that's all. I busted my ass to give you the best life possible. Ever since my mom passed, I've...we just need to get back home and sort this thing out. I promise things will be different, better. You'll see."

He picked at a strand of my hair and tucked it behind my ear. I appealed to the man I once knew, the one who'd vowed to love me for better or for worse, but he was long gone. In his place wassomeone I didn't recognize, a complete stranger, led around by his short hairs. *Delusional.*

"My home is no longer in Sorensen, Ryan. My place is here," I insisted. "Taking me back with my hands shackled won't keep me there. I'll find a way to escape again, I promise you that."

He grabbed me by the arms and shook the shit out of me. My head bobbled back and forth as I lost my footing and stumbled.

He screamed in my face.

"Oh, I know what you've been doing, True, and who you've been doing it with. My father always said you were a whore who needed to be kept on a short leash. Maybe if I had listened to him, you wouldn't have strayed off like a cat in heat, spreading your legs for that tattooed scum."

"He's a liar, Ryan, can't you see that? *He's* the reason why I ran in the first place. He was tearing us apart, tearing *me* apart," I protested.

"Don't start that shit again. You've always hated him for being a caring and involved father to me because you never had one of your own! Doesn't make him the devil because he never abandoned me, True. Get over yourself." He shoved me towards the bathroom. "You've got five minutes. Make it count."

I shuffled into the revolting box they called a restroom—no locks or windows, a men's urinal that had seen better days, and a sink so black with dirt it looked pained on. This time, I didn't try and hold back the sob that broke free, followed by a wave of flowing tears. Five minutes wasn't long enough for my one-man pity party, but I had to make do. Mace was gone, my baby was without her mother, and to top it all off, no one was coming to save me.

Well, shit.

That pretty much summed it up, and it only took two minutes.

I wasn't feeling particularly brave or tough in that moment. Scared shitless was more like it. I reached down deep and called upon my friends for an ounce of their strength. Kaden, for his inappropriate wit that hid his dark menace. Jerome, for his boyish charm that made me feel warm all over. Thinking of him took away the bone-deep shiver that'd been constant since my abduction. Jagger, larger than life with a heart to match. I'd give anything to see the brunt of his full strength unleashed on the animals holding me, including my husband.

Angelica, deserving of love, her spirit eclipsed only by her beauty. She was a fighter, and I only wished I could be half as tough as her when it came to protecting my family.

Mace, who saw in me what I never saw in myself. The world was a sadder place without him.

And finally...Dead Man.

I knew who he was the second I looked into his eyes. They'd changed so much since he was a young boy, harder, less inviting, but not enough to fool me. All the years of wondering what happened to him, and I finally had my answer, only for the joyful reunion to be taken away.

I will see them again, I swore under my breath, *in this life or the next.*

When the five minutes were up, Ryan appeared to take me back out front where I'd been forced to sit quietly and wait. His smug expression enraged me beyond common sense, so when he turned his back, I attacked that fucker with deliberate intent. Before he could figure out what was happening, I had my bound hands wrapped around his neck from behind, squeezing for dear life. He struggled against my hold not knowing I had a secret weapon at my disposal, all thanks to a crazy blond tattoo artists who'd taught me what to do. Our height difference gave me the clear advantage, and when I pressed my chin into the small of his spine, Ryan went down like a ton of bricks. He swung left and still, I held on, tight, and I pushed down harder, applying more pressure. I nuck-chucked the shit out of his ass, and it felt fucking great.

"Get the fuck off me, you crazy bitch!" he yelled, flailing his arms.

"Like hell I will," I growled.

The grunting and shuffling must've alerted someone to the battle. Boots pounded against the wooden floor, coming our way. My strength started to wane. Since my face was buried in the small of Ryan's back, I couldn't get a good look at who was approaching until it was too late.

Pain shot through my ribcage as I was kicked in my side at full force. The air left my lungs in a whoosh. At the same time,

Ryan lifted my arms from around his neck and threw me to the floor. I curled my body into a protective ball while my assailant lifted his foot and stomped downward on my face. Stars danced behind my eyelids in dazzling bursts of light. The metallic taste of blood filled my mouth as I squinted into the eyes of the cruelest man alive. My father-in-law smiled in triumph as he watched me wither in pain.

"Stay...away...from...me." I struggled to warn.

"Now, now, True. Is that any way to talk to your betters?" He smirked as he leaned down to eye level with my prone body, whispering so Ryan couldn't hear. "Missed you something awful, girl. Prepare to pay for the shit you pulled, running away as if anyone but me would want your ass."

"Fuck you," I managed through a cough.

"Soon, darling, soon," he replied sinisterly.

As always, I waited for my husband to come to my aid, and once again, he managed to disappoint me. When I was yanked to my feet by my hair, he stood by and watched, unfazed. When that bastard backhanded me across the face and threw me head-first into a chair, Ryan didn't even have the balls to hand me a napkin to wipe away the blood. When his father gave him a cruel look of disappointment, the only thing my husband did was lower his head in shame.

Mace was one hundred percent right.

Ryan was a new brand of pussy.

When he flashed a look of regret my way, I laughed bitterly to myself, shook my head, and concentrated on breathing through the pain as I calculated my next move. I had no intentions of going back to Sorensen or any other place that involved keeping company with my soon-to-be ex-father in-law.

The bikers got a kick out of seeing the left side of my face swell up like a balloon. One even commented how he wouldn't mind taking a turn, which he was quickly denied. One thing I could say about Rich Boardman, he always was a possessive sonofabitch. He preferred to be the one doling out the punishments himself in most cases. I could tell by his posture and the noticeable hard-on in his pants that he couldn't wait to get me alone. Meanwhile, my husband was too busy rubbing at the welts around his neck to even notice.

Typical.

As expected, my father-in-law took control, settled his debt with the bikers, and announced that we would be moving within the hour. One step closer back to hell.

I sent up a silent prayer to Mace knowing he was in heaven looking down on me, watching as I was being dragged from one place to another.

Give me the strength to be a real tough chick.

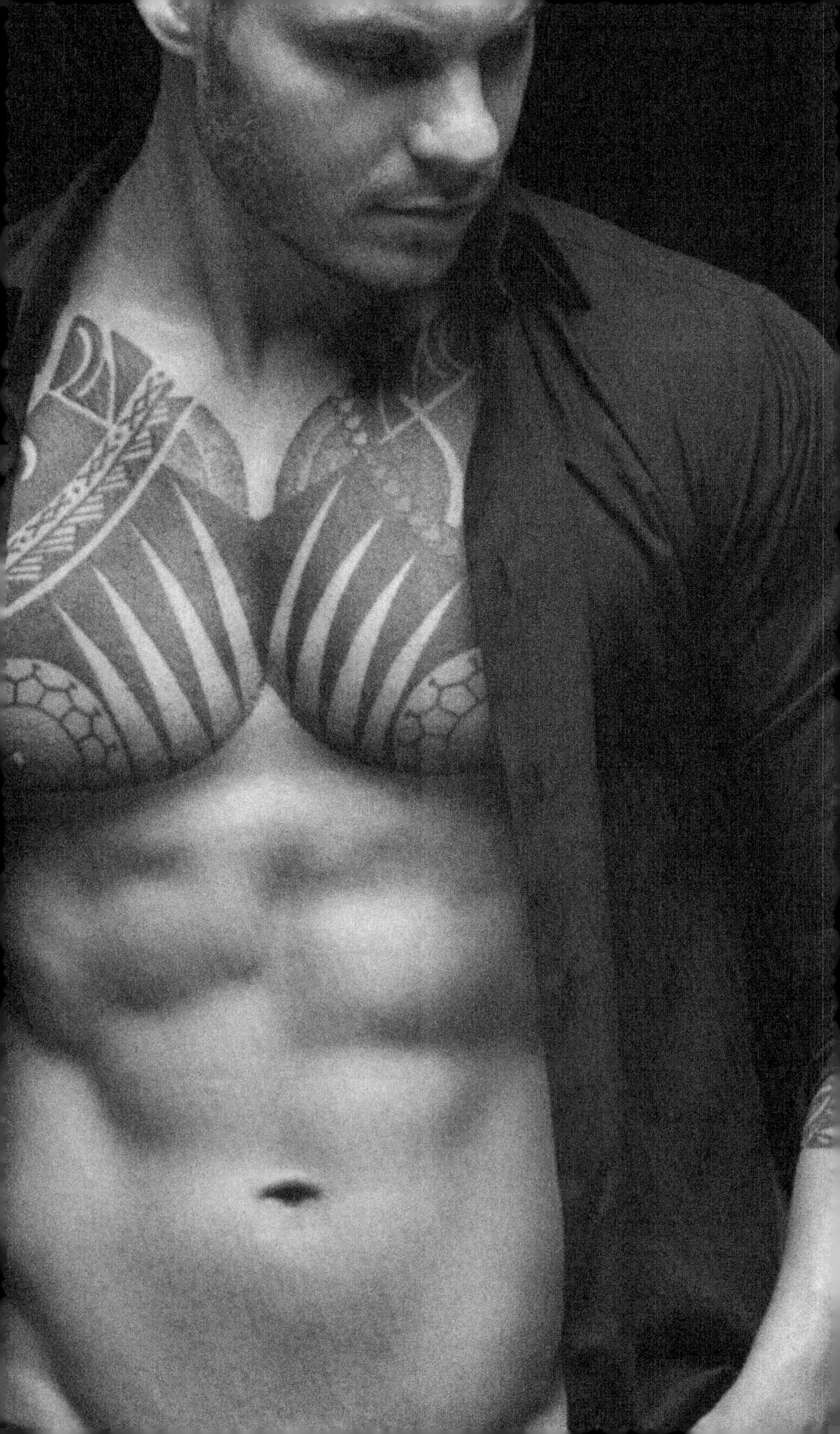

Chapter Thirty-Eight

Mace

"They're using the underground for transport, not staying in one place for longer than a few hours. Local crew is responsible for safe passage, maybe twenty strong on a good day. Your boy's been making deals all up and down the east coast trying to get back west. Bitch must be really special if he's willing to divvy up his share of ice distribution for a piece of that pussy."

"Seems we're not the only ones looking for that fucker. After the shit he pulled at my shop, FBI would like a word, and they aren't asking. Don't think he wants to take a chance on dragging a kidnapped woman around an airport or bus station," I remarked.

"Who's with you for backup?" Python asked.

"Dead Man," I told him. "The rest are watching over my people at the hospital. I got two down in bad shape, but we're hoping for the best."

"That ain't enough to take them down, and you fucking know it, Cochise."

"Well, it's what I got, so I'm rolling with it. End of."

"You are one stubborn sonofabitch, Mace. Gonna get you killed, fool."

"Do you want to help me or fuck me, Python?" I shouted.

I heard a deep growl on the other end of the line, followed by a frustrated string of curses. This wasn't the time to go toe-to-toe with him over how much fire power I had at my disposal. As president of a one-percent biker club, Python's solution would've been to ride in quiet, shoot EVERYBODY, set the place on fire, and blame it on a natural disaster while claiming innocence. Another time and place, I would've welcomed his high-handed intervention, but I couldn't risk True losing her life through friendly fire. Getting her back safely was my highest priority.

Kaden was able to narrow down the location of a safe house from a money trail sent from Boardman to the president of a local MC using an offshore account. His intel was limited to the only technology he had on hand at the hospital, which wasn't much, so I had no choice but to reach out to an old friend with some serious connections. The same old friend who was currently giving me shit on the other end of the phone. He was lucky the situation was dire and Kaden was understandably distracted, or I would've ended this five-knuckle shuffle ages ago. As things stood, I needed him if I had any hopes of finding True alive.

We made it to a cabin that belonged to the Seven Devils motorcycle club on the outskirts of town only to find it empty. By my estimation, we'd missed them by a matter of minutes judging by the warmth of half-stubbed-out cigarette butts thrown across the floor and a fresh blood stain on the shitty bathroom tile. It wasn't enough for a fatality, that much I knew, but someone had taken a beating. I felt my heart drop, thumping wildly in my chest as I imagined some prick with his hands on True, making her bleed, making her hurt. If the place weren't such a pigsty already, I would've taken a grenade to it like I did that meth house. Death would not come swiftly to anyone who dared touch what was mine. Time was running out.

"You must be stuck on stupid if you think that's even remotely a good idea, Mace. Two men against an army is suicide. No pussy is worth that much. Hell, my own momma ain't worth that much, and I happen to love the bitch."

"Just get me what I need, Python. You got ten minutes."

I hung up in time to see Dead shaking his head from side to side, taking it all in. He'd been kicking himself in the ass ever since I told him the truth about Boardman on our way out of town. I had to pull him back from the edge a few times in the last few hours, his thoughts as well as my own set firmly on the trauma surgeons working to save Jagger and Sal. He received an update from Dread while I was on the phone with Python, and it wasn't looking good judging by his curled lip and balled-up fists.

"What's the word?" I asked.

"Jagger is stable," he replied. "Angelica showed up, lost her shit, and damn near had to be sedated. Belinda was there, thank fuck. Had her back, settled her down, but she's in a bad way. Dread had to pull her off Kira's ass more than once before someone called the cops and got them all kicked out. It's a shit show."

Fucking hell.

"And Sal?"

Dead got quiet, the kind of quiet that would scare the shit out of anyone within range of his ominous vibe. His emotions were buried so deep that I couldn't remember the last time I heard him laugh or take pleasure in the little things like a good cup of coffee in the morning, a sunset, or a beautiful woman freshly fucked and sated. It was the quiet before the storm. The slight twitch of his eye was the only tell that he was about to deliver more bad news.

"She's in a medically-induced coma with a traumatic brain injury," he said, barely above a whisper. "We need to hurry this shit along, Mace, fuck this motherfucker. He deserves to be on a T-shirt or have a tree planted in his name before sunrise."

I couldn't argue with that.

"We can't go in halfcocked, Dead, not knowing what that bastard has planned for True. He's obsessed with her, the 'I'll kill her and then kill myself' kind of obsessed. Could get off a lucky shot if he gets spooked. The shit he said to me on the phone was next level crazy, and that makes him a loose wire."

He rubbed a hand along his buzzed head.

"They have to make it, man, Jagger and Sal. I can't stop thinking about what he said to me lying on that cold-ass floor shot to shit." He looked to the sky for help. I'd never seen him so conflicted.

"What did he say?" I asked.

"That it was up to me to be the might, that he was counting on me to protect the crew until he was able to do it himself, especially Angel. I won't let him down, Mace, he's…"

"He'll make it, Dead. They both will, believe that shit." I reached for his arm.

"I want to…but…"

The sound of an incoming text interrupted what he was about to say.

Python had come through big time.

"Got the next location. Let's roll. Save your anger for Boardman."

The coded message consisted of GPS coordinates, estimated headcount, a short dossier, and an emblem of a human skull which he used to symbolize death. It was a warning, his way of telling me that the crew of the next safehouse was heavily armed and I should expect a firefight. His admonishment meant nothing to me. I was going to get True back no matter what.

Boardman was smart, I had to give it to that old fucker. His exit strategy was impressive, using outlaws for cover, causing a distraction by shooting up my place on one part of town while wrecking Sal's ride and snatching True on the other. Might've even worked, too, if it weren't for one thing—the lengths I was willing to go to protect a member of my family. He had no idea the level of pain I planned to rain down on him and his bitch-ass son.

We hauled ass to the next stopping place, two wheels, ass smoking. I killed the lights and pulled the truck behind an abandoned supermarket. The shitty little town of Piccolo was on the border of West Virginia, population less than three thousand, all living below the poverty level. The MC that ran the place was aptly called the Deadly Miners, a homage to the once thriving industry before it all went belly up. The crew dabbled a little in prostitution, but their biggest trade was meth, which was probably why they took Boardman up on his offer for protection. They needed his resources to expand their distribution. It was a smart move.

"We going in or, are we just going to sit here holding our dicks?" Dead growled.

"You take the back, I'll take the front. Recon only. With luck, we'll catch these motherfuckers sleepin' and be able to get in and out without them knowing. Locate True, give the signal, and meet at the rally point, bug the fuck outa here back to Remington."

"Roger that," he agreed.

We did a weapons check, loaded up on additional ammunition. The sounds of metal sliding into place as we advanced the bullets into the chambers were the only noise made inside the darkened cabin of the truck. One quick fist bump, and we were off.

Dead didn't need any last-minute instructions. As an ex-Army Ranger, he moved like a shadow in the night taking flank on the left side. My job was infinitely harder. As I approached from the front, I saw a chain link fence surrounding a warehouse. Next to it was a smaller structure, a house I could barely make out in the darkness. Two prospects were on guard duty, a task usually given to them to prove their metal. They'd earn their patch tonight.

I approached the fence with my head down.

"Hey…" I slurred. "Looking for Benny. He said to meet him here. Open up."

"Nobody here by that name, motherfucker. Move along," one of the prospects ordered.

"Open up!" I pulled out my wallet, grabbed a handful of bills, and waved them around, dropping a few on the ground for show. "I got his money."

I stumbled around, swiped at the bills, missing on purpose. Their eyes got big as saucers pegging me for an easy mark, and just like I thought, the stupid bastards opened the gate and stepped forward, eager to collect their prize. I struck fast, disabling one with a roundhouse kick to the face while I spun on my heels, wrapped my arms around the other fucker's neck, and squeezed until he went nighty night. I dragged the bodies off to the side and closed the gate as if nothing happened in case anyone was watching.

Now to locate True.

There was a row of about twenty or so Harley Davidsons lining the cement driveway. If they decided to give chase, they were going to be shit out of luck. I used my knife to slash the tires. The wheeze of the seeping air filled the courtyard and kept my legs moving faster. I listened for the call signal from Dead letting me know he was in position. When none came, I kept pushing.

Adrenalin pumped through my veins as a light sheen of sweat started to form above my brows. Rock music blasted from the warehouse, which made it easier to maneuver around the perimeter of the camp. Armed brothers hung around drinking beers, smoking a blunt, and shooting the shit. The conversation caused my knees to weaken. I stuck my head around the side to get a better look, banking on the darkness to keep me covered.

"Do you really trust that pig to stick to the deal?" one of them asked.

"Fuck no. That fucker is slicker than a can of oil," came the reply.

No shit, dumbasses.

"Did you see the way he handled that bitch? Shame to fuck up such a pretty mouth. Bet she gives great head. If that was my old lady, we'd have a fucking serious problem, that's for damn sure. Guess pigs don't follow the code of the brotherhood. Old ladies are supposed to be protected, not used as punching bags."

"What the fuck do you know? Get an old lady first, then you can talk."

They all laughed and headed back inside, tossing their empty cans and butts two inches from my face, never once bothering to look where they landed. My mind raced with rage. True was hurt, that much was clear, but I didn't know how badly. I couldn't wait any longer; I had to go in. I got to my feet and pressed my back along the wall, turned, and came face to face with the barrel of a nine-millimeter pointed right between my eyes. *Fuck me.*

"Drop the weapon, cocksucker. You picked the wrong night to come skulking around my clubhouse looking for gash. My guess is you're a long way from home, Dorothy, which either makes you stupid or the hero. My left nut says you're the hero."

I dropped my gun, slowly placed my hands on top of my head, and squared my shoulders in surrender. A growl emanated from my chest at having been caught, not to mention I wasn't really fond of some prick threatening to kill me. I noted that the patch on his cut read *President* stitched in bold. He puffed out his broad chest with pride. The two teeth missing in the front of his mouth took away from his winning moment. I couldn't stop staring at that raggedy shit.

"You must be the head pussy in charge. It'll almost be a shame when I snap your fucking neck and skull fuck you to death," I mocked.

That little dig earned me a punch to the stomach that barely ticked my navel.

I wasn't impressed but held back my retort.

"Just as I thought, the hero. Pat him down and tie his ass up. We move out in an hour. Tell the pig we got company," he ordered.

The bulk of his crew fell in line at his side while one of the others felt me up, searching for weapons and the size of my dick. I was pretty well fucked sideways. It was now up to Dead to locate True and get her the fuck outa here without being discovered. All hope rested on his shoulders.

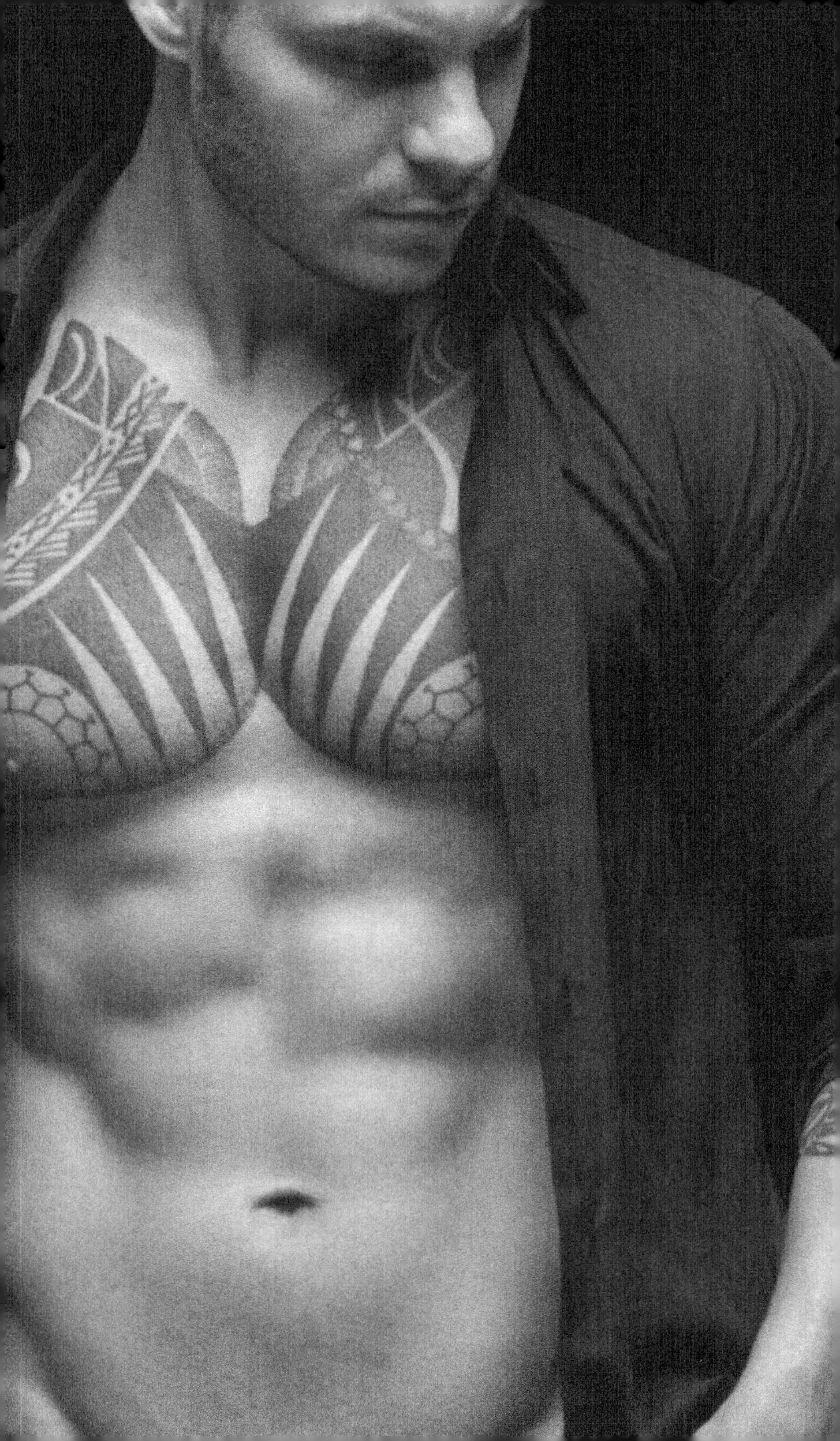

Chapter Thirty-Nine

True

"When I get out of these restraints, I'm going to kill you, Ryan," I threatened with as much venom as I could muster through a busted lip. The skin around my eye felt stretched to its limits. Even without touching, I knew it was swollen and blackened. I could've definitely used an ice pack or a bag of frozen peas, but did I give a shit? Hell no. I was too busy talking shit to my dumbass husband.

"That's no way for a woman to talk, True," he chastised. "I know you're angry, but in time, you'll see it's all for the best. My father can be extreme, but he's a good man, cares about his family, and whether or not you want to admit it, that does include you. He only wants what's best for the two of us, and that's to get back to our lives in Sorensen so we can put all this drama to rest."

After the bathroom episode, I was dragged outside to a piece-of-shit van that whisked us away to a second location. By my estimation, we drove for about an hour before pulling into yet another club place, clubhouse, or whatever the hell you called it. This one was slightly better than the last but still your typical dilapidated fuck shack. A new group of bikers took charge, while most of the others went their separate ways, leaving a few behind for extra muscle, or so they said. I still hadn't figured out a way to break free from my captors, a point that left me stewing in a vat of bitterness which I directed towards the only other person around. Ryan.

"You have no idea what's going to happen to me once we get back to Sorensen, Ryan, you don't! You think this whole thing is about some twisted family loyalty? Open your eyes for once and look at what he's done to us, to me!" I yelled.

"If you hadn't been acting so crazy, this never would've happened. It's your fault things got out of hand, True. All you had to do was act like a real wife and not some emotional basket case. All you ever did was complain when you should've had my back," he replied.

The longer I stared at the weak-minded man while he sat watchdog on his father's orders, the more my anger spiked to epic proportions. He deserved to know that my shortcomings as a wife had everything to do with his failure as a husband. He never loved, honored, or protected me as he'd vowed when we were married. I wondered, and not for the first time, if he ever really loved me to begin with, or was proposing to me a way to appease his parents? I tried reasoning with him ad nauseam, and frankly, I just didn't have it in me anymore to give a shit. I gritted my teeth and told him the truth and hoped he choked on it.

"Ryan, our marriage was over the night you left me alone to *service* your father."

There, I'd said it, and it felt damn good.

"Is that what this is about?" He sighed in disbelief, throwing his arms out to the side. I always hated when he did that. It made him look so childish.

"You're damn right, it is." Raw anger shot through me.

"Jesus Christ, True, it was one time five years ago, a small gesture to lift the spirits of a grief-stricken old man. You've always hated him, and now I know why, but if you want to blame someone, blame me. I was the one who asked you to do it, not him."

I was going to be sick.

He had no idea.

Since only my hands were tied, I stood from the ratty couch I had been sitting on and approached him with tears in my eyes. I had to see for myself, up close, if he was completely out of touch or using his doltishness as a way to get inside my head.

He glowered at me before taking in my sorrowful gaze.

"Ryan…not only was it not just the one time, he took possession of my soul that night and never gave it back. Didn't you notice the difference in me over the last five years? Weren't you curious as to why I wouldn't be in the same room with him, let alone speak to him? Why we all but stopped making love as husband and wife, or why I hated your touch?"

He reared back as if I'd slapped him.

"Well, I've been busy with the department, working extra hours. I…"

"And who sent you on those assignments, Ryan? Stakeout after stakeout, graveyard shifts, follow-up reports. There isn't enough crime in Sorensen to justify the manpower, unless there was a reason you needed to be kept away. Where do you think your father was when all of this was going on? He planned it that way. For God's sake, open your fucking eyes!"

He appeared stunned, turning over the facts in his mind to make it all make sense. I mourned right along with him that loss of a dream, that moment when you realized everything you thought was real was nothing but a big giant pile of lies and life had its knee in your balls. I reached up with bound hands and touched his cheek through an overwhelming need to comfort him. This couldn't have been easy to hear. The truth never was when you weren't expecting it.

I thought we'd crossed a bridge, until he shoved me away with so much force, I hit the ground sideways, unable to break the fall. Pain so sharp shot up my elbow, I knew my arm was broken or at the very least sprained. I cried out in horror, helpless to reach for the source of the injury. Ryan hovered over me, enraged.

"You expect me to believe that bullshit! You're a lying bitch, True. None of that ever happened."

Deny. Deny. Deny.

It was his father's way.

"Ask him yourself." I wheezed. "See if his eyes can convince you of the truth, Ryan."

The door to the house swung open, and in walked the man himself looking as smug as ever. His ensuing chuckle was evidence enough that the sight of me lying on the ground brought him great delight. Then again, my suffering always did.

"Damn, son." He turned his smirk to Ryan. "What did I miss?"

"Nothing." His ire weakened to a snivel. "Just having a word with my wife."

I righted myself on the floor, careful not to extend my shoulder any further than it already was. The two men paid me little mind as they exchanged glances with one another, silently conveying a message. I dared him. With two words through gritted teeth, I implored.

"Ask...him."

Ryan flinched, then shook his head.

"What?" my father-in-law snapped. "She talking shit about me again?"

"It's nothing... false accusations about you and her after... you know, the night that Mom died. She wanted me to ask you about it, but I said it was all bullshit."

"Hmm."

Ryan paused. Something in his father's reply didn't sit well. He turned to the older man and waited for more of a denial, which never came.

"It *is* all bullshit, right, Dad?" he pressed.

Instead of answering, he turned his attention back to me. My heart pumped furiously in my chest as his top lip curled above his teeth in a sinister snarl. He took two steps and advanced, and with a slip of the wrist, grabbed a fistful of my hair down to the root. I screamed out, but with only one good arm, it was useless to try and break his hold. I dangled like a puppet in his grip, lost in the pain, controlled by a monster.

He got right in my face, so close I could see his pupils.

"We're heading back to Remington," he hissed. "Seems we left something behind."

My legs gave out from under me.

"Noooo…please." He'd discovered my secret.

His darkened eyes glared at me, calculating and evil.

"Thought you could hide her from me!" he roared, spittle flying. "Stupid bitch! You always thought you were too smart for your own good."

"What the fuck are you talking about?" Ryan asked. "What did we leave?"

"One of the bikers was at that shitty little tattoo shop the night she arrived in Remington. Said she had a kid with her, a tiny baby. She kicked up the shit when someone tried to take it from her. She had a kid, Ryan, and never said a fucking word about it. I knew something was off about her pussy when I…"

He'd said too much.

The fucker finally stuck his foot in his mouth.

"What the fuck did you say?" Ryan shouted at his father, distraught.

"It doesn't matter, son. Don't you see? She lied and hid a member of our family from us. She's a goddamn whore who needs to be taught a lesson! One I plan on delivering myself once we get the kid back."

"You leave her alone, you bastard!" I cried.

I was fighting with everything I had left in me. The shoulder pain ceased to exist after a rush of adrenalin. The more I struggled, the tighter his grip gained purchase on my scalp, but I refused to give up. I was a momma bear protecting her cub from a snarling wolf masquerading as a cop set to eat her alive if he stepped any closer. The scuffling got worse as he tried to lift me up, and that's when I heard an inhuman wail from somewhere above. I stopped moving once I spotted a gun that was pointed at my father-in-law's head.

Ryan's chest heaved as he tried to control his rage.

"Let go of *my* wife, you decrepit piece of shit."

He pressed the butt of the gun harder against the back of his father's head, jerking it forward. Rich's hands raised high in surrender, and I was let go. My first instinct was to attack, which was exactly what I did, slapping that prick so hard across the face my palm stung. I could tell he wanted to retaliate but held himself back.

"You take this bitch's side against me?" he roared towards his son. "You really are a worthless piece of shit, you know that, Ryan? Too much of your cunt mother in you, boy, diluted the Boardman bloodline."

"Shut the fuck up." Ryan reared back and struck him upside the head, causing a massive gash to burst open and blood splatter along the nape of his neck. Wish I could say I was sorry, but I wasn't. It was a long time coming.

"True, get behind me," my husband ordered.

I skirted around Rich and stood behind him. His free arm went around my waist and kept me close as we started to back our way out towards the door. We were almost there when we heard the bang of gunfire happening outside and Ryan took his eyes off his father for a split second. A single shot rang out and hit him in the throat. He collapsed on the floor, taking me with him. The fumes of the smoking gun held by his own father engulfed the room.

"Noooooo!" I screamed.

Blood saturated the front of his shirt as he dropped his gun and tried to cover the wound with his hand. Wave after wave ejected from the large hole as more filled his mouth and overflowed to the ground. Ryan looked at me with pleading eyes while the life drained from his body. He tried to talk, but I shook my head no.

"It's okay, you're going to be alright," I soothed, knowing it was a lie.

"I'mmm sorrryy," he gurgled through a glob of blood.

"I know you are, Ryan. Please don't try and talk."

His breathing slowed, and I knew it was just a matter of time, so I did what I do best.

I lied to him.

"You have a beautiful baby girl waiting for you," I whispered. "Her name is Kayla, and she is amazing, bright, playful. She even has your eyes. You're going to love her, Ryan, you'll see. We finally have our own family."

I finished the tale with a watery smile that soon turned unbearably bleak once I realized he'd long ago taken his last breath. I hugged him to my chest. The tears that flowed were not only for the loss of life, but for the ultimate betrayal that pit father against son. He didn't deserve this; none of us did. There was only one person to blame.

"You killed him, you disgusting bastard, your own son," I hissed towards my father-in-law, who was peering through the window trying to see where the shooting was coming from.

"Yeah, bitch." He rushed along from window to window. "Fuck with me, and you're next."

I scooted away from Ryan's body, ready to run, ready to scream my head off, when his next words stopped me cold. He was close. The hairs on the back of my neck stood on end as my heart beat wildly in my chest. I heard his forked tongue slither with disdain.

"Now…let's go get *my* daughter, whore."

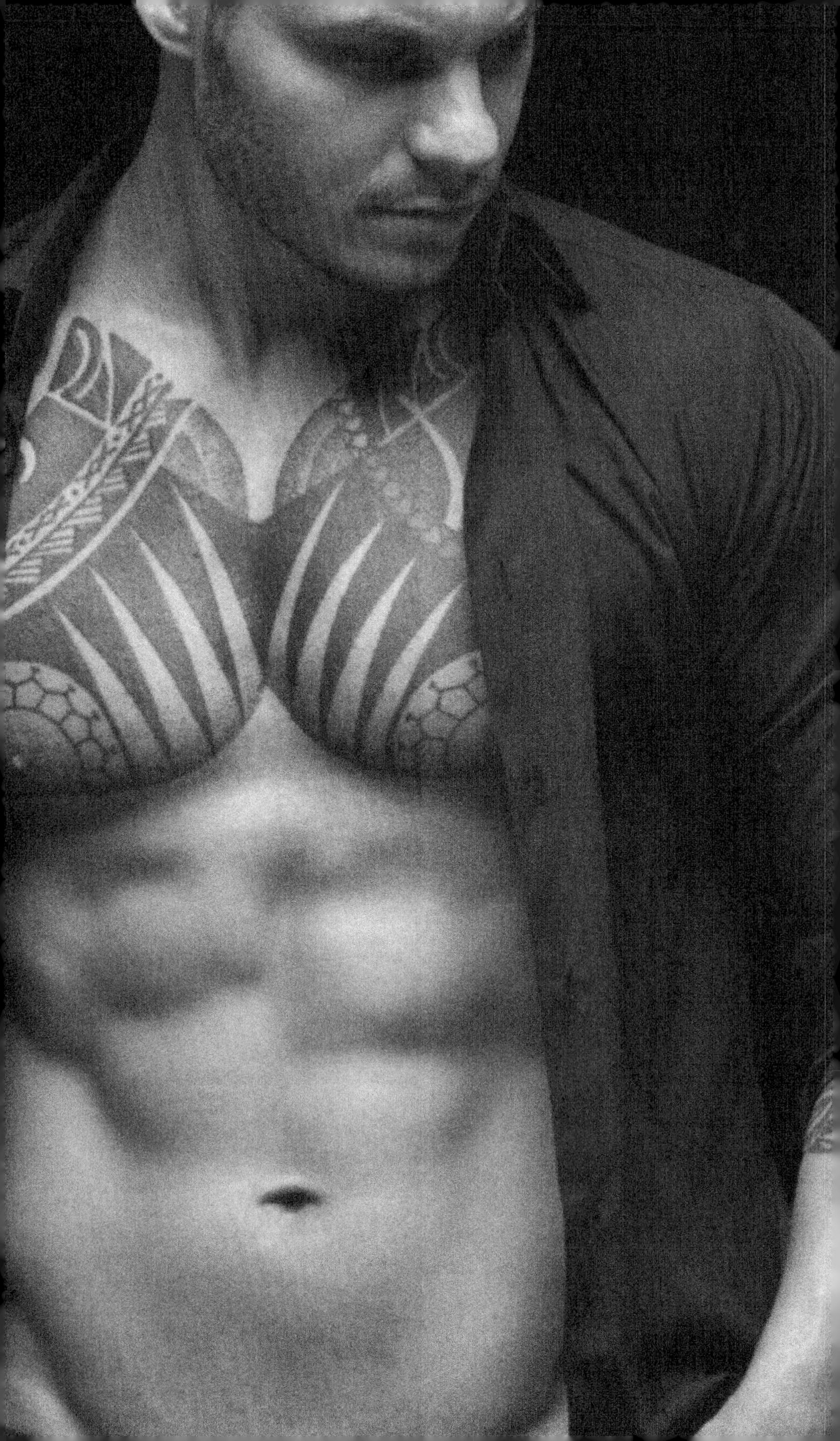

Chapter Forty

Mace

I heard a little birdy sing.

That's what it sounded like to anyone who wasn't part of my crew. Three quick tweets followed by two shorter ones rang out into the darkness of night. Dead was near and tracking. The next burst of chirps was a warning to get ready. I discreetly worked at the zip ties around my wrists. From experience, I knew that I could break them, only I had to do it quietly. My intent was to stall long enough for Dead to make his move. If they managed to get me inside that clubhouse in front of old prick Boardman, I was done for.

"Where the fuck are you taking me, douchebag?"

"Inside to meet the man. Said we might see some trouble tonight," the leader clipped.

"Don't know no *man*. Just here to purchase product. Heard you were the outfit to connect with, so I came out to do business. Big misunderstanding here, boys. Gonna leave some coin on the table if you don't stop and think about this."

"I'll take my chances," the president remarked. "Besides,

don't know you. You're too clean to be from around these parts. Means only one thing: you're here for the bitch, and that ain't my fucking problem."

I kept my eyes straight ahead as the biker cunts escorted me single file towards their clubhouse. Four at my back with their guns trained on my head, two leading the way, including the president. Two more quick tweets, and my shoulders bunched readying for battle. We stepped a few feet from the door, and I heard a whizzing sound somewhere behind me, a loud thump, then one of the four guys at my back hit the ground with the full force of his body weight. The other men took position, hunched down, scared shitless, at the same time fired off a few rounds into nothing. They couldn't see a fucking thing and were essentially wasting their time. The president ordered one of the men to check on their fallen brother.

"Carbon is dead, boss," he reported back.

What is with these idiots and their dumbass coal miner names?

"Keep your eyes peeled. Somebody is out there shooting at us. Probably came along with this motherfucker." He grabbed the back of my neck and shoved me forward to keep moving.

"No bullet hole, boss."

"What the fuck you say?" the president whisper-yelled.

The guy turned his friend over on his back, swiped his hand over the dead guy's chest, and out stuck a long-ass arrow, center mass, like something out of an old western movie. I only knew one man who was proficient enough to hit a moving target with a bow and arrow, but I couldn't get my hopes up that he was somewhere around here popping off bikers to save my ass, not after everything that went down at Buck's junkyard.

The gunfire brought out more men from the clubhouse, each carrying automatic weapons and vicious scowls on their faces. I counted fifteen, not including the five who hadn't been shot by a wayward arrow. The leader barked out orders to the men, sending some to secure the gates, others to locate Boardman, and a few more to secure the back of the premises in case they needed to escape. Once they all took off, it was back to a five count and better odds to make my move. One final twist, and I felt my hands freed from their bindings. The whizz through the air sounded again, and another man fell to the ground. I made my move.

I swung on the leader, breaking his nose while sending pieces of the bone through his brain, the crunch alerting his boys. There was an animalistic roar before a dark shadow descended upon the crowd, slashing at will, automatic. Dead Man appeared out of nowhere with his blades in hand doing God's work.

I grabbed the gun from the outstretched hand of the leader while he lay lifeless on the ground. Dead had his back turned and didn't see the two guys headed towards him on his right. I shot and hit one, but the other had enough time to raise his own gun and aim it directly at Dead's flank before a third man arrived on the scene. He was dressed in all black, wearing a mask that hid his face. He carried an old-fashioned bow and arrow. Quicker than shit, he pulled back the strings and let one fly, hitting the man in the forehead, killing him instantly. He approached me cautiously, hands raised, weapon in the air, and used his other hand to lower his mask just so.

The breath left my lungs in shock. *What the fuck?*

It couldn't be.

"For my woman."

It was the only thing he said before he collected his arrows from the flesh of the bikers on the ground then took off running towards the entrance. There would be time enough later for explanations, but for now, I let him go without saying a word. One thing was certain: I owed him a debt of gratitude for saving my life.

Dead and I did a once-over to make sure none of us were hurt, surveyed the carnage, and crept towards the clubhouse in search of True. We weren't out of the woods yet. Armed killers were running around on their boss' orders looking to fuckstart our heads. Once they caught on that he was dead, there'd be nothing stopping them from going full rogue out for blood.

We stared through the windows of the single-story clubhouse. It was clear that it was bare, with the exception of a few beat-up couches and a folding table used to hold beer. I turned to Dead, frustrated we came up empty.

"We need to split up, cover more ground," I insisted.

"Fuck that, Mace. We stick together, or these fuckers will pick us off like fish in a barrel," he replied, wiping the blood from his blades on the grass at his feet.

We were looking for a needle in a haystack, blindfolded, with one arm tied behind our backs. Meanwhile, True was out there somewhere being terrorized, beaten, or worse by old fuck Boardman. We were outnumbered and outgunned, stuck in one position holding our dicks. If we moved and were spotted, they'd descend on us quicker than a rabbit gets fucked. It was a goddamn suicide mission, but I'd already given my life over to someone I cared about once; doing that shit again was nothing. I couldn't expect the same level of commitment from a man who felt hollow most days.

"I need to find her, Dead. Won't ask you to risk your life going against these fuckers. Get to the truck, put it in gear, and get the fuck out of here. I'm going to look for True alone."

He got quiet.

Scary quiet.

"You got the fucking balls to say that shit to me, Mace?"

"We got no chance here, Dead. If I go down, at least you'll be…"

He took a second, closed his eyes, breathed in deep, and when he opened them, I saw the pain radiating from his pupils as clearly as if it were daylight. I knew his story; it was a long sad tale that was as fresh for him today as it was when it all happened. He had a stake in finding True, sure enough, but mine was different, and because of that, it was my call to make.

I stood, ready to bolt towards the old house in the distance when Dead grabbed my hand.

"Wait....do you hear that?" he asked.

I listened closely, and sure enough, in the distance, the roar of motorcycle engines coming down the road sounded off like an earthquake. Headlights lit the way, two by two, as they assembled along the fenced -ff grounds. Those fuckers must've called in reinforcements. Whatever hopes we had of escaping were shot to hell by the time a chain was wrapped around the galvanized steel and yanked to the concrete. They piled in, hooting and hollering, guns blazing, damn near surrounding the entire encampment. I braced, knowing in a matter of minutes, they'd be set upon us, savage and murderous.

"We're not going out like a bitch," I told Dead. "We take out as many of those fuckers as we can. Spare no one. I'll see you on the other side, brother."

He growled low in his throat. "Fuck, yeah."

Closer they came, until a voice shouted out a command.

"B9's... Make your brothers proud!" I heard bellowed.

Relief flooded my senses, along with every other emotion. The night turned out to be full of fucking surprises. Python's men filtered out in different directions, taking down the coal miners' daughters, driving a few of them away on their bikes, kicking the shit out of the rest. He was a welcomed sight, dressed in his colors, not giving that first fuck if he was recognized. I couldn't stop the smile that formed on my lips as he pulled right in front of us on his gleaming Road King looking like a total badass from a movie set.

"Man, am I glad to see you, hoss. Thought my goose was cooked," I greeted him with a handshake and a hard pound on the back.

"The boys were restless. Thought we'd lend a hand," he replied.

"Python," Dead growled.

"Dead Man." Python tipped his chin.

"Where do you need us, Mace?" Python inquired.

"Handle the renegades. I'm going after my woman. Dead, stick with Python. Check the rest of the grounds while I search that other building. Shoot once in the air if you find her before I do and keep your fucking heads down."

Dead started to object.

"End of," I growled.

I took off running, stopped when I heard my name being called.

"Watch your ass, Cochise," came from Python.

I gave him a solute and kept it pushing.

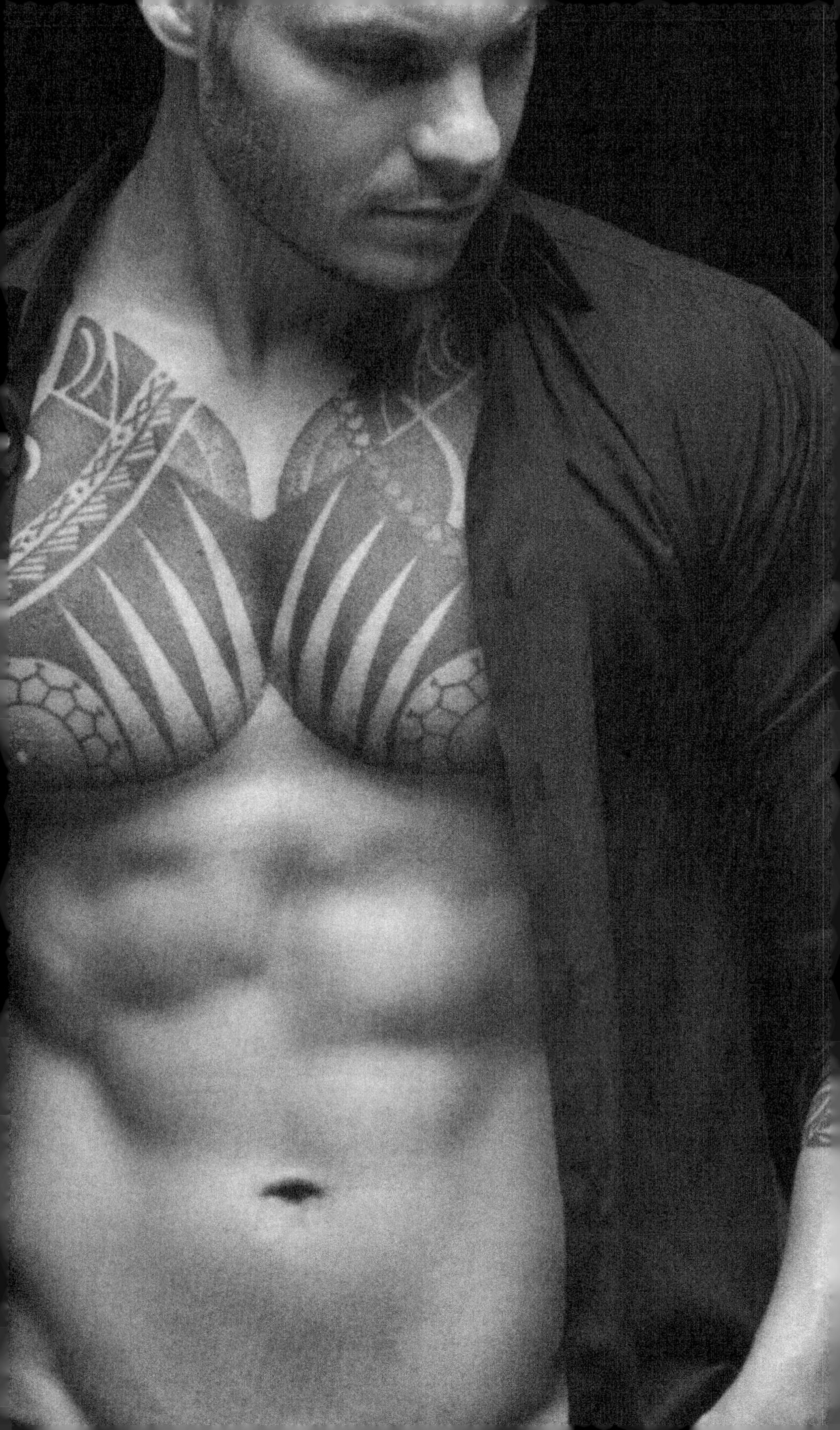

Chapter Forty-One

True

I WAS BEING DRAGGED by my poor battered scalp. The hair had long since been ripped from the roots judging by the wetness and streaks of blood running down my temples. The more I tried to resist, the harder he pulled, until finally, I couldn't take it any longer and went with it. There was still a shit ton of shooting going on, coming from all directions, but not close enough to cause a concern. Not that my father-in-law gave a flying fig; he was too busy gloating about killing his son and how things were going to be better now that he didn't have to come up with excuses to fuck me whenever he wanted. I cursed him, his tiny dick, his greasy grandmother, and his one-legged dog. No one was spared from my wrath.

The whole thing was surreal and as useless as a white crayon in a box of sixty-four. The man had no feelings other than lust, but that was the least of my worries. I couldn't allow him to take my daughter from me, not now, not ever. I told him so in as many ways as I could think of to deter his steadfastness, but the fucker kept charging forward.

"People are going to find out what you did to Ryan, and you'll go to prison," I told him.

"People will believe what I want them to, sweetheart. Two days from now, they'll find him in a crack house with his throat slit and his pants down around his ankles. Killed in the line of duty. My spin will make it stick," he argued. "It wasn't hard to convince the townsfolks that my perfectly healthy wife died in her sleep now, was it?"

"Whaat?" My steps faltered, and I recoiled in his grasp.

"Knew the only way to get my dick in you was to convince my kindhearted son that I was on the brink of suicide from grief. I went to Ryan after the funeral, tears in my eyes, snot running down my nose, the whole nine yards, laid it on him thicker than quicksand. You should have seen him scrambling around trying to find ways to help his dear old dad stay afloat. The second he suggested your pussy, I knew I had his ass."

He snickered to himself as if it was the funniest thing in the world. His breath wheezed from his chest as he struggled with talking shit while dragging me along a darkened path. I dug in my heels, realizing that once he put me inside that truck, it was all over for Kayla. He'd proved himself to be maniacally calculating in his pursuit, going so far as to commit not one, but two murders, all in the name of sexual desire. Perhaps it was the control over another human being he craved. Regardless of his sick motIve, I wouldn't allow him to subject my daughter to his cruelty or his twisted game of familial possession.

"You're a sick bastard, you know that? You used his love to manipulate him into doing the unspeakable. He had no idea you kept coming back, bringing your friends, threatening our home and our very lives!" I screeched. "How could you be so heartless and cruel?"

"If it weren't for me and your mother, he never would have married you in the first place, sweetheart. She sold your ass for top dollar when you were fourteen, guaranteed he'd be getting some virgin tail to break in. I didn't mind sharing with him; he was my son, so it was essentially my dick inside your pussy until I could have the real thing. Now, shut the fuck up and move your ass. My daughter's waiting."

Something deep inside of me broke free.

I was a mother now, and that alone made me prone to acts of violence where my child was concerned. *Keep fighting till the whistle blows*, I heard Mace's voice in my ear. The need to protect superseded my self-preservation. I raised my bound hands and scratched my captor across the eye, drawing blood. He let out a yelp, ground his teeth together, and shook off my assault with ease.

"You stupid bitch! You'll pay for that." He groaned.

"You'll get a lot more if you go anywhere near my daughter!" I screeched.

He slammed me against the side of the truck with one hand and delivered a punch to my gut with the other. The air left my lungs in a whoosh as I doubled over in pain. Thank God for the extra shot of adrenalin flowing through my veins; it helped me recover faster than he was expecting, making my delivery of a kick to his shin that much more brutal.

He didn't hesitate.

He pulled the gun from his holster, cocked back the hammer, aimed it over my head, and squeezed the trigger. I shrieked in surprise and froze solid in my tracks. The echo from the blast caused my ears to ring from its closeness. He grabbed me by the face and leaned in.

"The next one will be in your head if you pull that shit again," he cautioned with a grimace.

"Please…don't," I begged.

He pointed the barrel at my face and motioned with a flick of his chin for me to keep walking. I marched to the passenger side door of the van on shaky legs, reached for the handle, and lifted it up until I felt a click. My breath shuddered involuntarily from the heartache of defeat. I stepped one foot onto the running boards before being yanked by the nape of my neck to a halt. My father-in-law was curiously distracted by something he heard coming from the woods. I twisted my spine in the same direction and squinted my eyes into the darkness of the forest. For a second, I thought it was just his psycho imagination playing tricks on him, until the tree limbs spread and revealed someone I thought was lost forever.

"MACE!" I screamed, taking in all that was him through blurred eyes.

He was alive.

Sweet Jesus, he was alive.

He charged straight for us, looking every bit the dark hero. My body slumped with relief at seeing his handsome face after believing he was dead from a sniper's bullet. It felt so surreal, as if a missing part of my soul had been returned to me after being stolen away. I knew I wouldn't truly feel whole again until I held him in my arms, breathed in his masculine scent, and tasted his luscious lips in a fiery kiss. Rich Boardman stood in the way of that. He gave me a violent shove, which landed me face first across the seats of the van. I struggled to right myself. The harsh grunting and flesh pounding on flesh hurried my attempts. I stuck my head out the open door and watched the two men square off with each other in a battle of good vs. evil.

My father-in-law was beat to shit, which filled me with more joy than I cared to admit. Bloody nose, busted lip, his brown uniform shirt ripped to shreds. Sadly, I realized he was also still standing on his feet. Mace, on the other hand, appeared perfectly unscathed aside from a few strands of hair that stuck out from the sides. He snarled at the older man, eyes narrowed, teeth bared, ready for the kill.

"Give it up, motherfucker. She's not going anywhere with you," Mace ordered.

"You think I would come this far without taking home the

prize? Thought you were smarter than that, Fox. Seems I overestimated you where pussy's concerned," Rich wheezed.

"I was hoping you'd say that, cum stain."

The two men grappled again. My father-in-law took a punch to the sternum and dropped to one knee. I watched in horror as he reached for something attached to his ankle, which turned out to be a second gun, a hold-out pistol he used to kill Ryan. I didn't think. I dove onto his back, knocking him to the ground, where he lost purchase on the weapon. *Oomph...that hurt like hell.*

Mace grabbed it, pointed it at the fucker but didn't fire. He looked down at me with a silly smirk on his face, almost as if he was fighting back his laughter. "Real tough chick," I heard him mutter to himself. It was then that two other guys showed up to the clearing, one I recognized as Dead Man, the other I had no clue. He was clearly a friend judging by his scowl and battle stance, a biker wearing different colors than those clowns who'd kidnapped me. As a side note, he was also sexy as all get out. The three of them together was a woman's wet dream, but I digress. Dead Man approached and released my bindings with a knife he was holding. I didn't wait. I took off running towards Mace with my arms spread wide. He caught me mid-air.

"I thought you were dead," I whimpered against his neck.

He held on to me as if I were the most precious of treasures.

"I'm alive, True." I pulled back just a little. "We're alive."

He stopped my heart with a kiss so demanding, so pure, so full of hope, I almost forgot to breathe. We only broke apart after a loud not-so-subtle throat clearing and a deep growl coming from behind us. He pinched my chin between his fingers and tilted my head from side to side, checking out the damage. His nostrils flared, and he was grinding his teeth so hard, I felt sorry for his molars. The other men had secured my father-in law, but he wasn't about to go out like a bitch. He cursed and hurled insults as if the roles were reversed and he was the one holding

409

the gun. Mace steered me off to the side as he advanced towards the seething man.

My father-in-law, never to be outdone, stuck out his chest like a proud peacock and went to town with his baseless threats.

"Better think long and hard about what you're about to do, Fox. It's not too late to walk away and save your ass. Do you realize how important I am? The people I have on my payroll? One word from me, one phone call, and all your shit goes boom. Your crew, your shop, even that fancy house your mother lives in, all neutralized on my say-so."

The man in the leather vest, also known as the unknown friend, barked out a humorless laugh, slapped Dead Man on the back so hard, I felt the blow in my knees. He pretended to wipe away invisible tears before straightening himself with a scowl.

"Keep talking shit, old man," he dared. "Got fifty men at my back who would like nothing more than to bend your wrinkled ass over and take turns pounding your insides out. Hell, you might even like that, you old dirty bastard."

I liked him immediately.

"Don't threaten me, scum." He raised his chin in challenge to the sexy biker.

"Not a threat, motherfucker; it's a goddamn promise. That's my friend you're talking to. Don't got a lot of those outside of my brothers. That said, you fuck with him, you fuck with all 'a us."

"You don't scare me. I'm the king around here, and don't you forget it," he balked.

"Just say when, you hairless twat, and I'll send up the call," the biker promised.

That shut his ass up.

Dead Man stepped forward with a knife in each hand, larger than a dagger. Its blades dripped with fresh blood down the handles and into his palms. It was the vacancy in his eyes that stole my breath. They were unseeing, a void filled with death and malice. He was years away from the boy I once knew, the one who disappeared without a trace, leaving me alone to deal with my upbringing. Time would come when he'd have to answer for his departure, but not now. Protecting my daughter was more important. I spoke up from behind Mace's back, surprising everyone.

"You should go back to Sorensen and forget you ever knew me, Rich. Tell whatever story you want about Ryan's death, my sudden disappearance, your sad tale of becoming a widower...it doesn't matter to me. What you're not going to do is attempt to lay claim to *my* daughter. You have this one chance to crawl back to that lonely place *you* call home and leave us the hell alone. Do it, or I'll make sure you'll regret ever knowing me."

Mace puffed out his chest proudly. "Yeah, cocksucker, what she said."

"No deal," Dead man growled. "I say we off this fool and leave his body for the wolves."

"Not our call, Dead," Mace warned.

I waited for my father-in-law's answer on pins and needles. His top lip curled above his teeth in a snarl. He looked between the men surrounding him, holding him off. I should've known better than to think he'd act reasonably.

"No one is gonna keep me from my kid, whore, not these motherfuckers,"—he jerked his head towards Mace—"not your greedy cunt of a mother, and certainly not the likes of you. I can get to her any time I please. She's my blood, and that makes her mine, and there ain't a damn thing you can do to stop me from taking her away. I'm the goddamn chief of police, and you're *nothing.*"

He laughed a throaty cackle that made my skin crawl like tiny little mice running along the column of my neck. He jutted out his chin, daring me to contradict him as if I had a leg to stand on. His words were like daggers, unfortunate truth bombs that exploded in my head. All four of the men were waiting for my decision, three I assumed because they cared, and Rich because he was a dick. I walked around Mace's side into full view of my father-in-law. He wasn't aware of how much I'd changed, from the scared little housewife afraid of her own shadow to that of a real tough chick able to survive on her own without fear of failure. He would learn today what that meant, and I would be the one to teach him.

I straightened my spine and approached.

Surveying the devil right in his eyes.

"True...don't," Mace warned.

Something on my face must've told him I had this. He took a step back, giving me a wide birth. I nodded my head in his direction and carried on. My father-in-law didn't seem so imposing now with his beaten-up face, torn shirt, and stupid-looking smirk. How had I ever been foolish enough to give in to the whims of this man? Well, no more.

"You once said to me that unless I agreed to submit to your abuse, you'd send Ryan into an active shooter situation, orchestrated by yourself, of course, refuse his back-up request if called, and take great pleasure in watching him murdered. Do you remember that?" I asked, making my way over to Dead Man.

"Fucking right, I do," he preened. "You needed an incentive to come up off that pussy a second time, so I gave you one. Worked, didn't it?"

"Good, that's good. I'm glad you remember because I believed you."

I held out my hand to the man I once knew as a child and tilted my head. His brows pinched together, and I could hear the grumble coming from his chest as realization of what I was asking for set in. He looked to Mace for permission; a quick lift of his chin gave it to him. His eyes darkening with uncertainty until finally, he sighed with resignation. I heard his huff as he handed me one of his blades. I grappled with the handle, feeling the weight of the weapon between my fingers, in awe of its potential.

"And when you told me that you'd see us homeless and destitute if I said a word to Ryan about what you were doing to me, I believed your black-hearted threat," I said with my back turned.

"My house. I could do with it what the fuck I wanted, sweetheart. You had no money, no friends. Where the fuck were you going to go? Back to momma?" he blustered.

I swung around to face him with hate in my stare.

"First, you took away my dignity." I stepped closer, calmly, and with my shoulders back. "Then you took away my husband once he finally saw you for what you really were, a crazed lunatic capable of great harm. So... when you say that you'll take my child away from me, I one hundred percent believe you'd try, Rich, and that is a very, *very* bad idea."

I raised the sharpened blade and dragged it along my father-in-law's throat, like a surgeon's scalpel. The initial slice barely bled. His eyes bugged out in surprise as he reached for the gash trying, without success, to stop the flow of blood that spurted from the incision. I watched as he teetered between life and death knowing that my daughter was safe, that we were all finally...safe. When I dropped the knife and ran over to Mace, I did it with a clear conscience and a sense of relief I never expected to feel from taking a life. The devil was finally gone.

A low whistle sounded from behind My head. "Fuck me, Dead Man, you see that shit?" I heard grumbled. "I need me a bitch like her on the back of my bike. A real tough chick that can handle a blade? That's old lady material right there!"

I snickered into Mace's neck at his compliment, 'cause what's life without a little inappropriate laughter after you just killed a guy?

"Like your woman, Mace. Got a nice set of balls on her," the biker uttered.

"Get your own, Python. This one's all mine," Mace grumped.

I couldn't help the smile that passed my lips listening to the stranger's praise. We were free, my baby and I, and I couldn't have been happier.

"You ready to go home?" Mace whispered in my ear.

"Home," I breathed.

Nothing ever sounded so sweet.

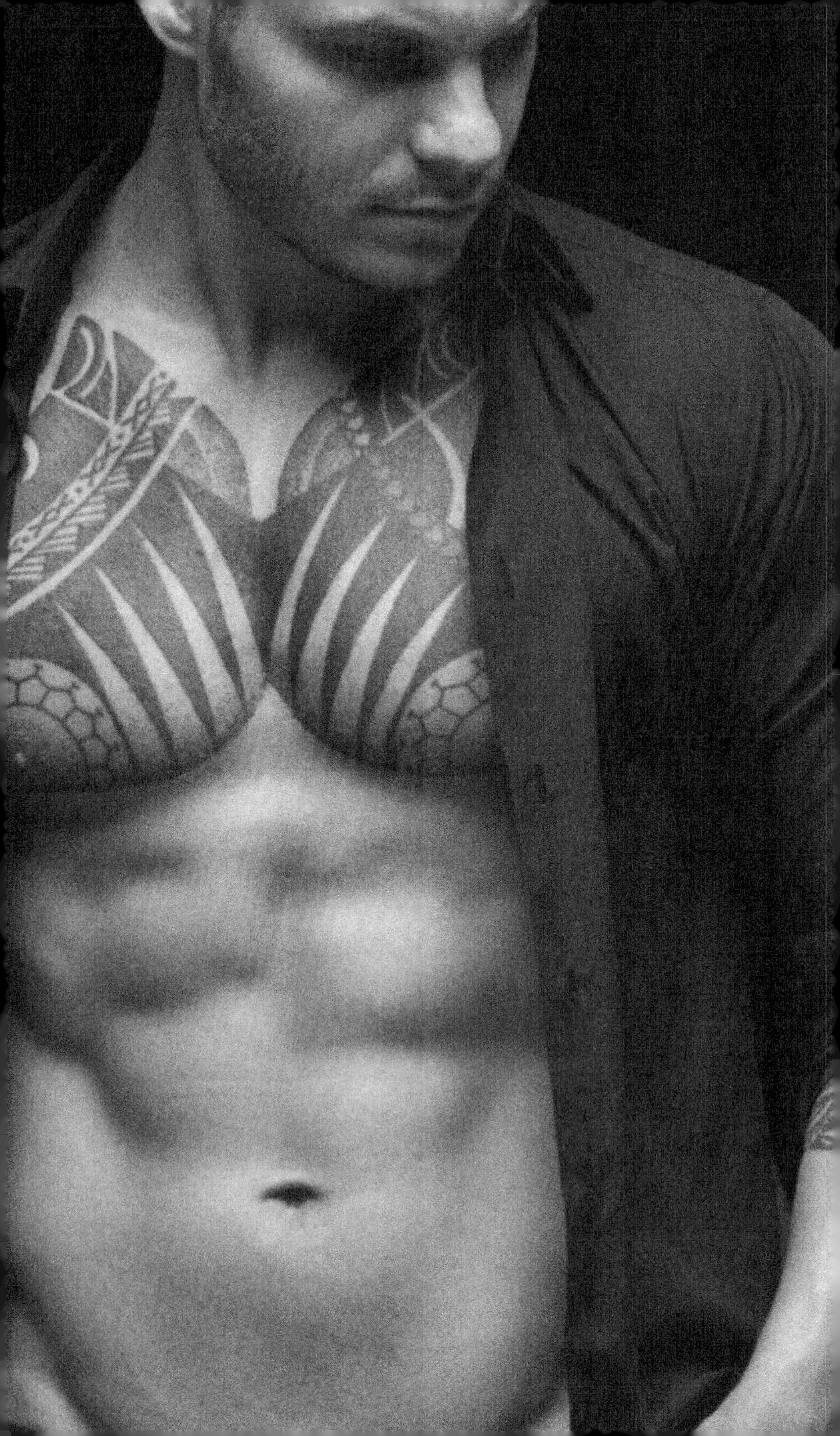

Chapter Forty-Two

Mace

WE LEFT the mess of dead bodies for the authorities to sift through. The so-called Deadly Minors had been on the local police department's radar for some time now, so blaming them for the carnage wasn't that difficult. Kaden used his savvy computer skills to create a roadmap connecting Boardman to their ice distribution in the west, and the whole affair was chalked up to the cost of doing dirty business. They never even knew we were there.

The one thing that True insisted on was that her deceased husband, Ryan Boardman, be made out the hero instead of a weak, spineless man child who couldn't protect his woman. She didn't want the world to know about all the fucked-up shit she'd been through. She felt that a tarnished past could affect her daughter's future, and she wouldn't jeopardize that for anything. It was an explanation I found hard to swallow but went along with, nonetheless. I had his body claimed from the morgue and flown back to Sorensen while his daddy was left unidentified to rot. Far's I knew, he was cremated with the rest of the unknowns and buried in an unmarked grave somewhere in West Virginia. A fitting tribute to a twisted piece of shit in my opinion.

In order to gain sympathy from the simple-minded folks of Sorensen, we needed a story that they would find believable but also painted True as an innocent casualty. By the time Kaden was done, Junior "bitch ass" Boardman was the saint who'd discovered his father's wrongdoings, went out of his way to confront him, and found himself in a drug war from which there was no escape. Mom agreed to watch the kid since she was still in Remington looking after Angelica, and the two of us hopped on a plane. Dead Man kept them both safe in my absence. I got behind the wheel of the limo that was waiting for us at the airport. It was the best way I could think of to explain my appearance at a funeral for a local town policeman. Looking the way I did, covered in tattoos, would've caused more speculation. That way, I was close enough to the action without being a part of it.

Long sleeves on her black dress covered her busted arm while dark sunglasses and a wide brim hat took care of the bumps and bruises. The entire farce was a shit show down to the grieving widow who mysteriously reappeared from her missionary retreat in Cambodia just in time for his funeral. That narrative explained True's long absence and why she wasn't aware of what her father-in-law was into. She buried her husband with all the pomp and circumstance befitting a fallen officer complete with a twenty-one-gun salute and an American flag draped over his coffin. We were in and out of Sorensen in less than two hours; would've been longer if True had told me the names of the other officers who'd abused her, but they weren't in the clear.

"Now is the time for healing, Mace," she told me once it was all over. "Past hurts and reminders of pain have no place in our hearts anymore. Let it go and live in the now."

I promised to drop it.

It was a lie, but it was for the greater good. End of.

That's how I ended up in my hometown a few days later.

I stood in the corner of a hospital room waiting for the nurse to finish her assessment and update the notes on the chart. She gave me a peculiar look, probably wondering if I were a family member or a close personal friend stopping by to show my respect. I was neither, but I kept that to myself. Coming here wasn't a priority on my to-do-list. The administrator who'd called said it was my choice, but after everything that went down, I felt it was the last chance I was ever going to have. She finished her duties and addressed me with a strained hospital smile.

"He's pretty out of it. The morphine drip is keeping him comfortable." She waved a hand at the IV poles that held more bottles of liquid than an Irish pub.

"Can he talk?" I asked.

She gave me a sympathetic nod. "Yes, but it's not always coherent. He's in the final stages now, so it's just a matter of time. He may say some strange things like seeing spirits or bright lights, but it's completely normal, so don't be alarmed. I'll give you two some space. Press the intercom if you need assistance."

"Thank you," I managed to reply.

The nurse stepped out of the sterile room, leaving us alone. Little did she know, I was the one person she needn't have wasted time explaining the intricacies of death and dying. I'd witnessed more men take their last breath than I cared to remember, some deserving, some not. The man lying stationary covered to his neck with a white sheet was definitely the latter, which meant I gave less than half a fuck if he was comfortable.

I pulled one of the plastic chairs closer towards the bed rail and took a seat. He looked completely different than the last time I saw him. Gone were the corded muscles around his neck and arms, a testament to his fit physique. That kiss of a tan that bronzed his complexion. The perfectly coifed hair that gleamed against the lights of the courtroom. That confident smile he wore as the verdict was read and he realized he'd gotten away with murder. In its place was a bald, emaciated man with yellowish skin, crusty lips, and dark splotches covering his eyelids who was about to do the world a favor by seeing himself out. *Pity.*

He must've sensed my presence in the room. His mouth gaped open, and his head lulled to the side.

"Did you see her?" he mumbled in a feeble voice.

"See who?" I asked.

"So... beautiful, my love. She's waiting for me in the glow of light."

A serene smile spread across his lips right before he started to cough uncontrollably. A pitcher of water sat next to his bedside on a tray. I grabbed it and poured some into one of the cups. The straw inside bobbled wildly. I held it in one hand and the back of his head with the other, giving him an opportunity to take a little sip. I laid his head back in the center of the pillow and waited until the spell had died down.

I was torn between feeling sorry for this motherfucker and yanking all the plugs that were keeping him alive out the wall. To think, a few weeks ago, I was content in the knowledge that by ending him, I, too, would end up a corpse. I was guessing I should have been paying closer attention to what was happening inside that prison, then I would have known that my sister's killer was battling stage four prostate cancer from his overuse of anabolic steroids.

Would it have changed anything?

Probably not.

Watching this animal decayed and fading, who would have been the same age as my sister had she lived, and the only thing I could think to say was *damn*. Couldn't have happened to a nicer guy. True had one thing right—it was time to put this shit in my rearview and get on with my life.

"Good luck in hell," I whispered in his ear, set to leave. "You deserved to die screaming, motherfucker. Look for me in the afterworld."

"Stay with me, please," he mumbled through pasty lips. "Maya, Maya, my love."

He drifted back off to sleep, maybe for the last time. *Good riddance.*

I pushed the chair back in the corner, stepped outside, and closed the door without so much as a backwards glance. Revenge was sweet, but karma was a cruel cunt who took my back and fought dirty. Now I was free.

I touched base with True and let her know that I'd made it back to Remington. I smiled to myself when she told me to be careful and that she'd be waiting for me when I arrived home. Moving her and the kid into my apartment with me was the easiest decision I'd ever made. She didn't feel comfortable living at Sal's place all alone, and I wanted, no, *needed* them close, where I knew they were safe. We weren't expecting any blowback from Boardman's murder, and I made sure that to everyone outside of our circle, she was Nancy Jennings, an accountant and a single mom recently relocated from Montana. To me, she was more.

To me, she was my home.

Home. It became our favorite word in the English language, and we used it often during our conversations. True used it as metaphor for lovemaking, our own filthy little promise that sounded unsuspecting to strangers but carried with it a whole heap of anticipation. Even now, I was sporting a semi just thinking about later on tonight once we put Kayla to sleep. I never realized fucking could be so much fun while at the same time trying not to wake a sleeping baby.

The repairs on the shop were completed a few days ago, and we were scheduled to have a re-launch party on Saturday night.

Even though one of our closest friends would be missing from the celebration, we decided to go ahead with it knowing she'd understand. It'd been three weeks, and Sal was still in the hospital undergoing treatment and rehabilitation for her injuries. We all felt her absence, Kaden especially, who refused to leave her side, threatening to lobotomize any motherfucker who so much as put a frown on her face—his words. He stayed at the hospital more than the shop, and nothing and no one could get him to leave. The weekend she spent at his apartment was obviously more than he'd originally let on, and I for one was here for it. He deserved a good woman, and she a good man. The lives they'd led, the pain they'd endured, if anyone deserved a lasting reprieve, it was them.

I parked my truck in its normal spot, made my way over to the front of Fosters Confections, stopped, and took a deep breath. I'd been putting this off until things died down a bit, but I could no longer avoid the inevitable. I swallowed down the thickness in my throat and shook off the nerves. After everything I'd done by freezing her out, refusing her visits, phone calls, or a simple wave in greeting, she had every right to tell me to get fucked. I'd been a cunt to her, and I deserved her ire. Sacrificing your life for the person you loved wasn't the betrayal I reasoned it to be, and I hoped Ashley Benjamin felt the same.

I stepped inside and grimaced when the loud-as-fuck cow bell sounded overhead. The sweet smell of cocoa assaulted my nostrils first thing. No wonder this place had been around for decades. Who could resist a dark chocolate truffle or a pecan caramel cluster? I sure as hell couldn't.

She was finishing up with a customer but noticed me right away. Her brows furrowed for a moment before she returned her attention to the man wearing a bow tie and suspenders. He gathered his package, politely patted the top of her hand, then skirted out the door, leaving the two of us alone. She opened her mouth to say something several times before closing it with a defeated sigh. I felt like an even bigger prick seeing the hurt and distrust in her eyes knowing I was the one who put it there. She was my friend, and I shat on her. We were beyond the words, the guilt, and the blame.

I opened my arms wide and waited, laying it out there that I was sorry for the way I'd acted, that even a hotheaded beast like myself knew when he was wrong. That my tragedy wasn't a good enough excuse to throw away our friendship because she acted the same way I would've given the same choice. It wasn't until her eyes filled to the rim, she let go of a sob, and crashed into my chest that I knew all was forgiven.

"Do me a favor, little troublemaker, will you?" I asked.

"Anything," she replied.

"Lay off the gum drops. I'm running out of room in the shop."

We laughed as friends…and it felt good.

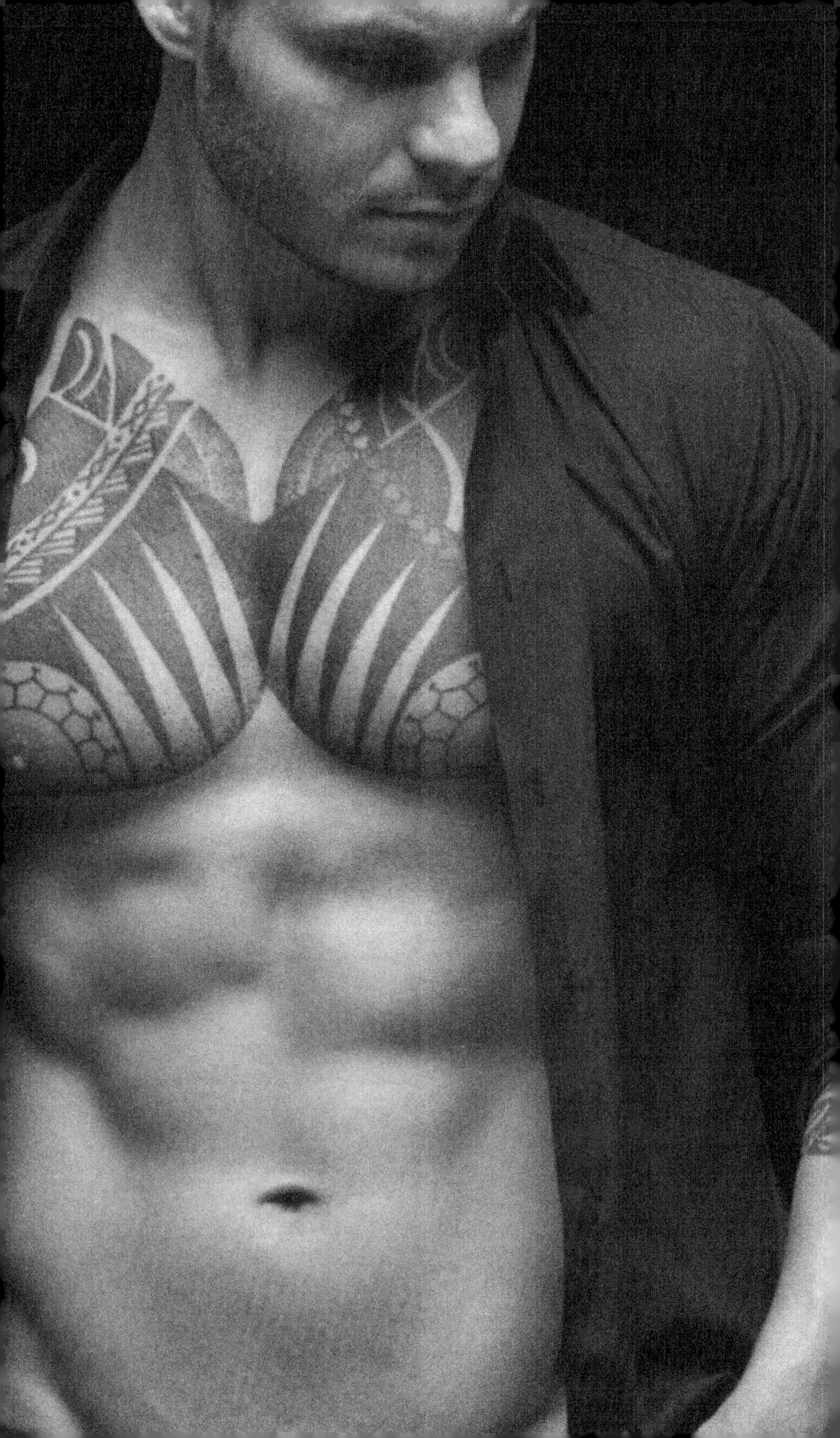

Chapter Forty-Three

True

Walt Whitman said, "Peace is always beautiful."

Now that I'd found some of my own, I believed that wholeheartedly.

The bodies were buried alongside the many regrets, secrets, and oodles of self-reproach. Through it all, the questions, the whispers, and the finger-pointing, I was left with a startling sense of rightness. My father-in-law deserved to die for what he did to me, but in order to protect my daughter, I would've cut his throat a thousand times over if it meant she was safely away from his grasp. Was I dismayed over the happenings that led me to this point in my life? Mace asked me that same question on our ride back to Remington after Ryan's funeral. The physical scars would heal with time, I told him, the emotional ones would linger forever, like that annoying fly you just couldn't seem to get rid of, no matter how hard you swatted at it. There was nothing else to be done about that now, and so I tucked it away along with all the other things we humans prefer to forget. Remington was my home. I chose it. At the same time, it chose me. I had my own tribe now full of friends and family whom I loved greatly. One person in particular would need me more than ever to see her through her recovery.

Visiting Sal in the hospital for the first time nearly broke my heart into a million pieces. Seeing her beautiful face marred by cuts and scrapes, a broken arm set proper with a cast, her head wrapped tightly in gauze while her brain function was being closely monitored hit me directly in the solar plexus. The guilt of knowing that my husband was the cause of her pain ate away at me during those early days. I sat by her bedside holding her hand, praying for her to wake up and speak to me. I'd cry for hours after leaving, wrapped in Mace's arms while he whispered empathetic words in my ear. They never helped. I wasn't the one who needed them, Sal was, but you couldn't tell that to the big muscleman. Watching me cry was akin to having his balls kicked repeatedly by a toddler in hard walking shoes, he'd complain. I resorted to crying in the hospital bathroom before calling him to pick me up. That was a few weeks ago. I was better now, and by the grace of God, so was Sal.

The first time she opened her eyes and called me *beloved*, I cried for a totally different reason, a joyful one, although the feeling was regrettably brief. The swelling in her brain was causing her long-term memory to be affected. The doctors weren't sure if it was something temporary or a glimpse into her new normal. Kaden thought they were all full of shit, Mace agreed, but Corrine and I were skeptical. Regardless, we would all be there to support her for however long she needed us. Sal was part of our family, end of, as Mace liked to say.

I'd heard that phrase, *end of,* growled so often recently I was starting to wonder why anyone bothered trying to have a civil conversation with the man. He used it when I objected to moving in with him at a moment's notice. He won that battle, but only because the shower in his apartment was the bomb and I had this thing about being clean. He used it again when he bought me a new car, citing convenience as the excuse to why I should take it. He eventually won that battle as well, but not before I forced him to return the Mercedes Benz SUV for something more befitting a working mother. Oh, he railed about safety for the *kid* and GPS tracking in case something happened, but in the end, I put my foot down and chose a perfectly awesome previously owned Chevy Trailblazer. I named her Sal, so we would always travel together in spirit. That earned me a deep growl and a pat on the butt. Score!

Mace Fox was a certifiable hard-ass, but he was *our* hard-ass, mine and Kayla's. He could be demanding, overprotective, and downright rabid, especially where our wellbeing was concerned. Case in point, Corrine needed to spend her time looking after Sal at the hospital, which meant she could no longer babysit during the day while I worked. Understandable, so I found a lovely in-home daycare center around the corner from Masonry Ink. Everything about it was perfect. Mace, of course, didn't feel the same way, especially once the sitter's dog, Puffy, greeted us at the door. He swore that the longhaired chihuahua gave Kayla the evil eye and was plotting to bite her once we turned our backs. Never mind that the animal was missing all but three of his teeth, which caused his tongue to loll around his mouth. He was a threat, and therefore, Mace wouldn't allow her to attend. The next day, the office at shop was outfitted with enough equipment that I could start my own daycare center, and she'd been with us ever since. See…hard-ass.

I had a few last-minute errands to run before the grand re-opening of Masonry Ink. Everyone was going to be there, and I looked forward to seeing Jagger in something more than a hospital gown. They really needed to consider making a big and tall version of that thing; it left little to the imagination in the bone department. Let's just say, Jagger had it going on down below, aside from the bullet wound and all. *Technicalities, True, technicalities.*

It was early afternoon, and I'd left Kayla with Mace fearing that the trip to the store would take twice as long carrying a cranky baby. I wasn't worried in the least if he could handle it; he was a natural, bowing to her every whim like a squishy little marshmallow. At bedtime, the spoiled little snickerdoodle wouldn't go to sleep without first hearing Mace sing to her. I was so surprised at the smooth baritone of the catchy little jingle; it was as if he'd written it himself. When I spoke to Belinda about it during one of our many phone calls since our visit, she told me he used to sing it to Maya when she was a baby. I boohooed for the entire rest of the conversation while my heart grew to the size of a melon. I never thought my life would be this full. I had a beautiful healthy daughter, a job I adored, and a man I found myself falling head over heels for more and more every day. If this was a dream, I hoped to never wake up.

The custom-made signage flapped in the wind announcing the night's festivities. I struggled to open the trunk of my car just as a tattooed hand reached out to lighten the load. I blew the wayward hair from my eyes; it was fairly warm out, and the strands were sticking to my sweaty skin. I assumed it was someone who had arrived early for the party and thanked them.

"Guess I should've made two trips, huh?" I mumbled to my savior.

I received a grunt in response, and that's when I looked up and saw Dead Man. He stood off to the side wearing his signature black. Black jeans, black hoodie, black boots, and a black duffle bag slung over his shoulder. I hadn't had the nerve to speak with him since the incident that shall not be named. Part of it was opportunity. I spent my free time seeing to Sal's recovery; nothing was more important than that. The other part was cowardice. I wasn't ready to be rejected by him for a second time; it was too great a loss the first go-around.

"You're…" I stammered. "I see you're not staying for the party."

"No, the fuck I'm not," he replied.

His coldness gave me pause, then again, it wasn't as if he tried to hide his disdain for me. If I walked into a room, he left it. If I passed him in the hall, he turned around and went the other way. If I said hello, he would pretty much scowl in my direction and then ignored my greeting. Kind of like today, minus the hand with the bags. He turned on his heels to escape me for the umpteenth time, but I had a trick for his ass, one that was as welcomed as flowers in May.

"I knew who you were from the start, you know," I called out. "That day, when the FBI came to the shop. It was your eyes that gave it away. They never changed."

He still wouldn't turn around, so I kept going.

"I waited for you, all that day and half the night. When your father came to visit my mother, I sat by the window expecting the boy who taught me to play Go Fish to show up, but he never did. Then one day, you both stopped coming. Why, Wenny?"

His shoulders tensed once he heard the moniker. When we met, I was too young to pronounce his given name, Rennick, so I took to calling him Wenny, and it stuck. His dad was one of my mother's many followers, an amiable man with a kind smile and good looks which his son inherited. Pity the bastard was a cheater like all the others. Last I'd heard, he'd died in a single vehicle crash off Interstate 40 in Sorensen.

"You were what, four, five? I'm sure you got over it," he snapped.

"You were my only friend, so no, I never got over it.

"Friend?" he said, slowly tilting his head to the side as he whipped around to face me. "Figures that stupid cunt never told you the truth, too busy sucking dick to fill in her own daughter. That bitch lied to you, and it cost a good woman her life, my fucking mother…slit her wrists in the bathtub when she found out that my father was cheating on her with the town whore. That's why *I* stopped coming. Can't say what did it for him."

He took a shuddering breath to regain his control. My legs began to tremble as I pressed my fingers to my gaping mouth. What was he saying? It couldn't be true. No way, it couldn't be...

I dropped the bags I was holding.

"Your mother killed herself because of us?" I cried.

Dead Man guffawed at my surprise. "Take care of the kid."

Then he turned and stalked away.

Holy shit. I felt sick to my stomach. How could she have been so selfish? Easily, I mused; it was in her hedonistic nature to inflict pain on others. I knew that firsthand. Still, Dead Man was leaving, and there wasn't a damn thing I could do to stop him. He wouldn't know that at Ryan's funeral, I told her how much I hated her guts and that I wished her dead. That I struck her across the face so hard with my good hand that she stumbled and fell to the ground. That I promised to ruin her life as payback for all the shit she put me through. He'd never know how much he meant to me or how much I missed him when he was gone.

It wasn't until I felt an arm drape over my shoulder that I realized I'd been standing in the parking lot watching an empty section of asphalt for several long minutes. I snuggled into the muscled chest, immediately recognizing the scent, and allowed the tears to flow freely. Kayla was strapped to his torso in her carry harness, fast asleep, oblivious to what was going on.

"How long have you known?" I asked.

"Since the beginning," Mace replied.

"Will he come back home to Remington?" I removed my face from his warm embrace.

Mace took a deep steadying breath.

"When he's ready."

"Then we'll be waiting to welcome him back."

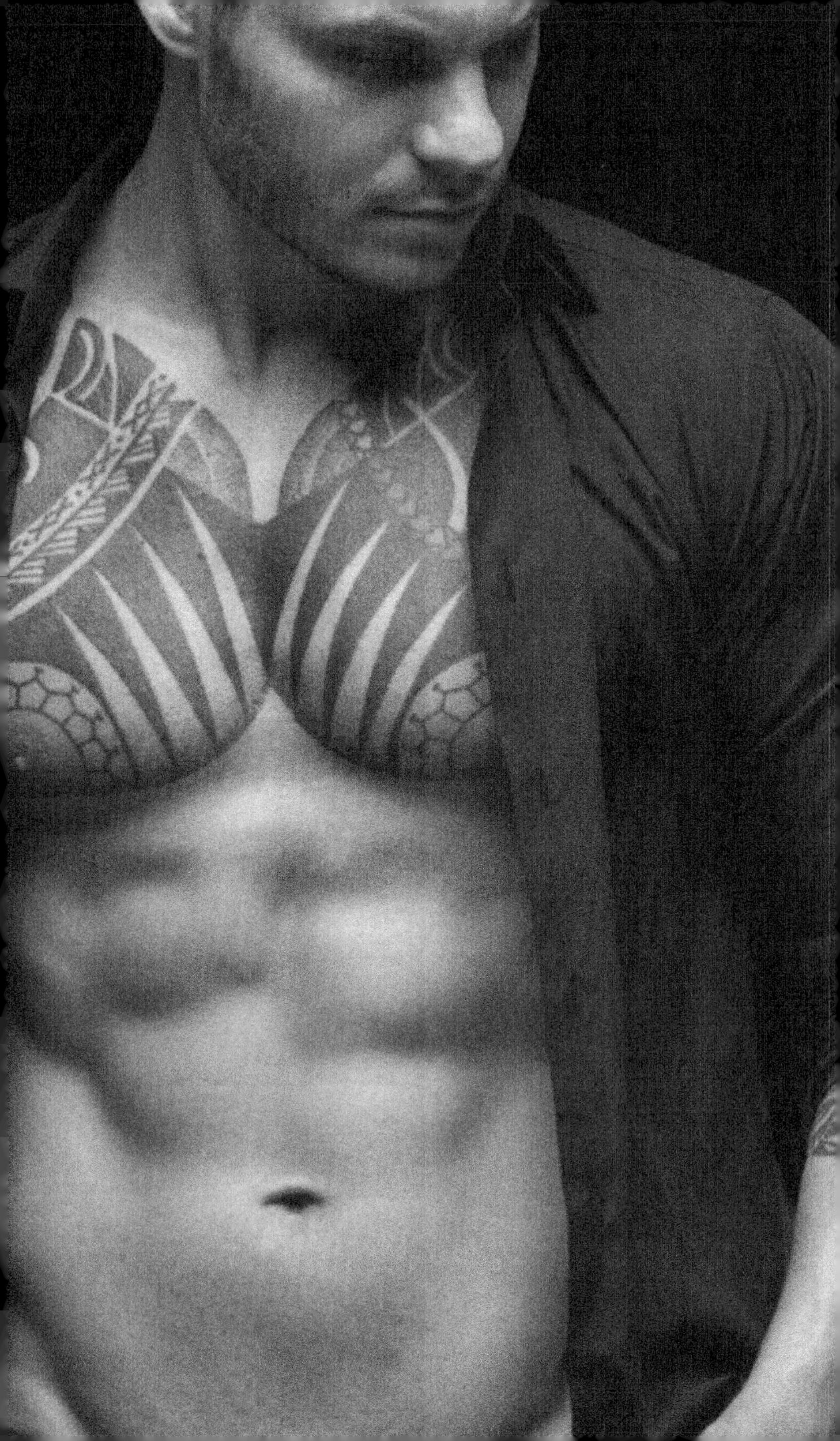

Epilogue

Mace

Masonry Ink was lit with excitement.

Everyone showed to lend their support, have a few beers, get inked, or kick the shit while listening to live music from one of the local cover bands. I walked around and took in the atmosphere, pleased as fuck at the new improvements that were made. Insurance covered most of the damage; the rest came out of a building fund which was the cash we copped from the dead bikers they'd left lying around. I gave a cut to Python and his boys, my gift for saving our asses, and the rest was left untouched as part of the crooked cop storyline. To think I nearly lost it all—my shop, my crew, even my fucking life. I had to do a lot of groveling and a whole hell of a lot of explaining over the last few weeks. Thankfully, I was somewhat forgiven for my actions involving the prison ambush, and tonight was all about celebrating.

Kaden stopped by for a few minutes, but his mind and spirit were elsewhere. Usually, a party wasn't a party until the blond chucklehead launched into one of his ridiculous stories about getting pussy, but on this night, we had to do without. Sal was out of the woods, thank Christ, and Corrine persuaded him to venture away from the hospital, noting a change of scenery would do him some good. He'd been at her side for weeks, and somehow, she was able to do for him what none of us ever could. She settled his demons, kept the crazy in check, and even managed to help the fool fall asleep, which was a feat in and of itself. I assured him that leaving wasn't a big deal and that he should follow his heart. He, in turn, told me to eat a dick and that I was starting to sound like a little bitch. Obviously, Sal had more work to do.

I peeped Jagger sitting on one of the new couches with Kira pressed against his side like a Velcroed patch. She might have been all about him, but his eyes were on someone else, a certain someone who was chatting it up with a newcomer. Young, handsome dude with a megawatt smile, brightly colored tats, and an obvious gift for the gab. I'd even go so far as to say that the man-boy was downright pretty in a Gap commercial kind of way. Angelica was definitely into him, leaning in slightly, flipping her long dark hair, touching his arm whenever he said something amusing. She'd changed since returning from her stay with Ma, less fearful and more willing to put herself out there. I felt like a proud papa watching her finally blossom into a confident young woman ready to take on the world. I wondered what finally did it?

The opportunity to fuck with Jagger was golden. How could I pass that up? I slipped in next to Dread and his woman, Michelle, who were standing in the corner within earshot of the big idiot.

"Who's the fuckboy with Angelica?" I asked.

Michelle piped right up. "Oh, that's Jess. He's my lab partner from school. He was in the market for a new tattoo, so I told him about the party tonight. I had a feeling the two of them would hit it off. I hope he asks her out on a date. She'd love that!"

"The fuck?" I heard growled as Jagger twisted around to face us. "Angel doesn't date, especially not some limp dick, pussy-ass motherfucker who couldn't tell a left hook from a slice of apple pie."

"Don't need a left hook if you got a big cock," Dread mocked.

Michelle playfully smacked her man on the chest.

"Don't say that! Angelica isn't looking for a quick lay. She's interested in a life mate, someone to be there for her when she needs them the most, not someone who bails on her for the first big-chested bimbo who walks by."

Damn, Michelle...who knew you could be such a savage?

"You're co-signing this bullshit, Mace?" Jagger bellowed.

He ripped his arm away from Kira, ignoring the pout of her lips. He stomped his way over to the three of us like a petulant child who just found out that his mother had fucked the mailman. He ogled the couple with pure disgust in his eyes, fists clenched at his sides. Given the size of his chest, I'd say the man was set to blow. I went for the dagger. Fuck it, he deserved to know just how badly he'd fucked up.

"Free country, brother. She's single, beautiful, smart. Any man with half a brain would be lucky to have her. Sweet boy over there looks like he's just about in there," I said, twisting the knife.

"Yeah, Jagger, what's with the cockblock? Don't you already have a girlfriend to worry about?" Michelle pointed to Kira, who looked as if she'd swallowed a doorknob.

He bared his teeth in response.

Too far gone to see his mistake.

"Fuck this shit." He shook with rage, shoving his way through the crowd.

I thought about stopping him, reeling his ass back in before he did something stupid, but I was having way too much fun, and like I said, he deserved it. Dread and I exchanged a knowing look before we stood by and witnessed the fireworks as they shot off around the shop in full view of everyone. Angelica, all of five foot nothing, squared off against a mountain of muscle, twisted her little finger around, and shot Jagger the bird before trapsing off towards the makeshift bar dragging Jess the college puke along with her. They say you never miss your water till your well runs dry, and right about now, Jagger was one thirsty motherfucker. My work here was done, but his work was just beginning. I left them to it sporting a triumphant smile.

That tasty little scene was solid and all, but I was past ready to call it a night. True had taken Kayla up to the apartment hours ago, and I found myself missing them like crazy. It was her idea to have this party, and she'd busted her ass for days to put it together. The few people she trusted to look after her child were on the north side of blotto, not that it mattered. She wouldn't allow anyone to sacrifice their good time in order to play babysitter. She took her duty as a mother seriously, which was one of the many things I respected about her and why I felt empty without her by my side to enjoy the festivities.

Despite the fact that I was surrounded by a room full of happy faces, my subconscious was firmly with my girls. By now, bath time was over, and Kayla's pink little bottom was greased and powdered to a soft glow. Her blonde hair, like her mother's, smelling of apples, her body wrapped tightly in footie pajamas decorated with yellow duckies. True had already sung to her about the beautiful princess loved by all the fairies in the land, and after all of that, her little ass was still wide the fuck awake. The image in my head warmed my insides.

My girls were waiting for me.

I swept past Ashley Benjamin dancing wildly on one of the new tattoo tables. Her man, Sebastian, stood on the sidelines and watched the little hellraiser act a fool with a bored look on his face. He was used to her bullshit. After the biker incident, I'd gone to the junkyard and thanked him personally for the backup. He played it just as I knew he would, with a furrowed brow, a hefty laugh, and a head scratch. He shrugged his shoulders, imparted some unsolicited advice on the side effects of using testosterone after the age of thirty according to his mother and Aunt Enid, and thanked me for stopping by. In other words, he didn't want or need my gratitude and preferred it if we never spoke about it again. He caught my eye as I passed, shook his head with exasperation, and went back to being Ashley's devoted sentinel, all in with her crazy and loving every minute of it.

I kept walking, ignoring all the pats on the back, the boisterous shouts of congratulations, invitations to *holla at me for a sec*. Determination quickened my strides until I had mother and child in my field of vision. Peace surrounded my core and shook me from the inside out. Minute by minute, the longer I watched, the harder it was to control my emotions. Any lingering doubts of failure for choosing not to avenge my sister's death blurred into mist. Renewed was my passion for life and living, my purpose stark with wonderment. They belonged with me, and I was born to protect them as my own.

True swaddled baby Kayla while she sang the princess song, and it was the sweetest sound I ever heard. She startled when she saw me standing in the doorway, relief evident in her smile.

"How are you able to get her down within five minutes, but she insists on torturing me half the night? I'm the one who carried her in my belly for nine months, the little traitor."

"Aww, come 'ere…let me show you how it's done."

She rose from the rocking chair and handed me the cranky baby, whose eyes lit up the second she saw me. I wrapped them both in my arms, looking into the baby blues like her momma's, and softly rocked back and forth.

Beautiful, beautiful princess, where have you gone?

Close your eyes and sleep while you listen to my song.
No goblins or ghosts can take you away.
I'll always be here to save the day.
Sleep, sleep, my beautiful doll.
Away, away, I'll watch till you fall.

"That's amazing, Mace. You truly have a gift," True whispered.

I placed the now sleeping Kayla in her crib, guided her mother out the door, and shut off the light behind us. She was in her own set of duckie pajamas, and I couldn't help the grin that spread across my lips at her cuteness. I swept her up into my arms and hugged her close, savoring the feel of her heartbeat next to mine, our breaths mingled.

"Is it wrong that I'm glad you ditched that boring old party to be here with us?" she asked against my chest.

"Not even a little bit. No place I'd rather be."

My muscles involuntarily stiffened, and True noticed.

"What's the matter?" she asked.

I reached into my back pocket and pulled out what I'd been holding for days. She looked confused for a second, untangled her arms from around me, then opened the envelope to read its contents. I started to panic when she didn't immediately respond.

"I know you never got the chance to make it official, so I had Kaden work his magic and process this one for the state records board. We can change it if you want…the name." I took a deep breath and let it out slowly. "She's mine, True. All my love, my heart, my honor, she has it, if that's what *you* want."

"Kayla Fox," she whispered, as her fingers brushed along the newly printed birth certificate. Tears flowed down her face in a rush and pooled at the apple of her cheeks as she smiled.

"Are *we* safe with you, Mace?" she asked.

"No, True." I ran a single finger over her lips before kissing her softly.

" You're *home* with me."
End of…

The End

CONNECT WITH AUTHOR SH RICHARDSON ONLINE:

https://www.facebook.com/authorshrichardson/?ref=aymt_homepage_panel
https://www.facebook.com/groups/185408491876707/?fref=mentions
https://www.goodreads.com/author/show/15174332.S_H_Richardson
Twitter @sharonricher1
Instagram @MrsbigT813
http://www.amazon.com/-/e/B01EG9K4RO?ref_=pe_1724030_132998070
https://www.bookbub.com/authors/sh-richardson
https://vm.tiktok.com/ZTdytgJv7/
http://bitly.ws/BBnx

DISCOVER OTHER TITTLES BY AUTHOR SH RICHARDSON

The Junkyard boys
Amazon US: https://amzn.to/2Q44MM0
Amazon AU: https://amzn.to/2MPEGyJ
Amazon UK: https://amzn.to/2PCogq7
Amazon CA: https://amzn.to/2MNn6uT
The Scrapyard Man
Amazon US: https://amzn.to/2wHucGC
Amazon AU: https://amzn.to/2NfZz5b
Amazon UK: https://amzn.to/2PzLJII
Amazon CA: https://amzn.to/2Q5CEIH
Refuse: A Junkyard Wedding
Amazon US: https://amzn.to/2MOYfHi
Amazon AU: https://amzn.to/2Q5kIO7
Amazon UK: https://amzn.to/2LVjsde
Amazon CA: https://amzn.to/2PEwcHB
Salvaging Max
Amazon US: https://amzn.to/2NNWlmu
Amazon AU: https://amzn.to/2MKajtg
Amazon UK: https://amzn.to/2wFjY9D
Amazon CA: https://amzn.to/2wBNXPC

DISCOVER OTHER TITTLES BY AUTHOR SH RICHARDSON

Recycled Memory
Amazon US: https://amzn.to/2Pnhrsp
Amazon UK: https://amzn.to/2wCijBP
Amazon CA: https://amzn.to/2C5qhcs
Amazon AU: https://amzn.to/2LI8dER

Dread: Masonry Ink by SH Richardson
Amazon US: https://amzn.to/2HWXCHs
Amazon AU: https://amzn.to/2KupN2l
Amazon UK: https://amzn.to/2Z48A3M
Amazon CA: https://amzn.to/2QRmaV2

48 Mac by SH Richardson
Amazon USA- https://amzn.to/3tkiP3K
Amazon UK- https://amzn.to/3pBnuMu
Amazon AU- https://amzn.to/3pEqhEQ
Amazon CA- https://amzn.to/2NT7Hut

Printed in Great Britain
by Amazon